The

Sweet Spot

Also by Amy Poeppel

Musical Chairs
Limelight
Small Admissions

The Sweet Spot

A Novel

Amy Poeppel

EMILY BESTLER BOOKS

ATRIA

New York   London   Toronto   Sydney   New Delhi

EMILY
BESTLER
BOOKS

ATRIA

An Imprint of Simon & Schuster, Inc.
1230 Avenue of the Americas
New York, NY 10020

First Emily Bestler Books/Atria paperback edition February 2023

EMILY BESTLER BOOKS/ATRIA PAPERBACK and colophon are trademarks of Simon & Schuster, Inc.

For information about special discounts for bulk purchases, please contact Simon & Schuster Special Sales at 1-866-506-1949 or business@simonandschuster.com.

The Simon & Schuster Speakers Bureau can bring authors to your live event. For more information or to book an event, contact the Simon & Schuster Speakers Bureau at 1-866-248-3049 or visit our website at www.simonspeakers.com.

Interior design by Lexy Alemao

Manufactured in the United States of America

1 3 5 7 9 10 8 6 4 2

Library of Congress Cataloging-in-Publication Data has been applied for.

ISBN 978-1-9821-7646-4
ISBN 978-1-9821-7645-7 (pbk)
ISBN 978-1-9821-7647-1 (ebook)

In memory of my parents,
Pamela and Jere Mitchell.

"The sweet spot is where duty and delight converge."
—*Thomas Mann*

"If you listen, truly listen, to an adversary,
you will probably find at least one goal on which you agree."
—*Gloria Steinem*

Prologue

Felicity had walked by the brownstone on Waverly Place dozens of times without ever noticing it. The homes in this neighborhood were charming, harkening back to bygone horse-and-buggy days, but this particular house, tired and unadorned, asked to be ignored. The building had reached a certain level of disrepair wherein it was neither eye candy nor an eyesore. It was simply unremarkable. But the location! Felicity could not imagine how a potter could have landed such prime real estate in Greenwich Village, the only corner of Manhattan—with its rows of town houses and its famous park, mews and alleys, elms and sycamores—that reminded her of the best parts of London.

Looking up to double-check the number next to the peeling red door, she wondered: Was the ivy damaging the brick facade? Was the interior equally shabby? If so, would they gut the whole building? Install central air? Would they kick out that dive bar in the basement and move the entrance to the lower level? Or dig deeper to build a garage?

As she climbed the worn stairs, her sandal caught on a broken step and the thin, blush-colored strap across her toes snapped. She took the shoe off, cursing under her breath, and rang the bell. She heard children shrieking from inside and placed a hand over her belly where her own little offspring, the size—according to her OB—of a turnip, was floating around obliviously, tethered to her insides.

When the door opened, a small girl (Five? Nine? Felicity wasn't especially familiar with the developmental stages of young people) and a large dog crowded the entry, both of them electrified by her arrival.

"Mommy!" the girl yelled into the expanse behind her. "There's a lady!"

Lauren came to the door, her hair half falling out of its clip. "Come in, come in!" she said, trying to restrain the dog from drooling on Felicity's tiered dress. "*Bumper, no!*" She clipped a leash on him. "We rescued him last week; he's three already, but you sure wouldn't know it. He's a handful."

"I apologize for inviting myself last minute," Felicity said, still standing in the doorway, "but I wanted to chat in person."

"No, I'm happy you came," she said. "We're in mid-move, so forgive the chaos."

Felicity was used to people apologizing for the state of their homes, even when those homes were lovely. It wasn't easy, she knew, to welcome a designer of some renown into one's living space. Felicity's TV show, still going strong after six seasons, demanded (for the sake of entertainment) that she say insulting things to the homeowner-victim-guests. But that was not, she had to explain all the time, *who she was*; that was only a persona. She was—in *reality* reality—perfectly kind and polite. Besides, Felicity had not come to the brownstone to judge.

"Watch your step," Lauren said as they entered the living room, and Felicity did, maneuvering around unpacked boxes, over stacks of books, and past dizzyingly unattractive seventies wallpaper. They went through the dining room and into the kitchen, with its avocado-green appliances and orange Formica countertops, to the back of the house, which had a door opening onto a deck. "I thought we could sit out here," Lauren said, "since it's so warm."

The children—there were three of them—were planting something in terra-cotta pots, their hands caked with dirt. The dog put his head in the watering can.

"Your sandal!" Lauren said, noticing that Felicity had one bare foot as she stood on the splintered deck.

"It broke," Felicity said with a little lift of her shoulders, the sandal hanging off her pinky. It wasn't tragic, but it was disappointing; she'd bought them last week on Bond Street in Mayfair.

"Charles," Lauren said to the tallest child, taking the sandal and putting it in his muddy hands, "be a clever boy and see if you can fix this." Lauren took that moment to introduce Felicity to her kids: "Charles, Harrell, Waverly, and, of course, Bumper, this is Mommy's new friend, Felicity."

"Did you say *Waverly*?" Felicity said. "Like your street?"

"Leo grew up here," Lauren said, running a hand over the girl's long hair, "and we always loved the name."

"It's beautiful," said Felicity.

"Leo's mother was Charley Aston," Lauren said. "I don't know if you've heard of her, but this was her house."

"Really? How remarkable." Felicity had indeed heard of Charley Aston, a pioneer of the American feminist movement, though she'd never seen one of her plays.

"We love the neighborhood," Lauren said, "but the noise at night takes a little getting used to."

"I live nearby, closer to the Hudson," said Felicity. "It's a smidge less lively."

"Oh, you're a neighbor," Lauren said happily. "I didn't realize."

The children were fascinated by the task of repairing a real shoe that was meant for a grown-up's actual foot.

"I know what to do," the shorter boy said.

"Surgery," said Waverly.

Felicity loved an original name, but she didn't love the idea of these scruffy children messing with her footwear. Before she could object, they took her sandal inside, conspiring about what would work best. A stapler? Duct tape? Glue? A soldering iron?

"They're between schools right now," Lauren said, as if explaining their availability to take on this job.

"I'm sorry?"

"We moved boroughs, and it got complicated to transfer schools so close to the end of the academic year. So we're homeschooling."

A little alarm went off in Felicity's head. Homeschooling was surely time-consuming. "Have you hired a governess or something? A tutor?"

Lauren laughed. "Nope, just me," she said, and indicated the soil on the deck and the seedlings in the pots with pride. She must have seen the look on Felicity's face because she quickly added, "Oh, it's only for a few months. They'll start at Perkins in the fall."

She gestured with her arm, offering Felicity a chair. Felicity brushed off the seat before she sat down, putting her Celine bag on her lap to hide her baby bump, and looked out over the barren yard; in spite of the unseasonable warmth, the trees had yet to put out a single leaf. There was opera coming from an open rear window of another brownstone across the way, a house that had been made over top to bottom with a copper PH Artichoke lamp hanging dramatically over the dining room table. Everything at Lauren's, on the other hand, from the rotting porch railing to the dog's smelly fur to Lauren's tired overalls, needed freshening. There were few arguments Felicity could come up with for conserving or treasuring the old and worn, and in this case, what she would do is blow out the whole back side of the house, replacing the north-facing wall with a Swiss-made, pivoting glass door that would let in the light and create a seamless transition to the outdoors.

"So," Felicity said, coming to the point of her visit, "your samples arrived at our office last week, and they're stunning. My team created an Instagram teaser to test the market, and it got over thirty thousand clicks in the first hours."

Lauren put her hands to her cheeks. She wore very little makeup. From the moment they'd met a few months before, Felicity had instantly liked something about this woman—her lack of artifice maybe. Her edginess was apparent only in the context of her work; she was the type of open, sweet human Felicity thought she *should* be friends with. And she likely knew a thing or two about mothering in New York City, a skill Felicity now considered interesting and even useful. Like this school—Perkins?—that her kids would go to; was it too soon to put her fetus on a waitlist?

"I'm not even on Instagram," Lauren said. "Thirty thousand sounds like . . . a lot."

"It's very promising," said Felicity. "And I'm not surprised. There's something about the way you combine the appealing with the abhorrent that speaks to the zeitgeist. People want joy, but they feel evil lurking. Or maybe they want to know beauty can exist in spite of mutating germs." Felicity felt she'd explained enough; she had a sense for what people wanted, and Lauren's pieces were going to sell.

"I made you something," Lauren said, "to express my gratitude for even considering my work." She looked giddy, almost childlike, as she reached beside her chair and handed Felicity a fat ball of newsprint. Felicity unwrapped the layers of wrinkled paper and found one of Lauren's pieces: a porcelain teapot with delicate sprigs of lavender hand-painted on the side and, of course, one of her signature grotesqueries: a revolting brown worm crawling along the spout. Felicity lifted the lid and to her delight, found a slug depicted on the underside.

"Oh, I love it," said Felicity. "It's classic *you*."

"The only bad part of moving to this house," Lauren said, her eyes still on the teapot, "is that my studio is way out in Brooklyn. It was only a block away from our old apartment, but it's going to be a tough commute now."

"You might want to find a new studio, then," Felicity said, "because I have an offer for you. We'd like to sell your pieces exclusively this fall. We'll feature them in our window displays on Mercer and Madison Avenue and possibly in LA too."

Lauren made a squealing sound. "Are you serious?"

"Quite," Felicity said.

Given the look of utter shock and disbelief on Lauren's face, Felicity hoped this ceramist was up to the challenge. An opportunity to be on the shelves of her store was far beyond any craft fair where Lauren had sold her pieces before, like at the holiday pop-up market where Felicity had discovered Lauren in the first place.

Lauren got up abruptly and went inside; was the pressure too much for her? Maybe her excitement needed to be expressed in private? Maybe she needed a moment to think? Felicity had no idea. The dog lifted his big head and drooled, watching her in a way she found slightly terrifying, his tail wagging through the wet potting soil the kids had splattered on the deck. Felicity did not move.

To her relief, Lauren returned. She had tears in her eyes and an open bottle of Freixenet under her arm. She handed Felicity a glass filled almost to the rim and held up another, saying, "This is unreal. I never in a million years imagined my stuff being sold at a place like Felicity."

"*Stuff*?" Felicity said as she placed her champagne on the table. "An original work of art like this"—she held up the little round teapot—"will be priced starting at five hundred dollars. You're going to be a household name. Well, an upper-class household name anyway."

"Incredible," Lauren said, wiping her cheek with the sleeve of her plaid shirt. She sat back down and took a sip of her champagne. The glass had red lipstick, clearly not Lauren's, ground into the rim. "How will I ever thank you for finding me?"

"I like to think we found each other," Felicity said.

"No, really," Lauren said, briefly placing a hand on Felicity's wrist, "I was starting to worry I'd never get my career back on track after having kids. They can really break up a trajectory, you know? And then you came along. . . . You amaze me, really, and not just because of what you're doing for me. When I think about all you've built in such a short time? It's phenomenal."

Felicity did not believe that children should ever be allowed to knock a woman's career off course, and she hoped Lauren's kids would not get in her way now; the order Felicity was placing would require Lauren to commit fully to her work.

"Leo!" Lauren said as a man came through the door and joined them on the deck. "Come say hi."

The dog, his leash dragging on the ground, bounded over to greet

Lauren's husband, who was wearing a helmet, the strap still clipped under his chin. There was some kind of zip tie around the right leg of his ill-fitting khaki pants.

"Hello there, yes, welcome," he said, shaking her hand too hard.

Where, Felicity wondered, would one begin to make over this man? The wire-rimmed glasses? The black tube socks? The T-shirt that had some kind of triangular diagram with the caption, *Here's looking at Euclid*?

He leaned over and hugged his wife, the top of her head lodged in his armpit. He smiled at his dog, at the unattractive porch, at the blue sky; Felicity had never seen a person look so utterly content with so little.

"Looks like you'll be in charge of the kids this summer," Lauren told him, "because Felicity here is putting me to work, starting . . . ?"

"Right away," said Felicity.

"How exciting," Leo said, straightening his back in an exaggerated way. "Corporal Aston reporting for duty." And he gave a silly salute.

Lauren did not seem the least embarrassed. "The kids are inside trying to repair Felicity's shoe," she said. "Can you make sure they're not going overboard with the hot-glue gun?"

Felicity flinched at the very idea, but Leo seemed intrigued, tapping his lips with his index finger. "Ahh," he said, "the craft of the cobbler," and he nodded wisely. He then pretended to doff his cap, saying in a lame attempt at a British accent, "At your service, m'ladies," and backed up through the kitchen door, opening it with his rear end.

Lauren was smiling. "If we give them enough time, they could probably replicate your sandals in the 3D printer."

Felicity doubted that very much; they were Alexander McQueen.

But something about the dynamic between these two appealed to her. Leo took orders from Lauren; did that come naturally or had she trained him? Or was it a perfect combination of nature and nurture?

"So, how does this work?" Felicity said, pointing from Lauren to the space her husband had just occupied.

"What do you mean?"

"Having a partner who's so dedicated to you? A supportive person by your side, day in and day out?"

Lauren looked confused at first, but then her eyes opened wide. "Felicity! Have you met someone special?"

Felicity felt herself blush. "Guilty," she said.

"Wow, that's great," Lauren said. "I somehow thought . . . On your show once—or was it in an interview?—you said—"

"I told the women on *The View* that having a life partner was not for me. And I meant it. But then I happened to meet this man, and things have changed, or it seems so anyway."

"That's wonderful," said Lauren.

Was it though? Felicity wasn't sure the specific circumstances would fit Lauren's idea of wonderful.

"It's a tad complicated," she said. "I've become involved with someone who's technically unavailable."

"Oh. Is he . . . *married?*" Lauren said, dropping her voice to a whisper, like she hadn't known such a thing was even possible.

"Unfortunately, yes."

Lauren seemed to require a moment to process that information, looking as though she were being asked to swallow the slug she'd painted on the teapot. "Oh, dear," she said.

"Their marriage is devoid of passion," Felicity said, "while he and I have this intense connection. He's so . . . solid, you know? He's a lawyer and absolutely brilliant. He adores me."

Lauren nodded, hanging on her every word.

"And then," Felicity said, "we were utterly astonished when—and this is confidential, so please keep this between us—I somehow got pregnant." As soon as the words came out, Felicity regretted sharing them. Aside from Russell, she had not told a single person this monumental news, not a friend and certainly not anyone she knew professionally. A baby had not been in her plans, but she also knew this would likely be her last opportunity to become a mum, which was something she thought she might like to do, though not something she wanted to do entirely on her own. With the right partner, however, it might be nice to push a pram down a New York City sidewalk, or snuggle a baby wearing one of the white French terry-cloth onesies she sold in her boutique, or share pictures of her pregnancy journey on Instagram.

"Gosh, Felicity!" Lauren was beaming at her, and Felicity wondered if she was *really* happy for her or if she was merely excited to have a minor celebrity confiding in her. "Congratulations," she said. "How far along are you?"

"Not far at all," Felicity said. This was not true, but due to the loose, graceful cut of her dress, her naturally slim hips, and her personal trainer, she was barely showing. "It took me—it took both of us—totally by surprise. He wants to leave her, his wife. But I said no, absolutely not. I cannot be responsible for the death of a marriage. And I *could* raise a child by myself."

"Of course you can," said Lauren with an encouraging nod of her head.

"But I don't especially want to. Given my rather *intense* career, being a single mother would present big challenges. And this lovely man keeps telling me how much he wants to be a father. That's sweet, right?"

Lauren looked down and patted her scruffy dog on his head. "Yes, well . . . If there's no passion between them, like you said, and if he really wants to raise the . . . boy? Girl . . . ?"

Felicity knew the answer to that already but kept it to herself. "He wants this baby more than I do," she said, and laughed, although she wasn't being funny; he actually did. "He's a sensitive, caring man, so he's in anguish about his wife, who sounds dreadfully dull." She sighed and waved a fly away from her face. "But what he wants most of all is to be the baby's father."

"How sad," said Lauren. "I can't imagine telling Leo that he's not part of our family."

"But that's exactly what I did," Felicity said. "Because I imagine his wife's situation, and I feel so . . . *bad*." But "bad" was not accurate. What she felt was more a nagging sense of being *supposed* to feel bad. It wouldn't be a good optics for her brand anyway; she was not a home-wrecker of *that* sort.

"Oh, how difficult," said Lauren, putting her hand back on Felicity's arm.

Lauren was looking at her so earnestly then that Felicity found it almost off-putting.

"I mean, people *do* get divorced," Felicity said curtly. "It's a reality. And the baby has me rethinking everything. Russell and I have tried to stay away from each other, but it's proving to be difficult, especially now, given the new circumstances."

"Of course. If you two—I mean, if you *three* are meant to be together, I don't know what choice you have."

"I could tell him to bugger off and raise the child on my own."

"I don't see how you can tell the father—especially since you seem to love him and all—that he can't be with his own baby," said Lauren.

And then she said, "You're kind of famous for having good instincts, right? I would trust those. Follow your heart."

Felicity put a hand to her chest, just as the baby caused some kind of faint flutter, a small ripple from deep within her. She did have good instincts; her entire career was based on her ability to know what was best. And her instincts were telling her that she needed him. If he would quit his job and agree to take the lead with the baby, then she would agree to be with him.

"My instincts tell me we should be together."

"Well, there you go," Lauren said.

Felicity sat back, tingling with resolve. "Thank you so much, Lauren."

"You're welcome," said Lauren.

There was the slightest wrinkle in her brow, Felicity noticed. A Botox injection would clear that right up.

"Yes," Felicity said, and she let out a huge breath. Her instincts had rarely failed her. "*Follow your heart*; oh, I love that." She slipped her foot out of her other sandal; she would take an Uber directly to Russell's, barefoot and pregnant.

Felicity picked up her glass of champagne. "I read that one little sip won't hurt."

Act 1

Chapter 1

What Lauren remembered most about their first summer in Greenwich Village was her absence. She spent those hot,
sticky days—away from her children and Leo—back in her Brooklyn
studio, where she shaped pieces and then painted them with ferns,
rabbit skulls, and quail bones. Petals, herbs, grasses, and leaves. Ants,
worms, millipedes, maggots, spiders, and flies. Molted cicada shells
and snake skins, cobwebs and beehives. She had several moments of
panic in June when she grasped the full scale of the order that Felicity
had placed and thought she'd never be able to finish by summer's end.
And she had several spells of elation in July when she'd completed
all the footed cake plates and serving platters. She'd screamed bloody
murder in August when she dropped a tray of coffee mugs on the
floor, just as she was taking them out of the kiln. Over the sound
of a fan blowing by the window, she played pop music and allowed

herself to feel the joy she'd experienced back in art school when she'd first worked with porcelain—volatile, yes, but silky and delicate. She thought of her kids and Leo settling into the brownstone without her, taking the train to Coney Island, going to the Museum of Natural History, and she worked even harder, knowing she was getting closer with every passing day to meeting Felicity's high and fabulous expectations.

Over the course of the summer, Lauren created something out of nothing, a collection of pieces she loved. Felicity, meanwhile, faded into the background, no longer checking in to give support or encouragement as she had at the outset of their collaboration. Rather, to Lauren's disappointment, she was put in touch with an executive at the company named Courtney who would call to discuss—in a breathy voice full of anticipation and possibility—deadlines and quantities, packing supplies and couriers. Courtney could talk about Bubble Wrap in a way that made it sound sexy.

At the end of Labor Day weekend—in the nick of time—Lauren sent off all the promised dessert plates, fruit bowls, teacups and saucers, mugs, sugar pots, and creamers that would grace the shelves of Felicity, a store Lauren admired but couldn't herself afford. Her hands were stiff, her eyes were strained, and her neck and shoulders ached. There wasn't enough moisturizer in the world to heal the deep cracks in her fingertips. She left her studio that day, feeling like her entire body was surrounded by a plume of clay dust. She was looking forward to shifting gears now, to settling into the house, spending time with the kids, cooking, and walking the dog.

• • •

On the afternoon before the kids' first day at their new school, Lauren was cleaning out the refrigerator when Courtney called to congratulate her: the pieces exceeded their expectations. Lauren took her phone outside and put her feet up on the back deck where she and Felicity had sipped champagne together on that warm day last spring. If she'd known then how much was going to be expected over the next several months, Lauren would have been in a state of panic that day rather than one of naive enthusiasm.

"We're obsessed with you and your whole aesthetic," Courtney said in her sultry voice. "So what we're thinking now is that we want you to round out the collection."

"I'm sorry, what?" Lauren sat up and put her feet back on the ground. "What does that mean," she said, "'round out'? Round out how?"

Bumper darted outside, carrying something in his mouth.

"Felicity has a new vision for your work. She doesn't want anything outside your sphere. Just a few additional decorative pieces to take you beyond kitchen slash tabletop. She wants you to create bookends, for example. Flower vases. Desk accessories, like paperweights, pencil cups, and handles for letter openers. Lamp bases."

"Sorry?" Lauren tried to open the dog's mouth to remove whatever he was chomping on, but he was too fast.

"Lamp. Bases," Courtney said more slowly, as though she were describing a hot man's body parts. "We'll provide you with measurements and specifications for the linen shades we have in mind. We also want large frames for mirrors and small ones for photographs. Knobs for furniture. I'll email a full list."

Lauren couldn't decide if she should whoop with excitement or burst into tears. What Courtney was describing would require hundreds of hours of work. "That's . . . amazing," she said, trying to stay calm. "And you would need these pieces . . . when exactly?" *Please say December*, she prayed. *Please say next year.*

"Before the end of October. So what do you say?" Courtney said, as if they were planning to run away together. "Doesn't that sound like fun?"

"Wow," Lauren said. "Just wow. Holy sh— Thanks so much."

As soon as they hung up, Lauren put her head between her knees. Bumper dropped Charles's retainer at her feet and licked her ear.

"Whatcha doing?" Leo asked, coming out to the porch. "Is that yoga? Doodlebug pose?" He patted her on the back.

"I didn't know you were home," she said, picking up the retainer, which was slobbery but unbroken, and sitting up. "I don't suppose you'd like to take a sabbatical? Spend some more quality time with the kids?"

"Sure would," he said, "and I'm due for one in about . . . three years."
Well, that wouldn't help. "Houston," she said, "we have a problem."

. . .

That night Lauren could hear the boys shouting upstairs over a game while she was rinsing Leo's late mother's plates in the deep cast-iron sink. Bumper was leaning into the open dishwasher, wagging his tail as he licked the remaining ketchup and salad dressing off the knives and forks Lauren dropped into the silverware basket. Leo and Waverly were sitting at the dinette table, working on a jigsaw puzzle they'd started weeks before. Lauren had insisted earlier that day that they finish the puzzle that night, not because she minded family meals on the back deck but because the kitchen would be the best place for the kids to do homework. But who would be overseeing the homework now?

"Is there any way you could work from home a few afternoons a week?" Lauren said.

"Not this semester," Leo said, studying the puzzle. "I teach a graduate seminar Monday, Tuesday, and Wednesday; I have faculty and committee meetings Thursdays, and lab meeting every Friday."

"I wish it stayed summer all year long," Waverly said. "I like it better."

"Not me," said Leo. "I *love* the start of the school year. I get new students to replace the ones who flew the nest. New pencils, new whiteboard markers. It's a fresh start every fall."

"What we need," Lauren said, scraping hamburger crud off a pan, "is a sitter who can pick up after school and stay until one of us gets home from work." Lauren pictured a wonderful, young freelancer, someone who loved algebra and baking and needed a stable weekly income.

"What if I don't make any new friends?" Waverly said.

"Of course you'll make friends," Leo said. They'd almost finished the puzzle but were still missing two shiny green beetles that looked enough alike in the picture that they were presenting a challenge. "Second grade is going to be great. Ah, I wonder what you'll learn this year. I hope you study photosynthesis. And paleontology. And Mesopotamia. Did you know the Mesopotamian number system was sexagesimal?"

"What?" said Waverly.

"A starving artist maybe," Lauren said. "Someone energetic and responsible."

"Sexagesimal," said Leo. "It means based on sixty. Babylonian astronomers figured out how to predict eclipses. Isn't that cool?"

Lauren felt Leo should be focusing on the problem at hand, but paying attention was not one of Leo's strengths. "I wish we had someone who could start . . . tomorrow," she said, and then she laughed because it was so utterly preposterous.

"Not tomorrow," said Waverly. "I want *you* to come get me."

"Of course," said Lauren, rinsing a coffee cup under the water. "I wouldn't miss pickup on your first day at your new school." Private school, and the price tag attached to it, had never been part of Leo and Lauren's plan. But when Phillip, Leo's biological father, invited them to Christmas at the brownstone the year before, he offered them a whole new life in Greenwich Village.

"Charley never wanted me to do anything for you," he'd said to Leo, as the kids made garlands out of ancient wrapping paper Phillip had found in the coat closet. "She told me I was not allowed to take on the traditional patriarchal role"—then he laughed—"as if I would. But your mother isn't here to lecture me anymore, and you're the only family I have." And then he offered them use of the brownstone—"I'm taking a new opportunity with an auction house in Berlin; I'll be away for a couple of years or so, popping back to New York very rarely"—and cash for tuition—"What else am I going to do with my money? The little scamps should have it." Phillip packed his bags that spring and handed over the keys, and Lauren and Leo, thrilled at their good fortune—a house! a yard!—adopted Bumper.

Lauren studied the cup in her hand before putting it in the top rack of the dishwasher, wondering how it was any different from a pencil cup. Desk accessories really weren't her thing.

The boys ran into the kitchen then, just as Leo was saying, "Leave it to me. I can find a babysitter in no time."

"I don't need a babysitter," Charles said.

"I do," said Harrell.

"It might take a week or so," Leo said, "but I can find someone who can do homework with you guys while Mommy and I are at work."

His confidence in the face of something so complicated irked Lauren. Some Mary Poppins, trained in CPR and crazy about kids, wasn't going to appear out of the blue.

"Who?" said Charles.

Indeed, who? thought Lauren. Leo was brilliant, but he wasn't always connected to the realities of life on earth.

Leo cleared his throat. "Put up an ad on the university list serve, I will, hmmm?" he said, doing his Yoda impression. "Easy, it is."

Harrell laughed.

"A student?" Lauren gently nudged Bumper's head out of the way to load a greasy plate. Her knuckles, so dried out from working with clay, were starting to sting from the water. "That's actually a great idea," she said. "But it's going to take time."

Her worry seemed to finally get through to Leo, and he looked up at the ceiling, thinking. Then he straightened his back and said brightly, "Evelyn!"

At the very mention of her mother, Lauren adjusted her posture as well. "What?"

Leo looked back at the puzzle and clicked two green pieces together, victorious. "Evelyn," he said, even more enthusiastically this time. "We could invite her to stay with us while we find someone." He switched back to Yoda's voice, saying, "Buy us time, it would."

Lauren dried her hands on the embroidered tea towel she'd tucked into the waist of her overalls and faced her husband. "You want my mother to come?"

Leo shrugged. "Why not? For the first time ever, we've got room for her. She can have the whole third floor to herself. And it would be nice to have her around."

"She doesn't like . . . New York." Lauren had almost said *She doesn't like* me, but didn't want to say such a thing in front of her kids.

"That's because she never stays long enough to get comfortable," said Leo.

Lauren disagreed; a longer visit would likely make things worse, not better. "I'm not ready to have her come here," Lauren said. "We're not at our best."

The faucet dripped behind her, and the yellow wall clock, which did not keep time accurately, ticked loudly.

"What do you mean?" Leo said.

The children were looking at Leo with the same expression as Lauren: as though they too were having a hard time imagining their strict grandmother in this rather scruffy setting.

Bumper pushed past Lauren to get to the other side of the open dishwasher, working another angle. The boys were eating ice cream out of the container and started sword fighting each other with their spoons.

"Hate this house, she will," Waverly said, doing her own version of Yoda.

Lauren did not disagree.

But Leo looked hurt. "How could *anyone* hate this house? My childhood home? Come on, it's a swell idea. The kids should spend some quality time with their only living grandmother. And we can reconnect with her, show her our life. It'll be fun, and, bonus, it won't cost us anything."

"Not monetarily maybe," said Lauren. She moved Bumper's head and closed the dishwasher. "I don't know how much help she would be. And she's not going to approve of"—Lauren looked through the kitchen and into the living room, where carpet frayed and the wallpaper peeled—"Phillip's decor."

There was a mangy, taxidermied hawk on the top of the bookshelf next to a broken lamp and a slide projector. There were board games and puzzles on the window seat and dog-eared anthologies of poetry and plays stacked under the coffee table. There was a sketch of a nude man, Phillip, by the look of him, although that had yet to be confirmed, over the fireplace. There were ashtrays—why were there ashtrays? No one here smoked—that still smelled of stale cigarettes, and there were framed pictures of strangers perched on every surface. The house was a time capsule from the 1970s, and even though they were living there for the time being, they didn't feel permitted to make changes.

"Evelyn is the perfect stopgap measure," Leo was saying.

"What's stopgap?" Harrell asked.

"A temporary solution, like using a generator in a power outage," Leo said.

Lauren's eyes settled on the broken table lamp in the living room. She got up and walked over to it: it was made with a celadon glaze, and there was a fine spiderweb connecting the shade to its very pleasing base. She put her hands on the cool, curved surface; she could try replicating its classic vase shape in her studio, if only she could get herself there.

"Teamwork," Leo called out. "We had a problem, and we came up with a solution, as a family." He was smiling, holding up his phone. "I sent her a text message."

"Wait," said Lauren, turning back to Leo in the kitchen. "No—"

"What?" said Leo.

"Too many emojis," said Charles, shaking his head at Leo's screen.

He'd already done it, but she supposed it didn't really matter; her mother would never accept his invitation.

. . .

The Aston-Shaws woke up the next morning as rain pelted against the windows. After breakfast, Lauren gathered the kids in the living room and took a picture to commemorate the first day of the school year, posting it on the family chat for her mom to see. They put on raincoats and headed out together in the storm.

At the corner of Waverly and Sixth, they split off. Leo, wearing a clear plastic poncho over his cargo shorts, took the subway uptown to the university, while Lauren, Bumper, and the kids walked a few blocks south to Perkins Academy.

Lauren was nervous. The school was housed in a lovely stone building tucked between long rows of town houses. It was known for its celebrity parents, its rooftop greenhouse, and its pedagogical resistance to grades of any kind. They'd chosen Perkins because of the science program (which Leo liked), the art program (which impressed Lauren), the gerbils in most classrooms (which appealed to the kids), and the proximity to Waverly Place (a bonus for Bumper).

It poured the whole way to school that first morning. In spite of their hoods, Lauren and her kids all arrived with wet, stringy hair. Their sneakers squelched as they walked through the Perkins lobby, past a crowd of noisy children with backpacks and confident mothers with sleek umbrellas. It was mayhem, and Lauren pulled Bumper close, hoping her kids would make friends there and be happy, once they adjusted. She held Waverly's hand, gathered the boys, and approached a man who was hunched over a computer at the imposing front desk.

He barely glanced up and yet scowled at the sight of Bumper. "Is that a therapy animal?"

Bumper shook then, sending a spray of water three feet in all directions, and rolled over to dry his back on the lobby carpet.

"Not exactly," Lauren said as Harrell leaned over to pat Bumper's damp belly. "Funny story, actually: the shelter told us he was three already, but our vet says he's not even one."

The man did not appear to find her story funny at all.

"We're new here," Lauren said. "As in *brand*-new. It's our first day."

"Who are you?"

"I'm Lauren Shaw, and this is Charles Aston, Harrell Aston, and Waverly Aston," she said, placing a hand on the top of each child's wet head in turn. "Grade six, grade four, and grade two."

He sorted through a box and handed her a fat envelope, just as there was a clap of thunder.

"Is this the bill?" she joked.

"Grade six goes to the fifth floor, grade four to the sixth, and grade two to the fourth. You have a required parent information session starting in fifteen minutes in the auditorium."

"Oh," said Lauren, looking around the lobby, noticing that the horde of parents was making no move to head back out into the rain. "Do you know how long the program will go?"

He didn't answer, but Lauren knew that the lamp base she'd been imagining in her head overnight would not be thrown on the wheel today.

She sat in the back row of auditorium flip seats, listening to presentations about the school's recycling program, field trip opportunities, and fundraising expectations, as Bumper grew restless and gnawed on her hand. At ten o'clock, she tugged him up two flights of stairs to attend the PTA breakfast, during which he ate an entire croissant right off the buffet when her back was turned and knocked over a teacher's full cup of coffee on the carpet. Lauren apologized profusely and offered to pay for the cleaning, solidly regretting her decision to bring him along. She rushed him home and returned an hour later, just in time for story circle in Waverly's class, which was followed by a middle school discussion with a psychologist who instructed the parents on how to combat drug and alcohol abuse, how to recognize signs of anxiety and depression, and how to advise kids against jumping off a cliff even when all their friends were lining up to do so.

At three o'clock, the program was over, and Lauren was flat-out exhausted. The kids came down to the lobby, and they walked home together on wet sidewalks under clear skies, the kids chattering about their first day.

. . .

Frances called that evening, just as Lauren was dumping a full box of pasta into a pot of boiling water.

"I think it's sweet you and Leo invited Evelyn for a visit," she said.

That her sister-in-law already knew about the invitation was unsurprising; she and Lauren's mother were, indeed, exactly that close. They saw each other several times a week and spoke on the phone—much to Lauren's annoyance—every single day.

"I think this is the longest I've ever gone without seeing her," Lauren said.

Bumper was pushing his empty food bowl around the kitchen, trying to get his dinner to appear.

"If she decides to come," Frances said, "maybe she could give you some advice on how to whip that house into shape."

"Oh, the house is fine," Lauren said, stirring the spaghetti with a wooden spoon. The range was an ancient Viking, permanently encrusted with decades of grease. The condition of the house was not something she wanted to discuss with Frances, who lived with Lauren's brother, William, the only son and undisputed favorite, in a fully updated four-thousand-square-foot home on Beacon Hill.

"I disagree," Frances said. "That picture you texted of the kids this morning? I noticed a lot of clutter in the background."

Lauren rubbed her forehead, wishing she'd cropped the picture more tightly.

"I'm just saying your mom is a good organizer," Frances said.

Frances, whose own mother had died young, had latched on to Evelyn from the day they met. The pair had a running joke about the necessity of talking to each other before going anywhere together because too many times, they exclaimed with a laugh, they'd shown up in the same shift dress and pearls. The chances of Lauren and Evelyn appearing anywhere in matching outfits were exactly zero.

Her mother was impressed by Frances's social circle, but even more so by her upper-crust, philanthropic, Kennedy-esque family. They had inborn political ambitions, which had rubbed off on William; he was actually talking about a potential run for political office. Evelyn would mention it to Lauren in hushed tones and coded language, as though the press had tapped her phone.

"What I'm actually hoping," Lauren said, "is that she'll hang out with my kids in the afternoons so I can work."

"You *still* haven't finished that order for Felicity?" Frances sounded alarmed, as though Lauren's delinquency would somehow reflect poorly on the entire family.

"No, I finished," Lauren said, "but they want more now. They're asking for pieces I've never even made before."

"Wonderful, Lauren. But can I be honest? Evelyn's not up to handling all three of your children by herself."

That comment struck Lauren as fundamentally unfair. "She helped out with your kids all the time when they were little."

"Sure, but that was years ago," Frances said, "and she had your dad to help then. You haven't spent time with her lately. Her sciatica alone would make babysitting a challenge, especially given how energetic your kids are."

William and Frances's kids were in high school already. Christopher was a senior at Andover, probably headed to Harvard, and Anne was a sophomore at Buckingham Browne and Nichols. Evelyn loved to brag about them.

"How are your kids doing?" Lauren said.

"Great," she said. "We're in the thick of college applications, so that's going to be our whole fall. Andover handles the process pretty well, but we've hired our own counselor, just to be sure."

"Sure of what?" Lauren said. *An Ivy League acceptance* was the likeliest answer.

"The essays, for one thing. Christopher is writing about your dad, did I tell you? It's all about how he wants to be a doctor like him and how deeply impacted he was by his death. I'll send it to you when it's done."

"Wow, really?" Lauren was jaded enough to believe that they were using her dad's death to write a moving essay. But then the alternative—that Christopher truly felt *that* close to his grandfather—made her feel even worse. Her own kids would never have such a deep bond to a grandparent. "Has my mom read it?"

"I'm sure she'll tell you all about it when she comes. It brought her to tears."

"I don't actually think she's going to come," Lauren said, wishing for the first time that she would. "We'll go to Wellesley soon enough anyway. Maybe for Thanksgiving."

"She told me she's on the fence," Frances said, "but don't take it personally. You know how many commitments she has here. Between her charities and her bridge club, it's hard for her to get away."

"She's with you guys all the time."

"Well, yes, but she's only half an hour away, and we don't ask anything of her. If you want her to come for a social visit, that's one thing. But as for the kids, you really should hire someone."

Bumper had nudged his bowl all the way over to Lauren's feet. She picked it up and filled it with a scoop of kibble. "We're working on it. Leo's going to find a college student."

"A student is not the way to go," Frances said. "What you need is a proper nanny. Or an au pair. I'll send you the names of some services that do background checks and screenings. You can't be too careful when it comes to your kids. You have a spare room now, right?"

Lauren knew the kinds of services her sister-in-law would recommend charged exorbitant finder fees. And the spare rooms they had were *not* the kind of accommodations Frances was probably imagining. The brownstone only had two and a half bathrooms.

"We don't need live-in help," she said, putting Frances on speaker so she could dump the pot of cooked pasta into a colander. The steam made her face damp, and she wiped her forehead on a crocheted pot holder.

"I disagree," said Frances. "With your kids, your career, and that house, not only do you need professional childcare, but you should hire an assistant, someone who can help you organize and throw out some of those stacks of magazines and books I saw behind your coffee table."

Why had she texted that picture? "We can't do that," Lauren said, looking at the orange vinyl dinette chairs, three of which were repaired with duct tape. They were vintage to be sure, but did Lauren love them? No, she did not. "Nothing here belongs to us. Not really, or not yet anyway."

"Then box it all up and store it. Did you have the place inspected for lead paint? Because I know this woman who moved into an old, un-renovated house like yours, and all her kids got permanent brain damage."

Lauren eyed the windowsills suspiciously. "Leo grew up here, and he doesn't have brain damage."

"Well, *may-be* not," Frances said, as though she were considering whether Leo's social eccentricities might have been caused by toxins.

"Oh," she said, suddenly rushed, "your mom's beeping in. I'll try to talk her into visiting you, but, Lauren, just don't expect too much of her."

Lauren didn't remind her that Evelyn was *her* mother, after all, and that she knew exactly what she could and could not expect.

· · ·

The heavy rain had cooled the air, but it still felt like summer. After dinner, Lauren, Leo, and the kids headed out to take a walk. There was a small crowd on the sidewalk directly at the bottom of their stairs, customers of the bar in the basement. Lauren was annoyed to see three young women actually sitting across their bottom step, smoking cigarettes.

"Excuse me," Lauren said as nicely as she could.

The women stood up and let them pass, fawning over Bumper as he went by.

"Looks like NYU is officially in session," Leo said. "The law school kids are historically the most loyal bar patrons, but I've been told Stern students tip the best."

"Whoever they are," Lauren said, "I hope they keep it down tonight."

They crossed the street and were passing under the arch in Washington Square Park when Lauren's phone pinged:

Lauren dear, Taking Amtrak early Thursday. I can stay through the weekend and that is all. This is your mother.

"Uh-oh," Lauren said, showing Leo her phone.

"Outstanding," he said.

Lauren wished she had as much confidence.

"In other good news," Leo said, "I already have two potential babysitters stopping by my office tomorrow to interview."

"Who are they?"

"Don't even worry. I'll prescreen them, and then bring home the best of the best."

As the boys took off for the fountain, Leo, Lauren, and Waverly stopped to watch three young guys playing jazz.

Leo walked up to them, reaching in his pocket for change, which he dropped in their open guitar case.

"How'd they get a piano out here?" Waverly said.

"Good question," Lauren said. "I actually have no idea." Waverly leaned against her, while Bumper sat on her foot.

Leo came back and put his arm across Lauren's shoulder. Rooted to the ground from all sides, Lauren looked over to see Harrell sitting on the fountain's edge while Charles was dipping his hands in the water.

"I think Evelyn will like our little corner of New York," Leo said, tapping his feet to the music, completely off the rhythm. "It's not fancy like Beacon Hill, but she might appreciate the vibe."

Lauren, too, felt a flicker of hope at the idea of her mother's visit. But right then a big group of skateboarders clattered past them, way too close for comfort, with a plume of pot smoke following them.

"I wouldn't bet on it," Lauren said.

"I have homework," said Waverly, "and I have to buy folders and notebooks and markers and colored pencils."

Lauren yanked her foot out from under Bumper's rear end. "By tomorrow?"

Waverly nodded.

Lauren turned to check on the boys again, only to see that Harrell had taken off his shoes and socks and was wading in the fountain.

"Let's go to Inkwell on Eighth," Leo said. "That's where your grandmother used to take me for school supplies."

"Grammy knew you when you were little?"

"No, I mean Charley," said Leo, "your other grandmother, *my* mother."

"And Phillip?" Waverly asked. "Did he take you too?"

"No, Phillip was just my biological father, meaning he donated—"

"We can explain all that later," Lauren said, concerned to see that Charles was splashing Harrell now with both hands.

"Charles," she called out, "that's enough."

"He likes it," said Charles with a shrug.

Harrell emerged from the fountain in a fit of laughter, water dripping down his bare legs onto the concrete.

He stopped laughing as soon as he discovered that his shoes were nowhere to be found.

Leo squatted down so Harrell could climb up on his back, and Lauren saw him wince slightly when he tried to stand up.

"Easy does it," she said, offering him her hands to pull on.

"Do you think Evelyn would like to take a tour of my lab?" Leo said, as they walked toward the west side of the park—past families, chess players, and weed dealers—and back to their house. Harrell's bare feet were swinging by Leo's hips. "I could show her our facilities and introduce her to my crickets." He looked at her, his glasses slipping down his nose.

"That's really sweet, Leo," Lauren said. "I mean it." She tried to imagine Evelyn taking any interest in Leo's research. "But no, definitely not."

Chapter 2

Evelyn did not take the train to New York. Rather, Frances booked her on the United shuttle and hired a limo service to pick her up at LaGuardia and drive her to Lauren's front door. Lauren stood on the stoop holding Bumper by the collar and waved as her mother got out of the back seat. Her mother looked up at the house, tightening the belt of her trench coat and running a hand over her hair. The driver carried her luggage to the top of the brownstone steps, and Evelyn tipped him with a crisp twenty-dollar bill.

"Isn't Frances clever?" Evelyn said, snapping her wallet shut. "That flight was so quick, and it was fifty dollars less than the train."

"I'm surprised she didn't charter you a private jet," Lauren mumbled as her mother put her wallet in her purse.

Lauren picked up the black Tumi suitcase and followed her mom across the threshold, watching as she took in her first glimpse of the living room. In that instant, it felt as if the composition of the air in the house changed, causing the wallpaper to wilt and the hardwood to buckle.

"So," Lauren said. "Can I get you something to drink, or should we start with the grand tour?"

Lauren walked her mother from room to room, while Evelyn—lips pursed, arms crossed—made only the occasional utterance: "My, my" and "Oh no." In another situation, her mother's relentless negativity might have amused Lauren, but she felt too defensive of Leo, Phillip, and of the house itself to find humor in her harsh judgment. She could only imagine what details Evelyn would relay back to Frances and William.

"You have simply got to be kidding me," Evelyn finally said, after they had climbed both flights of creaky stairs and arrived at the largest of three spare bedrooms on the third floor, the one with the multicolored hook rug and the Victorian wingback chair in front of the window.

Lauren went in with Bumper, pushing aside the long strands of beaded curtains that hung in the doorway, and slid a throw blanket over the chair's torn seat.

"Please don't say mean things, because we really love it," she said. And it was true, they did. Maybe not everything about it, maybe not the thick red velvet curtains in the living room, or the bright orange Formica countertops in the kitchen, or the faded theater posters—advertising plays from now-defunct East and West Village venues—thumbtacked onto the walls of the stairwell. Maybe not the sloping floors or the windows that would not open when closed or close when opened. But they loved—what did people always say?—the bones of the house. Its past. Its soul.

"I don't know if you realize, but this house is a pretty important place, historically speaking," Lauren went on, lifting her mother's suitcase onto the foot of the bed. "Charley was a visionary. And she hosted all kinds of interesting people here, theatrical types, mostly. Robert Brustein, Jane Fonda, Richard Pryor. Plus, Leo has such happy memories from his childhood. This was his bedroom, once upon a time. If it's too noisy you can take a room on the back of the house, but I don't think it would make much difference. And anyway, the sounds are all part of the fun of living in the heart of the Village."

Lauren threw open the yellowed curtains in the window. When the rod fell down, she kicked off her sneakers and stood on the wrought iron bed to reattach it in the brackets.

Evelyn was still standing just outside the open door frame, watching her through the strings of beads, the handle of her Chanel purse over her wrist, eyebrows raised as though all her aesthetic sensibilities were under assault at once. "Am I to understand that my room does not have a door?"

"No, but you have the whole floor to yourself," said Lauren. "It's private."

"My God," she said, parting the beads and seeing the rusted air-conditioning unit. "You don't have central air?"

"It's an old house, built pre–climate change."

"But surely Leo could remove that monstrosity from the window now that summer's over. It's blocking the light."

As Lauren climbed off the bed, a movement caught her eye, and she spotted a mouse as it ran across the landing directly behind her mother's Ferragamos.

"We're thinking of getting a cat," Lauren said. "Charley always had a few. You're not allergic, are you?"

"Lauren," her mother said sternly, "do not take on more to manage than you already have: three children, an untrained dog, a demanding job, this . . . dwelling, *and* a husband like Leo. I think that's quite enough. I always tell your sister-in-law: 'I don't know how Lauren does it.'"

Lauren sat on the bed and slipped her feet back in her worn sneakers. Maybe her mother would ask to take a rest. Lauren tried to calculate how much time she could have in her studio if she left right away. "Frances has more to deal with than I do," she said. "She and William have the busiest social calendar I've ever heard of."

"Her situation is somehow more . . . civilized," said Evelyn. "Did you know she has two assistants, a personal trainer, a housekeeper, a dog walker, and a nutritionist? She and William take very good care of themselves."

"Well, good for them," Lauren said, standing up and clapping her hands together one time. "The bathroom is off the hall. I think there are towels in there, but I'll double-check."

"Does the bathroom have a door?"

"Of course," said Lauren, her voice snarky like a teenager's. "Your closet is kind of full of Charley's clothes, but Leo pushed them to the back to give you room to hang your stuff."

"*Charley's* clothes?" her mother repeated in disbelief. "I had your father's clothes packed up and sent to charity within a month after he died."

"A month seems unnecessarily efficient—"

"A million dollars," her mother said.

"Excuse me?"

"On first glance, I'd say this house needs a million dollars poured into it."

"Yeah, well, we'll just take it as it is."

"The whole place should be stripped down to the studs."

Lauren could not imagine erasing so much history. "We wouldn't want the house to lose its character."

"There is such a thing, dear," her mother said, finally stepping fully into the room, "as too much character, and that kitchen is stricken with it. Now how much time is there before pickup at school?"

"Five hours," said Lauren.

"Excellent," Evelyn said. "That's plenty of time to enjoy the day at the Metropolitan Museum. We have a reservation for lunch at twelve thirty."

As badly as Lauren needed to go to her studio, the lamps and book-ends would have to wait; her mother had made plans. "I haven't been to a museum in months," Lauren said, brightening at the thought. "Maybe it would be good for me. Spark a little creativity?" Walking through the Greek and Roman wing sounded like heaven.

"And I'd like to treat you and Leo to a nice adult dinner this week," her mom said, "preferably somewhere uptown."

"What's wrong with downtown?" Lauren said.

"Nothing," her mom said, "but Frances gave me a list of recommendations. If there's time this afternoon, we should have tea at that Viennese café in the Neue Galerie."

Her mother's plan for the day was so lovely, so out of the ordinary that Lauren walked right over and gave her a hug, which Evelyn responded to by leaning toward her but going completely rigid, making Lauren think of the ironing board attached to the wall in the laundry room that had recently fallen open all by itself and knocked her on the head.

"I'm glad you came," Lauren said.

"I can only stay until Monday," her mother said, patting her on the back. "I promised Frances I'd go with her to a charity luncheon at her club next Wednesday."

Frances, Frances, Frances. Lauren felt a childish stab of jealousy. "I know," she said, "but you're here now."

She went to her room and put on her dressier sneakers for the museum.

As their cab sat in traffic on Park Avenue, Lauren looked out the window, thinking about the little paper clip dishes that Courtney had put on the list. Maybe she would start with those; the shape would be familiar.

• • •

They returned from the museum to find that Bumper had pooped on the kilim.

"Honestly, Lauren," her mother said, "can't you hire a dog walker?" She stepped over the mess on the rug and went upstairs. "I need to freshen up before we go."

Lauren picked up the poop, washed her hands, and put Bumper on a leash. She called upstairs to her mom. When she didn't answer, Lauren climbed the two flights, leaving Bumper tied to the banister. He barked as if to tell her she was going the wrong way.

Lauren found Evelyn sitting on her bed, taking off her shoes.

"You'll have to go get the children without me," she said, reclining on top of the faded green coverlet and propping up the pillows behind her. "I need a catnap."

"Do you feel okay?" Lauren said.

"I was fine at the museum, but as soon as I walked back in this cluttered house, I got a sharp pain behind my right eye. I would think a man who traffics in the world of expensive antiques would have a better sense of style in his own home."

Lauren had wondered the same thing about Phillip, and more specifically, why the place looked as though Charley still lived there, a full decade after her death.

Evelyn rearranged the pillows behind her head as the sound of voices drifted up from the street. "Are the pedestrians always so noisy? I don't know how you stand it. When I was unpacking, I could hear a couple fighting on the sidewalk, cursing like sailors. I think these windows are single-paned."

"Probably," said Lauren. The windows were drafty and made a high-pitched whistling sound whenever the wind picked up.

Evelyn dabbed her nose with a tissue. "And I may need an antihistamine. Has the house been tested for mold in the past thirty years?"

The high Lauren had felt walking through the Asian art collection at the museum was wearing off. She wished her mother would at least acknowledge the molding in the brownstone along with the mold, the grand size of the house along with microscopic allergens.

"Not that I know of, but I'll ask Leo."

"You're going to need a good cleaning woman to get this place out from under the dust," she said. "Someone who's young enough to drag a vacuum cleaner up and down all those stairs. Can't Phillip give you the name of a maid? And where is he anyway?"

"He's traveling before he starts his new job. He went to an ashram in Tamil Nadu."

"What's that?"

"A yoga retreat."

"At his age?" Evelyn said, her voice going high in pointed disapproval.

"I think he's going to Finland next to visit friends before he settles down in Berlin."

"Your father and I always thought he was a pompous windbag."

Lauren doubted her father had given Phillip much thought at all; it was her mother who'd been consumed with Leo's unconventional family. At the bridal shower, Lauren could see Evelyn's embarrassment when she attempted to explain the circumstances of Leo's birth.

"I find it sad," her mother said. "He's alone in the world now because he never fathered poor Leo the way he should have."

"He has more friends than anyone I know," said Lauren. "And Charley didn't let him be a traditional dad; she didn't believe in that kind of family structure." She checked the time on her phone to make sure she wasn't late to get the kids. If she walked fast, she could get there in seven minutes.

Her mother looked confused. "I don't understand the nature of their relationship."

"It's pretty simple: they were best friends." Lauren had had this very conversation with her mother more times than she could count, and yet each time it was as though Evelyn were hearing the information for the first time.

"I'd say they were more than friends given that they had a baby together."

"Well," said Lauren, trying to be patient, "biologically speaking they did. But Charley wanted to raise Leo by herself, as a single mom. Phillip agreed to help her make that happen."

"But who would do such a thing?"

Lauren wasn't sure if she was referring to Charley wanting to raise Leo alone or Phillip donating sperm, or both.

"And now he's moving to Germany," her mom said, trying to puzzle the situation out, "while you're living in the house at his invitation. Does he see you as caretakers?"

"I don't think so," Lauren said, although she supposed it was a reasonable question. "He asked us if we wanted to live here since he'll be away for a couple of years. We said yes, of course. Our place in Brooklyn was tiny and expensive—"

"I remember," said Evelyn.

"So we're pinching ourselves."

"But the arrangement sounds complicated. Didn't Charley own

half the house? Is it in a trust? Should you be doing something to offset inheritance taxes down the road?"

"I really don't know, Mom," Lauren said, taking a step toward the door. She could not be late for pickup. "Leo will inherit it eventually, I guess."

"I wouldn't hold my breath," said Evelyn, "unless you've seen it in writing. Phillip could have bequeathed it to some distant relative. And anyway, my poor bridge partner Helen got her house in the divorce, but then she couldn't afford to keep it. Her sister had to take her in. Now, you don't want to become a burden to William and Frances someday, do you? You really must discuss all of this with an estate planner. I can introduce you to mine; Peter could help you sort through this mess, but I assume you have one already."

Lauren didn't confess that she and Leo did not have an estate planner. The closest they'd come to planning for some type of unanticipated tragedy was when Lauren had swilled a couple of glasses of wine and said to William, "So if Leo and I ever croak, you guys will take care of our kids, right?" and William had nodded solemnly, saying, "Of course."

Those two had surely done everything responsibly and legally, made a will and set up trust funds for the kids and assigned guardianship in a manner more binding than a haphazard, tipsy, verbal agreement. It occurred to Lauren then that her brother had never asked if she and Leo would take care of *their* kids if the unthinkable were to happen.

"We're Phillip's only family," Lauren said. "And anyway, he's paying some of the kids' school tuition."

"Ahhh, we wondered how you and Leo were going to manage that," she said, as if a great riddle had been solved. "No offense, but Frances was saying that the schools in Manhattan are exorbitantly expensive. I'm amazed, frankly," she added. "I didn't take Phillip for someone who would do such a thing. He struck me as so . . . self-involved."

"Are you sure you don't want to come along?" Lauren asked her mother, who had closed her eyes. The house itself seemed to be tiring her. "It's a short walk."

"I'll stay," Evelyn said. "I need to rest before my grandchildren arrive."

Lauren went down the stairs—much to Bumper's delight—and headed outside with him, locking the door behind them and dropping her keys in the pocket of her jeans. They headed west on Waverly, walking past the entrance to the bar, where someone had either spilled food on the sidewalk or thrown up. Lauren pulled Bumper away from the mess, hoping it was the former. She also hoped her children would be on their best behavior that afternoon. She then scolded herself for imposing her mother's unrealistic expectations on her darling little kids. So what if they ran circles around the house, got into fights over nothing, and spilled their milk at the dinner table? They were children after all. They weren't the problem.

· · ·

On the way home from school, an argument ensued over what to cook for dinner. Harrell wanted pancakes, Charles wanted roast chicken, and Waverly wanted macaroni and cheese. There seemed to be no meal on earth that could meet her mother's exacting expectations, her children's picky demands, and Leo's newfound commitment to a predominately plant-based diet. At Gristedes, they finally settled on spaghetti, again, and meatless meatballs. She hoped her mother wouldn't be able to tell the difference between ground beef and pea protein.

When they got home, they found Evelyn had positioned herself in the living room like a queen, ready to receive her subjects, three gift bags on the coffee table before her.

The kids hugged her, and she embraced them all at the same time, not stiffly as she had Lauren, but warmly, adding kisses to the tops of their heads.

"Let's remember," she said to Harrell, as she released him, "how important it is to bathe every day. Now, who wants a present?"

She'd bought them matching accessories from Brooks Brothers: navy-blue-and-white-gingham ties for Charles and Harrell and a blue-and-white silk headband for Waverly. Harrell mistook the headband for a frisbee and threw it across the room, where it ricocheted off the portrait of the nude man who was probably Phillip. Lauren picked it up and placed it on Waverly's head.

"Ow," said Waverly, and she put it around her thigh instead.

"Tell me all about your new school, one at a time, please," said Evelyn. "Have you made new friends?"

"No," said Charles, "but it's only been, like, a few days."

"It's only been a few days, not *like* a few days," said Evelyn.

"I made a friend today," said Harrell, attaching his tie to Bumper's collar. "Me and Curtis played soccer and—"

Evelyn held up a finger. "Curtis *and I* played soccer. . . ."

Harrell looked surprised. "*You* played soccer with Curtis today too?"

Lauren stepped in to explain. "She means you should say 'Curtis and I' to be grammatically correct."

"Oh," said Harrell. "Well, I hope there's a game tomorrow with Curtis and I."

"With Curtis and me," said Evelyn.

"Huh?" said Harrell.

"I'm glad to know you're cultivating friends," said his grandmother.

"What's cultivate?" said Harrell.

"Acquire," said Evelyn.

"I'm doing choir," said Waverly.

"No, what Grammy means," said Lauren, taking a spot on the floor, "is it's nice to make friends."

Bumper came over and sat on her lap. She shifted his weight so she could breathe and unknotted the tie from his collar.

"Grammy," Waverly said, running her hands across the fabric of her grandmother's pleated skirt, "why are you so fancy?"

"Am I?"

"Are you going to a party?"

"I dressed for our dinner tonight," Evelyn said, her back straight and her ankles crossed.

Lauren considered the meatless meatballs thawing on the kitchen counter; they were sure to disappoint.

"One should never look slovenly," her mother added.

"Do I look sluvvelly?" Waverly asked, standing up to show her leggings, sweatshirt, and signature mismatched Keds.

"Of course not," said Lauren, who happened to love the way Waverly put an outfit together. "You look very comfortable."

"And at your young age," said Evelyn, "you're still allowed to put comfort over occasion."

Lauren tucked the tail of her flannel shirt into the back of her jeans. This was about as dressy as she ever got.

• • •

Leo came home from work early that evening with his first babysitting candidate: a student from Ohio named Nate. Leo introduced him to Lauren and then to Evelyn, who eyed him skeptically, which for some reason made Lauren all the more determined to like the young man. He had a preppy style and seemed very engaged.

"The kids are upstairs doing math homework, or I hope so anyway," Lauren said, restraining Bumper from jumping on him. "I'll call them down in a minute."

Lauren wished her mom would go upstairs as well, but instead she sat in the window seat and pretended to read a *New Yorker* from 1982.

"I was pretty good at math," Nate said. "I mean, I was an okay student when I was a kid."

"Charles and Waverly are self-directed," Lauren said. Then she whispered, "Harrell, not so much, but we're working on it."

Leo seemed pleased with himself for finding Nate, and he smiled at Lauren as they took their seats in the living room. "Nate's free every afternoon, and he can stay as late as we need," he said.

Lauren imagined hours of uninterrupted time in her studio, checking the items off Courtney's list one after the other. "What led you to come here," she said, "all the way from Ohio?"

"New York wasn't really in my plan," Nate said. "But turns out, I like it here."

"What do you think of college so far?" she said. "Are you worried about the workload? Juggling a job downtown could be tricky."

Nate shook his head. "No, see, I'm not actually a student . . . per se. I hacked into my girlfriend's account to get access to job listings."

"Sorry, what?" said Lauren.

"I know all her passwords," he said, tapping his temple. "We've been together since we started high school, and she thought she could break up with me before she left for college. But it all worked out because I followed her here to keep an eye on her. I hang out on campus, outside the library or her classes, just to let her know she can't get away from me that easy." He smiled and turned to Leo. "Women, am I right?"

Nate was dismissed.

"What a lunatic," Lauren said, bolting the front door and then leaning against it. She wished her mother hadn't witnessed that debacle. Evelyn had turned in the window seat, looking out on the street to make sure Nate was actually leaving the premises.

Leo had a stunned look on his face. "He's a stalker," he said. "I brought a stalker into our home."

"You didn't know," said Lauren. "How could you possibly know?"

"I knew," said Evelyn. "From the moment he walked in, I could tell he was hiding something. He didn't take off his baseball cap, he couldn't maintain eye contact, and his khakis were badly wrinkled. I think he's on drugs."

"Well, I don't know about *that*," said Lauren, "but he's definitely a bad guy."

"Really bad," said Leo. "But the next one will be much better—"

"Now, listen to me," said Evelyn, standing up and planting her fists on her slim hips. "Frances said you should be using one of those agencies. I assume you two will listen to her after what just happened."

Lauren had thought that was overkill before, but now she was thinking Frances was right.

"Give me another chance," Leo said. "I've got two more people already lined up, and they seemed great when they emailed. I'll make sure they're actually students this time."

"You can't be serious," her mother said, directing her exasperation solely at Leo now. "It would be worth every penny to have proper background checks done. You can't rely on your instincts when it comes to the well-being of your children."

"I won't," Leo said, chastened. "I'll do more thorough research next time."

Lauren felt caught in the middle, but she saw the judgmental look on her mother's face and immediately took Leo's side. "That was a fluke. Leo will find someone perfect." She gave his arm a squeeze. "Won't you?"

"Absolutely," he said. "Meanwhile, I need to call and report Nate to the campus cops."

Lauren quickly escaped to the kitchen, leaving Leo to deal with her mom.

• • •

She was making coffee the next morning when her mother came into the kitchen, already dressed and wearing understated lipstick. Lauren was still in pajamas. Evelyn sat down at the kitchen table, exhaling as though she'd just come in from a hike. "I could barely sleep last night," she said, sitting even more stiffly than usual. "Your radiators make such a racket."

"You turned on the heat?" Lauren said. She hadn't even known the heating system worked, since they'd never tried it. "But why?"

"It got very chilly up in the attic last night. Wait until you're my age and see how cold you get."

"A walk will warm you up," Lauren said, handing her a coffee mug that featured a millipede crawling on the rim. "You can go with me to take the kids to school."

"I can't," she said, showing Lauren that she could barely turn her head. "I have a crick in my neck. As soon as you're back, I'll need you to show me how to call one of those Uber cars. Frances is making a massage appointment for me at the Carlyle. Why don't you come along? I know spas aren't really your thing, but perhaps you'd like to get a facial."

A love of beauty treatments was yet another thing her mom and Frances shared, along with dieting, Chanel, and monograms on literally anything. Lauren would have tolerated a pedicure, but she needed to work. She had no idea how long it would take her to make a single letter opener, nor could she imagine who in this world would actually use one.

After dropping off the kids, installing the Uber app on her mom's phone, and seeing her off, Lauren took the R train to her Brooklyn studio. It took her forty-five minutes to get to Greenwood Heights, leaving her only two hours to work before she would have to head back to the Village.

She'd left the space in disarray, and yet she was happy to be back. She stood in the doorway for a moment, closed her eyes, and smiled as she breathed in the earthy smell. Then she opened the windows and got to work, spending the little time she had cleaning up and preparing to begin the new projects. Madonna was playing on a speaker down the hall while Lauren scrubbed her tools, sponged down her wheel head and splash pan, and vigorously swept the floor. She sat on her stool and went over the email Courtney had sent and tried to come up with a reasonable schedule: when to wedge, when to throw, when to trim, when to fire. Which pieces would be hand-built? She'd never made candlestick holders in her life. How should they look? What clay should she use? Lauren put her head on her arms and tried to picture them, how they would fit into the rest of the collection, what kind of critter would take up residence on the surface. She made no progress, even in her mind.

. . .

Evelyn looked radiant when she returned to the brownstone that afternoon, having gotten her hair and nails done in addition to her massage, and Lauren half wished she'd gone along. Her own hair could use a trim and her nails were, in fact, chipped and split, clay packed permanently underneath them.

When Leo came home that evening, he had a student with him named Sasha. Lauren offered to take her jacket, but before the young woman could even respond, she sneezed hard into the crook of her elbow. And then she sneezed again, pointing to Bumper, who was bounding in circles around her, his fur flying. The girl quickly backed out of the house.

"I'm so sorry," she said from the stoop, reaching in her backpack for an emergency inhaler, "I forgot to mention, I'm *severely* allergic to dogs."

Lauren thanked her for coming and shut the door.

"Yeah, that's unfortunate," Leo said glumly. "She had terrific references."

"It's okay," Lauren said, patting him on the shoulder and trying not to lose all faith. "You can't possibly think of everything."

Her mother walked by them on her way to the kitchen and didn't say a word, and yet to Lauren, her silence spoke volumes.

An hour later, the next candidate, a young woman named Kat, arrived. She sat on the floor talking to the kids. Kat had a small silver stud in her left nostril, she had read all the Harry Potter books, and she put her arms around Bumper when he came over and sat on her lap.

Lauren and Leo sat side by side on the couch, watching her talk to the kids. Leo reached over and took Lauren's hand, and Lauren leaned in and whispered, "Well done." She kissed him on the cheek.

That was when Kat burst into tears.

"Oh dear," said Lauren. "Did— I mean, are you okay?"

"My family was just like this once," Kat sobbed, wiping her face with the sleeve of her denim jacket as the kids looked on with bewildered expressions, "but my parents are getting divorced. You all seem so happy."

Evelyn came in from the kitchen with a box of tissues, gave Lauren her *I told you so* look, and took the kids upstairs. Kat wept for fifteen minutes, while Lauren patted her back and listened to the young woman vent about her mother's new boyfriend and the custody fight over the family dog.

Lauren was annoyed when Leo walked away from them and opened his computer, leaving her alone to assure Kat that her parents' irreconcilable differences were in no way her fault. But then he returned a few minutes later, giving Kat the number of the university counseling office.

"Good thinking," Lauren said after Kat left.

Leo often came through with the right solution at the right moment, and she appreciated that about him.

"So what do we do now?" she said. "Because I'm starting to think that the timing for this commission is just plain . . . bad, and maybe I should call Courtney and turn the whole thing down." She felt sick saying it, but it was true. Leo could not quit his career, with its steady salary and benefits, but she could take a break again from hers.

"Absolutely not," he said. "No, I don't accept that." He pushed his glasses in place and took her hand. "Take tomorrow, take the whole weekend at your studio. I'll do stuff with your mom and the kids. If you get started, you'll feel better about all this, and it's not like we can't find a sitter. We just have to keep trying."

It wasn't a long-term solution, but it was what she needed to hear in the moment. Time alone in her studio? She would take it.

Chapter 3

Alone at last! Lauren worked methodically, almost aggressively, at her studio. She decided to begin with what she thought would
be the most pleasant and familiar item to make: a small, shallow dish
to hold paper clips. Desk accessories weren't a thrill, but at least this
was a vessel, a piece designed to contain something, and that was what
Lauren did; she made pieces to be handled, filled, and used. Bookends,
furniture knobs, and paperweights were new to her and would have to
wait until later. She threw three dozen little bowls on the wheel that
day. They would need to be trimmed, once they were leather-hard, but
meanwhile, she placed them in rows on a shelf, feeling no small sense of
satisfaction in the accomplishment.

On her way home, she checked her email and saw that Courtney
had written, adding three dozen "decorative tiles" to the list.

• • •

At five the next morning, hours before anyone was up, Lauren rushed off in the dark to her studio, where she trimmed the paper clip holders, feeling pleased with their saucerlike shape. Next she began making vases—also vessels! Lauren imagined the flowers that would go in them and took great pleasure making one after another, lining them up to dry. When she was done throwing a dozen of them, she washed her hands and looked at her work. It was a start at least. It wasn't enough, but she was satisfied.

She arrived home just before noon to find Leo making pancakes. The boys were sitting at the table doing homework.

"All hail the conquering hero," Leo said as Lauren sat down. He pretended to blow a trumpet, and then said, "Good for you. The early bird gets the worm."

"I have to go back tonight to trim," she said, rolling her stiff shoulders, "but I got a good start."

Charles said, "Is that true about early birds? Or is that a myth?"

"Actually, it's true," said Leo. "Or sort of. Some biologists in Germany found that great tits who sleep in late—"

"You said tits," said Harrell, laughing uproariously. He started drawing a large pair of breasts on his math homework.

"Are more likely to be cuckolded by their mates *and* more likely to get stuck caring for chicks who aren't their own."

"Cuckolded? What's cuckolded?" said Harrell.

This conversation was too much for Lauren, who only wanted to go upstairs and crawl back in bed. "It's hard to explain," she said. "And I don't think your teacher's going to appreciate your artwork. Where's Waverly?"

"I sent her upstairs to get Evelyn, speaking of sleeping in late," said Leo as he mixed batter in a faded Pyrex bowl. "She hasn't even come downstairs yet. I think we wore her out at the Bronx Zoo yesterday."

"That's because I scared her so bad when I got lost," Harrell said, coloring the bosoms. "She said I gave her a heart attack."

"You got *lost?*" said Lauren. "Where? And for how long?"

"It was only for a few minutes," Leo said, dismissing her concern with a wave of the spatula. "We accidentally left him behind in the World of Reptiles, but a security guard found him in the Sea Bird Aviary."

"Leo!"

"What?"

"Can we have chocolate chip pancakes?" Harrell said.

"No," said Charles resentfully, "because of Waverly. What kind of monster doesn't like chocolate?"

"Don't call your sister a monster," Leo said, putting a colander of blueberries on the table.

"You *lost* Harrell?" Lauren said.

"Harrell, tell Mommy what happened," Leo said. "It was a very short-lived crisis, and he was perfectly fine."

Lauren's mother came into the kitchen then. Where was her lipstick? And why was she still in a bathrobe at almost noon? "Ah, you're home," she said, seeing Lauren. "I just got off the phone with Frances, and she is of the firm belief—"

"Yes, we know," said Lauren wearily. "Frances thinks we should pay a fancy company to find a *real* babysitter instead of—"

"That's not what I was going to say," Evelyn said as she took a seat at the table. "I was going to say that Frances thinks you should inquire about the noise regulations in the neighborhood. I was kept up half the night by all the shouting and music. I drifted somewhere between wide awake and dead asleep all night long."

"Ah, the Sweet Spot," said Leo, as he poured Evelyn a cup of coffee and handed it to her.

"I wouldn't call it *that*. It was more like purgatory," she said. "Or hell."

"Nay, lassie, I'm referring to the Sweet Spot, the highly respected establishment beneath our wee feet," Leo said, using some kind of Scottish or Irish or maybe Cockney brogue for no reason that came to Lauren's mind; it wasn't like the bar was trying to be a British pub. Charles looked up from his homework and Harrell from his boob drawing, both delighted as always with Leo's various character voices, but Evelyn was staring at him with a baffled expression. For some reason, he switched then to a Southern accent. "That thar drinking hole has been 'round since I was a pup."

"You should file a complaint with the city immediately," Evelyn said, setting down her cup. "That kind of ruckus should not be allowed in a residential area. You have children, for goodness' sake."

"Oh, I could never lodge a complaint against Dan," Leo said in his own voice. "I've known him pretty much my whole life; he's a great guy. And the sound doesn't bother us, probably because it feels so familiar."

"It bothers me sometimes," Lauren said. "But Dan's a family friend, so we wouldn't want to make trouble for him."

"Who's Dan?" Evelyn asked suspiciously, as though they had dropped the name of a neighborhood thief.

"The owner," said Leo. "He was friends with my mother. Funny story, actually: Phillip was a witness at Dan's marriage ceremony to Meg. And Phillip—not a fan of babies, by the way—held theirs while a shaman did the honors, and she spit up all over his seersucker suit."

"Whose baby?" said Evelyn. "What shaman?"

"Dan's and his wife's baby," said Leo. "Well, ex-wife now. Meg met the shaman after a mud flow in Colombia. And anyway, Olivia's all grown up now and living on her own somewhere nearby. Nearby here, I mean, not in Colombia."

Evelyn sighed impatiently. "I don't understand a single word you're saying," she said.

Leo placed a platter of pancakes in the middle of the table. "Bon appétit!" he said, in a falsetto voice à la Julia Child.

Lauren smiled, although she wasn't over the matter of Harrell getting lost at the zoo.

"Mommy," said Harrell, picking up a pancake with his fingers, "how come you never do voices like Daddy?"

"I'm not any good at it," Lauren said, passing him a fork. She recalled then a formal Thanksgiving at her brother's house—complete with silver serving dishes, crystal glasses, and a staff to serve the twenty-some-odd guests—when Leo insisted on speaking like the dowager countess from

Downton Abbey every time food was being served. Lauren had caught Frances rolling her eyes.

"The pancakes taste different," said Harrell.

"They're vegan," said Leo. "Less dairy means less methane and carbon dioxide emissions and a healthier planet."

"Plant-cakes," said Charles.

"Good Lord," said Evelyn.

Waverly came into the kitchen then and leaned on her grandmother's shoulder. "What are we doing today?"

"Interesting question," said Leo. "A Sunday in New York City in the fall. The possibilities are endless."

Lauren put her head down on the table.

"Build a drone," said Charles.

"Pottery painting?" Waverly asked.

"Dim dum in Chinatown," Harrell said with his mouth full.

"Dim *sum*," said Charles, shaking his head. "*You're* dim dumb."

"Don't call your brother dim or dumb," Leo said.

Evelyn perked up. "I would like to go to Central Park," she said.

"Aha," said Leo, squinting his eyes in approval, "the jewel of Mannahatta."

• • •

Instead of taking the nap she wanted, Lauren went along with her family. She couldn't trim the vases until that evening anyway, and it was her mother's last day in New York after all. Of course, Evelyn refused to take the subway to Central Park; Lauren gritted her teeth as they sat in traffic in an Uber that took twice as long and cost four times as much. She tapped her feet together impatiently, looking down to see a smattering of clay dust on the floor that her sneakers had tracked all the way from Brooklyn.

Leo and the kids took the 6 train and were waiting for them when they got out of the SUV at Madison and Seventy-Fourth, Evelyn in gabardine slacks, her Chanel handbag over her wrist.

They strolled down the park's crowded, leafy walkways to the pond where Leo and the children rented a model sailboat. Lauren sat with her mother on a bench to watch them.

"I've always thought that this part of Manhattan is the finest," Evelyn said with a look of approval. "You've got the Frick. And the Guggenheim. Excellent restaurants and tea at the Mark Hotel. It's all so polished. But I have to admit, I've come around a bit this week. Greenwich Village is grittier, smellier, and less elegant in general, but I can see why you and Leo fit in so well there."

"Thanks, Mom," Lauren said. She laughed, but the comment stung. She hadn't managed to meet her mother's approval since she was fifteen years old, when she agreed—for the last time—to wear the green taffeta dress she was assigned for their annual Christmas party.

"Since I couldn't sleep last night," Evelyn said, "thanks to all the drunkards, I passed the time reading one of Charley's plays I found on a bookshelf. Her dialogue is obscene, and how on earth is it appropriate to talk about menstruation onstage?" She lowered her voice then, looking over at Leo. "If you want my opinion, her brand of feminism did absolutely nothing to advance what I assume was her cause. She comes on too strong."

"Maybe her ideas aren't your cup of tea," Lauren said with a touch of condescension.

"Whose cup of tea are they? I'd like to know."

"Lots of people," said Lauren. "Critics. The committee that grants Tony Awards."

"She may have been nominated," said her mother, holding up a finger, "but she never won. Because she was overly provocative and contrary."

Lauren had heard this all before. The months surrounding her and Leo's wedding had been a nonstop flow of disapproving remarks about Charley's unfiltered cigarettes, her penchant for wearing men's clothing, her pixie haircut, and her refusal to settle down with a man.

"Mother," said Lauren. "You can criticize her all you want, but it doesn't change the fact that she was an icon. Still is. I don't know why you insist on judging her, or Phillip either."

Evelyn lowered her voice again, brought her fingertips up to the pearl necklace at her throat, and said, "There's something about Phillip I never told you."

Lauren stopped watching the kids and turned to see her mother looking at her as though she were about to announce a fatal diagnosis.

"Years ago, when you and Leo got engaged," her mother said, "Phillip propositioned me."

Lauren could not help but smile. "I don't think so," she said.

"That shows what you know," she said. "Not all men are as morally steadfast as Leo and your father."

Lauren looked back at Leo, who was showing Waverly something in the palm of his hand. A cicada shell? An acorn?

"Phillip called me at the house just after the engagement party," Evelyn said, tipping her head closer to Lauren's, "and invited me to go to New York and attend the theater with him, *alone*."

Lauren had not heard this story before, but it made her like Phillip even more for attempting to make inroads with her family, especially after the stodgy party her parents had hosted at their Wellesley home. The two mismatched families had stood awkwardly around the formal living room, attempting to make conversation, until Phillip tried his best to lighten the mood by clinking his Baccarat glass and making a toast, taking all the credit for the union as the person who had—loosely anyway—introduced Leo to Lauren in the first place.

"Mom," Lauren said, annoyed by her mother's serious expression, "you know perfectly well Phillip is gay."

Evelyn shook off Lauren's explanation. "I don't care what he says he is. It was not appropriate for him to ask me out without your father, and you know it."

Lauren could not remember her father without picturing him in a navy blazer; he'd worn one with everything, except pajamas. He was also the only person in the family who wholeheartedly supported her decision to go to art school. "I'm still using the cup you gave me," he would say every time she visited, holding it up with pride as he filled it with coffee.

"Phillip," Lauren said, "was only being nice. He was trying to get to know you."

Evelyn sat up straight. "I would have considered going if he'd invited your father along, but I certainly couldn't be seen out alone with another man. Can you even imagine the things people would have said?"

"What people? You should have gone. You might have enjoyed it."

"I doubt it," Evelyn said. "But I loved going to the theater with your father."

Her dad's death had been such a shock, and Lauren was crushed to think her kids would never have the chance to know him better.

"I miss Dad too," she said. She scooted closer and looped their arms together, feeling the sharp point of her mom's elbow in her side.

"You were very lucky to grow up with a loving, steady father," Evelyn said, giving Lauren's hand a little pat as they watched Leo calmly negotiate what looked like an argument between the boys over the remote control. "I think it's remarkable Leo turned out as well as he did, given his lack of a stable male presence."

Lauren braced herself for yet another tirade about Charley's selfish, feminist agenda. But instead her mother squeezed her hand and said, "The point I'm trying to make is that I think you and Leo are doing a very good job, and my grandchildren are turning out to be just wonderful."

Lauren almost fell off the bench. For someone who didn't care about what people thought, she relished this stamp of approval from her own mother. "Thank you," she said. "We're doing our best."

· · ·

When the kids finished sailing the model boat, they all walked toward Lexington Avenue on Seventy-Second Street. At the corner of Madison, Lauren grabbed Leo's arm and gasped. There, in the storefront of the uptown Felicity boutique, was a large wood tray holding one of Lauren's teapots along with two cups sitting on their delicate saucers.

"Mommy," said Waverly, standing on her tiptoes to get a better look.

The boys put their sticky hands on the plate glass window. "That's you!" said Harrell. And it was. Seeing her pieces, brightly lit and artfully staged with high-end cream-colored linens and ornate silver place settings, took Lauren's breath away.

"What a shame they're closed," said her mom. "I'm so proud of you."

"Crickets," Leo said, looking at the teapot, "and there's your name too."

And indeed, there was a little sign that read: *Handmade ceramics by Lauren Shaw.*

Lauren felt a swell of pride. She wanted to thank Felicity and wondered if she'd had her baby already. Lauren could only imagine how perfect her nursery would be: an eco-friendly, Scandinavian crib with tastefully embroidered French linens.

Lauren got her phone from her back pocket, scraped a bit of clay off the screen, and took a picture of the window display. Then she sent a quick email:

Dear Felicity,

Consider my mind officially blown—I'm standing in front of the uptown shop where I just spotted my pieces in the window. Holy moly, how cool! To see my porcelain sharing the spotlight with glasses by Simon Pearce, silver by Georg Jensen, place mats by Sandy Chilewich . . . well, it's pretty spectacular. A million thanks for this opportunity. Meanwhile, I'm working away . . . xoxo

• • •

Late that afternoon, Evelyn went upstairs to pack. Before heading back to Brooklyn, Lauren read with Harrell so he could write a book review entry on the online class blog. When they were done with the chapter, Harrell, with a couch pillow balanced on his head, typed into his iPad: *Ok so far!*

"Come on, Harrell," Lauren said. "That's not enough."

"Why not?"

"Because your teacher asked for your reflections. You need to do more than the bare minimum."

Harrell looked at the book cover and added, *But not my fave.*

"And . . . ?"

"And I don't feel so good," he said, taking the pillow off his head.

Harrell was not an especially strong student, and giving up quickly was one of his classic moves.

Waverly, who was dressed like a pirate, was the only one who had finished her homework. She jumped around the room from floor to chair to couch, sword fighting a phantom enemy with an antique walking cane she'd found in the umbrella stand. Leo was kneeling at the coffee table, helping Charles make a model of stratigraphy for his science class.

Lauren, still glowing from the glimpse of her pieces in the Felicity storefront, wanted to instill in Harrell the joy of doing one's best work. "Come on," she said. "You'll feel so satisfied if you write something meaningful. I want three more sentences, okay? Make yourself proud."

"It's not fair," Harrell said. "Charles has fun homework."

Charles was trying to line up a rectangle of white foam board with a rectangle of green felt with a rectangle of yellow poster board, all before the glue hardened. When he tried to let go of his cross section of earth, the pieces stuck to his fingers.

"Arrgghh," he said, shaking his hand.

"Hang on," said Leo, carefully peeling the material away from Charles's thumb. "Don't move."

Waverly leaped on the couch and thwacked a throw pillow with her cane.

"Not so rough," Lauren said. "Inside playing, okay?" Waverly settled down, and Lauren checked the time on her phone. She was surprised to see that she'd already gotten a response from Felicity. The message was brief but had a powerful effect on her already anxious state of mind:

:) Wonderful! How are the new pieces coming along?

She couldn't tell the whole truth, so instead Lauren emailed back, plagiarizing her son:

Ok so far!

When Lauren turned back to Harrell, she found he'd abandoned his iPad altogether and had curled up in a ball on the floor.

"No, come on, Harrell, get up. All you have to do is say something about one of the characters or about what you think of the setting."

Harrell didn't answer.

"Maybe we should take a break," Leo said, placing the gluey layers on the table to dry. "We could even finish up in the morning."

It was an unsurprising suggestion coming from Leo because he was an early riser, but Lauren didn't like the idea. Mornings were chaotic under the best of circumstances. She was about to say so when, to Lauren's astonishment, Harrell began vomiting onto the carpet.

"Oh, Harrell," said Lauren, kneeling on the floor beside him and rubbing his back. She tried to guide him onto his feet and to the bathroom.

At the sound of her brother retching, Waverly spun around to see what was happening, knocking Charles in the face with the cane she had in her outstretched hand. Charles made a yelping sound, and they all turned to look at him as he sobbed, his hands covering his face. He looked up at Lauren and moved his hands away, and she saw a surprising amount of blood running down his cheek. Harrell saw it too and vomited again.

Leo sprang into action, but before he got anywhere, he made a sound that was hard for Lauren to place: wounded seal, maybe? Rather than help Charles, Leo remained bent over, one hand on his hip, the other on his knee. His glasses fell off, and he didn't make a move to retrieve them from the floor. The second she saw him frozen in that stooped, tabletop pose, Lauren knew his back had gone out again.

She took the sweatshirt from around her waist and pressed it to Charles's face. Harrell was throwing up again on the floor, and Leo was leaning over the chair, still as a statue, his face contorted in pain. Telling

Charles to hold the sweatshirt in place, Lauren stepped over Bumper to reach Harrell and felt a muscle pop—how else to describe the twangy, sharp pain that shot through her calf? Harrell was crying, and she hobbled over to him, helping him lean into the bamboo umbrella stand so he could throw up somewhere other than the floor. It was a poor choice, Lauren thought as Harrell heaved into it, given that it was entirely open on the bottom and possibly a valuable antique. Leo, bent at a ninety-degree angle, asked Charles to come to him so he could get a closer look at the bleeding wound. Waverly—the last family member standing—was wailing.

Evelyn's voice suddenly filled the room: "What on earth is going on in here?" She charged into the room to find the cause of all the tears.

"It's okay," said Lauren, patting Harrell on the back as Waverly cried, clinging to her leg. "We're all okay."

"You don't look okay," said her mother, wiping Harrell's mouth with a tissue.

"It was an accident," Waverly cried. "Is Charles going to die?"

"What happened to Charles?" Evelyn said, going to check on him.

"No one's going to die," said Lauren, but as she looked around at the pandemonium, dumbfounded that so much had gone so wrong so quickly, she could not think of a single intelligent thing to do. Bumper wandered around the room from one victim to the next, knocking the jar of paste off the coffee table with his tail.

"Sit!" her mother commanded. Bumper sat. "Nobody move unless I say so."

Lauren watched as her mom put an arm over Harrell's shoulders. "Well, my goodness," she said, leading him to the bathroom. "Come with me, poor boy." Without Harrell to lean on, Lauren hopped to the couch and sat down, gingerly touching the back of her leg to find out what on earth she'd done to it.

Evelyn returned with damp paper towels from the kitchen, sat Charles down, and showed him how to hold them firmly to his cheek. Next, she helped Leo down onto his hands and knees, the only position that seemed to ease the pain in his back, and handed him his glasses.

Lauren watched her mother in awe. Perhaps it was her years married to an internist, or maybe it was her experience as a mother, but Evelyn triaged each case while remaining remarkably calm.

"This," she whispered as she helped Lauren lie back on the couch, placing an ice bag under her injured leg, "is what Frances's children would call a 'clusterfuck.'"

Lauren started with a quick inhale of her breath; her mother never cursed.

"Now," Evelyn said, examining the bloody paper towels on Charles's face, "Charles very likely needs stitches."

Charles's eyes opened wide. "Rad," he said. "Will it hurt?"

"Not too much," said Evelyn. "Leo, give me your insurance card."

Leo, still on his hands and knees, nodded over his right shoulder, and Evelyn pulled his wallet from his back pocket.

She parked Bumper next to Lauren by the couch and took Waverly and Harrell upstairs.

Lauren patted Bumper's head, wishing she could help her children up to their rooms and tuck poor Harrell into bed.

When her mom came back down, she called an Uber while helping Charles into his jacket. "I put a plastic pail next to Harrell's bed," she said, "and Waverly is watching *Frozen*. Will you manage to stay out of trouble until we get back?"

"Of course," said Lauren.

"We'll try," said Leo.

"Maybe I don't want stitches," said Charles, still holding the paper towels to his face. "Or do I?"

"We'll leave that to the doctor," Evelyn said, studying the screen on her phone. "Off we go. Johnny B and his silver Rav4 will be here in two minutes."

"You'll be fine," Leo said to Charles, and gave him a shaky thumbs-up.

"I love you!" Lauren called after them.

Charles smiled nervously and waved.

The door closed behind them, and Lauren climbed down onto the floor next to Leo. "Are you okay?" she asked, holding her leg as she rolled over onto her back.

"It's pretty bad," he said, wincing as he tried to drop onto his elbows, an awkward attempt at child's pose. "You?"

"It doesn't hurt much when I'm completely still, but I can't put any weight on my leg."

"Well, this is a setback," he said, reaching out a hand to pat her on what turned out to be her face.

"My pieces," Lauren said sadly. Her vases would be too dry to trim if she couldn't get back to them. "I was finally getting somewhere."

"This sucks," Leo said, exhaling through the pain. "Should one of us go upstairs, in case the kids need something? I think I can get there."

"How?"

"Very slowly," he said.

"I'll stay here and wait for Charles." She watched as Leo got to his feet, stooped over like an old man.

"This might take a while," he said.

Lauren sat up on the floor with her back against the couch, thinking she would call her mother in half an hour for an update. What would they do about dinner? She closed her eyes, hoping that Charles wouldn't mind too much when he felt the prick of the needle numbing his cheek, that the anesthesia would work well, that the doctor would stitch him up neatly with a steady hand.

· · ·

Bumper woke her up, barking at the sound of Evelyn and Charles's return.

Lauren hobbled to the door to greet them. The sharp pain in her calf jolted her fully awake.

"How was it?" she asked, holding on to the beadboard wainscoting for support.

"You should have your leg elevated," her mother said. "Charles is fine. He was very brave. Tell her."

"I got six stitches," Charles said, and turned to show the bandage on his face.

Lauren flicked on a light to get a better look and then kissed the top of his head. "Did it hurt?"

"Yes," said Charles, touching his fingertips to the gauze. "It feels like I'm gonna die."

"No need for histrionics," Evelyn said. "Your parents are likely in worse pain than you."

"Are you?" he said, his eyes wide with worry.

Lauren leaned against the wall, so exhausted she ached. "I'm okay," she said. "I tore a muscle or something." She turned to her mom, suddenly close to tears with gratitude. "Thank you for saving us. Are you completely done in?"

"Me? I didn't throw up or injure my back or cut my face, so there's no need for anyone to worry about *me*. I was happy to be able to help." She reached out and gave Lauren's hand a squeeze.

"Is it late?"

Evelyn checked her phone. "Eleven thirty," she said. "How's everyone here?"

Her poor mother had spent almost six hours in the ER. "Sleeping, I hope," Lauren said. "Harrell's definitely staying home tomorrow."

"What about me?" Charles asked.

"No school for you either," said Lauren, ruffling his hair. "You need a day to heal."

This pleased Charles immensely. He whooped and hugged her, almost knocking into her bad leg. He ran up the stairs, tripping while taking them two at a time.

"Chip off the old block," said Evelyn.

"Me?"

"I meant his father. Warmhearted and knock-kneed." Evelyn smiled. "Now, to bed!" she said, louder than their proximity warranted.

Lauren felt too wiped out to make the trip up the stairs. "I think I'll sleep on the couch in Charley's atelier," she said.

"In her what?" said Evelyn.

"Her office, of sorts."

Lauren had hoped her mother would never see this particular room, but there was no avoiding it now. Evelyn put out her arm and helped Lauren hop through the kitchen.

"I just assumed it was a storage closet back here," Evelyn said.

The accordion door was stuck in its tracks. Lauren jiggled it, but it wouldn't budge.

"The first thing I would do if I moved into this house," said Evelyn as she gave the door a hard pull, "is take out every relic from the seventies. Surely Phillip would understand. You just call him up and say, 'Phillip, we're going to have to . . .'" She turned on the light, letting her voice trail off as she caught sight of the interior of the room. "You have got to be kidding me."

As much as Lauren wanted to give an explanation, there was no way she could justify the situation in Charley's former office. The most glaring peculiarity was a mannequin that looked a lot like Charley herself, wearing a short platinum-blond wig, bright red lipstick, and a man's suit. She was sitting in a row of three theater flip seats in front of the large rear window, an unlit cigarette dangling between two plastic fingers, a disco ball directly over her head. Two of the walls were covered with gold-and-silver metallic wallpaper that had a geometric zigzag pattern, and the third wall was cork-tiled and covered from the crown molding to the rolltop desk with drawings of theater sets, reviews clipped from newspapers, and dozens of photographs of Charley, her many friends, and costumed actors from her circle, all tacked with pushpins and in disarray. In one picture, Charley was posed in the nude; Evelyn's eyes flew open when she noticed, and then she quickly looked away, as though she'd invaded Charley's privacy.

"Well, I really don't have the words," Evelyn said, as she looked at the spiral-bound notebooks piled halfway to the ceiling. "It's no wonder you kept this from me. What was this room originally? Maid's quarters? A butler's pantry?"

"Maybe Leo knows," Lauren said, settling onto the tweed couch while trying to keep her leg as stationary as possible.

"If this room is any reflection of her mind, then Charley Aston was off her rocker."

"It could be the nicest room in the house if it were cleared out. And there's a positive energy in here anyway, don't you think?" Lauren said. "In the whole house actually."

Her mother shook her head as she gently placed a cushion under Lauren's leg. "I'm detecting a negative, narcissistic energy, but don't let me sway you."

The pain in Lauren's calf muscle was now radiating down to her foot. Leo had called this situation a setback; that seemed a major understatement. "Clusterfuck is right," Lauren said. "I don't even know how we'll get Waverly to school tomorrow. Stick her in a cab?"

"Don't be silly," her mother said, unfolding a throw blanket and draping it over Lauren's legs. "I'll take her."

"But you're leaving—"

"What kind of mother would I be if I abandoned my child's family in such sorry condition?"

"Are you sure?"

"I can stay a bit longer, just until you're back on your feet."

"Thank you, Mom," Lauren said. And then she stretched, careful not to move her leg. "While you're in savior mode, could you pop in to my studio and trim flower vases for me?"

"No, darling, that I can't." Evelyn turned off the overhead light. "Sleep well," she said, and then she wrestled the accordion door closed.

In the dark Lauren could see the silhouette of the mannequin. What would she do with this space if it were hers to change? She tried to imagine putting her own mark on the house, gutting the master bathroom with its turquoise pedestal sink and matching turquoise toilet, but then she dismissed the idea. The bathroom also had a cool, claw-footed antique tub, and they just didn't make stuff like that anymore. She was lucky to be living here at all and did not need a single thing to change.

Except for maybe the wallpaper, she thought, as she fell deeply asleep.

Chapter 4

Melinda had never worked in a noncorporate setting before or with this particular software platform or with a clientele under the age of fourteen, but already she could tell: this job was going to be ridiculously easy. The tasks sounded simple, and the computer system was intuitive. As an added bonus, the bar for doing this job well was about as low as it could possibly be, since the employee she was replacing had been fired for some kind of borderline criminal activity, although no one would tell Melinda exactly what he'd done.

She was no criminal. She was a functional human being, and that alone was miraculous given that her entire life had been blasted to smithereens. As a woman who'd gotten divorced three days shy of her thirtieth wedding anniversary, wrecked her own career, and moved from a large apartment in one part of Manhattan to a small one-bedroom in another, all in a matter of six horrendous months, the last thing she needed was stress over work. There was only so much shock, heartbreak, and upheaval a person could take before she eventually cracked up, and Melinda had cracked. Now she was trying to rebuild, to stay calm and centered, and not to feel so grief-stricken and full of rage that she went around smashing things.

She arrived early on the first day of her new job. The principal greeted her at the door and held out the school handbook, saying, "I hope you're a quick study." Then she walked Melinda over to the reception desk that was situated front and center in the lobby and pulled out the chair for her. Melinda would have preferred working in a closet somewhere in the basement of the building, but so be it. She took her seat.

Within one hour, Melinda had read the school handbook, familiarized herself with the online attendance and phone systems, made nice with the administrative staff, learned how to use a walkie-talkie (for fast access to the janitor, the security guard, and the school nurse), and settled into her post in the lobby of this prestigious kindergarten-through-eighth school.

Now the students began to drift in, and Melinda watched them scan their ID cards, their names simultaneously popping up in a window on her screen. Justin Melia was officially in the building. Carson Moss, present and accounted for. She entered the password she'd been given for the attendance email account and began to log absences: Fifth grader Ryan Loeb had the flu and would be out for at least three days. (Thank God she'd gotten her shot.) First grader Chloe Thomas was in mourning over the loss of a guinea pig named Milk Dud (a rodent; Melinda was not moved). Eighth grader Angela Donahue had cramps and might be in later, but maybe not, it really all depended on the efficacy of Advil, which last month had worked quite well, but during this month's cycle, who could be sure? (TMI.)

But Angela's case gave Melinda pause: Did she mark the girl absent or not? Was there a holding cell where Melinda could put her name? She was irritated by this mother who couldn't make up her mind if her child was coming to school or not, but then Melinda half smiled as she remembered: the stakes were so low, it really didn't matter. Mark the period girl absent, and if she showed up later, deal with it.

That was when she noticed a nicely dressed, salt-and-pepper-haired woman coming in through the heavy glass door, tightly holding the hand of a little girl. Melinda wouldn't have paid any attention, except that they had a big shaggy dog with them, and Melinda had seen nothing in the school handbook about pets. Was that beast allowed in here? Weren't some snot-nose kids allergic? She hoped both the woman and the dog would leave as quickly as possible so that Melinda could go back to the mind-numbing task of clicking the absent box next to student names.

The little girl scanned her ID, looked directly at Melinda, and said, "Uh-oh."

"What's wrong?" her chaperone asked, stepping out of the way as the dog ran in a circle around her and then sprawled out on the carpet.

The girl pointed. "That lady's not the normal man who sits there."

"She's not what?" the woman asked, trying to get the dog back on its feet.

The young girl spotted a friend and ran off with her without so much as a goodbye.

"I'll be back at . . . ," the woman called after her. "What time . . . ?" But the girl was already gone.

Tugging the scruffy dog behind her, the woman approached Melinda's desk.

Go away, thought Melinda.

The woman greeted her with a formal "Good morning," and a nod of her coiffed head.

"May I help you?"

"Yes, you may," the woman said, her voice nasal and snobby. "I've delivered the youngest Aston child this morning, and she's gone off to class."

Did she want an award or something? Melinda didn't need this information, as the computer had already handled it. "Fine," she said. *Run along.*

"Her siblings, however, will not be attending school, as they are incapacitated. I took the eldest to the hospital to get stitches last night, poor dear."

Whoop-dee-doo.

"And the middle child," the lady went on, "has fallen victim to a stomach bug. Is there a form to fill out or . . . ?"

Apparently, this woman was newer to the school than Melinda. Her smelly dog sat and used a back foot to scratch his head. Melinda wanted him and his fleas gone.

"Name?" she asked, her fingers poised over her keyboard.

"Evelyn Shaw," she said, clasping her fingers around the leash. The dog rubbed his ear on her skirt then, knocking her momentarily off-balance.

Melinda checked—there was no Evelyn Shaw in the system. Or Shah. Or Shauh. Melinda felt annoyed that this simple task wasn't yielding an instant result.

"What grade is she?" Melinda asked, trying to search by first name: Evelyn? Eva Lynn? Nothing.

"Who?"

"The kid with the stomach thing."

"It's a he."

Melinda stopped typing and looked up. "A boy named Evelyn? Like Waugh?"

"Excuse me?" the woman said.

"You said Evelyn had a stomach bug."

"I most certainly did not," the woman said, pulling her shoulders back haughtily.

Melinda closed her eyes, inhaled deeply, and then slowly released her breath to a count of five. This was a new technique she'd learned from an anger-management TED Talk she'd watched online. It was supposedly an effective strategy for people whose tempers spun out of control. She wondered if it would work.

Melinda opened her eyes again to find the woman staring at her. "Maybe we should start over from the beginning," Melinda said.

The dog slumped down on the floor and closed his eyes.

"First of all, are you"—she glanced up with an eyebrow raised—"the parent?"

The woman scoffed. "At my age? How absurd," she said. "Obviously I'm their grandmother."

She was right about that; it would be absurd. Melinda took off her reading glasses and leaned in, saying, "At sixty years of age, every man alive on this planet should be required by law to undergo a vasectomy. Or be castrated. No exceptions, no anesthesia." She tapped her glasses on the desk. "That's what I think."

The woman was looking at her now as though she were out of her mind, and Melinda wondered if perhaps she had overshared. She put her reading glasses back on, took a piece of paper from the printer tray behind her, tore it in half, and put it on the desk. "Write down the names and grades of your grandkids who aren't coming to school today with a *brief* explanation."

The woman did as she was told, writing in a neat, tight cursive, and passed the paper back to Melinda. "And can you tell me what time I should return to retrieve Waverly?" she said.

Melinda was starting to get sick of this stuck-up grandma. "Who?"

"My *granddaughter*."

"Are you authorized to pick her up?" Melinda asked.

"I don't know," the grandmother said curtly. "Can my daughter deputize me?"

Two parents were lined up behind her now, and Melinda had had enough. "Tell her to send an email," Melinda said, trying to mask her impatience.

"To whom? Or to where?"

Melinda had several conflicting urges. She wanted to throw her heavy stapler through the plate glass window facing the street. She also wanted to grab her coat, walk out the door, and curl up under the blanket on her bed for the rest of the day. But mostly, she wanted to scream at the top of her lungs and hear her voice bounce off the walls of the lobby. Instead of doing any of those things, she attempted a smile. It was hard to do, and she tried to relax her cheeks so as not to appear aggressive.

She spoke slowly and calmly. "Tell the mother or the father or whoever's legally in charge of the kid to email me right here at the front desk of the school." She tapped the screen of her computer. "I'll figure it out."

"Thank you," said the woman politely. She pulled on the leash to wake up the dog. "In that case, my daughter, Lauren Shaw, will be emailing you this morning to grant me permission. She injured her leg last night and can barely walk. And her husband's back is acting up."

Melinda did not give a single shit. "Buh-bye," she said.

"Goodbye," the woman said. The dog was not reading the cues, and the woman finally took hold of his collar and pulled him to his feet.

Melinda saw there were now five parents waiting to talk to her, each looking harried and self-important. She willed herself to keep her cool through each stupid request, excuse, and explanation. She would wait until the end of the day—no, the end of the *week*—before she decided if taking this job had been a colossal mistake.

Chapter 5

It didn't take until the end of the week or even until the end of the day before Melinda knew that the position at Perkins wasn't what she needed it to be. No, Melinda figured that shit out by two in the afternoon on her very first day. Parent emails—nonsensical, self-involved, and utterly complicated—were ruining what was supposed to have been Melinda's ideal job at this particular juncture in her life.

She put on her reading glasses and tried to untangle the absurd messages flooding her in-box.

Hello! I wrote earlier to say that my daughter Maggie won't be at the play auditions this afternoon because of a tutoring appointment. Thank you for agreeing to arrange a special audition slot for her tomorrow. But it turns out she might be at the audition today after all because I can maybe bump the appointment to next week, but I'm not 100% sure on this . . . the tutor is hard to pin down :) What should we do?

Huh?

Max's dad here. Max will be at soccer practice today unless he won't. A friend of a friend is moving mountains to get him in to see this rock star orthopedist for his sore knee, but we're waiting to hear back if it's actually happening, all depending on the timing of the orthopedist's wife's C-section. Please keep Coach informed and stay tuned!

What?

My aunt in California is expected to die any day now. Jack will miss four-ish days of school for the funeral. Quick question: depending on when Aunt Hazel dies, Jack might miss the bus for the 7th grade trip to Washington, DC. If that happens, can he meet the class there? FYI—we may not actually go to the funeral at all because while I'm super close to this aunt, I'm not feeling all that close right now because rumor has it she decided to leave all her money to Habitat for Humanity after making a lot of concrete promises to the family re: inheritance. Also, she may not die anyway, in which case this will all be moot. Please advise.

Why did these people have to be so stupidly complicated? As Melinda tried to decipher the messages, her breathing became shallow and her face turned red in aggravation. She wasn't in a frame of mind to handle bullshit.

Not the case before! Melinda had been expert at solving problems. She'd spent years appeasing difficult personalities, soothing the fragile egos of privileged men in suits from her position in human resources. She settled disputes between employees and helped workers communicate without using acts of aggression—passive, micro, macro, or otherwise. She was widely considered levelheaded, objective, and empathetic, and she'd convinced many a headstrong employee that a transfer to another department was a bad idea.

So why was she caught completely off guard when her own husband of thirty years requested a transfer out of their marriage?

The unraveling of Melinda's perfectly satisfactory-enough life had begun during an evening stroll the previous winter. Her husband, Russell, never mentioned another woman as they walked down Fifth Avenue that pivotal night, his arms moving stiffly by his sides. Rather, he said he was feeling "off," restless, out of sorts, and in need of some alone time. It was temporary and nothing at all to worry about, he'd said. They walked back into their Upper East Side apartment, and—to her horror—Russell packed a suitcase, and left for an Airbnb in the Meatpacking District, leaving most of his belongings behind. His behavior was so wildly out of character that Melinda knew he'd be back to himself soon. He needed her. They loved each other. He was just going through something, a late midlife crisis. She gave him the space he asked for.

Two weeks later, he called, asking to see her, and Melinda almost collapsed from relief.

"Oh, phew," she said. "I'll cook dinner. Any requests?"

There was a pause, during which she wondered if he would ask for her roast chicken or shrimp scampi. And then he said, "Actually, I think this is too hard to do in person."

"What is?"

"I have to tell you something: I'm seeing someone."

"What do you mean?" Melinda said. She wasn't being coy; she actually had no idea what he meant.

"I met a woman, and we've developed feelings for each other. I can't help it, but I've fallen in love."

Melinda's legs wobbled, and she sat down on the hardwood floor.

"Maybe you remember my mentioning Felicity Wynn?" he said. "She was a client of mine at one point."

"Of course I remember," Melinda said. "The design guru. She had a dispute over one of her retail spaces—"

"Exactly."

Melinda began to understand. "How old is she?"

"How old? Oh, I don't know exactly. Does it matter?"

"Yes," said Melinda, in a voice an octave deeper than her normal one, "it matters."

"Around forty. And this isn't easy for me, Melinda, any of it, and I'm sorry, but I . . . I have to follow my heart: I want to be with her."

Melinda didn't say anything. She felt all the air being sucked out of her lungs.

"And I think we can keep this amicable, don't you?" he was saying. "It's important to me that we remain friends. I never meant for any of this to happen, of course, but—and here's the other thing, it's a miracle really—" He cleared his throat dramatically. "It seems I'm going to be a father."

Something of an occult force entered her body then, impregnating her with a hate-baby of her own that implanted itself in her soul. On the living room floor, she held the phone to her ear as hot flames of fury rose in her chest, her brain, and the room around her. She got to her feet and tugged at her shirt as though she were bursting out of it, like the Incredible Hulk popping the seams of his clothing. She saw dark red blobs in her peripheral vision.

"You don't like children," Melinda said, speaking sharply into the phone through her clenched teeth. "We never wanted children. *Ever*, you said. You always insisted—"

"I know!" he said, sounding positively delighted at his ability to re-invent himself so completely, even at his age and practically overnight. "It's incredible to me as well, but you know what I discovered?"

Melinda was silent while he paused theatrically.

"I'm finally ready," he said.

"Excuse me?"

"I'm finally ready to be a father."

"*Finally ready?*" Melinda said. "It's *too late*. You're almost seventy! You're three decades too old—"

"I'm sixty-seven—"

"You're old. And you know how I know? Because *I'm* old, and I'm a decade younger than you! Jesus, Russell, what are you thinking? You won't be able to play golf again, *ever*, I hope you realize that. You'll never get another good night's sleep for the rest of your life. You'll be over seventy-five before the kid's in braces. What the hell are you doing?"

"I don't think that's—"

"You'll be tottering around at high school graduation with a walker, if you're not already dead by then. Don't be a fool."

Russell was quiet for a moment, and Melinda hoped she would wake from this nightmare; they saw the world the same way, after all. They always had. This conversation simply could not be happening.

"It's not like you to be cruel, Melinda."

She choked. "Cruel? You think *I'm* being cruel? *You're* the one who cheated, and that makes you a mean, stupid fuckwad."

Russell sighed. "Can't we be mature about this? I had assumed, given all our years together, given our friendship, that on some level, you'd be happy for me."

Melinda almost blacked out at the word "happy." She began ranting into the phone, cutting him in ways that were deeply personal, exaggerating specific parts of his aging anatomy in ways that only she, after almost thirty years of marriage, could: How did this young woman feel about his nose hair; his slightly sagging bottom; his limp, elongated testicles? Was he swallowing his weight in Viagra? Melinda used the word "flaccid" over and over again.

Russell hung up on her.

She couldn't sleep that night. She smashed their wedding china in the bathtub. She put Russell's Harvard ring in the blender and watched it ricochet off the blades. She googled the connection between old sperm and autism, the effect of newer, younger sexual partners on erectile disfunction, and the statistics on divorce rates in second marriages. She scrolled through comments in a divorce group on Facebook and found similarly enraged women, many of whom wished their ex-spouses a slow and painful death. She cried because she wanted Russell dead. She cried even harder because she wanted him back.

The next morning, she could not eat or drink. She got up and went to work at the insurance firm, wearing the sweatpants she'd slept in, open-carrying her anger up and down the hallways, firing out criticism, snapping at coworkers, and finally losing all her composure over the state of the shared kitchenette.

"WHY" she typed out in an email to "all," "is there OLD tuna—*TUNA!*—stinking up the refrigerator? And gross, EXPIRED, half-eaten yogurts? You are all DISGUSTING!!! I counted five (5!) coffee mugs in the sink and eleven spoons. WASH your SHIT, people. HAVE. YOU. NO. SHAME??????????"

Retirement had not been on the table for Melinda, but she suddenly found herself on the wrong side of the HR desk.

"You know what?" she told the male coworker who'd called her in and suggested she take a leave of absence. "I'm not interested in getting a lecture on behavior from anyone around here, least of all you. I've bailed *your* ass out of three separate sexual harassment claims."

"Those were workplace misunderstandings," he said, unable to meet her eyes. "I have never *harassed* anyone."

"Oh, puh-*lease*," she said, and let loose a menacing laugh. "You're a *serial* harasser, and I doubt your wife appreciates the way you hit on every new young employee who walks through the door."

That was Melinda's last day at work.

She put her longtime marital condo on the market, moved to the first one-bedroom apartment she saw, and took what she'd hoped would be a mellow job. She did not think she would ever recover from the pain of being left to grow old alone. She despised her ex-husband. She also missed him as though she'd lost a limb.

• • •

At a quarter to three, Melinda began to prepare for school dismissal. She tidied up the lobby, putting a Yankees baseball cap in the lost and found and some candy wrappers in the trash. She removed the tacky back-to-school decorations left by her predecessor. She opened the attendance program on her computer, knowing the children would soon swarm into the lobby and swipe their IDs as they left the building. What was she supposed to do if anyone missed the scanner? Would she have to walk through the building looking for strays?

When she spotted a tall, gangly boy chewing gum as he lingered by the door, she marched over—all five feet ten inches of her—from behind her desk to reprimand him, grabbing Kleenex from her desk.

"No gum," she said, handing him a tissue. "Spit it out."

"Come on," the boy said, "I'm about to leave."

"*Now*," said Melinda.

The boy took the tissue but continued chewing as if to get the most flavor out of it before complying.

Melinda felt her blood pressure rising. She got the school handbook from her desk, flipped to the relevant page, and pointed her finger to the place where it alerted members of the community about the gum policy.

"It is forbidden," she said. "It says so right here, in black and white."

He wadded the tissue around the gum and said, "You're kinda making a huge deal out of nothing."

"Nothing?" said Melinda. "You think rules are *nothing*? Let me tell you something: an institution requires rules in order to function. And every person who has agreed to be part of that institution, like you, has to adhere to the agreed-upon conditions of the union, and to respect right from wrong, or the whole system collapses."

"Fine, I already—"

"When we make promises to each other, when we vow to respect certain sacred . . . creeds, we should keep our promises. But then you come along, throw in the towel, and say, 'So what if I made you a promise? I'm going to break it willy-nilly!' You think it's okay to let people down? To betray the trust they have in you? No, sir, not on my watch."

The boy was staring at her as though she were holding a bomb.

In a calmer voice, she said, "And why are you leaving school before dismissal anyway?"

"My mom's picking me up early for a dentist appointment."

"Aha!" she said. "I don't think your dentist wants you chewing gum either."

He held out the pack. "It's sugar-free Trident," he said. "My dentist recommends it."

"Hmm," said Melinda. And then she wasn't sure what more there was to say.

"Can I go now?"

She took the wastepaper basket from beside her desk and held it out to him. He dropped the ball of tissue in it. "Now, remember what I said. You look like a responsible young man, and I'm sure the younger children look up to you. So . . . go forth and set a good example."

"Sure. Whatever," he said, and walked out.

Melinda turned back to her desk and set down the trash can. If she was going to keep working at this stupid school, she would have to start picking her battles more carefully.

Chapter 6

Melinda lasted the day and then she somehow made it through another. At the sound of the dismissal bell on her second day, she watched the students flood out in chaotic fashion, emitting a slightly gamey smell. For the next hour, she remained at her post, tracking their comings and goings, immensely relieved to have almost reached the end of another day. A few minutes before four, she made a trip to the ladies' room, and when she returned, her hands still damp, thanks to the ineffective "TurboWind" air dryer, she stood completely still with her back to the school entrance, fists planted on her hips, glasses hanging on her chest in limbo. She waited, watching the monitor on the wall behind her desk as it flashed pictures of soccer games, art classes, and choir rehearsals. A girl concentrating in front of a canvas, a boy playing Daddy Warbucks onstage, tipping his top hat. By the time it cycled through to the announcement about the upcoming fourth-grade field trip to the

Brooklyn Botanic Garden, the digital clock at the top right of the screen finally reached 4:01. Melinda pulled the readers off over her head, tossed them in her bag, and put on her jacket, hoping to say goodbye to absolutely no one on her way out of the building, not to the young girl with braces scrolling through her phone on the bench in the lobby, not to the father who came in looking harried, and certainly not to the short-haired teacher who cheerfully called out "Later!" as she held the door open for Melinda.

Stepping out into the cloudy fall afternoon, Melinda zipped up her jacket and walked, head down, to the intersection at Sixth Avenue. As soon as the pedestrian light turned, she crossed, heading west, in the direction of Cornelia Street. And then—nightmare of nightmares—she spotted them, walking directly toward her.

It was too late to run or hide.

"Oh," Russell said, looking up at her with a pained expression. "Melinda."

Melinda glanced down again, scanning the ground for a manhole or a storm drain that she could use as an escape. Instead, what she saw was her dinghy-shaped shoes—nondescript loafers that added as little to her height as possible.

"This . . . ," he said awkwardly, turning to indicate the woman by his side, "is Felicity."

"Mmmm," Melinda said, unable to speak his name aloud or the name of the diminutive British bimbo with dewy cheeks and bright blond hair. She was even more perfect than she appeared on TV, which made sense, given the cosmic torture that was Melinda's new life. In sync with her entire brand, the home-wrecker was chic and sleek and slightly edgy. Melinda despised her with her entire body and soul.

"So . . . how are you?" Russell said, forcing a smile. He seemed as uncomfortable as she was, which was some consolation. His muscular hands were clamped onto the handle of a baby stroller, and—adjacent to a cuff button she'd resewn herself—there was a brown, braided leather bracelet wrapped around his wrist.

Russell wearing jewelry? Melinda suppressed her gag reflex.

She'd stopped breathing. She forced her mouth into a smile and gave a thumbs-up.

"And what brings you downtown?" he said, as though they'd divided the city into zones, like Berlin at the end of the war. Russell was now living in some loft on Riverside Drive, so Melinda could have asked him the very same question. She stared at his lips, too unnerved to speak. Russell's features were so familiar, so attractive, the sight of his face caused a jolt of nerve pain to shoot from Melinda's heart to her abdomen and then radiate outward. There was a single, long golden hair fluttering on the shoulder of his Brooks Brothers blazer, and she had to stop herself from reaching out to pick it off.

It was none of his business that she'd impulsively sold the Upper East Side condo they'd shared for twentysomething years and moved to a rental in Greenwich Village. Averting her eyes from the sight of the happy family, Melinda looked into traffic, saying, "I have a new job, so I work here. Or, well, I work there actually," and she waved her hand in the vicinity of the school behind her.

The woman standing next to Russell was wearing pale taupe boots that went up to her knees, a tan suede skirt, and a cream-colored sweater. She was evil incarnate, masquerading in expensive, tasteful neutrals. The boots didn't have any kind of visible zipper; how in God's name had she wrangled them on? Melinda squinted at the impossibly soft-looking sweater, wondering what animal contributed to such a luxurious, finely knit fabric.

"A new job?" said Russell, tilting his graying head. "That's a surprise."

She imagined a garbage truck running him over, first the front wheels—*BA-BAM*—followed by the back—*crunch*.

"What strange timing," said the tart, "isn't it, darling? For her to be starting a new job when you've just retired from yours." She looked up at Melinda and said, "They threw him a big party last night. It was quite a to-do."

Retired? Melinda could not imagine Russell with endless free time on his hands. What would he do with himself, other than play golf? *Oh*, she thought, *he'll have sex all day long.* She bent her knees slightly, feeling monstrous next to her replacement, and suppressed the desire to kick her in the shins. She knew all of Russell's partners at the law firm, and it pained her to imagine them being nice to this bitch who'd stolen her husband out from under her. Loyalty was dead.

"After twenty years in the same firm, I'm sure they were quite happy to see me go," Russell said in a faux humble manner.

"Oh, Russ," the home-wrecker said, feigning pity, a pouty little frown of her pink lips. "They were quite sad, everyone said so." She gave him a gentle pat on the arm.

Russ?

He then added, with a slightly embarrassed shrug, "We're going away for a spell to mark a new beginning."

Melinda felt a stabbing sensation in her chest, sharp enough that she had to press her fist into her diaphragm to counteract it. *Don't look in that stroller,* she told herself, *don't you dare fucking look.* She glanced up at the darkening sky instead, as though searching for a lost pen that had defied gravity.

"Tomorrow morning," the harlot said. "We're going on a cruise in the Caribbean—well, a private one. I have a friend lending us her yacht."

May you get dysentery and shit your bikini. Had she said that aloud? She was fighting the urge to cover her ears with both hands and shout *la la la la* to block out their voices.

"Ten days out on the open sea," Russell said proudly, as though he would be the one steering the ship, like he was Captain Cook himself. "It'll be a grand adventure."

Had he forgotten who he was talking to? She wanted to ask what he planned to do about his motion sickness and whether he'd packed enough of his statin, losartan, Flomax, Nexium, and the SPF 50 that didn't cause him to break out in a rash, but she kept her mouth shut, leaving them all to suffer through an awkward pause.

"The timing's fortuitous," he added with a half smile, "because the baby's *almost* sleeping through the night."

Melinda felt another wave of red-hot anger, like she was the one floating on a roiling sea. *Babies and cruises and sex, oh my.*

The blonde twisted her lips, conveying— Wait, was it annoyance? All at once, Melinda was on high alert.

"I think that's a little overly optimistic," Felicity said, running her fingers through her impossibly glossy hair. "The truth is, babies are . . . a lot."

"Oh?" said Melinda.

"A lot of work, a lot of trouble, a lot of everything," she said.

"But you have to admit, it's getting easier," Russell said with a little lift to his voice. "We'll be catching up on sleep any day now."

Melinda looked into his eyes for the first time and noted the dark circles, the slightly swollen lids, the bloodshot whites. What was this baby doing to make Russell age so quickly? And why did Felicity look so rested?

"In any case," Felicity said, "we've got a proper nanny starting as soon as we're back. It took me weeks to settle on the right one, but he came from this reputable agency, and he'll be worth every penny."

"She must have interviewed ten people before she decided on an Eton-educated British manny," said Russell proudly, but not without mischief.

"Fifteen," said Felicity without a trace of humor. "No one was good enough until I found Liam." Felicity turned, eyeing the school. "Are you teaching there or . . . ?" she said, with what sounded like genuine interest.

"I'm an administrator," said Melinda. "A receptionist actually. It's great. I love it. Kids!" It was so obvious she was lying that she tried to cover it by adding something truthful: "The guy before me got fired. I hear he was a despicable, immoral, utterly heinous person." Melinda stopped, knowing that the edge in her voice was revealing her low opinion of the despicable, immoral, utterly heinous couple standing in front of her.

Just then, the thing in the stroller let out a wail, a shrill, snotty, ear-piercing desperate sound that gave Melinda goose bumps.

"Oops," Russell said, "well, here he goes."

A boy. Russell had a son.

The baby's mother did not make a move. Instead, it was Russell who sprang into action, leaning into the stroller to fuss over the screaming creature, lifting its tiny, fleece-clad body and jostling it up and down. The sight of Russell being paternal made Melinda want to step in front of an oncoming bus. He'd never even wanted a cat all the years they were together. Houseplants were a responsibility not to be borne.

As the baby hollered, he tried to switch positions, to cradle the thing instead, but he was clumsy with the bundle and started making ridiculous, singsong sounds Melinda had never—in their three decades of marriage—heard him make. She wondered if she could pick up the empty stroller and smash the child's mother in the face with it. It looked like it had some heft, like it could cause some real damage if weaponized.

Wait, Melinda thought, *how is it possible that the devil's spawn is even here already?* Unless it was born two months prematurely, its existence made no sense according to the timeline Russell had laid out when he'd dumped her. She counted on her fingers inside her jacket pockets and was certain the brat should not exist yet. *Lies, lies, lies!* Not that it even mattered anymore, but *my God*, what a damned, no-good liar Russell had turned out to be. She made fists with her hands and took a step backward in the direction of her apartment.

The mother of the crying brat did nothing to help Russell, who was rocking his whole body from left to right in an effort to lull the infant. Rather, she continued looking with exaggerated curiosity at the school across the street. Was she hoping Melinda could secure a spot for her brat when the time came? *Fat chance.*

Melinda cleared her throat. "So, I'm late for a thing—"

"You know, I just realized something," the haughty bitch said. "That's Perkins Academy."

Duh. Melinda tried not to watch as Russell fumbled around with the baby as though he were holding a greased piglet, gently thumping its back.

"What a coincidence," Felicity said. "That's so funny."

Melinda could not see what was funny about any of this. She wanted to go home, crawl in bed, and hold a pillow over her own face until she expired. She'd had enough of this punishment.

"I just realized—my friend is a parent there," she said. "You must know her. Lauren Shaw? She's got . . . two children. Or no, three!" And she laughed as though losing track of the number of children one's friend had was amusing. "She's an artist, a ceramist actually, very talented."

"I don't know anyone there," Melinda said bluntly. "I only started this week, so I haven't met people yet."

"It's just that I have this store, you know," she said, "or maybe you don't. Two in Manhattan actually, and we sell Lauren's pieces there."

"Mm-hmm." *Shaw. Lauren Shaw.* The name vaguely rang a bell.

"Long story but Lauren Shaw's kind of the reason Russ and I . . ." She paused, placing her hand on Russell's shoulder, nails like little pink shells against the navy wool.

Melinda's face was hot, and her mouth slightly agape as she tried to comprehend another woman touching her husband, ex-husband, that is, as though this behavior was anywhere in the realm of acceptable, as though she knew him better than Melinda.

"What I mean is, if it weren't for Lauren's encouragement, we probably wouldn't even . . ." Again she let the sentence drift off unfinished.

Why did this slut think it was appropriate to bring up the how or why or because of whom she and Russell had ended up together? If the universe itself had a handbook, this asshole was breaking every rule in it.

Russell stooped to lower the small lump of baby back into the stroller. "We'd best be off," he said. "Little Horatio needs his bottle."

Melinda was 100 percent sure she'd misheard. "Sorry?" she said. "Little what?"

"Horatio," said Russell, his cheeks flushing slightly.

"My friend—the one I was telling you about," said Felicity, "named her daughter after a street. I loved the idea, and since I was living on Horatio when Russell and I met—"

"It has a certain gravitas that we like," Russell said.

"It's *original*," Felicity said, as if correcting him. And then she said, in a clipped tone, "We need an Uber."

Melinda worried she might actually combust from the gathering, incandescent rage in her chest. She wanted to say, *Way to wreck a child's life!*, followed by *Eat shit, motherfuckers!* Instead, she called out, "Later," and abruptly spun around.

She zombie-marched away from them in a haze of anguish, hearing what she thought was the deep, ugly bass of a passing car stereo until she realized the throbbing sound was coming from inside her brain. Humiliation and outrage overwhelmed her, causing her vision to tunnel, the edges darkening, until it felt like she was looking out the porthole of a submarine. She was sure she would pass out, if not from the irregularity of her own breathing, then from the sharp pain in her temple or maybe just from the sheer humiliation of it all. She rounded the corner and once she was out of earshot, she started imitating Felicity, exaggerating her upper-crust accent: "Oooooh, *dahling*, I have this amazing shoppe, did you know? And I'm so goh-geous, look at my peh-fectly peh-fect tits. You can watch me on the telly!"

Melinda thought of how Russell had fallen for her whole *thing*, and she started railing: "*Russ*? You hate being called *Russ*. You hate jewelry. You hate babies. You love your job! A *yacht*? Who the fuck, even, are you? God, I hate you, you cheating, lying stupid piece of shit! You dumb, disloyal . . . *man!*"

A young woman turned to face her, calling out, "You tell him, lady! Way to vent! Get it all out!" and put a hand up in the air for a high five.

Melinda hadn't realized she'd been speaking out loud.

"You're leaving me hanging?" the woman called after her. "Cold!"

Melinda did not think of herself as cold. She certainly didn't feel cold. It was forty-six degrees outside, and she was steaming under her jacket, sweat rolling down her back. Russell didn't think of her as cold, she was almost certain. So, what *was* wrong with her? What did that bitch have that she didn't? Perky boobs. Youth. Overactive ovaries. Fame. A chain of stores. A television show. Russell.

A lot actually. British Bimbo Barbie had a lot Melinda didn't have.

She slowed her breathing and with shaking hands took the key from her pocket as she reached her building. She didn't know how long it was going to take to recover from this hideous setback: from the sight of Russell paired with his new lover, from the actuality of her ex-husband as a father, from the existence of his progeny, from the very fact of Russell's new, full, happy life. But the small bit of her that wanted to survive made her swear that no matter how defeated she felt, she would get up in the morning and go to her stupid new job. At least those bratty students, those entitled parents, and even that insufferable grandma with the stick up her ass would serve as a distraction from her pain.

The grandmother! It came to her then: the email she'd received, granting permission for that uptight, elderly woman to pick up her grandkid, some lengthy, ridiculous tale filled with so many excuses (a pulled muscle, a bad back, stitches, puking) that Melinda had doubted the entire absurd story. The email had come from a Lauren Shaw.

Melinda did not know what role Lauren had played in her divorce, but Lauren was Felicity's friend, and therefore, she was now Melinda's mortal enemy.

She burst into her apartment, lit up with fresh purpose and intention. She would no longer be a victim. She would destroy Felicity, in every possible way she could think of, and she would make Lauren Shaw's life as perfectly miserable as her own.

Revenge was new to Melinda. She needed a plan. She changed into sweatpants and sat down on the couch with a legal pad and sharpened pencil.

• • •

According to their own admission, Russell, his repulsive offspring, and its despicable mother were cruising around on a borrowed yacht somewhere in the Caribbean. Melinda found this information somewhat freeing. At least she had Manhattan to herself and, for now anyway, didn't have to worry about running into the happy family again.

But knowing the pair were off on a vacation together was also vomit-inducing. Everywhere she went, she kept imagining the two of them, lolling on lounge chairs and gazing at each other lustily, touching each other, waking up in each other's arms. She felt sick with sadness and anger. One afternoon she tried to conjure their first meeting as they sat together in his office. Had she flattered him? Had she been impressed by his view of Battery Park? Had he dared to flirt with her first? That notion made Melinda want to choke a parking meter with her bare hands. Instead, she gave herself a pep talk: *Come on, Melinda, pull it together! Focus!* She was on a mission to concoct a plan to destroy her enemies; there was no time to indulge in sloppy, emotional thinking.

The first idea she came up with seemed like pure genius. From the couch in her depressingly empty living room, she compiled a list of uptown nanny agencies. Starting at the top, she made calls, using a deep voice and pretending to be Felicity's assistant. "Felicity would like to make a change in Liam's start date," she said.

The first four agencies said they had no Felicity Wynn as a client in the system. Melinda apologized for the error and hung up. But the fifth agency on the list said that, yes, Liam was flexible and ready to move in anytime.

Melinda hadn't realized the nanny would be living with them.

"I'll have him call her today to discuss timing," the woman said on the phone.

"No!" Melinda snapped, panicking. "Ms. Wynn does not wish to be disturbed on her vacation. She'll call him when she's available."

Melinda hung up and cursed her carelessness. She hadn't thought this through well enough, never imagining she would succeed in finding the agency so quickly. And why had she called from her own phone?

The next day after work, she googled how to block her phone number from showing up and called the agency again. This time she'd written a script and had practiced her British accent. "Halloo, Felicity Wynn here," she said. "My assistant called yesterday, mentioning a change in Liam's start date. I'd like him to move in tomorrow, please."

"Of course," said the woman at the agency. "I'll pass the message along."

"But I do have a few requests," said Melinda, trying her best to sound like Emma Thompson, "regarding Liam's attire. Whenever he's in my home, I'd like him to wear . . . as little as possible."

"Excuse me?"

"Does he own a Speedo? If not, I'd be happy to provide him with one. Maybe with the Union Jack flag on it?"

There was silence on the other end of the line.

"He needs to wax his chest regularly. And I've got a full gym here, so there's no excuse for him to get flabby," Melinda went on. "I like a taut buttock."

"Ms. Wynn," said the woman, "you can't possibly—"

"If this is going to be a problem," Melinda said sternly, "then you can cancel my contract. If you can't work with me to meet my predilections, I'll find an agency that will."

"You won't get your fee back," the woman said coldly. "The ten thousand dollars were nonrefundable."

Ten thousand! Melinda was having fun now.

"I don't care about the piddly money, you twat," she said. "All I want is a hot, young Brit with six-pack abs and a thong. If you can't handle such simple requirements then— Hello?"

The line was dead.

Maybe it had worked? Or had she gone too far? She had a nagging sense that the woman knew it was a prank call. And then Melinda wondered if she'd broken any laws (impersonation of an enemy? slander? fraud?). She imagined a Page Six article outing her as a malicious, spurned lunatic.

She would have to be subtler. Why was it so hard to ruin someone's life? What was the best way to create mayhem, to rankle, to ruin relationships while still keeping her hands clean?

Melinda was determined to do better at doing bad.

• • •

On Friday, she got another idea. She wrote an email to Lauren Shaw that was sure to cause distress, but just before she hit send, she considered the fact that this act could cost her her new job. She changed the subject line from "Classroom Gerbils" to "Long Weekend" and sent it anyway.

She was nervous afterward, and she took her bad mood out on the parents of Perkins. She snapped at a father who tried to leave his car in the fire lane. She scolded a mother who waltzed in with a special treat for her son's birthday: a tray of cupcakes with pistachios sprinkled on top. Nuts! When it said very clearly on page three of the school handbook that they were forbidden! Parents kept asking her to excuse absences that were inexcusable, and Melinda was having none of it.

"My seventh grader needs to miss afternoon classes because her favorite instructor is teaching at SoulCycle."

Absolutely not.

"My eighth grader is missing school next week to go on a West Coast college tour."

Hell no!

One girl came to the lobby asking to use Melinda's desk phone to call her father's work phone so he would bring her iPhone.

"Why?" said Melinda. "You can't use a phone during school hours anyway." She pointed to a sign she'd taped to the front of her desk that had a picture of a cell phone with a red *X* over it. "Now go back to class."

The girl burst into tears as though Melinda had just informed her of a death in the family.

"Oh, come on," said Melinda, handing her a tissue. "No need for that."

The girl continued to cry.

"What's your name?" Melinda asked, with an exhausted sigh.

"Silvestra," said the girl, sniffling.

Silvestra? Horatio? Waverly? "Seriously? Why?"

"Why what?" Silvestra said.

"Never mind," Melinda said and sent her back to class. Unfortunately, she would remember this girl's name forever whether she wanted to or not; maybe that was the point.

• • •

The principal stopped by her desk just after dismissal. "Melinda," she said, with some hesitation in her voice, "let's recap your first week. Is there anything you think we should discuss?"

Melinda wondered if Lauren had turned her in already. "I think I'm getting the hang of things," said Melinda with a false confidence. She patted the handbook. "I'm enforcing law and order. No breaking rules on my watch. Some of the parents think they can pull the wool over my eyes, but I'm no dummy."

"There's no need to be *overly* strict," the principal said with a worried smile. "Just remember: you're the face of the school. You should project our friendly spirit of community. The rest—tardiness, gum chewing, cell phone use—really isn't your domain. The teachers and I can tackle the various disciplinary issues."

Had the gum chewer lodged a complaint? Had Silvestra tattled? What little turds.

"Sure, sure," Melinda said. But she had a list of better goals to tackle from her post in the lobby: number one, she would bring the parent body to its knees, and number two, she would make Lauren Shaw a pariah among them.

• • •

Melinda left work and walked south down potholed, cobblestone streets until she was standing across from Felicity's SoHo boutique. She felt her courage wane and considered aborting the mission, going home, and watching Netflix on the couch. But Netflix was streaming *Felicity at Home*, all six seasons as it turned out, and Melinda had made the mistake of bingeing them all, stunned by how nice her cohost was—the funny and handsome Zach—and by what a stone-cold bitch Felicity was to the poor home owners who already knew that they had no style or taste; that's why they'd hired her in the first place. Melinda despised her.

She stood on Mercer Street, fists on her hips, watching people come and go through the royal-blue door. *Courage*, she told herself.

She put on a pair of oversize dark glasses, waited for a truck to pass, and then crossed the street. Looking in the window, she spotted a couple of women, standing together in the back, talking, and one well-dressed man browsing. She would go in and look around, do a little reconnaissance. What was the big deal with this shop anyway? Why was it so popular? And was there some way she could make the place go bankrupt by stopping people from buying things—starting with Lauren Shaw's stupid pottery?

Melinda put her hand on the shiny chrome doorknob and pushed hard. At the sound of a bell tinkling, she walked into a world of fine, sparkling, breakable objects, wishing she'd brought a baseball bat.

Chapter 7

The second Olivia stood up from her desk at Felicity headquarters, Courtney looked up and cleared her throat.

"So," she said, almost in a whisper, "where are you off to?"

"Nowhere," Olivia said. "Just stretching." And Olivia raised her arms over her head and bent to the side, as if to prove it.

Courtney was a powerhouse, as committed to Felicity and the store's mission as Felicity herself. Perhaps more so, since Felicity's attention was split between her shop and her show. Courtney could discuss, at length and in detail, any product they sold, much like a parent might gush over a child. Or more accurately, like a woman might gush over her lover. She could make a stainless steel serving spoon sound so positively alluring, a customer could not help but buy it. Olivia was learning a lot from her.

But she didn't love working under her relentlessly watchful eye.

Olivia couldn't even go to the bathroom without some kind of commentary.

"It's just that if you're going out to grab coffee," Courtney said, "I wouldn't mind a triple-shot skim latte."

"Oh," said Olivia. This was how quickly a conversation with Courtney could turn into a minefield. "I hadn't planned on it, but if—"

"No, it's fine," said Courtney, checking her Hermès Apple Watch. "I was just thinking I could really use some caffeine while I fix the marketing material you sent."

Fix? "I'd be happy to go to Common Ground if you want a coffee."

"Only if you're getting one for yourself."

Olivia had been Courtney's assistant before being promoted to a new position that involved doing a little bit of everything, but Courtney was still very much her boss and often had her doing things that were more in line with her former position, which had not yet been filled.

"No problem." Since she'd been sitting in front of her laptop all morning, writing online copy for the new line of ceramics, Olivia realized she wouldn't mind a little fresh air. She got her purse.

"Venmo me," Courtney said.

"Sure. And I'll put this beauty back in the window on my way out," she said, picking up a three-tiered porcelain cookie plate that was on her desk. She'd finished the short description of it that would serve as a caption on Instagram, if and only if Courtney approved it.

"Just don't drop it," Courtney said, and laughed like she was making a joke. She wasn't though, not really. Olivia knew all too well that Courtney would never, *ever* let her live down that one time last year when a delicate hourglass, etched comically with breasts and a belly button, slipped through her fingers and smashed on the floor, a pile of glass shards and pink sand at her feet.

She held the plate carefully with both hands and watched her step as she went down the stairs from Felicity headquarters to the boutique below. This piece, priced at $650, was part of her line now, one of the four she was officially managing. Her recent promotion came with a small raise, a desk next to a window on Mercer, and a minor say in the aesthetic principles of the Felicity brand. And she would travel!—the flagship store on Mercer and its sister shop on Madison were only the beginning; she would now be sent to LA, and eventually to San Francisco, Miami, and Chicago, where new stores would be opening. There were murmurs about a shop in Felicity's hometown of London.

Thanks to this promotion, Olivia could not only afford her Brooklyn studio but she could also breathe a bit. With some careful budgeting, she could eat out once or twice a week, maybe, depending on the restaurant, and she could treat herself to clothes, if only at the kind of secondhand places she usually shopped. The entire outfit she was currently wearing—bargain that it was—was new.

She walked into the shop with its bleached oak floors, strategically placed mirrors, and soft lighting that made not only the products but even the shoppers look their most stunning. The salesgirls rushed over to her as soon as they saw her. Olivia would never want these two to know that when she'd first met them, they'd seemed interchangeable with their matching long, straight brown hair and their designer clothes. Fortunately, since Jennifer was from Texas and had a high squeaky voice and Jessica was from New Jersey and smoked half a pack a day, Olivia learned to tell them apart just by listening. Todd always referred to the pair as Jennica.

"Babe!" Jennifer squealed, "We heard! Oh mah God, are you okay?"

"Oh, Olivia," said Jessica, punching her affectionately on the shoulder as Olivia tightened her grip on the cookie plate. "The fuck happened?"

Had she been diagnosed with an illness and no one bothered to tell her? "Sorry?"

The girls looked at each other. "Gurrrl," Jessica said, taking Olivia's hand, "we know about Todd."

How on earth had *that* news traveled?

"He stopped by," said Jennifer, tightening her ponytail and blinking her cartoonishly big eyes, "and dropped off somethin' for you. I stuck it in back."

"Explain it to me like I'm dumb," Jessica said in her raspy voice. "Why'd you break up with him? He's hot, and he's into you."

They were five years her junior, recent NYU grads who shared a pretty apartment in Chelsea that their parents obviously subsidized. They went out most nights of the week, dropping a hundred bucks on sushi dinners like it was absolutely nothing. Olivia liked Jennica, even if they were spoiled rotten.

In Jennica's world, a breakup at Olivia's ripe old age of twenty-seven probably seemed like a catastrophe. But Olivia had felt proud of herself when she'd ended things with Todd. Sure, she'd taken the subway to her studio in tears, acknowledging that she did, in fact, very much like his face and his humor and his cooking and his company, but she was glad she'd been honest about how mismatched they were. He still shared an apartment in the East Village with three other guys, while she had long outgrown communal living. She paid her bills on time and was working to improve her credit score, while his student loans were staggering, even compared to hers. He was uninsured. He hadn't registered to vote until Olivia shamed him into it, too late, as it turned out, for the last election. He was a freelance sound engineer who often worked in the middle of the night, slept in late, canceled plans with her when he got work, and got high when he didn't, while she had a stable career. It was nearly impossible to spend time together because her schedule was normal, while his was irritatingly upside down.

The final straw came the day before when he was offered a nine-to-five job with benefits at a commercial studio, and he told her nonchalantly that he'd *turned it down*, saying it was not his "dream" to write jingles.

"Maybe not," she'd said, so frustrated that it was hard to get the words out, "but couldn't a real job lead you closer to the vicinity of your dream?"

"I *have* a real job," he'd said, shooing his roommate's cat out of his room before she used his laundry pile on the floor as a litter box again. "Why would I work for some company when I can be my own boss? Yeah, I get more work some weeks than others, but I'm building something. And anyway, I'm resilient. You know me: I'm like a camel. Or a cactus. I'm built for dry spells."

Through the wall, she heard one of his roommates cough three times and then flush the toilet.

"Sadly," she'd said, "I'm . . . What's the opposite of a cactus? The idea of a dry spell gives me hives." She wanted them both to be working toward something attainable, like renting a decent apartment together, buying cool, mid-century furniture, and planning trips to places they'd never been, but hearing that he turned down a good job made Olivia realize that Todd actually preferred his life in the unstable gig economy. The last time he'd gotten a fairly hefty payment for recording a band, he didn't save the money, or pay down his debt, or even buy a piece of recording equipment. No, he'd spent it all on a tattoo.

Jennifer and Jessica were staring at her now with matching expressions of concern and fear. Olivia put the cookie plate down on a shelf.

"Oh, *that*," she said, as if her stomach hadn't been reminding her about it all day. "No, it's for the best, really. Todd and I have such different lives. I need someone more grown-up, a man who's actually ready to talk about our future."

"But y'all were so cute together," said Jennifer.

"Man, to be single and starting over again . . . ," Jessica said, shaking her head and letting her voice trail off. Olivia knew she'd stopped herself from adding *at your age* to the end of the sentence.

"There's nothing wrong with being alone," Olivia said, hoping to impress the girls with her independence. "I'm going to focus on me for a while."

Looking at their worried faces, she could tell that they thought she'd made a huge mistake. She had wondered the same thing that morning in the shower, and on her walk to work, and at her desk that morning.

"But what was actually *wrong* with him?" Jennifer asked in a quieter voice as the only customer in the store, a cool-looking man in a tweed blazer, wandered toward them.

"I'm just saying, he looked so freakin' sad," Jessica whispered.

"Let's talk later," Olivia said, picking up the cookie plate. "Courtney's waiting for me to bring her a coffee."

Jennica backed off at the mention of the retail manager's name.

"Drinks after work," Jessica said, and she turned to Jennifer. "What was that place we wanted to check out?"

Jennifer looked as serious as if Jessica had brought up a major news event. "The rooftop bar of that new hotel in Tribeca. The one with the cool mixology menu. It was just written up in the Style section. Let's Uber there, y'all, as soon as we get off work."

Drinking twenty-dollar cocktails was not Olivia's favorite way to spend an evening, but she agreed; being home alone sounded worse.

"Yuge favor," said Jessica, pulling a lanyard over her head and holding out her keys to Olivia. "Can you stay on the floor with Jennifer for a sec? I gotta pee."

"Sure," said Olivia. The store had a hard rule that two staff members had to be on the floor at all times. Even when the store was completely empty, the sales staff wasn't allowed to eat or drink, make personal calls, or scroll the internet. One guy got fired for reading a book during a lull.

Jennifer approached the customer who was browsing tailored table linens from Japan, right beside the Norwegian textured barware. Olivia went to the front window to place the off-white tiered plate—which featured a line of tiny black ants crawling up the crackled stem—with the rest of the new porcelain collection. Everyone knew Felicity was a diva, but she sure had great taste. What Olivia admired most about the brand was that it did not take itself too seriously. There was whimsy throughout the store, not obvious in every piece, of course, but just enough to say to the customer, *Don't forget: this is supposed to be fun.* There were cheese spreaders with wooden handles carved in the shape of dachshunds. There were throw blankets made of the softest Irish cashmere imaginable, with embroidered stitching near the fringe that read: *Too fucking cold.* Olivia's studio got miserably uncomfortable in the winter, and she wanted to take that blanket home and wrap herself up in it. Unfortunately, it was way out of her budget.

Olivia followed Felicity's personal Instagram with keen interest and envy. She'd recently posted a gorgeous, perfect picture of her baby, dressed in a cream-colored onesie with a matching cap, sleeping peacefully on her chest. Felicity's gorgeous hair was cascading around her face, and her glossy lips were poised to kiss the baby's forehead. The caption read: *Who says you can't have it all? #FelicityatHome.*

. . .

Olivia was used to being the shortest person in the room, but the woman who walked into the store just then was objectively, markedly tall. She was wearing flat shoes and dark glasses, and when the door closed behind her, she let out a lungful of air as if she hoped to knock someone over with it.

"Welcome," said Olivia. "Let me know if I can help with anything." She glanced at the other pieces of the new porcelain collection, counting how many Instagram captions she still had to write.

The woman came up beside her, lowered her clunky sunglasses down the bridge of her nose, and leaned in to see the signage that had the ceramist's name. "Aha," she said.

"Excuse me?"

"Lauren Shaw," she said, scowling. She had a strong jawline and was clenching it so hard, the muscle in her cheek twitched. "Stinking rotten, putrid, heinous . . ."

Olivia thought the customer was making a reference to the maggots painted on the sides of the teacups. "She's a local artist," Olivia said. "Every piece is hand-painted at her studio in Brooklyn, where she juxtaposes morbid or repellant images with beauty in a way that's delightfully comedic." Olivia had written those exact words for the website and was rather proud of them.

The woman picked up a dessert plate. "Disgusting," she said loudly, peering at a decomposing mouse skull painted in the center. "Why would she do that?"

Not everyone liked whimsy, apparently.

"It's her style, to add funny little grotesqueries to her pieces."

"Well, I can see that, can't I?" the lady said, setting the plate down with a thud. Her height was intimidating, but her apparent anger was incomprehensible. "Lauren Shaw is obviously deranged," the customer said.

Olivia thought she was projecting and took a few steps back.

The door opened, and another shopper walked in. She spotted Jennifer, and met her over at the everyday china on the left side of the store.

This woman looked more like a typical Felicity customer: she was wearing a Burberry trench coat and a Louis Vuitton cross-body. She had expensive-looking auburn highlights, and her diamond engagement ring was probably worth enough to buy out the entire store.

"I suspect," the angry lady was saying, waving her hand at the porcelain, "that every bit of this stuff is tainted with lead and toxic glazes."

"Oh, gosh, no," said Olivia. "We set exceptionally high safety standards for all our products."

Olivia kept an eye on the woman as she began wandering around with her nose in the air.

"What is that sickly smell?" she asked, gagging dramatically next to the collection of baby products.

"That's probably our signature verbena-scented candle," Olivia said. She turned her back and quickly texted Courtney upstairs:

Weird hostile customer in shop, possibly drunk?

She put her phone back in her pocket and pretended to fold the French terry-cloth onesies.

"How stupidly impractical."

Olivia jumped, startled to hear the woman's voice coming from directly behind her. She reached over Olivia's shoulder and grabbed the plush fabric.

"Why would anyone put a kid in a pricey outfit that it's just going to poop in?"

She wasn't entirely wrong. Olivia tried to catch Jennifer's eye, but she was absorbed in talking to the bride about the new line of British stoneware. The tweed-clad customer was in his own world, consumed with the Georg Jensen silver.

What was taking Jessica so long?

When would Courtney come down?

"Are you freaking kidding me?" the woman said, holding up a wooden block in her palm. "Two hundred dollars for a stupid *toy*? How ridiculous."

Her anger seemed so out of proportion. Why in the world did she care?

"Well," Olivia said, trying to remain calm herself, "this set of building blocks is hand-carved in the Black Forest by a German family that's been in the business since 1890." Olivia picked up another block and pointed out the detailing, leaves carved on one side, a squirrel on another.

"So?" the woman barked.

"Well, I was speaking to the craftsmanship, in case you were interested," said Olivia. "The toys are all made with organic berry-based stains, so they're completely free of toxins, and the wood is sustainably sourced, of course."

"Oh, *of course*," the woman said, in an unnaturally high voice, mimicking her.

How rude! She reminded Olivia of a heckler she'd once seen at a comedy show.

The woman carelessly put down the block, only halfway on the shelf, and it fell on the floor. "And this?" she said, turning to her other side and picking up a fragile, iridescent carafe with a glass stopper. "I bet you're going to tell me that *this* garbage thing is handblown by virgins on a remote island, and that's why it costs"—she consulted the pale pink price tag attached with twine—"*two hundred and sixty dollars?* It better do a lot more than hold liquid."

Olivia picked up the block and checked the edges for damage. "That carafe *is* handblown," Olivia said warily, hoping the lady wouldn't drop it as well, "by artisans in Vermont." The word "booze" was etched in cursive on the side.

"I seriously don't give a shit who's blowing what, where," the woman said, gesturing angrily with the carafe, its glass stopper teetering. "How on earth can this stupid store be successful? It's filled up with a bunch of overpriced, unnecessary, bourgeois shit, and—as a sales clerk—you should be ashamed of yourself to be working here. Don't you realize there are homeless people in the world, in *this city?* And you're encouraging people to spend their money on crap they don't need."

Olivia did not know where to begin. She was proud of the role she played in selling these high-quality goods. Art, actually. "When we source our products," she said defensively, "we consider labor practices and reduction of waste. . . ." Was there really any point in defending the company to this nutjob? There was no other recourse she could think of, so she went on. "If you look at our website, you'll see that Felicity gives back a percentage of profits to several initiatives that benefit the environment, that advocate for incarcerated women, that fight hunger—"

"Blah blah blah," the woman said, waving her arms in circles.

Olivia kept her eyes on the carafe as it, too, circled through the air.

"You think you're above criticism?" The woman backed into a shelf then, an actual bull in a china shop, causing a velvet stand of men's jewelry to wobble. She gasped and reached out with her free hand to inspect one particular braided leather bracelet that caught her attention. "Holy fucking shit," she said. "Oh my God."

Olivia assumed the woman had noticed the five-hundred-dollar price tag. "Look," she said quietly, dropping the sales pitch entirely, "you obviously don't care for our merchandise or our store. So unless there's something I can actually help you with, why don't you . . . go." And she indicated the door.

"Are you throwing me out?" The woman narrowed her eyes. "You little snob, with your fancy designer dress and your platform shoes, you think I'm not good enough for your hoity-toity knickknacks?"

Snob? Olivia had bought her shoes for 70 percent off at a Stuart Weitzman sample sale—one of the perks of having size-6 feet—and the dress was a crocheted seventies classic from a secondhand shop in Brooklyn—one of the perks of being a size 2. "You don't know anything about me, lady. But I know one thing: this store isn't a good fit for you."

"Meaning what exactly?" The woman was gripping the carafe like she was holding it hostage.

Where the hell was Jessica? Olivia spotted the male shopper on her left, wandering into the war zone. She needed to put a stop to this situation at once, before the madwoman started throwing things. "What I'm saying is, you need to calm down."

"*Calm down?*" the woman said, her eyes wide in fury.

Olivia gestured in the direction of the door. "Yeah, and get out." The woman didn't budge, so Olivia decided to try another tactic by giving the kind of speech Felicity would make at an all-company meeting: "Look, we target a very specific demographic: wealthy, educated people with a deep appreciation for luxury goods, customers who want high-quality pieces and appreciate the tasteful curated collection we offer. We're about well-designed and beautifully made *extravagance*. We don't offer bargains, and we're sure not targeting a woman like *you*."

The woman's face hardened. "Oh, I see," she said, putting the carafe down on the shelf. Olivia was hopeful, thinking maybe she'd succeeded in diffusing the situation. "You're telling me I'm too poor, too tacky, and too ignorant to shop here?"

"Well . . . ," said Olivia, "I'm saying you'd fit in better at a different kind of store. Like HomeGoods. In any case, you need to leave."

"You are so mean," the woman said, sounding pitiful now instead of angry.

Olivia turned to see Courtney, Jessica, Jennifer, and the shoppers gawking at her, as one might at the scene of a car crash.

Next thing she knew, Courtney was stepping in to offer the aggrieved customer her sincerest apologies and a complimentary eighty-nine-dollar verbena-scented candle.

"And as for you," she said to Olivia through clenched teeth, "upstairs, *now*."

Olivia's face was bright red as she walked past her friends toward the stairwell in the back. She could not imagine how she would possibly explain herself.

Chapter 8

Olivia stood with her hands at her sides in front of her boss's desk.

"I'm simply aghast," Courtney said for the fifth time in what was without a doubt the shittiest conversation Olivia had ever had. "You used our own marketing strategy *against* us. How could you talk to a customer that way? You made that poor woman cry! What brought on such an onslaught of snobbery?"

Olivia stood there, mortified and sweaty, and took it. "I'm really, really sorry," she said.

"I'm going to have to think this over and come up with a plan," Courtney said. "Maybe I promoted you too quickly. You need more training, on sensitivity, on customer care, on our mission. But I can't even deal with this right now because I'm swamped and I've lost an hour."

"I'm so sorry," said Olivia again. "That woman was—"

"Get me that coffee," she said, turning back to her computer. "My head is killing me. Actually, no, go to Balthazar and get me the marinated beet salad and one of those little bread things I like. Then pick up coffee before you come back so it's still hot."

Yep, she was definitely being demoted. And now, to add to the humiliation, Olivia had to slink down the stairs and back into the shop in order to exit the building.

"Babe, I'm so sorry," Jennifer whispered, her voice thick with its Texas drawl. "First a breakup, and now *this*?"

"That sucked," said Jessica, putting a heavy hand on Olivia's shoulder. "What the fuck even happened? I wasn't gone *that* long."

"I don't know," said Olivia. Her heart was pounding. "I let that customer get to me."

"Ah, shit," Jessica said, rubbing her forehead. "It's all my fault. I never should have asked you to stand in for me."

It had not escaped Olivia's attention that Jennifer had done nothing to help. "Didn't you see how belligerent that woman was? It was like she stormed in looking for a fight, and I just happened to be the one standing there."

"I'm sorry, Liv, I was helping that bride add all kinds of stuff to her registry," said Jennifer. "I just wasn't paying any attention at all to what was going on up front."

"That had to be a phony name she gave, right?" said Jessica. "'Silvestra Perkins'? I mean, come on."

Olivia raised her shoulders helplessly. "I think it's kind of pretty. It sounds like a soap opera character or an actress."

"Courtney knows how good you are," Jessica whispered. "It's not like you work the floor anyway."

"She's right," Jennifer said, squeezing her hand. "I'm sure this whole thing will blow over before you know it."

Olivia wanted to believe that, but as she walked down Mercer, she had a knot in her stomach and a nagging sense of evil lurking, a darkness that took the shape of that horrible woman as she'd stormed into her life.

. . .

Olivia walked to Balthazar and then eight blocks in the other direction to Common Ground. The baristas were so slow, Olivia had to ask twice if they'd skipped her order.

When she finally walked back in the store, Jessica shot her a look of warning. There was Courtney, waiting for her by the checkout counter, her face contorted in anger. Olivia offered her the coffee and the bag with the salad, apologizing for taking so long, but Courtney held up a hand to stop her. On the counter next to her was a cardboard box containing everything Olivia had had on her desk.

"I don't understand," Olivia said, her entire body turning cold. "I thought I was getting sensitivity training—"

"Your tirade blew up in our faces," Courtney said. She held out her phone and there on the screen was Olivia herself, in profile, leaning in with a finger pointed, lecturing. She looked like a little girl playing teacher in her mother's shoes. The crazed shopper was not in the frame. Courtney hit play and Olivia heard that the sound quality was, unfortunately, outstanding. She could hear herself: "We're about well-designed and beautifully made extravagance. We don't offer bargains, and we're sure not targeting a woman like *you*." And lest there be any confusion at all, Olivia's speech was printed on the reel, unfurling diagonally, one word at a time. She'd been filmed—out of context!—but nevertheless saying the actual words she'd said, all in the right order. "Get out," she'd said. What defense could she possibly give?

"This is a PR nightmare," Courtney said, picking up the cardboard box and shoving it in her arms. "I've got to go clean up this mess. You're done here."

She turned and stormed up the stairs.

Olivia thought she might throw up. She looked down with blurred vision into the box, where she saw her phone charger, a box of tissues, a bottle of Advil, a tin of peppermint tea.

The girls rushed to her side, both gripping their phones.

"I'm so sorry," Jennifer said. "This is just the worst."

Olivia put down the box and gasped for air, her eyes stinging with tears. "Should I try . . . ? How can I . . . ?" She looked at them, feeling absolutely frantic. "What do I do?"

"Nothing," said Jessica, scrolling on her phone. "The video's gone viral."

"It must have been filmed by that man who was here," Jennifer said, "but I never saw him get his phone out."

"This can't be happening," Olivia said, shaking her head as if to wake herself out of a nightmare. "So, what, I just go home? That's it?"

"Wait a sec," Jennifer said. She opened a cabinet under the counter and placed a paper bag into the cardboard box. "From Todd," she said, looking like she might start crying herself. "So, listen, we'll see you at around six at that place in Tribeca."

"I can't," Olivia said. She put her purse in the box as well and grabbed a tissue from it. She backed away from them, stumbling in her shoes. "I'm going to this other bar, and I'll text you later. If you want to meet there, great, but it's not the kind of place you two normally go. I'm warning you, it's a dive."

"Authenticity," Jennifer said, and gave her an encouraging smile, "you know we love it."

"We'll go wherever you say," Jessica said, wiping a tear from her own cheek. "And the drinks are on us."

Sweet, thought Olivia, as she turned to leave, closing the shop door behind her for the last time. But there was no need for them to treat; she knew the owner.

• • •

It took some rejiggering of Olivia's brain to accept that she had a free afternoon. She had a free week. She had free time, in fact, for the foreseeable future.

Rather than take the subway home to Brooklyn, Olivia carried her box along Mercer Street and then cut over to West Broadway. She had to stop now and then to wipe the tears from her face and adjust the weight of the box. Her student loans! How would she pay off any of her looming debt? She would have to tell her parents. She would tell

Todd too, and he would be nice about it and overly relaxed. *Todd.* She stopped short; Todd was no longer her boyfriend, Todd was no longer there to be sweet and supportive, to tell her—in his unfailingly optimistic way—that something better would come along, not to worry. She'd been judgmental of him, but at least Todd *had* a job, unstable though it might be.

She put the box down on the sidewalk and opened the paper bag he'd left for her at the store. On the outside of the bag, he'd written in green marker: *Some of us like dry spells* and he'd drawn a heart. Inside the bag was a small, potted cactus. He'd gotten her a breakup present.

"Todd," she said sadly, taking the succulent out of the bag.

A man walking by in an AC/DC T-shirt stopped beside her. "Todd won't ask for much," he said.

Olivia turned to him, holding the cactus with both hands.

"But whatever you do," the man said, "don't overwater him," and he kept walking.

Olivia felt sick. She was no cactus. Being unemployed was the worst thing she could imagine. Would she even be able to pay her rent next month?

She put the cactus back in the box and got her phone out of her pocket. She found the video and watched it again. Her outfit was, in fact, fabulous, while everything else about the video was humiliating and just plain awful. Her voice was snooty, her face prissy and self-righteous, and the words themselves unforgivable. The video had garnered hundreds of comments in the last hour, all dissing the inherent elitism of Felicity's brand and the rudeness of Olivia herself.

What a frickin' bitch!!!

Hey little girl shut your face lol

Felicity is garbage!!!!!Total snob bullshit :(Never shopping there.

Ha busted! That rude salesgirl is toast.

Olivia sputtered and wiped her nose on her own sleeve. She was despised!

She checked the Felicity Instagram page and saw that Courtney had not yet posted any kind of apology. She was probably on the phone with Felicity herself, strategizing the best response.

She texted her dad: On my way. Have some bad news :(

She wound her way through Washington Square Park, turning onto Waverly Place. As soon as she walked down the well-worn stairs to the Sweet Spot, she started to feel comforted. The warmth of this place, which felt like her second home—with its battered wood floors, the pungent smell of beer, the rickety tables with matchbooks under the legs and unlit votives on the tops, the song "You Can't Always Get What You Want" playing in the background—was exactly what she needed. The room was empty, which wouldn't last long. The Sweet Spot would be buzzing by late afternoon.

And there was her dad, at his post behind the bar. He was standing with his palms on the counter, his black apron around his waist, looking up with his kind eyes as she came in. He dropped his shoulders and extended his arms. "Hey," he said. "What happened?"

Olivia put her box down on the first table as her dad came to her from behind the bar. She dissolved. He hugged her and rubbed her back, saying, "Okay, now. It can't be that bad."

"I got fired," she said, her nose running on his rumpled button-down shirt.

"No," Dan said, his voice revealing his utter shock. "But why?"

"I messed up," she said. "I was really rude to this customer. And—"

"I can't imagine *you* being—"

"And someone in the store filmed the whole thing, and I've gone viral for being an asshole."

Her father's eyes were wide. "Is your name on it? Anything to identify you?"

"Other than my *face*?" she said ruefully. "The store is getting hammered, and I'm the poster child for snobby jerks everywhere."

Her dad was shaking his head. "I can't picture you being rude to anyone."

"I'm so screwed," Olivia said, dropping her head. She was starting to get a dull headache behind her eyes. "What am I going to do?"

"Come on, it'll work out," he said, leading her to a barstool and handing her a cocktail napkin.

"I like working for Felicity," Olivia said. "I mean, the brand *and* the person. She's a force, you know. She's a really big deal." She blew her nose as Dan sat down beside her.

"Courtney wasn't always easy," he said.

"Yeah, but I think she was starting to respect me," she said. "I was getting pretty good at all the writing." She wondered how many people were watching the video at that very moment. "Do you want to see me showing the world what an awful person I am?"

"No, let's not add to the views," he said.

Olivia almost smiled; her dad really could be adorable. "One more won't make a difference."

She opened TikTok and played the video.

"Can I be honest?" he said. "That's not you at all."

"Except that it is. What if I interview somewhere and the person recognizes me?"

"What got you so riled up?"

"This woman! Who's conveniently *not* in the video. She was like a tornado. She came in like she wanted to wreck the place. She was like ten feet tall and ranting and angry, bumping into things."

"She sounds scary," he said.

"Oh, you have no idea. I'll find her." Olivia googled *Silvestra Perkins*, hoping she could find a picture of this raging amazon of a woman who'd cost her her job. "I'm not sure how to spell her name," she said. "I've never heard of a Silvestra before, have you?"

"No," he said.

"I'm only getting Sylvester Stallone. Maybe it's *Sylvestra* with a *y*? Anyway, she was completely out of control."

"Was she on drugs or something?" asked her dad, getting up and walking to his side of the bar.

"I have no idea," Olivia said, putting down her phone. "But she had this palpable fury, like she hated the very ground the store stood on. It was like a PETA activist in a fur-coat store."

Dan smiled, the corners of his eyes creasing. "Thrown into a rage by decorative pillows? She sounds like she has issues."

Olivia knew her father didn't appreciate the exorbitant prices or the frivolity of home decor. Nevertheless, he'd been proud of Olivia for landing a good job and getting promoted so quickly.

"Can I help?" he said.

She removed the small laminated menu that was stuck to her elbow and glanced at it. "I'll take the happy hour red."

"It's a pretty bad merlot," he said. "Start with a club soda; you're probably dehydrated." He reached for a glass, added a scoop of ice, and filled it from the soda tap. He dropped in a lime and placed the glass on a cocktail napkin next to her.

Olivia took one sip and then put her forehead down on the sticky bar.

"Have you called your mom?"

"She's in Haiti," she said, dreading that conversation. "I'll tell her when she gets back."

"And Todd?"

Olivia didn't want to talk about it. Her dad liked Todd almost as much as she did. She lifted her head and said, "Any chance you might need a waitress?"

"Olivia, no," he said, "you don't want to come back here." He leaned on his forearms. "But what if I hire you to set up one of those accounts for me, on whatever site is in these days."

Olivia put down her glass. "I really hope you don't mean a dating site, because that would be super awkward."

"Not for me. For the bar."

She'd been telling him for years that he needed social media for the Sweet Spot. "Of course," she said. "That's long overdue."

"I'll pay for your expertise to get me set up."

Olivia knew he was just throwing her a bone. "Why now?"

"The bands I hire are getting annoyed that I don't do anything to advertise when they play," he said. "And in the event I have to relocate, I'd like to be able to do more than stick a farewell note on the door."

"Relocate?" she said, looking around the room where she'd practically grown up. "Why would you ever leave?"

Dan pointed to the ceiling. "Charley Aston's son, Leo, and his wife and kids moved in upstairs. Who knows if they'll want to keep some old bar in the basement."

"This place is an institution," said Olivia. "I can't imagine they would displace you; they'd be reviled by everyone in the neighborhood—"

"Not by the people who make the noise complaints," he said with a smile. He reached his hand over the bar, and without even looking, he turned the volume down on the Rolling Stones.

"Charley will haunt the place if they kick you out." Olivia hadn't seen Leo for years, but he seemed like a good-enough guy, a serious science geek who studied something to do with bugs. And she'd grown up revering Charley Aston: a legend, a woman at the crossroads of seventies feminism and funny but socially conscious theater. Sitting at this very bar, her history textbook open, music playing from a jukebox, long since defunct, Olivia would listen to Charley preach about how important it was for women to be financially and emotionally independent. Her words had made an impression.

"Maybe they'll let me stay," said Dan, "but I need a backup plan in case."

Olivia looked around the dark, wood-paneled room: it was not an attractive space, but it had a rich history; the Ramones, Blondie, and Sonic Youth had all played there back in the day. She tried to imagine her dad setting up shop anywhere else and simply couldn't. This grungy hideaway was his habitat, his home.

The door to the bar opened then and an older woman marched in, looking rattled. She was dressed in a pleated skirt, twin set, and pearls, and she was holding the hand of a small girl on one side and of a young boy on the other. A third kid with Band-Aids on his cheek stood behind them. By the look on the woman's face, Olivia was certain that she was there to lodge a noise complaint herself. She was willing to bet this lady was about to shout, *I'd like to speak to the manager!*

But instead, as her dad turned down the music even lower, the woman apologized for interrupting and asked if there was someone there named Dan.

"That's me," her dad said, getting to his feet. "Can I help you?"

"My daughter and son-in-law live upstairs, and Leo said you might have a spare key, or that Phillip keeps one here? I went to pick up the children from school, and I stupidly locked us out." A few strands were loose from her bun, and her eyes revealed a low-level panic.

Dan went into a drawer behind the bar and pulled out a key attached to an old-fashioned brass key chain. "And you are . . . ?"

"Evelyn," she said formally. "I'm the grandmother. I came in town for what was supposed to be a short visit but—well, there was this series of catastrophes, and I had to extend my stay to help with my grandchildren. I'm not quite used to their routine, and we went to the park, and we desperately need a restroom. . . ."

Dan handed Olivia the key. "My daughter can let you in." He turned to her. "You don't mind, do you?"

"Not at all," said Olivia, getting up from her barstool. The tension from her miserable day had worked its way into her neck. "I'm Olivia," she said.

She saw then how tightly the little girl was crossing her legs. Since the bar's bathroom was, frankly, too gross to offer, Olivia moved quickly to the door.

They hurried outside to the brownstone steps, Evelyn trailing behind as the rest of them took the stairs two at a time. Olivia wasn't sure if she should be the one to unlock the door, or if she should wait to hand the key to the grandmother. But Evelyn waved her hand, letting Olivia know she should go ahead. As soon as she opened it, the girl rushed in, just as a large, shaggy dog came bounding out, leashless and wild. He took off down the sidewalk, stopping briefly at the nearest fire hydrant before recklessly crossing Waverly Place and continuing on his way to Washington Square Park, as though he had no use whatsoever for a human chaperone. Olivia caught sight of a red leash hanging on the inside of the doorknob, and, imagining the cabs speeding down the neighborhood streets, she grabbed it and ran after him. The last thing she wanted was for this shittiest of all days to end with some rando dog getting hit by a car.

Chapter 9

That dog was fast. Olivia lost sight of him at the entrance to the park and thought she might not be able to track him down at all. She walked as far as the fountain and then returned to the west side again, thinking he might stay closer to home. One of the chess players noticed her carrying a limp leash and pointed in the direction of Bleecker Street. She walked south, asking people along the way if they'd seen a lost dog. A woman suggested she check the dog park, and she finally found him there, panting by the gate, barking at his friends on the other side. Winded from her sprint, she took hold of his collar and clipped on the leash. "Bumper"—according to the imprint on his tag—seemed perfectly happy to have a complete stranger take control of him, but when Olivia encouraged him to walk along with her quickly, thinking the children were probably worrying, Bumper let her know he had his own plans for the outing. He stopped every two feet to sniff the ground and pee, refusing to move no matter how hard she tugged on his leash. She got him halfway through the park when he stopped again to poop, right in front of a family eating pretzels on a bench. They gave her a dirty look, got up, and left. She had no bag to clean it up, so she stood there, hoping some dog owner would come to her rescue. A man walking a pack of poodles reluctantly gave her a bag and then scolded her for not having her own.

"What a totally shitty day," Olivia said as she leaned over and picked up the pile of poo.

Bumper looked up at her, panting while Olivia dropped the bag in a garbage can. As they walked back toward the arch, she opened her phone and checked Instagram again. Courtney had posted a response, simple white lettering on a plain blue square:

> We at Felicity pride ourselves on living the values we hold dear—inclusivity, beauty, and artisanship.
> We are aware of the video circulating on the internet, and we disavow in the strongest possible terms the language used and the attitudes expressed by one of our employees.
> Because we have zero tolerance for elitism and poor customer relations, we terminated the employee, effective immediately.
> We hope to earn your trust as we continue to source beautifully made products to warm and brighten your home.

The comments under the post were brutal—*Glad you fired that bitch!*—and Olivia was absolutely horrified, dropping down on a bench to absorb how reviled she was. And as for her job? There wasn't enough groveling in the world for Courtney to take her back. Her life at Felicity was over.

She wiped her eyes with her sleeve and patted the big dog on his side. She was unemployed, starting all over again, without even a reference. This just plain *sucked*.

She got up and walked with Bumper to Waverly Place, climbing the steps when they reached the brownstone. She still had the spare key in her pocket, but it didn't feel right to let herself in. She rang the bell instead, and Bumper sat down to wait.

After she rang the bell a second time, the door opened, and the girl wrapped her arms around the dog's neck. "Bumper, you dumb dumb," she said. And then she yelled into the apartment behind her, "Bumper's back."

Evelyn came to the entry, looking flustered but immensely relieved. "Oh, thank goodness you found him," she said. "I'm too old to keep up with him. He's badly behaved, but for some reason, the family is attached. You're not allergic, I hope."

"No," said Olivia, wondering if her red, puffy eyes had prompted that question. She unclipped the leash and hung it back over the doorknob where she'd found it. Olivia hadn't been in the brownstone since one of Charley Aston's epic birthday parties over a decade before and was astonished to see how little had changed. The living room sofa she'd sat on as a girl was looking the worse for wear, as were the upholstered chairs and the threadbare carpets. The house didn't smell *bad* exactly, but there was a layering of odors—wet dog, dry laundry, burnt cheese, stale perfume—that Olivia found slightly unpleasant.

The girl ran off in the direction of the kitchen, as Evelyn said, "Well, I can't thank you enough, for both the key and the dog. It's all just too much for me." Olivia noticed that Evelyn's cardigan was inside out. "I've been in charge of everything here for an entire week, and frankly, I'm exhausted."

"It was really no problem," Olivia said. Her phone was buzzing in her pocket, and she wondered if friends were texting about the video. Had she been tagged? She took her phone out and shut it down.

"Don't you look darling," Evelyn said. "Such interesting style. Who do you remind me of?" She pondered that, and then said, "I've never been good at remembering the names of celebrities."

Olivia would have been happy to hear any one of a number of names: Olivia Newton-John, Twiggy, Ali MacGraw, Goldie Hawn. She waited to see what this woman would come up with.

Instead, Evelyn said, "Are you a waitress?"

Olivia hesitated. Was she? She certainly didn't work in retail anymore.

"The bar downstairs?" Evelyn said. "I thought maybe you work there."

"I used to," she said.

"I don't suppose you want a job walking Bumper?"

"Oh, no, but thanks," she said. She would not be reduced from assistant buyer at a high-end boutique to pet wrangler in the course of a single day. Waiting tables would be a hard enough transition.

"It's only that you seem to know your way around a dog," Evelyn said, "and my daughter and her husband both managed to injure themselves and are hobbling around. Bumper's sweet, but he almost knocked me off my feet this morning."

The little girl came running back in and pulled on her grandmother's skirt. "The kitchen's getting smoky."

"The oven!" said Evelyn, and she rushed away, the tag of her cardigan showing just under her bun.

"We're having dinner already," the girl said, and without another word, she took Olivia's hand and led her to the kitchen. Olivia was curious to see more of the house. As a girl, she'd wandered around during parties and took no small interest in the naked drawings on the walls, the couples making out in doorways, the smell of pot and incense in the air.

They entered the kitchen, which looked charmingly retro and wholesome. She had not remembered it that way, probably because she'd always seen it full of people smoking cigarettes and mixing martinis while they waited for the second act of a staged reading to begin. This time the kitchen had a grandma in an apron fussing over a casserole dish at the gas stove.

The younger of the two boys was sitting at the kitchen table, an open math book beside him that he was decidedly not studying; he was concentrating instead on making a drawing of something that looked like either a robot or a large root vegetable. The kid was no artist.

The back door was wide open to the deck, where the boy with the Band-Aids was reading. Olivia remembered sitting on that very chair while her father walked through the whole house flushing the toilets and running the taps as a favor to Phillip and Charley when they were both traveling.

"Do you like macaroni and cheese?" the girl said, pulling her by a sticky hand to the table.

Olivia had not eaten anything that day other than a yogurt at her desk, and that felt like a lifetime ago. "Sure, who doesn't?"

The girl went to the counter and whispered in her grandmother's ear. Evelyn took a stack of rimmed bowls from a cabinet, filled one, and gave it to the girl, who used two hands to bring it over to the table. "You can have more if you want," she said.

"What's your name?" Olivia asked.

"Waverly." She dropped a pile of spoons and napkins on the table.

"Well, thank you, Waverly," Olivia said. She wanted to take a bite but waited; no one else had been served. The boy next to her dropped the drawing and the open math book onto the floor between them and leaned his forearms on the table to put a spoon at each seat.

"And who are you?" Olivia said.

"I'm Harrell," he said.

"Harold," Olivia said, putting out her hand to introduce herself, "nice to meet you."

"Har*rell*," he said, shaking her hand in an exaggerated way.

Evelyn brought bowls for Harrell and Waverly and went back to the stove. "Leo and my daughter met at a bug museum in New Mexico called Harrell House," she said with her back to them. "The place is special to them." She looked over her shoulder and raised her eyebrows at Olivia, as if to say she did not approve. "*Charles!*" she called out to the boy on the porch.

The boy on the porch came inside and took a seat across from Olivia.

"Hi," Olivia said. "I bet you were named after your grandmother Charley."

"The *other* grandmother," mumbled Evelyn, keeping her back turned, "and I won't speak ill of the dead."

Watching Evelyn putter around the kitchen, Olivia noted that Charley and Evelyn could not have been more different. Charley, for example, never wore a bra, while Evelyn looked like someone who slept in one.

"Thanks for inviting me. I'm Olivia, by the way. My dad runs the bar downstairs."

Harrell put his napkin on his head and stuck his arms out like a zombie.

Waverly tapped Olivia on the shoulder and said, "Grammy says the bar is not a sweet spot at all because there are too many drunks making noise there."

Olivia suppressed a smile as Evelyn dropped her big wooden spoon on the floor. "That's not *exactly* . . ." She shot Waverly a look as she dampened a paper towel to wipe cheese sauce off the linoleum. Bumper beat her to it and licked the floor clean. "I only said that your new neighborhood is a bit raucous for my taste. I prefer life in the suburbs. But that's just me." She brought a platter of broccoli to the table, pulled out a chair, and sat with them. "Bon appétit, everyone."

Olivia took a bite of her macaroni and cheese. She closed her eyes. It was classic comfort food, warm crunchy bread crumbs on top, cheesy and decadent underneath, exactly what she needed after such a miserable day. She swallowed, feeling ever so slightly cheered. In a little while, she would go back downstairs with a full stomach, have a glass of wine with her dad, and the next day, full steam ahead, she would look for a new job.

"Who started homework?" Evelyn asked. "Because when your parents get home from physical therapy, I want—"

"What's physical therapy?" said Harrell.

"Your mommy and daddy hurt themselves last week," Evelyn said, "so Aunt Frances recommended someone who can help them get better. Isn't that wonderful? When they get back, I want to be able to tell them your homework is done, or close to it."

"But it's the weekend," said Charles, taking a retainer out of his mouth and putting it on the table.

"And you don't want it hanging over you, do you?" Evelyn said.

"I started my math," said Harrell. "It's easy."

"Good boy," she said, passing him the broccoli.

Olivia glanced down at the open book on the floor and saw that Harrell had only solved three multiplication problems in a set that had twenty. All three answers were incorrect.

She took another bite and then another. *Ah, carbs*, she thought, and she scooped up the last of the elbow noodles, thinking she would not turn down seconds if they were offered. But her eyes widened when she saw what remained in the bottom of the bowl: there, crawling under the end of her spoon, was a perfectly depicted, utterly realistic, hand-painted cockroach.

The girl noticed Olivia noticing the bug. "It's not real," she said, giggling. "Don't worry."

"Oh, dear," said Evelyn, seeing the expression on Olivia's face, "unappetizing, isn't it? I've told my daughter time and time again that her dishes would be so much more attractive if she made them without those ghastly little additions, but she won't listen to her mother."

"Are you going to throw up?" Charles said, looking at Olivia with delight. "Harrell threw up six times the other day."

"Charles," said Evelyn, "please don't talk about such things at the dinner table."

Olivia put down her spoon and looked around the kitchen, letting the knowledge of who lived there sink in. She was in Lauren Shaw's house. She was in the kitchen of the woman whose entire line she'd been in charge of—the commissions, the marketing, the placement, the sales in each Felicity boutique—and she'd lost the opportunity to prove herself, all because some horrible, unhinged, mean woman had wandered into the store at the worst possible moment.

The dog was begging on her right, the boy who couldn't do simple math was on her left. The girl started telling a story that made no sense about crickets having ears, probably because Olivia was struggling not to burst into tears in front of them all.

She stood up, and without even clearing her plate or saying thank you, she rushed out of the kitchen to the entry, with the dog trailing behind her. She left the house, closing the door in Bumper's confused face.

Out on the stoop, where the sun was setting over the West Village, Olivia stomped her foot on the sandstone step and cursed that Silvestra Perkins for barging in the store.

She wanted to call Todd.

She thought of the crackled, ant-covered cake plate she'd placed in the window of Felicity. She heard Bumper scratching on the door behind her and wondered if there was maybe some way she could fix this whole mess by ingratiating herself with Felicity's new artist. If she got to know Lauren, if she became her friend even, or if she was especially nice to Evelyn and that drooling dog, maybe Lauren would see her way to putting in a good word with her former boss. At the very least, she could get a reference. Lauren was a neighbor after all; they were practically family, sort of.

She wiped under her eyes, shook out her hair, and turned around. And—to Bumper's delight—she let herself back into the brownstone.

Chapter 10

Lauren and Leo's physical therapist was wearing nothing but a sports bra and tiny bike shorts. After introducing herself, she took a step back and looked them up and down. Lauren tugged on the waist of her sweatpants and sucked in her stomach. The girl assessed them as they limped and hobbled through a special circuit in the modern, state-of-the-art gym Frances had recommended on the Upper East Side, trying their best to follow her instructions.

"You are so freaking cute," she said to Lauren, who was most certainly not looking cute as she attempted to lunge, lost her balance, and tipped over on the mat. Lauren wanted to go home.

At the end of their evaluation, the physical therapist sat Lauren and Leo down on yoga balls and stood in front of them, saying they both needed to commit to a rigorous strengthening routine. She told Leo his back had gone out because he had "no abdominal musculature to speak of," and she told Lauren it was imperative to avoid injury "at her age." In the cab on the way home, they decided never to return.

"You do, too, have a core," Lauren said encouragingly. "You just weren't flexing."

"We're not *old*," Leo said. "We should avoid injury because, well, shouldn't everyone avoid injury?"

They were sulking as the cabdriver took a right onto their street, hitting a pothole and making them both yelp. Lauren's leg ached more now than it had before, which the therapist had claimed was perfectly normal. Was it though? Lauren had her doubts.

Leo opened the front door, calling out a loud "Hello!" Bumper and Evelyn came in from the kitchen, Evelyn drying her hands on a tea towel and gesturing with a wooden spoon.

"Well, we've had the most eventful evening," she said. "She fled. She simply got up from the table and left the house as if the whole place were on fire."

"What fire?" Lauren said. "Who fled?"

"Olivia. We met her at the bar this afternoon."

Lauren tried not to smile; her mother was becoming a whole lot more comfortable in their neighborhood. She had memorized the routes to the school, the drugstore, and the playground, and the previous night, when they'd run out of milk, she'd gone to the corner bodega, all by herself and in the dark.

"We were locked out of the house," she said. "Waverly was about to tinkle in her pants, poor thing, and then Bumper ran away. One thing led to another, and Olivia joined us for dinner—there's plenty left on the stove. But then out of nowhere she got up and stormed out."

"Dan's Olivia?" Leo said.

"I don't understand," Lauren said, watching Leo lower himself onto the floor and try to do the cobra pose he'd been taught. "What happened exactly?"

"I have no idea! I was worried I had said or done something to offend her," Evelyn said, "because it didn't seem possible that the cockroach alone could have caused such an extreme reaction. One minute, she was enjoying her dinner, and the next, she just ran out."

"Maybe she's lactose intolerant," Leo said. "I suspect I am."

"I've been telling you that for years," said Lauren.

"So there we were," Evelyn continued, "flabbergasted that she'd rushed out in a seeming huff since we had gone out of our way, if I may say so, to be hospitable, we really had. She's a family friend, after all, isn't she? We welcomed her to have dinner with us. I even offered her Bumper."

"Excuse me?" Lauren said, placing her hand on Bumper's head. She felt something weird—a piece of tape maybe—stuck to his ear and picked it off.

"Not to *keep*," said her mother, "but you two certainly can't walk him five times a day. And he's too much dog for me. I thought she might want to make a little extra money."

"I'll be able to walk him again soon," Lauren said, putting her heel on a tufted ottoman and stretching her bum leg. She had been improving, but even so, the only way she could walk was if she pointed her foot out at a ninety-degree angle and didn't bend her knee.

"I don't think Olivia would be interested in dog walking," said Leo.

"Well, that shows what you know because all of a sudden she came back! And she's the most wonderful girl—smart, funny, attractive. College-educated! And this is the best part of my story: it just so happens that she's freed up at the moment and she adores dogs *and* children. So I hired her."

Lauren looked down at Leo and then up at her mom. "I'm sorry, what?"

"Olivia will be taking care of the children *and* the dog every afternoon from school pickup until after dinner, starting immediately."

Lauren hoped Leo would jump in and say something, but instead he rolled over onto his back, bent one leg, and clasped his hands behind his knee, grunting.

"Mom, you can't just— We have to interview her first," Lauren said. "I've never even met her."

Leo inhaled slowly, looking up at the ceiling. Bumper went over to lick his face. "Last time I saw her," he said, "she was in her teens."

Lauren had lost faith in Leo's ability to find someone at the university, but she also wasn't ready to hire Olivia sight unseen. "I hope you didn't promise her a job," Lauren said.

"Your sister-in-law simply cannot believe you have no help with the children, no help with this house—"

"Please don't talk to Frances about—"

"And while I'm perfectly happy to lend a hand with *certain* tasks," Evelyn said, "I can't walk that dog, I won't break up sibling fights, and besides, I need to go home. Let's be honest, your attempts at finding a sitter have been an abject failure."

Leo winced, whether because of his back or Evelyn's reprimand, Lauren wasn't sure. "Why would she want to babysit?" Leo said. "Dan said she's in marketing or something."

"We'll ask her that question when we interview her," Lauren said.

Evelyn dismissed her comment. "No need for formality," she said. "She's a darling girl and she's starting Monday."

"Mom!"

"You can think of it as a trial," Evelyn said, waving the tea towel at her, "but believe me, you'll love her."

"Actually," said Leo rolling over again and getting on all fours, "it's not a bad idea. We know her, we know her family. Did I ever tell you her mom is the world's expert in the shit hitting the fan?" He exhaled loudly as he arched his back.

"She's the what?" said Evelyn.

"She studies disaster management, like hurricanes and earthquakes," Leo said. "Avalanches."

"It's settled, then," said Evelyn. "With a mother like that, she'll be well equipped to handle the crises in this household."

Lauren felt a little glimmer of hope; maybe this Olivia was the answer to their problem. Lauren was sick thinking about the vases she'd never trimmed and the pieces she hadn't even begun. She was also getting overwhelmed by the tricky Perkins emails that filled her in-box: Harrell was supposed to bring empty tennis ball canisters to school next Wednesday. Where would she get those? She and Leo had to complete an endless SurveyMonkey poll on the newly proposed number of required student community service hours. Starting immediately, all three children needed to start bringing Perkins gym clothes to school (Waverly on Tuesdays and Fridays; Harrell on Mondays, Wednesdays, and Thursdays; and Charles on Mondays, Tuesdays, and Fridays), pricey outfits that needed to be purchased right away via the link on the school website. There were constant calls for volunteers. And then there was the oddest email of all, one that came from the new school secretary to Lauren directly: something to do with gerbils and the long weekend coming up.

Her phone rang, and Felicity's name appeared on her screen. Lauren's stomach dropped. She limped to the kitchen to take the call.

"Felicity," she said. "How are you?"

"I'm sorry it's taken eons to check in," Felicity said, her voice chiming through a crackle on the line. "You simply can't imagine how busy I've been."

"How're you feeling?" Lauren sat on a stool at the counter. "You must be pretty far along by now."

There was a pause, and then Felicity said, "Oh, *that*. I already had the baby."

"Well, congratulations!" Lauren counted in her head; unless the baby was premature, Felicity had been about halfway through her pregnancy when she'd come to the house the previous spring. That flouncy, gorgeous maxi dress had hidden what must have been a sizable bump. "Boy or a girl?"

"Boy. I took your advice and named him after a street."

Lauren was certain she'd given no such advice, and she started to say so, when Felicity cut her off.

"Darling, I'm calling from a yacht, and my service is iffy. Did you get the instructions about expanding your line? You need to keep producing those quirky, wonderful pieces, understood? We've got big plans for you, and there's an unexpected rush on this now."

Lauren, simultaneously elated and panicked, inhaled sharply. "What kind of plans?"

"I've got some exciting news. The new season is going in a slightly different direction. Instead of dealing with regular people, my cohost and I are taking on the second home of some *very* important celebrity clients. It's all hush-hush for now, so don't even ask. But think famous Hollywood couples, only much bigger and add a big splash of royalty, if you—"

The line went quiet. "Felicity?" Lauren said. Her heart was pounding, blood pumping in her ears. "Felicity? Did I lose you?"

"Can you hear me?" Felicity said, and Lauren heard her mumble, "*Goddammit—*"

"No, I can hear you, Felicity, and that sounds amazing," she said, unable to keep her voice steady.

"Yes, so if all goes well," Felicity said, "you're going to be featured in several episodes of the new show. But there's a twist, Lauren: I need you to go *desert* with these new pieces of decor."

"Did you say desert or dessert?" Lauren asked.

Felicity's voice was coming and going, crackling like she was underwater.

"Desert, darling. Think West Coast when you add your little horrors. I want scorpions, that kind of thing." A baby started wailing in the background, and then Felicity said, "I'm heading straight to LA in the morning, and I need you to produce, produce, produce, all right? Are you making good progress?"

"Sure," said Lauren. "Absolutely. My pieces are going to be on TV?"

"I can't say anything more until it's official, but I need you working at a fast clip," she said.

Olivia was starting to sound like the perfect solution.

Lauren thought Felicity had hung up already, when her voice came back again, clear as could be. "And that's when the wildest thing happened. You'll never guess who Russell and I ran into."

Lauren could not possibly guess. She could barely even deduce who Russell was.

"Sarah Jessica Parker?"

"I like your thinking, but no. We ran into Russell's ex."

"Ohhh," Lauren said, wondering why Felicity would share this with her. She got a spoon from the drawer and went to the stove to take a bite of her mom's macaroni and cheese right out of the pot. "He's divorced already? That was quick."

"Oh, yes. He's a lawyer, so he fast-tracked that whole thing."

"And you two . . . ?"

"Married? No. *No.* So anyway, we ran into his ex on the street, and you'll never guess where she works."

Again, Lauren could not possibly. "I really don't—"

"Where was it you said your kids are going to school now?"

"Perkins Academy."

"Right, so we were walking past Perkins, and there was his ex-wife, on her way home from work. She used to be head of human resources at this massive firm, and now, poor thing, she's a school secretary."

None of this information seemed relevant to the highly charged, somewhat urgent conversation they'd been having about the television show and Lauren's porcelain, and Lauren had no idea how to react. "You don't say." She got two bowls from the cabinet and turned the heat on under the pot.

"Or maybe she said 'receptionist.'"

How many receptionists were there? The only person Lauren had met was a man her mom had told her was no longer working there. A new woman—Melinda—was apparently manning the desk now, and she'd sent Lauren a few curt emails, including the weird one that had landed in her in-box that day about the gerbils. Lauren put Felicity on speaker and found it. The innocuous subject line was "Long Weekend."

"Is his ex named Melinda?" Lauren asked, reading the sender's signature.

"Melinda, yes! Anyway, I accidentally let slip that you're the reason Russell left her."

Lauren put her phone back to her ear. "*Me?* That *I'm* the reason . . ." She forgot herself and put too much weight on her bad leg, immediately regretting it as a sharp pain shot up her calf. "Why would you tell her that?"

"Because it's true. When I came over last spring—remember?—I confessed everything about Russell and the baby, and you said all those wonderful things about trusting my instincts and following my heart. I'll never forget it. I left your house that day and went straight to see

Russell, and I told him what you said. And he got very determined and called Melinda and told her he wanted a divorce. Honestly, Russell is so grateful to you. You gave him the courage he needed to end his thirty-year marriage."

Thirty years? Lauren turned off the stove; she'd lost her appetite. "I take it Russell's a bit older than you?"

"He's very young at heart," she said.

"Wait." Lauren didn't know what question to ask first. "You told the receptionist at my kids' school that *I'm* the reason her husband of thirty years left her?"

Felicity laughed. "I'm afraid so," she said. "So you might want to watch your back next time you see her. Kidding, of course. But not really. Russell says she didn't used to have much of a temper, but she sure does now. She has not taken the divorce well."

Lauren didn't blame her. "Yikes," she said. She put Felicity back on speaker and skimmed the email from Melinda: It said that Lauren's name had been selected at random to take all the school gerbils home for an upcoming long weekend. There were twelve of them.

"Maybe she won't even remember your name," said Felicity.

Three of the gerbils, it said, needed a daily anti-diarrheal medication to treat wet tail. One was presumed pregnant.

"She remembers," said Lauren.

"Well, even so, I'm sure she'll behave professionally," Felicity said. "But I wanted to warn you, in case."

"In case what?"

One of the rodents, the email warned, was known to be aggressive.

The line crackled again. "Felicity?" From upstairs, she could hear what sounded like a fight brewing between her boys.

"Anyway," Felicity said, "motherhood has not changed me or my focus on my brand, not one single bit. I won't be back until I finish filming and make you the most coveted name in household goods."

"Amazing," said Lauren. "Thank you." Motherhood changed everything; surely Felicity would realize that soon enough.

"Meanwhile, you've got work to do. Don't let me down. I need these pieces, like, yesterday. Ciao," she said, and hung up.

Lauren took a wineglass and a bottle to the living room, where Leo was now doing wobbly pliés, his hand on the back of a chair.

"There's nothing like ballet if you need all-over strengthening," Evelyn was telling him. "Your physical therapist is right about how you got yourself into this predicament: lack of muscle. You don't want sloppy posture, do you? Now, Frances has perfect posture because she was a dancer as a child."

"Mom," Lauren said, "you know that lady at Perkins named Melinda?"

"The front-desk woman?" Evelyn said, instantly frowning. "What about her?"

"What's she like?"

"Rude, short-tempered, humorless. Tall and snappish. Slightly terrifying. Why?"

"I think she might have a vendetta against me."

"That sounds a little paranoid," said Leo.

"Apparently," said Lauren, trying to shrug it off, "I might possibly have accidentally, inadvertently, that is, wrecked her thirty-year marriage?"

"Oh dear," said Evelyn, taking her attention off Leo and his barre exercises. "How on earth did you do that?"

"It wasn't on purpose," she said. It simply had not occurred to Lauren at the time that Felicity would pay any particular attention to what she had to say. "Felicity confided that she was having an affair with a married man, and I guess I kind of told her she should . . . go for it. Well, I didn't say it directly, but I said something like she should follow her heart."

"Excuse me?" said Evelyn archly.

"That doesn't sound like you," said Leo. "It's a little sappy, no?"

"Not to mention bad advice," said Evelyn.

"I know," said Lauren. "It was just kind of off the cuff, you know. I didn't expect her to *act* on it. But now she told Melinda that I'm the one who encouraged her husband to leave her."

"Oh my," said Evelyn, sitting on the couch, her brows furrowed. "I wonder if she cast some kind of spell on you; you've all suffered quite a bit recently."

Lauren looked over at Leo, who was dipping low into a graceless squat. "I don't think one thing has anything to do with the other," Lauren said.

"Of course not," Leo said, straightening himself up. "Those events aren't causally linked."

"But what if they're karmically linked?" Evelyn said.

"I don't believe in curses," said Lauren. But then she remembered the gerbils. She was in for big trouble anyway. "She could do a lot of damage if she wanted."

"Melinda is . . . ," said Evelyn, looking at Lauren as though she were actually afraid. "Well, Melinda might just be the last person on earth I would want on my bad side."

"Oh, great." Lauren moved to Leo's yoga mat and began stretching her bad calf exactly the way the physical therapist had recommended, pointing and flexing her foot.

"Look at you two," said Evelyn. "Taking care of yourselves. Well done."

Lauren concentrated through the pain. "In case Melinda comes after me," she said, "I need to be able to run."

Chapter 11

Lauren rehearsed apologies in her head as she got the kids ready for school.

Hello, Melinda. You don't know me, but I kinda wrecked your life.

Too general?

Hi there, I'm Lauren. I really didn't mean to tell Felicity to steal your husband.

Too blunt?

There was no easy way to face this woman.

"Make sure no one's standing around her desk who can overhear anything," Evelyn said, clearing the kids' cereal bowls. "She's testy."

"Right," said Lauren. She was running a brush through Waverly's hair. "What does she look like?"

"Ow," said Waverly, covering her head with her hands.

"Sorry." Lauren handed her the brush and began putting the bowls in the dishwasher.

"Severe," said Evelyn. "She could probably be quite attractive if she got rid of the permanent scowl on her face."

Bumper began licking the dishes, and Lauren pretended it wasn't something he always did.

"Bumper, stop," she said.

He looked up at her, cocking his head in confusion.

Waverly ran off, her hair still tangled.

"Tell your brothers to pack their stuff up before they come down," Lauren called after her.

"I was up half the night worrying about this," said Evelyn, leaning against the counter.

Lauren smiled; at least her mother cared enough to lose sleep over her.

"But here's what I finally determined," Evelyn said. "That man— Russell?—he's the only person responsible for the collapse of his marriage. Whether you gave a nod of approval or not is irrelevant. Men his age are stupid and prone to flattery, especially when the flattery is coming from a younger woman. Felicity is glamorous *and* she's a celebrity of sorts; Frances tells me her show was very popular among the crowd she runs with—"

"You told *Frances* about this?"

"So along comes this young, beautiful woman who sweeps him off his feet, and he would have done anything she told him to. Why? Because he's a fool, like so many men are fools, and therefore, this isn't *entirely* your fault."

"Really?" This was exactly what Lauren wanted to hear. "So you're saying Melinda won't blame me."

"Oh, no," said her mother, "she'll definitely blame you."

Lauren felt sick. "I'm going to have to deal with this woman every day for years. I'll be calling her to explain absences, showing up with the kids' homework when they forget to bring it, asking for help every time Harrell loses something. I need to fix this with an apology."

Evelyn looked unconvinced. "Let's hope you catch her in a reasonable mood. Though it would be the first time since she started working there."

Lauren was troubled by her mom's generalization about men. "Do you think Leo's a fool?" she said. "Is he going to dump me for a thirty-year-old assistant professor when I'm in my mid-fifties?"

"*Leo?*" Evelyn started laughing.

"What?"

"No, not Leo."

"Why not?" Lauren asked, wondering what could be funny about such an awful possibility.

"Leo loves you. And he has his crickets, his hobbies, and a fold-up bicycle; he's got quite enough foolishness to keep him busy and satisfied."

Lauren knew this was insulting in a certain way and also not necessarily true. Of course, it could happen to her. It could happen to anyone. Was Melinda as utterly miserable as Lauren would be in the same situation?

Her mother was still laughing.

"What's so funny?" Leo asked coming into the kitchen, barefoot with his laptop open. His hair was more disheveled than Waverly's, and he was walking stooped over, his free hand edging along the counter.

"My mother assures me you won't leave me a decade from now," Lauren said.

Leo looked up. "To go where?"

"Never mind," Lauren said. "Can you go with me this morning? I don't want to face Melinda alone."

"I'm not so sure I can walk that far," he said. He poured himself a cup of coffee without taking his eyes from his computer screen, spilling some on the counter.

Lauren had a feeling there was more to his refusal than a bad back. "We could take a cab," she said, testing him.

"We don't fit in a cab."

That was unfortunately true. "What's going on, Leo?" she asked. "You've got that look."

"I was up almost all night," he said, tilting his computer toward her. "Check this out. Pretty exciting, right?"

He scrolled and scrolled through lines of code while Lauren nod-ded at the screen, having no clue what he was showing her.

"Awesome," she said, with a lift to her voice, trying to sound sup-portive.

"It could be. It really could," he said. "I mean, game-changing, if I'm right." He leaned over his laptop awkwardly and started typing.

"And there goes his back," said Evelyn.

"You need a standing desk," Lauren said.

Her mother patted her on the shoulder, saying, "I'll take the chil-dren on my own." She turned to put on her trench coat. "It will be better for a third-party to negotiate a truce. I can be very diplomatic, and I'm old; she won't bully me."

"I thought you were taking the train to Boston this morning," Lau-ren said.

"Well, I can't very well leave my daughter in the midst of all this hostility," said her mom. "I'll stay another day or two, just while we sort out this mess."

Lauren could not imagine her mother would stay away from her beautiful home, from her bridge club, or from her busy social life a minute longer. The fact that she was willing to stick around felt like some kind of victory over Frances, even though her reason for staying was because Lauren was perpetually in a fix.

"I'd love that," Lauren said, "but I'll handle Melinda on my own. How bad can she be?"

"Bad," said Evelyn. "Very bad. We'll go together."

• • •

There was a scramble to find the right jackets, but they still managed to head out ten minutes earlier than usual. Lauren's mom shepherded the children down the sidewalk at a quick pace, while Lauren limped along behind them. She'd put on jeans and a cashmere sweater, one of the few that wasn't flecked with clay, in hopes of looking like any other respect-able parent. She kept picturing Melinda blowing up at her and flipping her desk in the lobby. If only Lauren had been around long enough to make friends among the other mothers; it would have been nice to have an ally in the building, someone other than her own mom. She took some comfort in knowing that Melinda was new to Perkins too; maybe that would level the playing field somehow.

Her mother stopped outside the building to wait for her to catch up, tightening the belt on her coat, and they walked in together. The lobby was fairly quiet. As the kids scanned their ID cards, Lauren reminded them: "That girl Olivia who ate dinner with you? She's picking you up today."

"Don't go with anyone else," Evelyn called after them. "She'll bring you right home."

Lauren had positioned herself behind her mother, and she peeked around her at the front desk: there was Melinda, typing angrily into her computer with a humorless look on her face. She was prettier than Lauren had imagined, high cheekbones, thick, dark hair swept up, and a commanding presence. Lauren was intimidated.

Her mother stepped to the side and gave her a little push. "Courage!" she whispered.

They approached the desk, and Lauren cleared her throat. "Hi, Melinda. I'm Lauren Shaw."

Melinda looked up at Lauren, then at Evelyn, and back to Lauren, her brain making the unpleasant association. She narrowed her eyes at Lauren in disgust. "Go away," she said, turning back to her computer screen. "I'm busy."

Lauren leaned in and said quietly, "I want to apologize and explain what happened, how my connection to Felicity—"

"Did you get my email about the gerbils?" Melinda asked, not even looking at her.

"I did, yes," Lauren said with a cautious laugh, "and I'm afraid that twelve gerbils are about ten more than we can manage. But we could maybe take one? Or two?"

"And what would you have me do with the rest? Euthanize them?"

"Certainly not," said Lauren with a confused smile; surely that wasn't a serious question. "It's only a three-day weekend, right? Can't they stay here at school?"

Melinda glowered. "They'll turn the heat down and the lights off to conserve energy, but if you want those tiny, innocent creatures to stay in a cold, dark building all alone, that's fine. I'll just write a message to the entire parent body explaining that you rejected our plan to care humanely for the animals."

It was perfectly obvious to Lauren that Melinda was messing with her, but she also didn't know what to do about it.

"Of course, I'm willing to take a *few* gerbils, a reasonable number—"

"And how many dead gerbils is reasonable to you?" Melinda said. She pursed her lips, waiting for an answer as the muscle of her sharp jawbone clenched.

"Sorry? Why would they be dead?"

"I wonder what the head of school will think about your callous attitude toward animals." And she picked up her cell phone, as if to text her right away.

"Hold on," said Evelyn, holding up her pointer finger over Lauren's shoulder, "what if my daughter agrees to take four gerbils off your hands? Would that be satisfactory?" Lauren's jaw dropped; was her mother really going to negotiate with this terrorist? This entire conversation was clearly a charade designed only to make Lauren miserable.

"I'll tell you what," said Melinda, crossing her arms and looking at Lauren through vengeful, narrow eyes. "*You* can be in charge of finding accommodations for *all* the little darlings. Thank you so much for volunteering. And just a reminder: there's also a ferret, two terrariums of snails, one gecko, and a clown fish."

Lauren swallowed. This task was impossible, and also . . . wasn't this entire conversation some kind of mean-spirited joke? Was Melinda going to let her off the hook and admit as much?

"Look," said Lauren quietly, "I want to apologize to you for my association with a certain woman we both know. The truth is, I had very little to do with whatever happened. I don't even know Felicity all that well, and I certainly have never met your husband."

"*Ex*-husband, thanks to you," Melinda said in a quiet but forceful voice. "Now, why don't you kindly fuck off?"

Lauren, shocked she would use profanity in the school lobby, backed away from the desk. Melinda had the most intense eyes, and they seemed to bore right through her.

Her mother stepped in again. "Lauren waded into a conversation with Felicity she should have stayed out of, and she's learned from the experience." She turned to Lauren. "Haven't you?" she said.

Ashamed, Lauren nodded and looked at the floor. She heard Melinda scoff.

Evelyn was undeterred. "Lauren knows she shouldn't have encouraged that home-wrecker."

Melinda made a sound then not unlike a growl.

Lauren tugged on the sleeve of her mom's blouse, as she had done countless times when she was young and wanted her to stop talking to a saleswoman at a store. Evelyn was still not swayed.

"But you must know, Melinda," Evelyn said, "your ex-husband is the only guilty party here."

Lauren glanced up at her mom, thinking that comment was for sure going to backfire.

"Shame on him, by the way," Evelyn went on. "He's a scoundrel to leave you after so many years of marriage. And to become a father at his age? Men are complete idiots."

Melinda looked pacified for a moment, like she might even agree with Evelyn, but then she shook off any possibility of commiserating and said, "What do you want?"

"I only ask," her mother said, "that you don't hold a grudge against my daughter because it really was unintentional."

Lauren was tempted to hug her mom right there in the lobby.

"Now," Evelyn added brightly, "on another note, we'd like to inform you about our new babysitter."

Melinda had not accepted Lauren's apology. She'd in fact told her to fuck off, but changing the subject seemed as good a move as any. "Yes," said Lauren, "a young woman named Olivia will be picking my kids up from school today, and maybe from now on—"

"Fine," said Melinda, slapping a piece of paper and a pencil on the desk in front of Lauren. "Write down her name, so I know who's coming in and out of my lobby."

My lobby? That was rich. "O-liv-i-a," said Lauren as she printed the name. "She's the daughter of a friend of my husband's . . . biological father."

"She's what?" Melinda tilted her head, looking at the scrap of paper. "She's the daughter of—"

"Just put down her last name. Or is she just 'Olivia,' like 'Cher'?"

Lauren looked at her mother, who simply shrugged. "I don't actually know," said Lauren, setting the pencil down.

"*You don't know?* How can you not know?" Melinda said, sounding appalled and yet somehow delighted at the same time. "This sounds like very irresponsible parenting."

"No, I mean, I know *of* her," said Lauren, taking her jacket off as she suddenly felt very warm. "She's a close family friend." That was stretching the truth a bit, but Lauren figured that the daughter of a friend of Phillip's was a friend of hers.

"*I* hired her," said Evelyn. "She's maybe twenty-two years old—"

"She's older than that," said Lauren. "She's probably twenty-six or -seven."

"Get your story straight, ladies," said Melinda, with a devious look. "Am I to understand that you've never met this person to whom you're entrusting your children?"

"Not exactly, but—" said Lauren.

"*I* met her," Evelyn said, "and she's a lovely girl, very petite." Evelyn put a flat hand to her shoulder to show how short.

"Have you at least googled her?" Melinda asked, crossing her arms, clearly enjoying herself now. "Or better yet, done a background check? Called her references? What are her skills? Does she have experience with children? Does she know CPR? These are basic steps to hiring a childcare provider, no?"

Lauren was too embarrassed to answer.

"They've known her father for years," Evelyn said.

"Oh?" asked Melinda.

"He runs the bar in the basement of their house," said her mother.

Lauren winced, as Melinda got a ballpoint pen and clicked it open by slamming the end on her desk. She wrote on the piece of paper, saying aloud, "Unknown daughter of barkeep to pick up Aston children. Got it."

"Good morning," said a cheerful voice behind them. Here was the principal, all smiles and a hand out to greet them. "Ah, and the grandmother too. So nice to meet you. How wonderful, welcome to Perkins. And how are the children enjoying school?"

"They're settling in," Lauren said, relieved to have a real authority figure step in. This woman was Melinda's boss, after all. Surely she could dilute the onslaught of unprofessional hostility.

"Mrs. Shaw," said Melinda, "has just presented an unusual childcare arrangement: a stranger—have I got that right?—will be picking up the Aston children starting this afternoon. This is a woman she hasn't met or vetted, but she knows *of* her from a guy who works at a bar."

Lauren felt her face flush and swallowed hard.

"I'm sorry?" said the principal, her voice full of alarm.

"Oh, no," said Lauren, mortified, "it's not quite like that. Olivia's actually . . . she's a close friend of the family."

"Right," said Melinda, holding her pen at the ready, "I just need her last name, so that I can make sure I send your children home with this very 'close' friend."

Lauren raised her shoulders slightly. "I'm afraid I don't know," she conceded, and then she smiled. "But she's terrific with kids."

The principal frowned. "We can't release the children without—"

"I'll come for pickup today," Evelyn said, a hand on her chest. "I'll meet Olivia here and introduce you to her myself."

"That works," said the principal, pacified.

"Fine," said Melinda, coldly. "And just as a reminder, Mrs. Shaw," she said turning back to Lauren, "from now on, could you please refrain from sending your children to school with Reese's Peanut Butter Cups?"

Lauren's eyes opened wide; she had done no such thing, *ever*. But Melinda put her hand out then: in her palm were three golden, foil-wrapped cups, little packets of death.

"Oh no!" said the principal, aghast. "We have students who are deathly allergic to nuts, right in Waverly's classroom, as a matter of fact. We require everyone's cooperation, of course. No exceptions."

"Gosh," said Lauren. "I didn't—" She looked at her mom, who shrugged as if to say, *I give up.*

"You're new," said Melinda, smiling condescendingly. "But you might want to take another look at the school handbook."

"Yes," said the principal, "our handbook is a very thorough resource for new families. Please do give it a careful read."

"I did!" said Lauren. "And I will, again. And I assure you, I'm not one of those 'fun' moms who hands out candy left and right. Processed sugar, ugh."

"Oh, you seem plenty fun," said Melinda, with a mean smile. "You must be since you've made a request to take all the school pets home for the long weekend, as well as during the Thanksgiving and winter vacations."

"Oh my," said the principal. "That's a tad excessive, Mrs. Shaw. Why ever would you want to do that?" She was looking at Lauren as though she were some sort of pervert.

Lauren felt as if her throat were closing up. She opened her mouth, but no words came out.

"That really wouldn't be fair to the other children who might want to take a furry friend home," the principal said, "and we want to give every family a fair chance to take a turn."

Lauren's head was spinning. Melinda was making her look terrible in so many different ways, she couldn't keep up. "Of course," she said. "There's been a misunderstanding. I only meant to say I'd be willing to take an animal or two home if there was ever a need."

"And if there isn't a need," said Evelyn, "it would be better for her not to take one at all. Lauren has quite enough chaos in that house of hers without adding rodents to the mix. Her dog is barely housebroken."

"Okay, then," Lauren said quickly, desperate to stop Melinda from torturing her any further. She tried to recap the miserable conversation by saying, "My mother will come for pickup today, I'll never send in nut products, ever, *ever,* I promise, and while gerbils are great, they're best in moderation, and I think we can all agree on that. Thank you and have a wonderful day."

She turned and limped out of the lobby. Melinda had won.

• • •

"Well, that went a lot worse than I expected," Evelyn said once they were outside, "and I was expecting it to be pretty terrible."

"That was possibly the most embarrassing moment of my entire life," Lauren said.

Her mother considered that. "Yes," she said, "you're right. I can't think of a more embarrassing moment, and I'm remembering that dance you and Leo did at your wedding."

They were passing the Greenwich Village Funeral Home, as Lauren let the insult slide. "She's going to make my life miserable. What do I do? Should I send flowers? Maybe I'll make her a coffee mug." Lauren imagined painting one for her with a big rat on the side, its tail wrapping around the handle. Her studio came to mind then along with Felicity's eager words on the phone: *I need you to produce, produce, produce.* Lauren tried to limp more quickly.

"You could forward the email she wrote you to the principal. That would at least clear things up about the gerbils."

"First I wreck her marriage, and then I get her fired? No way," Lauren said as they weaved around a woman on the sidewalk who had a cat on a leash.

"Then give her space and wait for this whole situation to blow over."

"But in the meantime, she could go around telling people I *ate* the school gerbils. And no one knows me there, so there's not a single person who would defend me. She could tell the teachers anything. Or what if she changes the kids' grades in the system or plants drugs in their backpacks?"

"I don't think anyone's *that* diabolical," said Evelyn. "Maybe write her a nice apology letter and leave it at that."

"I have to do more than a gesture. I need to think of some real way to make it up to her."

Bumper came running to the door when they got home, happily showing Lauren where he'd peed on the rug. Leo was still in the kitchen working on his laptop, gingerly bouncing on a big green yoga ball.

"Leo," Lauren said, snapping her fingers to get his attention, "you forgot to let Bumper out."

"Sorry, what?" he said, lost in whatever digital world he was in. He didn't take his eyes off the screen, and Lauren could see he was feverishly writing code as fast as his fingers would allow. "I'm telling you, if I'm right about this, my idea could be very, *very* important to the field."

"Right about what?" Lauren said.

He stopped typing and ran his hands through his hair, causing it to stand up in all directions. "Well," he said, "it's a little hard to explain, but I think my crickets are generating sounds at a frequency that could be highly useful if exploited for artificial intelligence." He glanced up at them, his eyes lighting up. "And you know what that means."

"I, for one, haven't the vaguest idea," said Evelyn, wearily, unbelting her coat and sitting down. "I need to rest from that hideous encounter. Melinda wore me out."

"It went badly with the school secretary," Lauren said as she took a wad of paper towels from the roll and the rug cleaner from under the sink. "Very badly, in fact. It was a catastrophe."

There was a crashing sound directly over their heads, like a box of plates getting dropped on the floor. Bumper looked up at the ceiling and wagged his tail.

"What on earth?" Lauren said, gripping the bottle of rug cleaner like a weapon.

Leo ignored her alarm and continued to work.

"Leo," she said, gripping his shoulder, "who's upstairs?"

Leo stopped typing and listened as well. Now there was the sound of stomping and something that sounded like a heavy piece of furniture being moved.

Evelyn looked terrified. She stood up and whispered, "Are we being robbed?"

Another sound, this time a man's deep voice, belting out a song.

"Oh!" Leo said happily, "I almost forgot: Phillip came home."

Evelyn scowled. "You've got to be kidding me," she said.

Lauren fumbled and dropped the paper towels, watching them unspool on their way across the kitchen floor. Phillip was supposed to be in Berlin, settling into his new job. Phillip was not supposed to have boomeranged back to the brownstone, not already.

"He was in Finland for a spell but had some time before he has to be in Berlin. So he's here."

"Well, how fun is that?" said Lauren, trying to sound sincere. How on earth was this going to work, her mother and Phillip sharing a bathroom? Sleeping across the hall from each other with nothing but beaded strings separating them? Her mother would not tolerate that arrangement for a day. "Won't this be interesting? Should we go say hello?"

Evelyn, her face pinched in irritation, followed Lauren out of the kitchen and up the stairs. At the top, Phillip popped through the beads in Evelyn's doorway, wearing nothing but a towel wrapped around his waist, and greeted them warmly. His white hair was slightly bedraggled, but he nevertheless looked dashing, even stripped down.

"How wonderful to have so much life in the house again," he said, his arms outstretched. "Toys everywhere, Leo hard at work. And how I love the third floor of this battered abode."

"Are you sure about that?" Lauren asked, trying to decipher his expression. "Or do you feel displaced?"

"Not at all!" He gestured to the room at the back of the house. "*That* was always my room, all through the seventies and eighties. I only moved to the second floor after Charley died and my knees were fighting me over the stairs."

"You remember my mother," Lauren said.

Phillip stood very formally with his hands clasped and bowed stiffly. "Evelyn."

She nodded, her expression icy. "I'll go pack my things," she said in lieu of a greeting.

"Oh," said Phillip. "But why—?"

"Mom, don't." Lauren hated the idea of her mother leaving in a huff. Also . . . who would pick up the kids that afternoon?

"I'm imposing," Evelyn said, averting her eyes from Phillip's bare chest. "This is your home, and I've overstayed."

"No! Imposing?" Phillip said, tilting his head. "This house is meant to be full of people. Back in the day we had houseguests galore, artists in need of a sofa, friends between apartments. It was musical beds, and we always made room. This is the way it's supposed to be."

"Please?" Lauren said to her mom. "Don't you want to make sure Olivia works out?"

"Who's Olivia?" said Phillip. "Dan's daughter?"

"Fine," Evelyn said primly, ignoring Phillip. "I'll stay until tomorrow morning."

"I had no idea I'd have the pleasure of seeing you, Evelyn. Look at you! You've still got that beautiful figure."

"Leave my figure out of this," said Evelyn sharply.

Lauren knew that if she let herself laugh, she would only make her mother sourer. "What brings you back to New York?" she said. "Not that you can't come for any reason at all, of course."

"I had a change in my schedule," he said, "and wanted to know how you were all getting along."

"And Berlin . . . ?"

"Will still be there," he said happily, "when I arrive."

"Well, it's good to see you," Lauren said. She wasn't being entirely disingenuous, but she felt awkward and wished she could pin down his actual plans. She didn't push any further though; the last thing she wanted was to offend him.

Phillip was gazing at Evelyn. "What an unexpected thrill," he said. "I've always wanted to be better acquainted with the mother of this amiable woman who has made our Leo so happy." He put an arm across Lauren's shoulder. Surely her mother couldn't deny how kind and charming he was.

"Not everyone finds me amiable," said Lauren, recalling the hateful look in Melinda's eyes. "I've made my first mortal enemy."

"Really? How exciting," said Phillip. "Does he or she know where you live?"

Lauren hadn't considered that and felt a wave of new anxiety. "Yes, I suppose she does. Or she could easily find out."

"I've arrived in the nick of time, then," said Phillip. "We'll batten down the hatches and prepare a counterattack."

Evelyn rolled her eyes. "All she needs to do is write a formal apology and let the woman cool down."

"Or perhaps a spicier response is needed." He waggled his eyebrows mischievously.

"How can you know what's needed?" said Evelyn. "You haven't even heard what happened."

"Let's all go to Lure for a sushi lunch, and you can fill me in."

"I don't eat sushi," her mother said, "and I never will. My husband always warned you get parasitic tapeworms from eating raw fish."

Phillip sighed heavily. "All right, then we'll go across the street to Babbo. They have a sublime spaghettoni with lobster."

"I can't," said Lauren. "I absolutely have to work today. But you two go."

At that, her mother shot her a withering look.

"No excuses, Evelyn," said Phillip, clapping his hands together. "Here we are, two companions in the big city. Let's have martinis. I'll take a quick rest, shower to wash the airplane off of me, and we can go as soon as they open. How does that sound?"

Evelyn sighed. "Fine," she said.

Lauren was deeply surprised to hear her mother acquiesce.

Evelyn held up a finger to add, "But I don't drink martinis, and I can't dillydally. I have to meet the children and their new sitter at the school at three on the dot."

"Our grandchildren," said Phillip with a smile. "I'll go with you."

"I'm perfectly able to pick up *my* grandchildren on my own," Evelyn said, rankled.

Lauren could feel her mother's discomfort; Evelyn, at least in her own mind, had been the only relevant grandparent, until now.

"Our three wonderful grandchildren!" he said. "And won't they love to see us together at last?" He turned to Lauren, just as his towel slipped from his waist and fell on the floor.

Evelyn shrieked and swept the beaded curtains aside to go into her room, while Phillip picked up his towel and retreated into the bathroom.

"Well, I'm off," said Lauren to the empty landing. "Desk accessories don't make themselves. Unfortunately."

And she went down the stairs, amused and slightly uneasy to think of her mother and Phillip spending the day together.

Chapter 12

Lauren sat at the dusty table in her studio, pencil in hand, trying not to worry about how her enemy might inflict more damage or what arguments her mother and Phillip were having over lunch. Instead, she sketched. *Desert*, she thought. *Heat, but a dry heat.* Her studio was actually chilly that day, and she buttoned up the cardigan she'd pulled on over her overalls. She rubbed her hands together and then she drew a single bookend in the shape of a tall cactus. It was tacky. She tried again, this time drawing a lumpy and unattractive mesa that looked like a pile of cow dung. Then she doodled an actual pile of dung. What was in a desert anyway? Cow skulls? Fence posts? Barbed wire? Lauren had spent very little time west of Philly. She started over again and drew an egg with a tortoise emerging from it. It was pretty good, but it couldn't be used as a bookend since it was rounded on the bottom. A paperweight maybe? She sketched a tire on a roadside; it was ugly.

A dated-looking suitcase with national park stickers; it was kitschy. A cowboy boot; cheesy. Even though it felt like cheating, she got her phone out to google images of bookends, when she heard a rapping on the door of the studio.

There was a young woman standing at the doorway with a bright smile. She was wearing a miniskirt, a crocheted vest, and biker boots. Her long hair was pulled up in a high ponytail, and her coat was over her arm. "Well, this is exciting," she said. "I finally get to lay eyes on the real Lauren Shaw, in person. Not the way I expected us to meet, but hey, this is cool anyway. Lauren, hello."

"Hi?" said Lauren.

"I'm Olivia," she said, "Dan's daughter."

Lauren thought they must have had a miscommunication. Had her mother given completely wrong instructions? She checked the time on her phone.

"Oh, don't worry," Olivia said. "I know I have to be at the school at three. I just thought I'd pop in here first since I live in the neighborhood. I wanted to introduce myself so you know who the heck is hanging out with your kids."

"Well, come on in," Lauren said, and stepped back from the door. Then she stopped, saying, "Wait, how did you know to find me here?"

"Well, it's funny, kind of," she said. "I had this address from when our guys picked up your pieces for Felicity last month. And, since I only live a few stops from here, I thought why not drop by the studio, say hello to the artist herself, and bring her a sandwich." She held out a brown paper bag. "Hungry?"

"I don't understand," Lauren said, taking the bag and looking inside. "You work for Felicity?"

"I did," she said, walking past Lauren. She hung her coat on a wall hook and put her bag on the stool. "In fact, up until last week, I was the new point person on your line of ceramics."

"I've talked to Courtney, sure," Lauren said. "But I had no idea you—"

"Neither did I!" the woman said with a lift to her already high voice. "I mean I certainly didn't know that *the* Lauren Shaw was living upstairs from my dad's bar."

"Sorry if I'm being slow here," Lauren said, trying to process what was going on, "but why are you babysitting?"

"Your mom told me you needed help. And since I just lost my job, I thought, here I am, free to lend a hand."

"Lost your job . . . why?" Lauren said, hoping Olivia hadn't done anything disqualifying.

"I mismanaged an irate customer," she said. "But the good news is I'm available to hang out with your kids while you work. I don't usually—I mean, I'm not the firing type normally, you can ask anyone. I accidentally said something stupid, and it was bad PR for the company."

"How bad?" Lauren asked.

"It's blowing over," Olivia said, "or I hope so. But I really wish I'd kept my mouth shut."

"I know how you feel," Lauren said. "I'm in a similar situation myself." Lauren certainly was in no position to judge anyone for making a damaging, offhand remark.

Olivia looked around Lauren's studio. "I may not be super experienced with kids, but I can read to them or play or whatever you need. And I have a feeling you might be under a lot of pressure because of that new order."

The shelves on the back wall were filled with the paper clip dishes she'd made. None of them were painted yet.

Olivia tapped her wrist as if she were wearing a watch. "How's it going with the new pieces?"

"Are you in touch with Felicity?" she said warily.

"Oh, gosh, no. I'm persona non grata over there."

"Well, to be honest, then . . . ," Lauren said. "*Can* I be honest? It's not going well at all. I haven't had enough time to work on or even think about the commission. And she just threw the West Coast thing at me yesterday."

"What West Coast thing?" Olivia said.

"Felicity called," Lauren said, "and said to think desert because of some celebrity client in LA."

"Did she say who it is?" Olivia said, her interest clearly piqued.

"She wouldn't tell me." Lauren suddenly wondered if she could trust this girl. "But keep that between us. Felicity said it's all 'hush-hush.'"

"A celebrity," Olivia said, and she got her phone out. "I wonder who. . . ."

"You're not texting anyone—"

"No, I would never," Olivia said. "I'm just checking her Instagram to see if there are any hints." She scrolled for a moment and said, "Looks like she's still on the yacht." She showed Lauren a picture of what were presumably Felicity's feet by the ocean, pedicured toes pointed over crystal blue water.

Lauren looked down at her sketches. "Some of these decorative pieces she wants," she said, "they're new to me."

Olivia put her phone away, and Lauren cringed while she looked at her hideous drawings.

Olivia laughed when she saw the cowboy boots. "That's not you," Olivia said. "Maybe you're overthinking it."

"I am?"

"Yeah, just do your sophisticated, clean look with the bugs. That's what attracted Felicity to you in the first place."

Lauren wadded up the drawings and threw them in the trash.

"No matter what she asks for, you should keep your style," said Olivia.

"I'd like to, but I can't picture some of these pieces."

"Well, take the bookends," she said, closing her eyes. "I'm imagining your usual color palette, the creams, the whites, the neutrals. . . ." She opened her eyes. "What if you made, like, a weighted, antique book, really simple, clean lines. And then you paint silverfish eating the pages."

Lauren could see it, sort of: a worn cover, deckled edges of the paper, the slinky, silvery legs of the insects. She felt a little jolt of excitement, and she got up, ready to get her hands dirty. "Right," she said. "Right, thank you."

"Happy to help," Olivia said. "Good luck."

As the young woman picked up her coat and walked out the door as quickly and assuredly as she'd come in, Lauren felt she'd just been visited by a young but wise guardian angel. A muse.

An hour later, when she found the turkey sandwich Olivia had brought, she ate it gratefully, realizing she'd forgotten to ask for her last name.

Chapter 13

Melinda was pretty damned pleased with herself. She was making solid progress on her two-pronged plan to punish Felicity and Lauren for their actions, and she was having fun to boot. Already, she'd gone on Yelp, Google, and Facebook and posted one-star reviews of Felicity's stupid store, adding comments like: *Snobby! Overpriced! Not worth the $$$$!* And: *Gross, it's like the worst of Goop but for the home instead of your vagina.*

That shopper's video! What a stroke of luck that had turned out to be, and all the more so because Melinda had been miraculously left out of the footage on that fifteen-second little TikTok masterpiece.

Meanwhile, she was coming up with a wide range of aggravations for Lauren, like cutting off her access to the school portal. She sent an email saying the school had never received any medical records or consent documents for the kids, making Lauren rescan and reupload all the immunization reports and forms. She hoped it gave Lauren a headache. That kid Harrell was an absentminded little dolt, and he left a trail of sweatshirts, shoes, and homework wherever he went. Melinda helped him dig his gym shorts out of the lost and found one afternoon, but then she snuck three stinky, mildewed, middle-school jock straps into the plastic bag for Lauren to find.

Melinda felt empowered, like a vigilante in the Wild West.

And the principal loved her now! She'd actually apologized to Melinda that day, saying, "I worried you might be a little too rule-focused initially, but I can see we need your special brand of parental oversight. Imagine: That Lauren Shaw could have killed a child if it hadn't been for you." And she walked away, mumbling, "Reese's Peanut Butter Cups" under her breath.

On Monday, Melinda put out fires here and there. When a seven-year-old kid on a visit with the admissions department got lost during his tour, Melinda was the one who found him hiding in the bathroom and coaxed him out to his upset parents. During lunch, a claustrophobic teacher got trapped in the elevator, and Melinda got on her walkie-talkie to alert maintenance and then talked to the hyperventilating teacher through the intercom while they waited for the repairman. A student she'd met before—the real Silvestra—came to retrieve her phone just before dismissal; she'd been caught texting in class.

"Now why would you do such a thing?" Melinda said, unlocking her desk drawer. "You know phones aren't allowed in class."

"It wasn't my fault," Silvestra said with a sulky expression.

"Come now," said Melinda sternly. "Take responsibility for breaking a rule," said Melinda, holding the phone hostage, "or I won't give it back."

Silvestra rolled her eyes and sighed. "The drama teacher said he was posting the cast of the musical this afternoon, and my mom kept texting me over and over all day, 'Did you get the lead? Did you get the lead? All those voice lessons, she better give you the lead,' so finally I texted her back, just to say, like, 'No, I *didn't* get the lead. I'm in the chorus,' and then *I* got busted for using my phone."

"I see," said Melinda.

Melinda handed the girl her sleek phone and then offered a Starburst from the pile of goodies she'd confiscated. "Being in the chorus could be fun," she said. "It's a lot less pressure."

"I'm fine with the chorus," Silvestra said, unwrapping the candy, "all my friends are in it with me. But my mom wants me to be like a child star or something and won't back off." She showed Melinda the notifications on her phone: sixteen messages from MOM.

"You tell your mother that *I* said to stop texting you during the school day. And if she has a problem with that, she can come see me."

"She won't care."

"May I?" Melinda asked, putting out her hand.

Silvestra handed her the phone and Melinda replied:

This is the receptionist at Perkins. STOP texting your daughter during school hours. It is a distraction, it is against the rules, and it reinforces bad habits. If you cannot control your urge to text, I will keep Silvestra's phone in my desk drawer every day for the rest of the school year. That said, if there is an emergency, you can always contact me or anyone at the school, using the appropriate channels. - Melinda

She hit send and handed the phone back to Silvestra, who read the text and started to laugh. "Oh my God," she said. "My mom is gonna be pissed. I hope she doesn't get you in trouble."

"Let her try," Melinda said, putting her palms on her desk, feeling like she was boss of the whole school.

The door was opening and closing now, mothers, a few fathers, and babysitters arriving for pickup. And there was an oddly familiar face. Melinda realized she knew the young woman who walked in, but she also felt *something not right*, like two worlds were colliding, as if the Roy family from *Succession* appeared in an episode of *Emily in Paris*.

The young woman caught sight of Melinda and frowned. She looked around, and then she narrowed her eyes in anger. "Silvestra," she called out accusingly.

The real Silvestra looked up from her phone, still chewing her Starburst. "Yeah?"

Well, this was awkward. Melinda wondered how on earth the young woman from Felicity had found her; was she here on official business, trying to stop the relentless onslaught of negative reviews? Melinda sat up straight, determined not to let those bullies curtail her freedom of speech.

The young woman approached the desk, looking enraged. "You," she said.

"Who are you?" Silvestra asked, putting her backpack over one shoulder.

This, Melinda thought, was going to be hard to explain. "She's talking to me actually," said Melinda.

"Why is she calling *you* Silvestra?"

"A little mix-up," said Melinda to the student. "Now run along. And show your mother our cell phone policy, page eighteen in the handbook."

Silvestra looked at the woman and then back at Melinda. "That's super weird," she said and walked away, flipping her hair and scanning her ID on the way out the door.

"So, what's your real name?" the salesgirl asked.

"What are you even doing here?" Melinda said, on the lookout for the principal. She didn't want her mission to sabotage Felicity to complicate her good standing at the school.

The woman was staring at her with a look of disgust. "I cannot believe they let someone as vicious as you work with children."

"Look, if this is about that video," said Melinda, "I had absolutely nothing to do with it. It was just a little added bonus from a stranger."

Two of the Aston kids, Waverly and Harrell, came to the desk then, looking wary.

"Hey, guys," said Olivia. "Where's your brother?"

"He gets out five minutes later than us," said Harrell shyly. "What are we doing this afternoon?"

"I have no idea," said Olivia, smiling at them, her expression—open and kind—the opposite of what she'd shown Melinda at the store. "What do you normally do?"

"'livia," said Waverly, "I want to go home and play."

"Wait," Melinda said, trying to put the pieces together. "*You're* the new babysitter?" she said.

Olivia bent down to look the kids in the eye, although she wasn't all that much taller than Harrell was. "Can you two go wait for me on the bench over there?" Olivia said. "I need to talk to this . . . *person* for a sec." She used air quotes on the word "person."

"You can all take a seat," Melinda said, "because none of you are leaving this building until your grandmother comes to identify this stranger. She could be a kidnapper for all I know."

The children opened their eyes wide and stared at Olivia.

"I'm not a kidnapper," she said to them, ruffling Harrell's hair. "We had dinner together, remember? Your grandmother asked me to pick you up."

"You're not leaving with those kids," said Melinda flatly, "until I get confirmation."

The children went to sit on the bench, but Olivia stayed where she was. "Thanks a lot for getting me fired."

Melinda started, noting the fury in the young woman's eyes and the rising color in her face. "I did? Well, that wasn't my intention. You were just a casualty of a completely different war I'm fighting."

"What war?" said Olivia, leaning toward her.

"I can't get into the specifics here," said Melinda, checking to see if anyone was eavesdropping on their argument. "But I'm seeking revenge on your old boss. And your new one, too, actually."

"Why?" said Olivia. And then she cocked her head. "Seriously, why were you so mad when you came into the store?"

"Look," Melinda said, "I didn't get you fired, okay? That's between you and that stupid store. And I certainly didn't mean for you to get stuck working for the second biggest asshole in this city. I mean, I don't know how you could stand working for someone like Felicity, but just so you know, that Lauren Shaw is a terrible person."

"*You're* a terrible person," Olivia said through gritted teeth. "You cost me my health insurance and probably my apartment."

Melinda recalled her behavior in the store with some degree of shame. "I'm sure you'll find a new job in no time," said Melinda, trying to play down what she'd done. "Lots of stores need workers."

"I wasn't a salesgirl," said Olivia curtly. "I was an assistant buyer. It was a great job."

"I assumed—"

"I want to know what you have against Felicity," Olivia said, putting her hands on the desk. "What did she ever do to you?"

"Something truly evil," said Melinda. "You'd be on my side if you knew the whole story."

"I don't think so." Olivia gave her a knowing look. "I think you've got psychological problems."

Melinda couldn't disagree with that; that Royal Crown Derby she'd smashed in the tub had been worth two hundred dollars a place setting, and there was one night when she was watching Felicity's Netflix show and she got so disgusted by Felicity's snooty attitude, she'd thrown her iPad out the window.

Charles came into the lobby then with the rest of the sixth graders, the gamiest-smelling grade of the student body, and Melinda saw a few parents waiting to talk to her.

"Look, I can explain what happened if you want to know," Melinda whispered, "but not here."

"You should feel guilty as shit," Olivia whispered back. "I'll bet you've had everything handed to you your entire life, but then you get me fired from a job that I worked harder to get than you can possibly imagine." She leaned over the desk and held up a finger right in Melinda's face. "You better stay away from me."

Evelyn came rushing up to the desk then, breathless. "I knew wine at lunch was a bad idea. Sorry I'm late, but I see you've met Olivia, yes? And Olivia, this is Melinda."

So much for anonymity. Melinda hated the idea that Felicity might find out who caused the scene in her dumb store.

"So, all's well, then?" Evelyn said. "Is she approved? Or do you need fingerprints?"

"It's fine," said Melinda. She wanted the whole damned family out of her sight. She wished it was her turn to go home.

Olivia turned and stormed away.

"She does that sometimes," Evelyn said, with pink cheeks and an apologetic smile. "We're not really sure why."

• • •

For the next hour, Melinda tried to put Olivia out of her mind. But at four o'clock, when she normally would have bolted out of the building, she was still sitting at her desk, thinking about the scene she'd caused that had cost that young woman her job.

Melinda gathered her things—her jacket, her tote bag, and the Reese's Peanut Butter Cups she'd hidden deep in her desk drawer—and went home to her bare-bones apartment, where she hoped to put the whole Olivia problem out of her mind.

Seeking revenge was proving to be more complicated than she'd anticipated. She felt guilty all evening, even as she tried to let herself off the hook. It wasn't as though Melinda had demanded a termination to make up for her treatment, and how could she have known some customer would film the whole thing?

Focus! she told herself. *Destroy Felicity!* She picked up the phone and left a message on an anonymous tip line at city hall saying she'd noticed a rat infestation at the uptown Felicity store while the staff served wine and hors d'oeuvres to customers— "Oh! Were they not licensed to serve alcohol?"

Tuesday, she signed Lauren up for an upcoming field trip at a food bank in the Bronx, even though none of Lauren's kids were going. On Wednesday, she opened a fake Instagram account (UpscaleShopper123) and left nasty comments on all the Felicity posts. And finally, on Thursday, she looked up Lauren's home address in the school computer and sent flowers with a message that said, "To Lauren, my darling: You are the sexiest woman I've ever made love to. With passion, Carlos." Lauren had ruined Melinda's marriage. So Melinda would do her damnedest to ruin Lauren's right back.

For some reason, none of these acts of vengeance were making her feel as happy as she'd hoped. She had little bursts of adrenaline when she came up with a new idea, and she would voice things like "So there!" or "Serves you right" to the walls of her near-empty apartment. But for reasons she didn't understand, all this hate and rage was leaving her even lonelier than she'd felt when Russell abandoned her.

Chapter 14

Melinda was facing yet another weekend alone. It was Friday evening, and she could not stop the flood of images in her mind: Russell holding Felicity's hand on the deck of a ship; Russell cooing over his baby; Russell happy in his new life; Russell not missing her at all.

She considered calling a friend, but they would probably encourage her to try online dating. Melinda would rather lie down on the subway tracks. She'd rather lick the bathroom floor in Penn Station. She would rather watch twelve straight hours of golf—a sport she detested—on television.

She poured a glass of wine, sat cross-legged on her new couch, and tried to put her ex-husband in the past by cutting up all of her wedding pictures. Bits of Russell's face and body began to pile up on the coffee table, his dark eyes, his thin lips, his formal shoes. She worked her way through the album, up to the cut-the-cake candids, and was trying to decide if she should throw away the scraps or make a collage of Russell in all the wrong order, his crotch on his head, for example, as a representation of how he let his sexual attraction to Felicity take over his brain.

Apart from the beautifully packaged Felicity candle on the coffee table and the photographs on the floor, her apartment was neat and practically empty. Everything Melinda had owned would have reminded her of her former life, so she had sold or given away most of her belongings before moving. She'd gotten rid of the painting they'd bought together at a little gallery in New Orleans on a trip they took to celebrate their tenth anniversary. She'd left their sofa behind—a soft, worn-leather beauty that would have made her long for the comfort of their daily life together. She'd even thrown out her favorite bathrobe because it was one of a matching pair. She'd taken none of her books, since each one sparked a memory of some part of their life.

Her personal life was an abysmal state of affairs, but at least she was warming up to her new job. A fifth-grade boy had approached her that morning, asking to go home.

"Why?" she'd said, ready to dismiss any lame excuses.

The boy was fighting back tears as he told her quietly that a girl he liked had rebuffed him.

Melinda said, "Uggh, God, isn't that just the worst feeling in the world?"

He nodded, wiping a tear from his cheek.

"Now listen to me: I understand, okay? And I may as well tell you— hard truth, okay?—it's not going to get better for a while. So just settle into the misery. The best thing you can do is find some kind of absorbing distraction, like a hobby. Do you . . . I don't know, draw or play soccer or anything?"

"I like to cook," he said.

"Well, there you go. Why don't you make something after school today, like cookies? Or, no, something harder, something with a lot of steps."

"Like Baked Alaska?" he said.

"Absolutely, kid, yeah, like Baked Alaska. That's a classic. Go for it.

And you won't have time to be heartbroken over this girl who probably doesn't deserve you anyway."

He stepped around the desk and hugged her. Melinda could not have felt more surprise in that moment, and it occurred to her that maybe some children weren't such terrible people after all. She asked his name and made herself remember it. *Connor, Connor, Connor.*

Now she was doing a hobby herself, one that was basically the opposite of scrapbooking. With surgical precision, she removed Russell's arms from his body; in this particular picture, he was standing at the altar, waiting for her. She stabbed the tip of the scissors into his eyes.

This past year had been hell, sure, but was Olivia right? Had things been handed to her? She'd gotten into college at a time when it wasn't so competitive to get in or cripplingly expensive to attend. After graduation, a full-time job, for which she was completely unqualified, fell into her lap. She could afford a small but nice apartment, and she put money into her 401(k) plan that her company matched dollar for tax-free dollar; it grew and grew. She met Russell, and by pooling their salaries together, they could afford vacations, a car, and a down payment on a condo. She had never really struggled to get ahead, and that clearly wasn't the case for kids these days as salaries stagnated while the cost of living soared.

She julienned Russell's legs and then put the scissors down. No, she should not have gotten Olivia fired. That was shameful.

She got her phone and looked up the online order for the flowers she'd sent from the invented lover, jotting down Lauren's address. She put her shoes and coat back on, got her purse, and locked the door behind her.

• • •

As she walked up Waverly Place, the late-afternoon sun at a low slant already, she sighed when she realized she was on the correct block, just steps away from Washington Square Park. Wow, what a lucky family. Each brownstone was more elegant than the next, right up until she found herself next to Lauren's. Looking up at the shabby facade with its ragged-looking stoop and air-conditioning units crammed into three of the front-facing windows, it occurred to her that the Astons were real people, and she felt a twinge of guilt over the stunts she'd pulled. Had she caused an actual fight between Lauren and her husband? She imagined those rather decent kids having to split their time between divorced parents. She'd already gotten one person fired; maybe that was enough damage for one lifetime.

This was likely a pointless outing; what were the chances she could catch Olivia alone as she left for the day? And what on earth would she even say to her if she did?

She was startled then to see the front door open as an uncoordinated man in glasses came outside. He was wearing . . . leggings under gym shorts? Standing on the top step, he put his hand on the wide stone railing and began to squat. Or no, he wasn't squatting really. It was more like ballet. Was he doing pliés?

And then to her horror, Lauren came out and joined him on the stoop.

Melinda crouched behind a blue mailbox, looking up and down the street for an escape. She could turn and try to sneak off in the opposite direction without being seen, or she could duck down the stairs to the bar directly next to her. A drink did not sound like the worst idea in the world.

She put her purse up to hide her face and slipped past the sign marking the door to the Sweet Spot.

Pausing inside while her eyes adjusted to the darkness, she could tell this was not a posh place. There was a long bar on the right side of the room and the opposite wall was covered in black-and-white photographs of Greenwich Village back in the day. There were dark wood tables in the center of the room, only two of which were taken. Melinda opted for a stool at the bar.

The bartender approached and handed her a small laminated menu. Melinda had forgotten her reading glasses at home next to the cut-up wedding pictures.

"White wine," she said, dismissing the menu. "Whatever's dry."

He smiled, his eyes creasing in the corners. "If you're sure."

Melinda wasn't in the mood for games. "Why wouldn't I be?"

"It's a Friday afternoon on a perfect fall evening in the Village," he said. "I'd get a manhattan."

For twice the price, probably. "No, thank you," she said, hanging her purse on the hook she found under the bar.

He shrugged, took a wineglass from the rack, unscrewed the cap from a bottle, and gave her a generous pour. This was no millennial bartender with a tattoo and a man bun; he was nicely dressed in a white button-down shirt. His thick hair, flecked with a bit of gray at the temple, needed a trim. He placed the wine in front of her on a cocktail napkin. "It's local," he said. "Cheers."

She nodded and took a sip, instantly wishing she'd ordered the manhattan.

The bartender went back to a dapper, white-haired man seated near her, who had wisely chosen a martini. "I wasn't sure when we'd get to see you again," the bartender said.

The gentleman waved him off. "I needed a bolus of New York cynicism to cleanse the palate. The thing about the Finns," he said, "is that they're so earnest. You should see them sing for each other around a campfire. Americans are too jaded to stand up and give a spontaneous, unrehearsed performance as a gift to other people. We're afraid of being mocked. But these people are authentic and raw. They just get up in the silence of the woods, and they sing. Of course," he added with a laugh, "we were all rip-roaring drunk by midnight, so no one was feeling the least self-conscious."

"And this was before the naked sauna or after?" the bartender asked, a look of boyish mischief on his face.

"After, of course," the man said.

Naked sauna? What kind of debauchery was this? Melinda took another sip of her wine, staring straight ahead and wondering how long Lauren and that guy—her husband?—would be doing ballet on the stoop.

"The scene: a full moon reflected on the surface of a lake surrounded by evergreens," the man said, gesturing. "A truly magical setting. And at some point, I myself was moved to sing. No, don't look shocked, you wouldn't be able to resist the pull either. So, I stood up, closed my eyes, and I belted out a tune."

"A cappella?"

"Of course. We were in the middle of absolutely nowhere. And the woman I mentioned earlier must have liked my baritone because the next morning, after coffee and rye bread, she came to my room and tried to seduce me."

The bartender tilted his head. "Why did she wait until morning?"

"I don't know, but I admired her for making the move in broad daylight."

"What did you sing?"

"'Fly Me to the Moon.' I sang like an angel and then broke her heart, poor darling."

Melinda scoffed. She didn't mean to. But she let out a sound that conveyed her disgust toward humanity at large and men in particular.

She glanced over and saw that they were looking at her. The debonair man drinking the martini was older than she'd first thought. And he was charmed by his own self; that was obvious.

"Sorry," she said, pointing to her throat. "I swallowed the wrong way."

"Now, what's your story?" the white-haired gentleman said. "You are"—he sat back and considered her—"not a tourist; I can always spot those. But you have never frequented this particular bar before or you would never have ordered that ghastly New York State house wine. And here you are . . . passing time. But you didn't wait in the park despite the lovely weather; you came underground instead. You chose to sit at the bar rather than a table. I'm guessing you've got a blind date, and you wanted less intense seating. So, who is he? Did you meet him online? You haven't sent him any money, have you? Scam artists love to go after people our age."

Our age? Melinda felt her face turning red. "I happen to be very wise to con men, and I'm certainly not on a blind date."

"A regular date, then?"

"Now, Phillip," said the bartender, "she doesn't have to tell us. Maybe she's meeting a friend or something."

"I'm not here with anyone at all," she said. "I'm by myself. Is there anything wrong with that?"

"I didn't mean to pry," the older man said. "I apologize. I'm just back in town from the Nordic wilds and overly comfortable on my regular stool. I've been known to loiter here since nineteen seventy-something."

The bartender was nodding in amusement. "Back when this place was the Underground. Hold that thought." He went to the far end of the bar and refilled beers for a couple of guys who brought them back to their table against the wood-paneled wall.

Melinda got her phone and opened a news app, signaling her desire to be left alone.

"Cheers," the man said, and he took the last sip of his drink.

"Sure, cheers," said Melinda, keeping her eyes on her phone, pretending to read an article about deep fakes and the risk they pose to politicians.

"Dan, my faithful friend and barkeep here," Phillip went on as Dan returned, "is about to offer me another martini." He pushed his glass away, saying, "So, tell me about you."

"Phillip," Dan said, getting the shaker out, "let her . . . be."

"What's wrong with conversing with a fellow patron?" said Phillip, looking a little hurt.

Melinda surprised herself, saying, "I was on my way to make amends, but I got waylaid."

"Well, now I'm intrigued," said Phillip. "Tell us. Whom have you wronged? I love a good amending."

Melinda thought this handsome, older man might be hitting on her, and something about that idea loosened her slightly, made her spine a little less rigid, her jaw less clenched. "It's a long story," said Melinda. How old was he, anyway? Seventy? Seventy-five? Too old for her.

"Start with the basics," he said. "Who are you?"

"I live a few blocks from here," said Melinda, pointing vaguely west.

"A neighbor! Marvelous."

"I moved downtown after my asshole, piece-of-shit husband left me for a much younger woman."

"Ah," said Phillip, "I'm very sorry. I really am. Recently?"

"Yes, and after thirty years of marriage," she said. She was spitting the words out, as though a champagne cork had popped, and the contents were pouring out. "I'd like to tear him to pieces actually, to destroy him. Especially now that he has a baby with the bimbo. He's ten years older than me, by the way. And we never wanted kids, so it's all a little hard to wrap my head around."

"I don't like babies either," said Phillip with disgust. "They're attention whores."

Melinda felt herself warming up to him. "They are," she said, "and they're mostly ugly, despite what everyone says."

"Same with cats," he added, swiveling his stool in her direction, as if they were in cahoots. "Entirely overrated."

"Babies aren't *all* bad," said Dan, pouring Phillip's martini from the shaker, "and some cats are as good as dogs." He gave Phillip his drink, and then he topped off Melinda's almost empty glass. "On the house," he said, and he winked at her.

Melinda was surprised by how welcome she felt, almost like she was among friends. "I should be moving on with my life," she said, "but instead I'm consumed with destroying him and the woman who stole him from me."

"How Shakespearean," said Phillip. "No, how Congrevian! Is that a word?"

"Not one I'm familiar with," said Dan.

"Restoration Period anyway. It was William Congreve who said 'Heav'n has no Rage, like Love to Hatred turn'd, Nor Hell a Fury, like a Woman scorn'd.'"

"Are you making fun of me?" Melinda asked. She sincerely hoped not, because the last thing she wanted to do was storm out of this bar in a huff. The bartender was looking at her as if . . . What on earth was that expression on his face? Disgust? Terror? Curiosity?

"Absolutely not," Phillip said. "If anything, I'm making fun of anyone who willingly signs up for a monogamist lifestyle. I think couples are foolish to think they can go a lifetime—thirty years, you said?— sleeping with the same, dull person."

"Wait," Melinda said, "I'm a fool? I'm dull?"

The bartender tried to get a word in, but Phillip held up his hand to stop him. "But it's not your fault," he said kindly. "The puritanical expectations society has set for us are absurd. My closest friend wrote the literal book slash play on this topic. *Women Unbound.* Perhaps you've heard of it."

Melinda turned to face him. "You were friends with Charley Aston? I saw that play years ago. She was radical." Melinda wondered if she should read it again, if she would see the dialogue differently now that Russell had abandoned her.

"Then you probably know she did not believe in marriage, and neither do I."

It occurred to Melinda then that those Aston kids were related to the renowned feminist. "Don't you believe in love?" Melinda said. "In loyalty? In commitment?" If these things weren't real, then what had Russell forsaken?

"I've been fortunate enough to love many people in my life, including one very handsome Finnish man named Väinö who recently wooed me in the sauna." He closed his eyes. "Väinö." He drew out the name in three syllables. "Is that not the sexiest name?"

He was not hitting on her.

Melinda's shoulders slumped, and she took another gulp of her wine. "My dumb ex and his young-ass ho? They named their kid Horatio."

"Look at you," said Phillip, "chitchatting in iambic tetrameter." He raised his glass to her. And then he said, "Horatio?"

"I suppose you think *that's* sexy, too?"

"I *knew* Shakespeare was somehow relevant to this conversation," said Phillip, confident and delighted with himself, "but no, that's not sexy. That's pretentious."

"It's embarrassing," said Melinda.

"Makes sense to me," said Dan, "if they wanted to name the kid after his mother, the ho."

Melinda found herself laughing, and the sound of it took her by surprise. When was the last time she'd been amused by anything? "Ho-ratio," she said. "Nice." The bartender was handsome actually, she noticed, slightly rugged and confident. His cuffed sleeves showed off muscular forearms, and that black apron was tied around some seriously slim hips. Was it the wine?

"Now back to making amends," Phillip said. "You were saying . . . ?"

Melinda was ready to spill all when the door opened, and—to her horror—Lauren's mother marched in.

"Evelyn, my love," Phillip said with a kind smile, "you've joined the party, at last."

Melinda angled her barstool so she was facing away, tipping her head down toward her phone, one hand up to hide her face.

"I'm not here to have a drink," Evelyn said. Her panties were in a twist, but it seemed Phillip was the target of her annoyance, which was interesting. "Would you go upstairs, please, and pick up your wet towel off the bathroom floor, and put my toiletries back from wherever you hid them? I can't even take a shower; all my things are missing."

"I'm sorry," he said. "There was such a vast array of bottles and tubes and sprays and compacts, I couldn't even find space to shave. I thought I would put your feminine wiles all together on a silver tray inside the armoire on the landing, right at eye level."

She paused. "It's all there?" she said.

"Yes," he said. "It's all there. Now come join us for a quick drink."

She hesitated, but then, sounding somewhat mollified, she said, "Fine, but I've only got a minute. I'll have a manhattan."

"Excellent choice. You know Dan, of course," Phillip said to her as Dan began making Evelyn's drink. "And allow me to introduce . . ."

But Phillip had never asked Melinda for her name.

Mortified, Melinda looked up at Evelyn with a tense smile, raising her shoulders up to her ears.

"Melinda!" Evelyn said. "Are you *stalking* us now? This is really too much, even for you. You need to leave my daughter alone, or I'm going to call the police. I think you've made your point."

"Sorry? I don't know what you mean . . . ," Melinda said, trying to make her voice light and innocent, although she knew how unlikely it would be that she could pass off her presence as pure coincidence.

"Oh, come on," said Evelyn, glaring at her. "What are you doing here?"

Melinda's face flushed. All three of them were staring at her as she stammered, "I'm not here because of anything to do with Lauren. I just wanted to talk to Olivia."

"I doubt she wants to talk to you," said Evelyn coldly.

"I'd like to apologize," Melinda said, trying to keep her voice steady so she wouldn't come across like a crazed lunatic.

"And by the way," Evelyn said, her posture and surly expression making her seem especially self-righteous, "we all know you're 'Carlos.' The night of passion and the sexiness and all that?"

Melinda looked at Phillip and Dan as though Evelyn had said something preposterous, like the moon landing had been faked. "Who?" she said.

"Don't play dumb with me, Melinda," Evelyn said, taking a step closer. "Now that's quite enough sabotage for one lifetime. I am very sorry that you married such a terrible man, but enough is enough."

"How do you know each other?" Dan asked. The humor he'd shown before was gone, and Melinda suspected he would soon be solidly on Team Evelyn. She wished she'd never left her apartment.

"She works at the school where my grandchildren go."

"*Our* grandchildren," said Phillip, quietly, as if she'd misspoken.

"In a manner of speaking," Evelyn said.

Melinda was having a hard time putting these characters in place. Was this nice, older gay man Evelyn's . . . ex-husband? She reached for her purse again, hoping she could pay and leave without getting berated any further.

"It all started," said Evelyn, pointing her finger at Melinda, "when she decided to wage a vendetta against my daughter. But it's time to let it go, Melinda. You have every right to be furious with Russell and with Felicity, too, I understand that, but you need to leave Lauren out of it."

"What's all this got to do with Olivia?" Dan asked, his dark eyes suddenly full of suspicion.

"You know Olivia?" Melinda asked.

"I'm her father," he said.

The barkeep. Melinda put her head in her hands.

"Tell him what you did to Olivia," said Evelyn, "or I will."

Melinda swallowed hard and forced herself to make eye contact with Dan. "It was an accident," she said, "kind of. I was at the boutique where Olivia works, and—"

"Worked," said Dan.

"Worked, right. And I'm the one who sort of . . . got her fired."

"Did you film that video?" he said, putting his fists on his hips. "She told me some angry customer came in. Sylvia or something—"

"I'm Sylvia, or Silvestra, or whatever," said Melinda. "I never meant for Olivia to lose her job. She was just collateral damage. I was looking for a way to punish her boss, who stole my husband."

"You mean your *ex*-husband, don't you?" he said.

That seemed cruel, but it was also just plain true.

"I'm really sorry," she said, "I was seeing red when I walked in the store, and then I spotted this leather bracelet Felicity gave him, a *brace-let*, for God's sake. Russell doesn't wear jewelry. And I just took it all out on Olivia. I came here to tell her I'm sorry."

"Does this mean you're quite done terrorizing us all?" Evelyn asked.

Was she? She was willing to let things go with Lauren, maybe, but she was absolutely *not* ready to let things go with Felicity. Her hesitation in answering seemed enough for Dan to write her off. He took her near-empty wineglass and put it behind the bar. "I think maybe you should go," he said, "before you see red again and somehow put me out of business."

"I'm sorry," Melinda said, a little tipsy and a lot miserable.

Evelyn was almost breathless with anger. "I'm not even going to tell Lauren you had the gall to show up at her home; she has quite enough to worry about. You are wicked, Melinda. And that stripper you sent? What on earth is the matter with you?"

"Stripper?" said Dan. "What stripper?"

Melinda was mortified and wanted nothing more than to make a run for it. The stripper had maybe been a bit much, and she couldn't begin to explain why she'd done it. Instead, she looked at Dan and said, "I've been a mess ever since my . . ." She was tempted to rehash her whole sad, sordid story, but she stopped herself. "Never mind. I never meant for your daughter to pay a price." She stood up and took her purse from the hook under the bar. "Sorry."

She got her wallet out, but he waved her card off; he didn't want her money. It took her a second to realize it wasn't an act of generosity.

She walked home alone, wishing she'd worn a warmer coat, sorry she had repelled the two men she'd met that night because she really had enjoyed their company. She had even laughed once.

Chapter 15

Melinda slept terribly. She woke up feeling like she was seeing herself for the first time in months, and she was not pleased. She'd cost a young woman her job. The disgusted look Olivia's father had given her when he sent her away was one of those rare glimpses into the soul of parenting; anyone who would harm his daughter was unworthy of sharing the air he breathed. And the three of them together—along with Lauren and Olivia—left her feeling like an outcast.

Melinda got up. Was there something she could do to fix this mess? Relieved it wasn't a school day, she put on sweatpants and sat down at the dining room table with a cup of coffee to think. A pigeon with a bum claw—a regular visitor on her windowsill—jerked its head toward her and stared.

"What?" she said angrily.

The pigeon pooped on the sill and flew away.

Melinda considered writing Olivia an apology. Or should she write Evelyn a detailed explanation? Or maybe a note to Phillip to thank him for making her feel welcome, if only for a few moments? She tried not to think about Dan at all. Was it that terrible, local wine that had left her head in such a fog? She recalled then a former employee at the insurance firm where she'd worked who left on perfectly good terms to take over a family vineyard on the North Fork of Long Island. He'd recently sent a bottle of rosé to Melinda as a gift, and Melinda had found it surprisingly good. On a whim, Melinda got her phone and called the vintner to thank him. After they caught up for a few minutes, she found herself talking about Olivia.

"She's a terrific young woman," Melinda said, "smart, industrious, and she lost her job in retail. I don't suppose you have any need for someone with . . . marketing and branding skills?"

"As a matter of fact," he said, with a laugh, "I need all kinds of help."

Melinda wrote down a few details about the company and how this man was trying, unsuccessfully, to get the name of his vineyard out there.

After they hung up, Melinda called another former colleague who now worked for a company that built solar panels. And another who made picture frames from reclaimed barnwood. She was anxious about calling one woman who was now teaching entrepreneurship at NYU Stern because Melinda had always found her to be cold, but she was lovely on the phone. Another woman she tracked down was now a headhunter. There was a man who owned an alpaca farm in Connecticut, a woman who ran a charity to promote underprivileged women in business, and one woman in tech who ran an environmental nonprofit in Brooklyn. Melinda discussed bits and pieces of Olivia's situation with each of them—sometimes, depending on the tone the conversation took, she hinted at the role she'd played in Olivia's current unemployment.

At ten o'clock that evening, Melinda fell asleep on the couch with her laptop tucked under her arm.

On Sunday, she woke up feeling energized with a sensation in her chest that almost bordered on . . . happiness? She spent the day making a few more calls and typing up the information she had gathered the day before. She went to a local copy shop, where she printed a spreadsheet, her notes, contact information, and company mission statements. Melinda had always been organized, and she enjoyed the act of putting labels on dividers and using colored stickies to differentiate business types. The poor pigeon with the deformed claw returned to her windowsill as she sorted all the material into sections, each one beginning with a paragraph that outlined her personal connection and the reason she had included it. Finally, she put all the documents in a three-ring binder.

She stood up, stretched her back, and went to the kitchen to eat a banana. Opening the window next to the one where the pigeon was squatting, she crumbled a slice of bread onto the sill and leaned out the window to make sure the pigeon was paying attention. It cooed in her direction.

"So now what?" she asked it.

The lame pigeon turned its back on her.

"Thanks a lot," she said, and shut the window. She could not stand the idea of approaching Dan after the way he'd looked at her. Nevertheless, she took a shower, put on jeans, a sweater, and boots, lipstick and mascara. She took her coat from the closet and her purse from the couch. She picked up the binder on her way out the door.

It was dark by the time she got to the bar. From the sidewalk, she could hear jazz playing from inside. She looked up at the brownstone above, wondering how any of them slept with this noise. There was a security guy at the bar's entrance charging a cover. Melinda paid the twenty dollars, worried that Dan might throw her out even as the bouncer was letting her in.

The room was considerably darker and more crowded than the last time she'd been there. There was Dan, working the bar, which was bustling with people ranging in age from barely legal to geriatric. Melinda was brought to a table in the back corner, where she anxiously waited for the set to end. A waitress was taking drink orders from the candlelit tables, crouching low so she could hear the customers over the saxophone and snares. Melinda ordered a manhattan. When the trio took a break between sets, she thought she would find an opportunity to approach Dan, but the bar became even more raucous. She watched him talk to a couple while he made their cocktails, his large hands gripping the shaker, his eyes scanning the room behind them. Before the icy vodka was even emptied into their martini glasses, he was already checking IDs of some young women next to them who'd called out their orders. It was hard to guess Dan's age, but he looked and dressed too young to be the father of a girl in her mid-twenties. Every now and then he would recuff his sleeves and push them up his arms.

There was a spending minimum, so Melinda ordered a second manhattan from the waitress who was rushed but polite. She called Melinda "sweetheart" when she set the drink on her table. Melinda took a sip, thinking Russell would have hated everything about this place. But Melinda didn't. It was interesting to watch people. She longed to fit in.

Dan never stopped moving. She watched him as he made his way down the bar from one customer to the next. He was known, he was liked, he was maybe part of the reason all these people were there in the first place.

The band played its last piece, the drummer holding an unlit cigarette between his lips, ready to head out to the sidewalk to have a smoke. When they finished, the crowd clapped, and Dan whistled loudly, two fingers in his mouth. The waitress came to her table, and Melinda paid and then got up to use the cruddy bathroom with its bare bulb hanging from the ceiling, its chipped tile walls, and broken toilet seat. At the top of the mirror, someone had graffitied in lipstick: *sweetest spot in town*. If the writer was referring to the bathroom, Melinda would have to disagree. The bar itself, though, was growing on her.

Standing beside her table, she waited, nervously touching the purse strap on her shoulder, until the crowd thinned, and then she finally approached Dan at the bar, just as the lights came up, harsh and bright, making her blink. She felt exposed.

Dan looked neither pleased nor surprised to see her, which made Melinda think he'd known she was there all along. "You're back," he said flatly, giving her none of the sparkle he openly offered to his preferred customers.

"Yeah, so, I was wondering if you could give Olivia something for me." Melinda held out the binder. "It's just a thing I put together for her. It's nothing really."

"You'll see her at the school," he said, wiping the counter down. "Why don't you give it to her?"

"I could," she said, "but she's so disgusted with me, I don't think she'll give it a close look."

The trio was standing by the door. "Should we wait for you?" the drummer asked.

"Meg'll let you in," Dan called back to them, and they headed out to the street.

Melinda was hugging the binder to her chest. "Look, I'd hate for this to end up in the trash; it's possibly . . . valuable."

"Valuable how?" Dan asked, squinting at her while he twisted a wet cloth into the sink.

"It's my attempt to make up for what I did to her. I can't talk Felicity into rehiring Olivia, for obvious, highly personal reasons, so instead I've done some research, and these companies are all open to hearing from her." She handed it to him. "She can call me if she has questions or wants to talk about any of these people; I know them all."

Dan took the binder in one hand, reluctantly. "She doesn't need you to save her. She's got pretty good connections on her own."

"Of course she does," Melinda said, hating for him to see her in such unflattering, fluorescent light. "But who doesn't want to widen their network? Really, it's the least I can do for my inexcusably shitty behavior."

She turned to go. At the door, she put her hand up to push it open, when she heard him say, "Hey, Silvestra."

She stopped in her tracks and looked back at him, her face turning red. "I deserve that," she said, "but I'd rather you call me Melinda."

"Do you actually like jazz, Melinda," he said, collecting empty glasses from the bar, "or did you just sit through all that so you could give this to me?"

"I liked it," she said, surprised he would even bother to ask. "I can't remember the last time I went to hear live music."

He stopped moving for the first time all evening. "Are you hungry?"

She was, but she wondered why he was asking. Was the question a setup for some kind of mean joke? She shrugged, trying to communicate indifference, dreading a punch line. "Maybe," she said.

"I'm meeting a few people," he said, focusing on the glasses again. "You can come along if you want. It's just an informal thing."

Melinda could not imagine why he was being kind. "I have work in the morning," she said. "I should get some sleep."

"Really? Or are you rushing home to concoct more dastardly plans to destroy your enemies?"

She sighed and leveled her gaze at him. "Touché."

He was right though. Given the chance, she would still love to take Felicity down.

"Come have some food," he said casually, handing the bin of dirty glasses to a busboy. "Trust me, this'll be better for you than revenge."

• • •

The smell of garlic and onions greeted Melinda as she followed Dan up five flights of stairs in a shabby Eighth Street building.

"Am I even invited to this?" she said, pausing on the landing to catch her breath. "Did you tell the host I'm coming?"

"It's my place," he said as he pulled his keys from his pocket, "so yeah."

He opened the door to his apartment; there was the jazz trio from the bar, the waitress who'd called her *sweetheart*, and the bouncer. Dan introduced her to a history professor from the New School, a neighbor from across the hall, and to a woman named Meg whom Melinda understood right away to be both his wife and presumably Olivia's mother. She was stylish and energetic, and she welcomed Melinda, taking her coat, and drawing her in without asking who the hell she was or what she was doing there. If this woman knew Melinda had torpedoed her daughter's career, she didn't seem to hold it against her.

The cocktails had left Melinda thirsty, so she went to the little kitchen for a glass of water. Dan was there pulling mismatched plates from the cabinet. He handed them to her along with a glass of wine, and she went back to the main room, where Meg was setting the table. When Melinda offered to help, Meg insisted she have fun instead, so Melinda nudged her way into a conversation with the pianist and the drummer, who were talking about a rat they'd seen on the subway earlier that evening, not on the tracks, but in their actual subway car. Melinda told them about the pigeon with a deformed foot that had made a home on her windowsill. Dan came out of the kitchen then and presented a feast: plates of anchovies, olives, sausage, and cooked potatoes spun on a big lazy Susan in the middle of the table. There was a platter of paella with shrimp and mussels and a ceramic pitcher of sangria. The bouncer from the bar was maybe twenty-three, the waitress fifty, and the bass player possibly ninety. Melinda did her best to remember their names.

Meg clapped her hands together and called everyone to the table, and Dan held out a chair for Melinda, placing a hand on her shoulder as she took her seat.

Meg and Dan were practiced at entertaining; there was no stress between them, plenty of food, and the whole production came off as effortless, which Melinda knew was seldom the case. Why hadn't she and Russell ever entertained this way—joyfully, generously, and with a purpose other than impressing someone?

Everything about the evening—from the spiciness of the food to the open window through which a stray cat entered from the roof to the people—made Melinda feel judgmental. Not judgmental of Dan and Meg and certainly not of the bouncer whose adorable boyfriend came halfway through dinner and regaled them with stories about being an extra on the set of *Law & Order*. No, she thought as she drank her second glass of sangria, she felt judgmental of Russell. He would have looked absurd at this table. He was a handsome man, sure, and successful, but he was so damned uptight. What was with his affected formality? His paisley ties and his prissy belts and his moles that needed urgent checking but never turned out to be anything. What was with his obsession with golf when he wasn't even all that good at it? His pathological need for a regular bathroom schedule. Why was he so slow to refill an empty Scotch glass when they had people over and so stilted when he told a story or, God forbid, a joke? Why was he not ashamed of his childish fear of dogs? He was so terrified of losing his hair, and he parted it low on the left in a way that was stiff and managerial. His chin was weak, his navel herniated, and his penis lacked charisma. He insisted on coasters. He flossed as though he were trying to get his hygienist to give him a trophy.

What had Melinda liked about him? So many things. He was brilliant, for one thing, and a highly respected attorney. He was nice enough to look at. She always liked the evenings they'd spent at one of their three tried-and-true restaurants, and mornings at the kitchen table with NPR on in the background. They enjoyed taking walks, Russell checking his step counter every few blocks. She liked holding his hand.

Dan interrupted her thoughts by offering seconds of paella and refilling her sangria. He leaned across the table and asked about her job at the school. She felt a warm glow every time he fixed his attention on her, his eyes brightening when he smiled. In turn, she fixed her attention on Meg, who was seated beside her, to make it clear that she would never, *ever* encroach on someone else's husband, unlike some assholes she could name.

Meg, charismatic and confident, told her about her job and what it was like to study communities right after they'd been devastated by some catastrophic force.

"Jeesh," said Melinda, "where were you the day my ex-husband blew up my life?"

"Oh, I don't work at that level," said Meg, causing Melinda's cheeks to flush in embarrassment.

"Of course not," Melinda said. "I was only kidding."

"Oh!" Meg said, and then she laughed, giving Melinda's shoulder an affectionate little push. "Too much sangria for me."

In the midst of the laughter, liquor, and talk around Dan and Meg's table, a thought popped into Melinda's head: *I am having a very nice time with these strangers.* The cat was passed from lap to lap, a glass of water was knocked over. The art professor lit a joint.

At around midnight, no one seemed even remotely interested in leaving. Melinda turned to Meg and said, "I should probably get going. I have to be at work before eight."

"You can't leave yet," she said, as if Melinda was her new best friend. "Dan made his flan; it's like velvet."

• • •

When she finally headed out, before anyone else had left, Dan escorted her down the five flights of stairs and opened the door out to the street. The cold air felt wonderful on her skin as they stepped out into the night. She was tipsy.

"Cab?" he asked.

"I'm only a few blocks away."

Dan zipped up his jacket and offered his arm. "We're pretty drunk," he said. "I don't want either one of us to fall down."

"I'm fine, really," she said, waving him off. "Go back to the party. And please thank Meg again for me."

He took a cigarette from a pack in his pocket and lit it. "What for?" he said. "I did all the cooking. She just warmed things up."

That seemed a little rude; Melinda had liked Meg and thought she was an excellent hostess. "I figured she did most of the work. Wives usually do."

Melinda watched him blow smoke into the air. Russell was so precious about his body. He talked about toxins all the time. There was something almost alluring about Dan's disregard for his own lungs, but she couldn't understand what; she hated the smell of smoke.

"Meg and I aren't together," he said, as if it were absurd she would make such an assumption.

"Oh," said Melinda, trying to rethink the entire evening and Meg's role in it.

"I mean she's great. We were married for about six years back in the day," he said, stepping back to make room for a group of guys walking down the sidewalk. "We're friends, co-parents. But that's it."

"I just assumed—"

"She's dating a climate scientist she met at some conference in Myanmar."

Melinda couldn't imagine talking about Russell this way. *La-dee-da, my ex is dating a celebrity.* "In any case," she said, confused but slightly electrified over the idea that he was unattached, "I don't need an escort."

"I always like to walk after dinner," he said, "but I don't have a dog or a destination. So which way are we headed?"

Melinda stayed rooted to the sidewalk. "Are you saying I'm the dog you'd like to walk?"

"No, I'm saying, I'd enjoy walking an attractive, mercurial woman home," he said. "May I?"

Melinda smiled and pointed west. They set off together, walking past closed shops, open food trucks, and sketchy tattoo parlors toward Sixth Avenue.

"Promise you'll give Olivia that binder?" she said. "I spent the whole weekend putting it together."

"What binder?"

Melinda turned her head so he wouldn't see her smile.

"Don't worry. I'll explain it to her." Dan took a drag off his cigarette. "And thanks."

"It was the least I could do. Olivia accused me of being the very worst kind of old, entitled, bitchy woman."

"Ouch," said Dan.

"And she's right. I behaved abominably."

"Insults aside, I think she'll appreciate the effort."

Effort was better than *gesture.* "She doesn't have to appreciate it," said Melinda, "but I hope she makes use of it, if she wants to."

The light at Sixth Avenue was red, but the street was empty. Dan reached for her elbow as they crossed.

"Meg thinks she should aim higher," he said, his hand wrapped around her arm as he looked south for oncoming traffic, "or find something less frivolous, maybe. We were talking it over yesterday."

A van drove past them, blasting heavy metal through open windows.

"Sorry, but it's a little disgusting how well you and Meg get along,"

Melinda said over the music. "I can't even imagine being in the same room with my ex-husband. The urge to remove his eyeballs from his face would be too tempting."

"I don't want to diagnose you or anything," Dan said, "but as your bartender, I'd say you've got a very long way to go before you're over him."

Melinda smiled at that, *her bartender*. "I'm working on it," she said. "It's just that—and I think this is part of the process, right? Especially when someone has been an unfaithful liar—I spend a lot of time thinking of ways to murder him."

"Poison?" he asked.

"No, I'd like to shove him out the window of a tall building. Watch him flail and kick on the way down."

"No weapons?"

"I fantasize mostly about bare-knuckled violence. I would enjoy punching him in the face." She took her hand out of her pocket and showed him her fist. "Or kicking him in the shin with some solid footwear. Like a lug-sole-boot. You never felt like that with Meg? Not even for a minute?"

Dan hadn't let go of her arm. "Not really," he said. "It was important to me that we remain friends, so that's what we did."

"It's a little hard for me to imagine any divorce being that easy," she said as they turned on Cornelia Street. "I don't know about you, but I had no plan B for my life."

"In our case, Meg was traveling all the time anyway," Dan said, "and we'd grown apart. So it was pretty painless. A little tough on Olivia, but not so hard for us."

"How old was she?"

"Seven when we split up. But even then, she could see we were still friends. Meg has never lived more than five blocks away, not that she's around much."

"Russell and I will never be friends." She got her keys out. "Thank you for dinner," she said, trying to give her most benign smile. "As my bartender, you should know that your bathroom needs upgrading. It's pretty disgusting."

He smiled at her, and she wished she didn't find him quite so attractive. "I appreciate the one-star feedback," he said with a smile. "Is this you?"

"Yep, this is it. Me and Taylor Swift, once upon a time," she said, pointing at the townhouse across the street. "Should I walk *you* home now?" she said.

"I think I'll be okay," he said, dropping his cigarette and stepping on it. He put his hand out as though they were ending a business meeting. "It was nice to . . . hang out with you," he said.

Russell had such overly soft hands, thought Melinda as she shook his; she felt an inexplicable urge to turn Dan's over and kiss his knuckles. "Thank you. Nice to hang out with you too."

"Good night, Melinda."

For a split second, she imagined pulling off his shirt and wondered if she should invite him in.

"Everything okay?" he said.

He looked worried. Melinda wanted to comfort him, to run her fingers over the furrow in his brow.

"Oh sure," she said. "Fine, fine." She fumbled with her keys but managed to unlock the door. She smiled at Dan one last time before tripping over the threshold, righting herself, and closing the door behind her.

•   •   •

The next afternoon at Perkins, Melinda, nursing a dull headache, watched Olivia as she walked into the school lobby wearing one of her typically retro outfits, like she was about to hitchhike to Woodstock. Was it too soon to hope for a truce? Melinda kept her eyes on her computer, glancing up quickly when Waverly came down and showed Olivia a scrape on her elbow. Harrell came soon after, touching the bangles on Olivia's wrist. Olivia listened to their stories and gasped over a drawing Waverly was holding; like Melinda, she seemed to be getting more comfortable with the company of children. She was wearing a loud, yellow vintage coat that Melinda would have never bought in a million years but somehow suited Olivia. Melinda studied her, curious to know what she'd thought about the list of contacts, if she'd made any calls, if she was angry Melinda had interfered, if she knew her dad had invited her for dinner.

Olivia caught her eye and frowned. No peace deal yet.

As Olivia and the Aston children left the building, a man walked in against the current, holding a flower arrangement. He asked Melinda to sign for it, and she did, taking a closer look when she saw that the card he gave her had her name on it, and her first thought was that Lauren and Evelyn were getting even with her for the Carlos stunt she'd pulled.

She opened the little envelope with shaky fingers: *Try not to murder anyone this week. Fondly, Dan. PS Would you like to go out for dinner with me?*

Melinda felt her stomach do an odd little twist, and try as she might, she could not suppress the smile that took over her face.

Chapter 16

Olivia was getting very good at ignoring Melinda when she walked in to retrieve the kids from school. She would scroll on her phone or chat up the nannies, anything to avoid eye contact with her nemesis.

That day it was especially easy to ignore Melinda because Harrell's teacher came right up to her with the kids in tow, handing Olivia a wire cage.

"What's this?" Olivia said.

"A gerbil," said the teacher, "to take home."

Lauren had not mentioned a new pet. "Does their mom know about this?"

"Oh, yes," said the teacher, stepping back as if to get some distance from the animal. "She made a blanket offer to care for any class animals when the need arises." She held up a bandaged index finger. "And this one's a biter. Tell Lauren we don't want him back."

There was a sign on the side of the cage: *Beware!*

"We get to keep him?" said Waverly, making kissing sounds at the aggressive rodent.

"Let's talk to your parents about that," said Olivia warily. She could only imagine Evelyn's reaction.

Olivia awkwardly carried the cage, holding Harrell's hand in her free one to keep him from hitting his brother, who was in a mood. She wished the kids wouldn't bicker with one another so much. They even fought over *her*, although she always tried to divide her attention in three equal portions.

In Harrell's other hand, he carried the gerbil's water bottle, so it wouldn't drip into the cage on the walk home. Olivia begged him to stop drinking out of it.

"Seriously, Harrell," she said, "I don't know what kind of bacteria or germs you could get from that."

He stopped and sprinkled the water on his head. When they arrived at the brownstone, she saw her dad sitting on the steps. And next to him—causing Olivia to inhale so sharply she choked on her own saliva and began to cough—was Todd, leaning back on his elbows, his face tipped up to the sky and his sunglasses on, taking advantage of this warm fall day.

He waved when he saw her coming. Olivia managed to clear her throat and smile with a nod of her head, since she had no free hand to wave back. If there was one thing her parents had taught her, it was that two people could end a romantic relationship and still remain friends. She would have to try.

"Who's that?" said Harrell, pointing at Todd.

Olivia switched the cage to her other hand and picked up the bag of gerbil food Waverly had dropped on the sidewalk. Todd stood up to say hello. He hadn't shaved, and his stubble was bordering on a beard. Olivia wanted to put her hand on his jaw. "You guys remember my dad, right?" she said.

"Good to see you, kiddos," Dan said.

"And this is Todd," said Olivia. "Todd, this is Charles, Harrell, and Waverly."

Todd stood up and said hello, flashing the kids his wide, lovely smile.

"Are you 'livia's boyfriend?" Waverly said.

Charles elbowed her, and Waverly pushed him.

"Stop it," said Olivia, separating them before Charles could escalate the tension. What must Todd be thinking to see her like this, a gerbil cage in one hand and three kids in her charge, running circles around her. Even her father was looking at her as though he had no idea who she was.

"Whatcha got there?" Todd asked, pointing to the cage.

"Pixel," Harrell said, trying to reattach the gerbil's water bottle. "We get to keep him."

"Maybe," said Olivia.

"Whatcha got there?" Waverly said, copying Todd and pointing to his arm.

He pushed up the sleeve of his jean jacket to show a tattoo of an audio cable that started near his wrist, wrapped around his forearm, and ended—past where they could see now—at the top of his shoulder, a spot Olivia had kissed a hundred times before.

"I stopped by to ask your dad if we could do a project in his space," Todd said. "He's letting me record a video of this new band I'm working with. They're getting a ton of recognition right now."

She was disappointed to hear his visit had nothing to do with her. "Cool," she said, feigning enthusiasm. Todd was often excited about up-and-coming bands. As far as she knew, none of them had ever made it big.

"Any morning," her dad said. "Just let me know what day you need it."

"I'll text you," Todd said, "but I'm thinking early Saturday." He turned back to Olivia, saying, "I think it's great that you found a new job so fast. Really sucks what happened at Felicity."

"Yeah, well," said Olivia. Had he seen the video? It was pretty likely given the absurd number of views it had racked up. How humiliating. "I guess my very stable job turned out to not be so stable after all."

"Sometimes change is good," he said.

Was he talking about work, or did he mean he was glad they broke up?

He was looking at her with such a kind, open expression, she wanted nothing more than to feel his arms wrapping around her. But he backed away, waving to them all before he left.

Dan reached out and touched her arm. "Can I talk to you for a sec?"

"Sure, let me get these guys inside," Olivia said. She took the kids and Pixel up the stairs and opened the front door. Evelyn, who hadn't left after all, and Phillip came to greet them, just as Olivia was putting the gerbil cage on the dining room table, out of Bumper's reach.

"What in God's name is that?" Evelyn said.

"A mean gerbil," said Waverly, as she and the boys ran off to the kitchen, Bumper following behind.

"Some teacher said Lauren agreed to take him," Olivia said. "Should I have said no?"

Evelyn looked furious. "That *Melinda*," she said, "I swear. I really thought I'd gotten through to her."

"You were very clear," said Phillip, "as well as formidable and slightly terrifying."

"Thank you," said Evelyn.

Olivia wasn't sure he meant it as a compliment. "When did you talk to Melinda?" she said.

"When I saw her having a drink at your father's bar," Evelyn said. "She's stalking us now."

"I wouldn't say stalking—" Phillip said.

"Sorry, what?" Olivia said.

"Oh, hell's bells," said Evelyn, a hand to her chest. "I wasn't even going to mention it."

"You may as well tell her now," said Phillip, taking a seat at the dining room table as the children sped past.

"Fine," said Evelyn. "Melinda came by Friday *supposedly* to apologize to you."

Olivia crossed her arms. "Well, I hope you told her to get lost."

"We did," said Evelyn.

"And I've been feeling badly about it ever since," said Phillip, shaking his head remorsefully. "I know you have every reason to be mad at her, but I hated to see anyone look so downcast."

"Phillip!" said Evelyn. "Whose side are you on here?"

"Wait, hold that thought," Olivia said, before the pair got into a tiff. "Can you watch the kids just for a couple of minutes? My dad wants to talk to me."

"Could they have nap time?" said Phillip hopefully.

"Good luck with that," Olivia said with a laugh. "Oh, and the gerbil bites, so don't touch him."

"As if I would," Evelyn said, scoffing at the idea.

Olivia went back outside to sit on the step beside her dad. He placed a black binder on her knees.

"What's this?" she said. "Your memoir? Your last will and testament?"

"Neither would be this thick. No, it's from Melinda. She came by the bar."

"I heard. Evelyn says she's full-blown stalking us now."

"No, she's not a stalker," said Dan. "She asked me to give this to you. It's a peace offering."

"Did she tell you—"

"Yes, she got you fired. But I want you to consider the possibility that maybe she's not *all* bad. Just take a look at this, okay?"

How had Melinda managed to win him over? Her dad may have been kindhearted almost to a fault, but he was also smarter than this. "She's *definitely* all that bad," said Olivia.

"She's letting her anger out in the wrong way," he said, "but she's doing the best she can to get over the trauma of her husband leaving her."

"Please don't defend that monster."

"She's no monster," he said, looking almost shocked. "Not at all. I had her over to my place for dinner."

Olivia was horrified. "You cooked her *dinner?*" She could not fathom the idea of Melinda sitting at their old wood table, eating off of their plates.

"She feels really bad about what happened. And I think," he said, tapping the binder, "this may be worth something to you."

"Not interested," Olivia said, handing it back to him.

"You should try to be a little less rigid, honey," he said. "You know people are complicated."

"I'm not rigid," she said defensively. She did not like the way this afternoon was starting out.

"Todd says you broke it off," he said. "I was really surprised to hear it."

"Well, you don't know all the details," she said. "I happen to think it was the right thing to do."

"Then I wonder why you didn't mention it to me," he said. He put the binder back on her knees, stood up, and offered his hand.

"Maybe . . . I'm still processing," she said, staying where she was. "Maybe I'm trying to make some sound decisions about my future."

"Or maybe you don't know yourself why you did it." He leaned over and kissed the top of her head. "You better get back to those kids. They're a handful." He turned and walked downstairs to the bar, his hands in his pockets, hiking his shoulders up as a gust of wind suddenly blew down the street. Olivia watched the leaves fly by on the sidewalk.

She pulled her coat closed and clenched her jaw; she wasn't rigid. And she didn't know why her father was taking Melinda's side after what she'd done. Instead of sipping tea and working in her nice, calm office at Felicity, Olivia was about to spend five hours in utter chaos. She picked up the binder without opening it and walked back upstairs.

• • •

When it was finally time to go home that evening, Olivia went to the kitchen to get her coat. Evelyn, Phillip, Leo, Harrell, and Lauren were all sitting at the table, watching the gerbil dash around his cage.

"At least he's quiet," said Phillip, as Harrell leaned on him. "Charley and I once took care of a diva's parrot that literally never stopped talking."

"What did it say?" Harrell asked.

"Mostly obscenities."

"Actually, Pixel is probably talking to us right now," said Leo, his chin on his fists as he watched Pixel tear up a toilet paper roll. "Some of his vocalizations are around fifty kilohertz, which the human ear can't process."

"Thank God for something," said Evelyn, shuddering as the gerbil popped his head up and looked at her.

"I think we're stuck with him regardless," Lauren said, and she laughed bitterly. "Thanks a lot, Melinda."

"Can I take Pixel up to our room?" said Harrell. "We did rock paper scissors, and I won."

"Sure, but be careful," said Lauren, sliding the cage toward him. "I don't want anyone getting bitten."

Olivia put on her coat, hoping Harrell wouldn't drop the cage on his way upstairs. She could just imagine the mess, cedar chips and gerbil poop everywhere.

"Why don't you stay for dinner?" Lauren asked her.

Olivia looked up to see they were all watching her.

"Yes, please stay, Olivia," Evelyn said, picking up her glass of wine, "because after today, I won't see you again."

"That's a little dramatic, Mom," said Lauren.

"I'm taking a train to Boston tomorrow morning," Evelyn said shortly. "And who knows when I'll ever come back."

Phillip, who was wearing gold cuff links with his tailored button-down shirt, refilled his wineglass and then hers. He shook his head doubtfully, catching Lauren's eye. "I'll believe that when I see it," he said.

"I'll have you know, I've got a very nice life waiting for me at home," Evelyn said, clasping her hands together. "And anyway, I've overstayed my welcome."

Olivia wondered if she was fishing for an invitation to stay.

"The Boston suburbs are skull-crushingly dull," Phillip said. "And I suspect you like our little village more than you're letting on. Charley always said she thought you had a fun side."

"I don't think Charley and I shared the same idea of what constitutes 'fun,'" said Evelyn tightly. "As I recall, Charley's idea of 'fun' was going to Lauren and Leo's wedding wearing a blouse so see-through, it showed her nipples."

"Just curious, dear," said Phillip, tapping his finger on his wineglass, "how much time do you spend thinking about Charley's nipples?"

"Oh God," said Leo.

"Charley's nipples are of absolutely no interest to me," snapped Evelyn.

Leo covered his ears. "Can we please not talk about my mother's nipples?"

Olivia was hovering at the door, smiling through the banter. The more time she spent with this family, the more she liked them.

"And anyway, I don't want you to leave, Evie," Phillip said. "I'd like to set you up on a date with a friend of mine. If you stick around, he'll take you to dinner and a concert next week."

"I'm not interested in going on a date," Evelyn said. "Who is he?"

"John Wingdale," Phillip said, picking up his phone. "Let's see if I can find a flattering picture. He's a retired travel and culture writer. He spent the sixties in South America and half of the seventies at a California nudist colony. He's seen the world, his three late wives were all wonderful, each in her own way, and he's got a terrific wit."

"A nomadic, thrice-widowed nudist? No, thank you," said Evelyn.

"He was at the commune for *research* purposes," said Phillip, showing her a picture on his phone, "not to embrace nudism, not that there's anything wrong with embracing nudism. But anyway, just consider it. I think it would be good for you to meet a man."

Harrell came running back into the kitchen then. "We let Pixel out for exercise," he said, "and now he's gone."

"Dear God," said Evelyn. "Gone?" She lifted her feet off the floor, placing the heels of her shoes on the chair rung.

"He's under the bed," Harrell said, "and we need a flashlight."

"I'll get the gerbil," Lauren said. "You all decide what we're having for dinner." She walked out of the room, putting on a pair of oven mitts.

"Can we get pizza?" Harrell said. "Plain cheese?"

"Perfect," said Leo, patting him on the back. "The less meat we all eat, the better."

"Oh no," said Evelyn. She turned to Phillip. "And you ask me why I'm leaving town?"

"I have a better idea," Phillip said, placing his hand on her back. "I'll take you out for sushi."

"I told you, Phillip," Evelyn said. "I don't eat raw fish. You can get parasitic—"

"Tapeworms, yes, you've said." He sighed. "Fine, there's a wonderful French place about four blocks away. They cook a sole meunière that will make you weep."

Evelyn got up. "Give me a few minutes," she said and then, to Olivia's surprise, Evelyn turned to her, saying, "He'll be less provocative if you come along, or I hope so anyway. Will you join us?"

Olivia started to decline, but Phillip said, "Yes, you'll bring the average age of our table down by about thirty years. It's my treat."

"Or are we too old for you?" Evelyn said.

"Not at all," said Olivia. "I'd really like that." Dinner at a nice restaurant, free of charge? That sounded better than pizza with the kids and *way* better than a can of soup alone.

●   ●   ●

Phillip took them to a place called Chez Luc on Thompson Street. When they arrived, Olivia realized that the restaurant was directly next door to the building where her mom had rented an apartment right after her parents split up. There were a lot of mix-ups in those early days, when Olivia wasn't sure whether her mom or dad would be the one standing outside PS 41 after school. It was usually her dad.

A chandelier dominated the center of Chez Luc, and photographs of showgirls covered the walls. It was by far the most elegant restaurant Olivia had ever been in, and yet it was in Greenwich Village, which meant there were people dressed in everything from denim to silk to leather.

"Tell us about Todd," said Phillip once they were seated at a candle-lit table in the window. "I hear he's smart and ambitious. So what happened with him?"

"Who's Todd?" said Evelyn, smoothing her hair as she settled in beside Phillip in the sleek black booth.

"How do you know about Todd?" Olivia asked. She pushed her tote bag farther down the booth beside her, wishing she'd left Melinda's dumb binder with her dad.

Phillip shrugged, placing his linen napkin in his lap. "Is it a secret? I would understand if it is. It can be painful to think about a breakup. Much less discuss one."

"Who's Todd?" Evelyn said again.

Olivia wanted to say as little on the subject as possible. "He's just a guy I went out with," she said, "until I realized he wasn't right for me."

"In that case, bully for you," said Phillip, studying the wine list. "Out with the old. Brava."

"Don't listen to *anything* this man has to say about relationships," said Evelyn. "He doesn't think people are meant to stay with the same partner, and his friend—? Girlfriend? I never understood what you two were to each other—anyway, Charley's entire career was based on that hogwash."

The waitress came to fill their water goblets, and Phillip ordered a bottle of wine.

"It isn't hogwash," he said after she left. "I believe in love and rela-tionships. But Charley and I always thought that lifelong monogamy is unnatural and unrealistic."

"As someone who was married for almost fifty years," Evelyn said, raising her eyebrows at him, "I happen to disagree."

"I was always in awe of Charley," said Olivia, remembering the way she would sweep into a room and plant a kiss on someone's cheek, leav-ing the smell of perfume and cigarettes in her wake. "But I kind of like to think that marriage *can* work if you find the right person."

The waitress returned, showing Phillip the bottle of wine he'd se-lected and opening it; Olivia suspected it cost more than her monthly loan payment.

He tasted it and declared, "*C'est merveilleux.*"

The waitress poured them each a glass, presented them with menus, and left a bread basket on the table.

Phillip raised his glass. "To the next irresistible man—or irresistible woman—who captures Olivia's fancy."

"Woman?" said Evelyn, putting her glass back down. "Why would Olivia be attracted to a woman?"

"Why wouldn't she?" said Phillip, taking a sip of his wine. "Why shouldn't she?"

"She was dating a boy before, so I think it's obvious."

While they argued over her sexuality, Olivia ducked behind her menu, scanning the list of entrées, all of which were written in French.

"Nothing is ever obvious when it comes to sexuality," said Phillip, lightly thumping his fist on the table. "If there's one thing I've figured out at my ripe old age, it's that I should never make assumptions about people. Why should I put heteronormative restraints on Olivia, or on anyone, for that matter?"

What the heck was a *flamiche*? Or *moules du bouchot*? And why had Olivia never studied French? She closed the menu and put it down, deciding she would order whatever Phillip and Evelyn were having.

Evelyn was whispering now just loudly enough to make herself heard. "Are you speaking about yourself, Phillip? Are you attracted to men and women? Well, I feel vindicated; I always suspected you were trying to have an affair with me."

"False," said Phillip, giving Evelyn a quick wink. "It was your handsome doctor husband I was after."

Olivia smiled at that, but Evelyn looked deflated. "Why not me?" she said, pivoting in the booth to face him.

"Well, don't be offended, darling," he said. "We're not each other's type. But I promise you this: you can always tell me who you think of when you turn out the lights in the bedroom of your white suburban colonial with the black shutters and the boxwood shrubs lining your perfectly straight walkway."

Evelyn, her eyes wide, was clearly taken aback. "You've never been to my house. How do you know—"

"Of course I have," said Phillip, "years ago for that humorless, stodgy engagement party you threw for Lauren and Leo."

Olivia could imagine Evelyn's house—grand and formal. She took a sip of her wine. To her, it tasted perfectly good but no better than the stuff she and Todd would buy for nine dollars at the shop near her apartment.

"And what's wrong with being somewhat conservative?" Evelyn said, flustered. "Some traditions—like marriage, which you scorn, even though Leo and my daughter seem to be making a very nice life together—are worth treasuring. Which is why I would like to know why Olivia broke it off with her fiancé."

"Oh," said Olivia, twisting her napkin in her lap, "he wasn't my—"

"She was ready to move on," said Phillip, taking the basket of warm rolls and offering it to Evelyn. "What would you have her do? Marry him anyway?"

They weren't even looking at her. Olivia tried to interject. "Todd and I weren't—"

"I would suggest she ask herself what she wants *long-term*," said Evelyn. "Does she want a life partner or not?"

"I kind of do," said Olivia, feeling like she was talking to herself. "I definitely do. And I could tell with Todd that there was going to be a problem."

"What do you mean 'going to be'? It wasn't a problem yet?" Evelyn said.

"I wouldn't spend energy worrying about future problems," said Phillip. "What matters is the here and now. Is there fun? Like-mindedness? Kindness? Sexual attraction? You should enjoy each other in the moment. Tell me: Where does it say one has to stay with the same person forever and ever anyway?"

"On one's marriage license," said Evelyn, with a deadpan delivery.

"Exactly," said Phillip. He offered a roll to Olivia. They were warm. "Consider Melinda. She put her relationship eggs in the marriage basket and look where that got her."

"Do we have to talk about Melinda?" Olivia said, reaching for the butter.

"Hers is a terrible example," Evelyn said, opening her own menu. "How awful to be starting her life over at whatever age she is."

"If her heart is broken, and I'm sure it is, she should mend it by having a passionate love affair to take her mind off the pain," said Phillip. "That's what I did with Väinö in Finland, not that it worked."

"What?" said Evelyn, looking up from her menu abruptly. "Who broke your heart?"

"No one," said Phillip sharply, his lips turning down at the corners. Phillip, whom Olivia knew as perpetually snarky and good-humored, looked almost as if he were about to cry.

"I'll tell you everything," Olivia said, eager to cheer him up. "And then you two can tell me if I did the right thing or if I made the biggest mistake of my life."

• • •

Later that night—after eating a dinner that included pâté and sole and crème brûlée and cognac, and after being told by Phillip and Evelyn that she'd been way too hasty ending her relationship—Olivia rolled over and settled into the crook of Todd's arm. "Let's not even talk about what this means," she said. "Let's just enjoy being together."

"Sure, okay," he said. "Believe me, I'm enjoying it. I found it pretty hard to see you today and not kiss you."

Enjoying the moment took willpower; it was so tempting for her to look ahead, to ask how long he wanted to share this shitty apartment with his buddies, if he thought he might be ready to have kids in four or five years. Olivia held it all inside and instead appreciated the simple joy of having her head on his chest, his arm around her waist, her body pressed against his.

"I bet you never expected to see me working as a babysitter."

"Not really, no," he said, one hand stroking her hair.

At some point every day, she would replay the video, always hoping it wouldn't be as terrible as it really was. "Did you see the TikTok?"

"Only with the sound off," he said. "You looked fabulous."

She appreciated the joke, especially since her words were printed on the screen anyway. "Well, I got pushed into a corner. That horrible girl ranting in the clip? That's not me."

Todd didn't answer.

She propped herself up on her elbow. "It's not, right? I'm not an elitist snob."

"You're not, no," Todd said, "but the store kind of is. Not that there's anything wrong with that necessarily, but everything you said is true. They do target rich shoppers."

"But I shouldn't have said it," she said, "even if it is true. I made the brand look bad."

"That's why it's better to be your own boss," Todd said. "You represent yourself. You run your business exactly the way you want."

"Some of us need a stable salary," she said. She didn't bring up again the fact that Todd didn't have health insurance because, now, she didn't either.

"If things are tight," he said, "I can help you make rent."

Todd. He couldn't possibly afford to do that. Or could he? In any case, it was perfectly in character for him to offer, generous and kind.

• • •

Early the next morning, she got up to use the shared bathroom. Whoever had been in there last hadn't flushed the toilet, and even more devastating, there was no toilet paper.

Todd was still Todd.

After running her fingers through her tangled hair and putting her clothes back on, she kissed Todd without waking him and took the subway back to Brooklyn, her unwieldy bag on the seat beside her. She opened it and took Melinda's binder out, thinking she would drop the thing in a garbage can when she got to her stop. But first, she opened it and leafed through as the train rumbled along. It was an organized, thoroughly researched dossier of sorts. Each section highlighted a business, and there was a note on the front of each divider with comments like, *I have talked to Ethan, head of development of the college, directly, and he needs someone with a background in marketing.* And *Although this is an environmental nonprofit, the director Janet says they need an employee with excellent communication, outreach, and people skills.* On each one, there was some version of *Olivia, I spoke to the CEO—he's looking forward to hearing from you.*

Fundraising? Lobbying? Melinda clearly didn't get Olivia, her goals, her skill set, or her interests. Who did she think she was anyway? If this was Melinda's attempt to make up for her shitty behavior, it struck Olivia as misguided and presumptuous. But it also had clearly taken a lot of time to put together. Why had she gone to so much trouble? As she considered Melinda's motives—one possibility being that Melinda had a conscience after all, another that this was an elaborate trick of some kind—she got so agitated, she missed her subway stop.

How was Olivia even supposed to respond? By thanking her nemesis? No way she could bring herself to do that. She got home and shoved the binder under her bed, hoping they would continue ignoring each other in the school lobby, averting their eyes and minding their own business.

But she didn't have to worry about it because when Olivia arrived for pickup at the school, Melinda was nowhere to be seen.

Chapter 17

Melinda wasn't at work on Wednesday. She wasn't there Thursday either. No one at the school would tell Olivia where she was or when she'd be back. They'd replaced her with a jolly middle school administrator who gave a vague but polite "She's out" when Olivia asked again.

The less she knew, the more curious Olivia became. She began to wonder if Melinda had quit. Or if she had been fired. Or gotten ill. Maybe she'd gone all the way off the deep end and gone on a crime spree.

Olivia herded her three charges out of the building Friday afternoon. They played every game in the house that day, from Monopoly to Twister to Clue, until Olivia was sick to death of playing. Why couldn't these kids ever watch movies like normal people? Their energy had no bounds. She wished she could hang out with Lauren in her studio instead, discussing the pieces she had left to make, the timing, the way the collection would be presented. Olivia finally got the kids to settle down by asking them each to write a long, funny story over the weekend that they could show her on Monday. When she heard Lauren come in—finally!—she left them upstairs scribbling away.

She found Lauren in the kitchen with Evelyn, who hadn't left for Massachusetts after all.

"Kids okay?" Lauren asked.

"Oh, sure," said Olivia. "How was work?"

Lauren had clay on her arms, face, and overalls, and her hair was a mess. "I spent hours painting these boring tiles today. Five-inch-by-five-inch squares, as commissioned. What are they even for? Are they oversize coasters? Trivets? And guess what, it turns out I despise scorpions."

"They make my skin crawl," said Evelyn, with a shiver.

"Me too," said Olivia.

"But Felicity wants scorpions, so I'm giving her scorpions. The problem is I can't get them right," said Lauren. "I can make the tail kind of threatening, sort of, but look," she said, reaching for her phone, which, like her nails, was caked in clay, "the pincers look like my predatory arachnids have oven mitts." She handed Olivia her phone.

Olivia zoomed in on the bugs. "They're a little cartoonish," she said, hoping not to hurt Lauren's feelings.

"Right?" Lauren said. "This one looks like Sebastian from *The Little Mermaid*."

Olivia thought of Mr. Krabs from *SpongeBob*, but there was no need to pile on. "Maybe it's the scale," she said, pointing. "What if you made these things smaller, what are they called?"

"I'm so exhausted," said Lauren, "I can't even remember the correct name. Pedipups? Or palipeds? And 'tail' isn't the right word either. Metasomething." She went to the cabinet to get a glass and filled it with water from the tap. "Meanwhile, I was up to my elbows in sludge and missed two calls from Frances and one from William. I tried to answer with my nose, but it didn't work."

Evelyn turned from the counter where she was chopping carrots.

"I'll call them back tonight if I get a chance. They left me messages too."

"Have either of you seen Melinda?" Olivia said.

"No, and I've been worrying ever since that stripper prank she pulled," Evelyn said.

"What stripper prank?" Olivia said.

"Melinda hired a stripper last week," Lauren said, "and sent her to Leo at the university in the middle of a department faculty meeting," Lauren said.

"How embarrassing," Olivia said.

"It would have been, but Leo's not exactly the stripper type," said Lauren. "Everyone knew right away it had to be some kind of joke."

Olivia thought of the binder under her bed and wondered if Melinda might be easing off on her mission to wreck Lauren's life. "Has she done anything terrible recently?" Olivia asked, "like this week?"

"Not yet," said Evelyn. "I do wonder what diabolical plan she's cooking up now. I find her disappearance very worrisome."

"Not me," said Lauren, opening the refrigerator and taking out a dozen eggs. "I'm hoping she quit and we never have to see her again. I've actually never had anyone hate me before. It's a completely horrifying experience."

Evelyn looked up at the ceiling and then said, "No, you've had people hate you before."

"Who?" Lauren said, sounding quite surprised.

"I can think of a few actually," said Evelyn, "but for example, there was that older girl who befriended you when you were in maybe sixth grade, and she was in William's class—"

"Lucy," said Lauren.

"Yes, Lucy."

"She didn't hate *me*, I hated *her*. She used me to get to William because she had a huge crush on him."

"Let's just say you hated each other," said Evelyn. "And what are we doing with those eggs?"

"Quiche?" said Lauren.

"Fine," said Evelyn. "I'll sauté an onion."

"There's something to be said for keeping your enemies close," said Olivia, putting her coat on. "I don't like Melinda's disappearing act. I want to know what happened and where she is."

"I bet a parent complained about her for scowling all the time," said Lauren, cracking eggs in a bowl.

"I think that's just her face," said Evelyn. "Here's a realistic possibility: Melinda murdered Felicity and has gone into hiding."

"Honestly, Mom," said Lauren. "That's a little dark."

"A crime of passion," said Evelyn, holding up a knife. "It happens all the time."

"Felicity's alive and well," said Olivia.

"How do you know?" said Evelyn.

"Instagram," she said. She opened her phone and showed Felicity's latest post with her handsome, very funny costar, Zach Murray. The two of them were in workout clothes, sipping green juice on a beach. The caption read: *Powering up for the best season of #FelicityatHome EVER!*

"At least we've got eyes on the home-wrecker," said Evelyn.

Olivia saw that Todd had posted on Instagram too, mentioning a band he was going to hear that night at a venue on the Lower East Side. "I've got to go," she said, imagining his smile when she showed up. Not that she had any business going to a club. At this rate, she was barely going to make rent.

"Have a good weekend," Evelyn said. "I'm going home to Massachusetts tomorrow morning, so I won't see you next week."

Lauren rolled her eyes.

"Well, have a good trip back," Olivia said. Olivia had said goodbye to Evelyn at least four times already. "It won't be the same around here without you."

• • •

Olivia walked past the uncarved pumpkins on the stoop and went down to the Sweet Spot. Her dad was at the far end of the bar, serving the happy hour crowd, so she slipped behind the counter and poured herself a glass of wine. When a patron asked her for a beer, she served him one.

"Make yourself at home," her dad said, tossing a dish towel over his shoulder. "Nice to see you."

"I was wondering," said Olivia, taking a seat on the other side of the bar, "if you've heard from Melinda."

He slid a cocktail napkin under her glass. "No. I was actually going to ask you the same thing."

"She missed four days of work in a row."

He looked up at her with surprise.

"It's weird, don't you think?" she said. "First she's on a mission of destruction, then she tries to befriend you, and then she vanishes."

"Hmm," her dad said. "I assumed she was just avoiding me because I sent her flowers."

Olivia put down her wine. "Seriously? Why would you do that?"

"I don't know," he said. "I guess I . . . thought she'd like it."

"You sent my enemy flowers?"

"Yes," he said, looking abashed. "And I never heard back from her."

"That's rude," said Olivia. "She didn't even say thank you?"

"Nothing at all," he said. "Is she out sick?"

"I don't know," Olivia said.

Her dad was rubbing his forehead above a deep wrinkle between his eyebrows.

"Wait," she said, "are you worried about her?"

"Maybe," he said. And then he straightened his back. "Yeah, I am," he said, looking . . . *What was that look?*

"Oh my God," Olivia said, leaning her arms on the bar, "you like her, as in you *like* her." Melinda was decidedly not her father's type. It would be hard to imagine whose type Melinda was. "You're so sociable and civil, and she's so . . . hostile."

He shook his head then, his face turning red. "She's not. You don't have a full picture of her."

"Do you?"

"No, but I'd like to. I even asked her out to dinner. Look, maybe you should go check on her," he said. "Stop by her place."

Olivia laughed. "Okay, first of all, no. Second, Melinda would find that unbelievably weird. And third, I don't know where she lives."

"I do," her dad said. "I walked her home from my place the other night." He got a pen and wrote an address on a cocktail napkin. "You're the one who came down here asking about her," he said, sliding the napkin across the bar to her.

She slid it back. "If you're so curious or in love or whatever, *gross*, why don't you go?"

"I don't want to come on too strong," he said, pushing the napkin back again. "She's not over her ex, and it would be better if you went."

She *was* curious, but going to Melinda's apartment seemed a little crazy. "I'll think about it," she said.

"If you find her," he said, "let me know. How's Todd?"

"We're just friends," she said. "Sort of."

• • •

Olivia woke up early the next morning with Todd sound asleep beside her. She'd met him at the venue the night before, they'd hung out with the band, and next thing she knew, she and Todd were making out in the back of a cab.

She stretched and looked around his tiny room from her side of the mattress on the floor. There was a Batman sheet taped over the window and a bulletin board that had concert tickets tacked up several layers deep. Todd would likely sleep most of the day.

Olivia slipped out of bed, put on the skirt and boots she'd worn the day before, and picked up her coat off the floor.

On her way out, she noticed that someone had vacuumed the living room since she was last there. The kitchen was clean too, and smelled like 409.

• • •

She put her hands in her coat pockets, finding the cocktail napkin with Melinda's address scrawled on it in her dad's handwriting. Olivia studied it for a moment, wondering if she might catch Melinda at home. Instead of going home on the subway, she walked west through the

Village. As she rounded the corner of Cornelia Street, she checked the address again and found the building about halfway down the block. Right there, leaning nearsightedly into the list of names beside the door, was Evelyn.

"Well, hi," said Olivia.

Evelyn looked up, turned around, and tried to act casual. "Oh, hello." In her tan trench coat and an old-fashioned, plaid brimmed hat, she looked a little like a detective.

"What are you doing here?" Olivia asked.

Evelyn waved her hand around. "Well, I decided this would be a good week to have the floors refinished in my house, so now I can't go back home for another week. My bridge partner is ready to kill me, and my daughter-in-law—"

"No," said Olivia. "I mean, what are you doing *here*."

Evelyn tightened the belt of her trench coat and took off her sunglasses, her eyes wide with intrigue. "I want to know why Melinda's gone missing." She paused and tilted her head at Olivia. "Why are *you* here? And—wait a minute—aren't those the same clothes you had on yesterday?"

"Maybe," Olivia said, blushing and pulling her coat around her. "I also want to know where Melinda is."

"I thought you hated her," said Evelyn, narrowing her eyes.

"I do. Or I did anyway." She gave the only other explanation she had: "My dad has a crush on her."

"Yes," Evelyn said with a smile. "I heard about the flowers."

"Gossip travels fast," Olivia said, looking up at the building.

"Dan told Phillip and Phillip told Leo and Leo told Lauren and Lauren told me. Melinda's an odd choice, if you ask me."

"It's more than odd," Olivia said. "So what are we doing exactly?"

"We're paying a visit." Evelyn turned to read the names again, searching for Melinda's. "Here she is," she said proudly. "Five-N." Instead of pushing the buzzer, she reached in her purse and put on lipstick.

"How did you know where she lives?" Olivia asked.

"I called the florist she used when she sent flowers from Lauren's fake Latin lover," said Evelyn. "I told them I was so thrilled, I wanted to send flowers back. Her address was on the order form."

A woman walked out of Melinda's building then, and Olivia caught the door just before it closed again. She held it open. "After you," she said, relieved to have Evelyn along in case Melinda reacted to the visit with her special brand of anger.

But Evelyn didn't go in. "Is this a bad idea?" she said.

"Maybe," Olivia said, "but Melinda might be trapped under a piece of furniture. We could be heroes."

"Hmm," said Evelyn, "that's one way to look at it." She put her lipstick away and followed Olivia inside.

They got off the elevator on the fifth floor and walked down the hall until they got to a door that had been gone over hundreds of times with thick black paint.

There was some kind of yelping coming from the other side. "Does she have a pet?" Olivia asked.

"How should I know?" said Evelyn, rapping her knuckles on the door.

They waited. There was a crash and muffled cursing. She was definitely home, but she didn't open the door.

"Melinda?" Olivia called. "It's me . . ." As if Melinda would have the faintest idea of who "me" was.

Melinda still didn't answer. Instead, a man opened the door. He was wearing khaki pants and had a thin belt flung over the shoulder of his kelly-green polo shirt. The sound was not a puppy, Olivia realized, but a baby, louder now without the buffer of the door between them.

"Yes?" he said.

"I'm sorry," said Olivia, checking the number on the door, "we thought this was Melinda's apartment."

"It is," he said brusquely.

Evelyn cocked her head. "Is she here?"

"No," he said, and started to close the door. Olivia put up her hand to stop it. From behind him, the baby's cries got louder.

"Who are you?" said Evelyn suspiciously.

"Who are you?" he said.

"I asked you first."

Olivia looked past the man and saw that the apartment was in disarray. There were piles of clothes folded on the floor, two open suitcases, and what appeared to be a crib or playpen in the center of the room. Olivia's first thought was that if Melinda lived here, she was a slob. And then, as she took in the man's age, his overly tanned face, the situation became clear.

"Are you Melinda's ex-husband?" Olivia said.

"Russell," Evelyn said, sounding almost triumphant, like she'd solved a case.

The man started to speak but then shook his head, confused, no doubt. "Have we met . . . ?"

The baby wailed.

Evelyn had apparently had enough. "Are you going to pick up your infant," she said, "or let him cry himself into a state of unconsciousness?"

Russell stepped back, and the women walked in, looking around at the apartment. The living room was spacious compared to Olivia's, and there was an open door revealing a bedroom. It was the perfect size for one person and far too small for three. Olivia would have happily traded her crappy studio for this place.

Russell was clearly at a loss. "Do you live in the building?" he asked. "Is this another noise complaint?"

Olivia had so many questions, it was hard to decide what to ask first. "Why aren't you in LA with Felicity?" she said. "Does she know you're here? Why the hell are you staying with your ex-wife? And where is Melinda?"

Russell looked stunned. "How do you know—"

Russell's gray hair was damp, his nose was peeling slightly, and his eyes had bags under them. Nevertheless, for an old man, Olivia thought he was decent-looking. "Melinda's gone to pick up diapers and such," he said, picking up a pacifier from the coffee table and leaning to put it in the baby's mouth. "I don't know what's taking her so long or why Horatio's crying again. He just finished a bottle a half hour ago." He looked frantically in the direction of the door. "I'm late."

"*Horatio?*" said Olivia.

"I don't understand," Evelyn said.

"I have to go," he said, trying to get the baby to take the pacifier. "Tee time's at ten."

"*Horatio?*" Olivia said again in disbelief.

"Your golf game can wait," Evelyn said.

Olivia was glad Evelyn said that because *tea* time had not made any sense to her.

"It's a work thing," Russell said. He brightened up then. "Melinda will be back any minute, really; I can't imagine what's keeping her. And since you're here to see her, you're welcome to stay and wait for her. I mean, you could watch Horatio until she gets home?"

"You aren't serious," Evelyn said.

Russell took the belt from over his shoulder and began threading it through the loops of his pants. Then he went to the mirror by the door and combed his hair, parting it low on the side. "Could you tell Melinda I was invited last minute to meet my former colleagues? She'll understand. I'll only be a few hours. She knows the drill."

The baby had spit out the pacifier and was crying frantically.

Evelyn gave him her most withering look. "You are not actually leaving your baby with two complete strangers to go play golf, are you?"

He took a thick, gold watch from a pile of flotsam and jetsam on the coffee table and clasped it on his wrist. "You're friends of Melinda," he said, tucking in his shirt, "which makes you friends of mine." He smiled.

His attempt to win them over was backfiring; Olivia did not like anything about this man.

"Just make yourselves at home. Melinda will be here before you know it." He put his wallet and phone in his pocket, put a baseball cap on his damp head, grabbed a sweater off the back of a chair, and walked out, letting the door slam behind him.

"What just happened?" Olivia said.

Evelyn smirked. "I wonder if he'll realize his fly is down before he gets to the club."

They walked over to the playpen, where the baby was lying on his back, red-faced and bawling. He was wearing a miniature tracksuit.

"Now, now," Evelyn said. "What's all the fuss?" She put her hand down and rubbed his belly. He punched his little fists, opened his eyes, and looked at them. Then he took a breath and cried even louder.

"My diaper days are over," said Evelyn, taking off her coat. "This is on you."

Olivia leaned over and picked up the baby, struck by the heft of him; what a sturdy little boy.

"That fool is too old to have a baby," said Evelyn over the wailing, "and I can't imagine what he's doing *here*."

Olivia reached back in for the pacifier. "Why would Melinda let him stay with her?" She cradled Horatio's soft, bald head and walked him over to the couch, where there was a bed pillow at one end and a blanket strewn across it. "Looks like Russell got the couch." The baby took a few jerky breaths as he calmed down. She sat down with him and put him on the pillow.

"Good," said Evelyn. "Do you realize he didn't even double-check that Melinda knows us."

"She doesn't know us," said Olivia wryly, "not really." Olivia covered her eyes and then peek-a-booed, smiling at the baby. He responded by jiggling his feet at her. His toes were cute; Olivia had to squeeze them. "You need a new name, little muffin," she said, wiping the tears away with her finger and stroking his cheek with her thumb. "I can't say *Horatio* and keep a straight face."

"I agree," Evelyn said, pulling a chair from the dining table to the couch. "How about Horace? Or Rory?"

"Horace is too formal, and Rory's kind of hard to say. Rory, *Rory*. Nah. What about Hank?" she asked. Her second-grade teacher had been named Hank; she'd always liked him and the songs he played on his guitar. The baby made a funny sound then, a cross between a squeal and a growl.

"Ray is a nice name for a boy," Evelyn said. "Or Hal? At least it's Shakespeare-related."

"Hello there, Hank," Olivia said, trying out the name she liked best. He had beautiful round, blue eyes, a little puffy from crying. "I think he's a Hank," she said. "It suits him."

"Hank it is," said Evelyn. She stood then and leaned over to get a better look at him. "But what I really want to know is where is Hank's *mother?*" She found diapers and a package of wipes and brought them to Olivia. "They're vegan," she said, looking at the package, "whatever that means."

Olivia pulled off Hank's tiny track pants and changed his wet diaper clumsily; he complained a bit but tried to be cooperative. When she was done, Olivia got up and carried him around the apartment, a bounce in her step. She liked the smell of his head. "What on earth are we doing?" she said.

Hank was starting to snivel again.

"I can't get over Russell being here," Evelyn said, poking her head into the bedroom.

"Don't tell me I'm stuck babysitting again," Olivia said with a groan, "and on my day off."

"What choice do we have?" Evelyn said. "We can't leave now."

Hank's cries were growing louder as Olivia felt herself getting sweaty and slightly panicked. She handed the baby to Evelyn so she could take her coat off and hang it on the back of a chair by the window. She wondered how angry Melinda was going to be when she got home and found them there. But wouldn't she be angry at Russell for leaving? Or would she reserve her fury for the women who had barged uninvited into her home?

Olivia looked around the apartment and then turned to the street-facing windows, to the blue sky and the bright yellow and orange leaves on the trees below. She spotted a stroller folded up against a wall by the door. "What if we took him for a walk? Maybe he needs fresh air."

"I know I do," Evelyn said, cradling the baby. She wrinkled her nose, probably at the dirty diapers in the trash can. "This place is a shambles."

Olivia began wrestling with the expensive-looking stroller. When she pushed the right button, it popped open like magic. She found an absurdly soft cashmere romper on the table and, with Evelyn's help, wrangled Hank's arms and legs into it. She buckled him into the stroller and put her coat back on, grabbing a few items on their way out: a hat, a pacifier, a beautifully made stuffed elephant she recognized from the baby collection at Felicity. In the midst of all the activity, Hank had stopped crying.

"When I came here this morning," said Evelyn, "this is not what I was expecting."

"Me neither," Olivia said. Just an hour ago, she was in bed with Todd. Now she'd somehow been saddled with yet another kid.

They took the elevator down to the first floor, smiling at Hank as he waved his arms excitedly. Olivia thought he looked like Felicity, his coloring and the sharpness of his chin.

They stepped out into the sunshine, stopping short when a teenager raced by them on a scooter. It wasn't until the door to the building closed behind them that Olivia realized they had no key to get back in.

Chapter 18

Was it kidnapping?

Maybe. But being inside the apartment had felt to Olivia like breaking and entering, so either way, this situation would be very difficult to explain to anyone.

Evelyn's phone pinged as they stood on the sidewalk outside Melinda's building. "I need to take my medication," she said, turning it off.

"Please don't abandon me with him," said Olivia. She was okay dealing with the Aston kids, but taking care of a tiny baby was way outside of her comfort level. And she sure didn't want to face Melinda alone.

"I won't, but I'm not sure what we're going to do now. Golf takes hours." Evelyn pushed the stroller as they set out.

"Let's ask Lauren to call Felicity," Olivia said. And then another good idea occurred to her, but too late. "We should have left Melinda a note."

"We still can," said Evelyn, turning the stroller back to Melinda's building. "We just need someone to let us back in."

They both looked through their purses for something, anything to write on. Evelyn found a slender gold pen, and Olivia found the cocktail napkin she'd gotten from her dad. On one side was Melinda's address, on the other side, Olivia wrote: *We have the baby.*

"That sounds like a hostage letter," said Evelyn.

It did. She added: *We'll bring him back.*

"Surely, Melinda's not going to want us to bring him back," said Evelyn, rocking the stroller gently to keep Hank calm.

"That's true." Olivia added: *When Russell is done playing golf.*

"Speak for yourself," said Evelyn. "I have an appointment at the hairdresser this afternoon."

Olivia crossed out everything and just wrote her cell number and *We are here with the baby* and circled the words "the Sweet Spot" that were printed on the napkin. They waited until a young man walked out of the building, and while Evelyn stayed with the baby, Olivia went back up to the fifth floor and slid the napkin under the door, worrying that Melinda would walk right over it, never seeing the message. She took the elevator back down.

"Now what?" she said.

"I'm sure my grandchildren will be very happy to have a new baby to play with while we figure out what to do next."

Evelyn's shoes clicked on the sidewalk as she walked, and she kept her purse tightly under her arm. Olivia pushed the stroller. They walked from Cornelia Street to Sixth, and at the intersection, Olivia leaned over to pat Hank on the tummy and talk to him, using a high voice he seemed to like. As they entered the park, Evelyn got testy when a guy offered to sell her weed. Olivia could not help but smile as Evelyn wagged a finger at him, saying, "Excuse me, young man, we have a baby here. And do I look like some kind of pothead to you?" Under her unbuttoned coat, Evelyn was wearing a pair of tailored slacks with a beige cashmere twin set and a string of pearls; no, she did not look like a pothead, whatever she thought that meant.

"Hey, I don't make assumptions," said the man, holding up his hands. "I have customers of all ages. I just sold to a dude old enough to be my great-grandpa. He looked pretty sharp, just like you."

"I bet it was Phillip," Evelyn said to Olivia as they walked away. "I thought I smelled marijuana coming from his bedroom last night. It's like living with a naughty teenager."

Olivia was still thinking about the predicament they'd gotten themselves into. "You don't think Russell and Melinda are back together, do you?"

"Melinda certainly doesn't seem like someone who's quick to forgive," said Evelyn.

Hank had abruptly fallen asleep. As they walked out of the park and onto Waverly Place, they spotted a small group gathered directly in front of the bar. There were people carrying gear from a van parked on the sidewalk down the steps to the Sweet Spot: guitar cases and a drum kit, amps and microphones. To Olivia's surprise, Todd came into view, looping a cable from the crook of his thumb around his elbow until it made a big ring that he put over his shoulder. She felt guilty for assuming that he would sleep all day, because there he was, a bright smile and disheveled hair, hard at work.

Olivia wasn't sure how to greet him. With a hug because they'd literally *just* slept together again? Or coolly because . . . no big deal?

Todd was talking to her dad when he noticed her and smiled.

"Good morning," he said.

Olivia tried to act as chill as she could. "He-eey," she said, and gave his shoulder a kind of awkward shove.

Dan peered into the stroller where Hank was sleeping with a peaceful expression. "Whose kid?" he said. "You got another baby-sitting gig?"

"Not exactly," said Olivia, gently rocking the stroller. "We sort of . . . found him." She did not want to tell her dad about Melinda.

"Well, we can't keep him," Dan said. "You know I'm allergic." He turned back to Todd. "Can I help you guys with anything?"

"I think we're okay," Todd said. "This should only take a couple of hours. Thanks for this, man, really."

"It's no problem," Dan said.

Now Todd leaned into the stroller. "Cute kid," he said.

"Thanks," said Olivia. *Thanks?* "I mean, we basically stole him, but yeah. Good luck with the recording today."

"You can come watch," Todd said, backing away.

"It might be a little loud for the baby." *God*, she was probably scaring him half to death. She watched miserably as he left, wishing she could go with him. *Stupid baby.*

Todd walked down to the bar, passing Phillip, who was coming out. When he spotted Evelyn, he said, "Oh, I'm so glad you're back. The band asked me to be an extra in their music video. I need your advice on wardrobe."

He spotted the baby. "Yuck," he said, "what's that doing here?"

Evelyn seemed eager to tell the story. "Olivia and I decided to find out for ourselves what happened to Melinda," she said, gesturing dramatically, "so we showed up uninvited at her apartment."

Dan perked up on hearing Melinda's name and took a step closer. "And?" he said.

"And to our shock," Evelyn said, "we discovered that her ex-husband has returned and is staying with her. It's a scandal."

Dan stiffened and instantly dropped his smile. "You've got to be kidding," he said.

Olivia saw his pained expression and wanted to apologize to him for Evelyn's bluntness. "I think he's sleeping on the couch," she offered.

"So," Evelyn said, "we're going to take care of her ex-husband's baby until Melinda gets here to pick him up, and then we can get some answers."

"I'm not taking care of it," said Phillip. "I'm in a music video."

Dan was still taking in Evelyn's story, pointing a finger at Hank. "That's Melinda's ex-husband's kid? The kid he had with the 'ho'?" he said, using air quotes.

"If by 'ho,' you mean Felicity, then yeah," said Olivia.

"Evie," Phillip said impatiently. "Worry about the baby later. Help me pick an outfit for the video. I can't be late for my cue."

"I'm not abandoning you," Evelyn said to Olivia. "I'll help as soon as I get Phillip camera ready. And in the meantime, just make yourself at home."

The two of them went up to the house, and Olivia stood with her dad, who looked deeply confused. "Man," he said, shaking his head, "if I were Russell, I'd stay away from any open windows." He looked down at the baby again. "And Melinda? Is she okay?"

"We didn't see her," Olivia said.

"So how did you end up with the baby?"

"Russell left to play golf," she said.

Dan's jaw dropped open. "But he doesn't even know you."

"I left Melinda a note, saying I brought the baby to the bar," said Olivia. "So be prepared. She'll show up here pretty soon. Or I assume so."

"Great," he said bitterly. "I'll let her know where she can find her ex's love child."

Olivia smiled. "You're the one who said people are complicated, remember? Don't be rigid, you said."

"Well, I just don't get it," he said. "I don't get *her*. She said she despises him."

Olivia put a hand on his shoulder, sorry to see him so disappointed. "Can you help me carry this thing up?"

She carefully lifted the baby out, hoping he would keep sleeping a little longer, and Dan picked up the stroller.

"Watch that broken step," she said, walking over the jagged edge of the fifth stair.

"I sure hope you brought a bottle along," Dan said, lugging the stroller up, "because babies always wake up hungry."

Olivia tipped her head back in aggravation. They had not.

When they got to the top, Olivia held the baby and looked down Waverly Place in the direction of Melinda's apartment, hoping to catch sight of her, her tall awkward frame hustling down the street in flats. But why would Melinda want anything to do with this kid? Why was her ex-husband staying with her?

And what on earth would they do if Melinda never showed up at all?

Act 2

Chapter 19

On the face of every golf club, there's a sweet spot, and there's really nothing like the satisfaction of hearing the *thwack*—when and if you actually find it—and watching the ball soar.

"Jesus H motherfucking Christ," Glen said, as Russell's ball sailed off into the woods. "You suck."

The men laughed.

"All right, all right," Russell said with a good-natured smile. "I'm out of practice. Gimme a break."

"I thought retirement was supposed to *improve* the game," Stan said.

"Sure," said Ken, "but Russell needs a hot pro to show him how to grip his shaft."

Ken had always been a Neanderthal prick, so this kind of commentary was perfectly in character. And though Russell considered Glen a friend, and an excellent attorney, he was, in fact, an arrogant son of a bitch who loved telling him how much he was now enjoying the view from what used to be Russell's corner office. Nevertheless, Russell had missed this kind of rapport, juvenile as it was. And Glen was right about one thing; Russell could not hit a fucking ball to save his life that day.

Russell put his driver back in the bag and adjusted his belt. *Goddammit*, his fly had been down for hours. He turned his back on the men and zipped up.

He thought of Horatio then, spending the day at Melinda's with her mismatched friends, and his mouth twisted in lingering guilt. But he'd been so excited to be asked to join these guys, he'd gone off to the club anyway. The invitation made Russell realize how much he'd missed conversation with men. Dirty jokes and current affairs. Interactions that didn't involve diapers or spit-up. No one had prepared Russell for how hard staying home with a baby would be. Until he'd become a father, nothing had ever made him long for the order and quiet of a functioning office.

The only thing better than a day with these knuckleheads was time alone with Felicity. No golf outing, even if he were playing well, could be better than spending an afternoon in bed with her. Sadly, he hadn't had that particular pleasure since the baby was born.

The yacht was a beauty, but the trip in every respect had been a colossal disappointment. From dawn to dusk, Felicity had worked. She'd taken calls, drafted proposals, made consequential decisions, solved problems, and managed a PR emergency. All the while, Russell had been stuck in tight quarters with Horatio (who fussed more and more with each passing day), while the staff zipped around him, offering shrimp cocktail and champagne. The boat rocked and swayed, making both father and son queasy.

When the offer came for the new version of her TV show, Felicity cut their trip short without even asking and announced her intention to fly directly to California. She would be in LA for a week or two scripting the series, and then she and her cohost Zach would go to Palm Springs for three weeks of filming, longer if they got off schedule.

He'd hated that she was going without him and for so long. He told her so as she hurriedly opened her empty suitcase on the bed of their stateroom.

"Babe," she'd said, packing her sexy bathing suits and sandals, "I can't be distracted. I need to take my mum hat off to do this job well." He didn't say so, but Russell had barely seen Felicity put a mum hat on. She was willing to hold the baby so Russell could shower, and she would rock him while he slept, and she was always happy to pose with him for Instagram photos, but Russell did all of the heavy lifting.

"I get that," Russell had said, pacing with Horatio over his shoulder, "but can't you cut some corners, truncate the time frame?"

"Excuse me?" Her eyes flashed with anger. "This show is a once-in-a-lifetime opportunity. I've worked my whole life to get this kind of respect for my vision. You're asking me to truncate my dreams! Honestly, Russell, I thought—"

"No, it's only that I like being together, as a family. Maybe Horatio and I could come along, or at least visit for part of the time?"

"You *know* I have to go alone," she said, taking dresses off of hangers. He did not know that. He didn't see why he and Horatio couldn't spend time with her after work.

"And you'll have plenty of help with Horatio once you get home," she said, sounding a bit condescending actually, "so don't you worry."

"I'm sure Liam and I will be very happy together," he said bitterly.

Felicity was focused on her suitcase, folding her short skirts and cover-ups and exercise clothes into neat piles. "Don't expect to hear from me often," she said. "I'll be completely swamped."

Russell felt utterly dejected. Still holding Horatio, he started to pack his own clothes with his one available arm.

· · ·

He climbed back into the golf cart now, and Glen drove them down the fairway. The air was chilly, and Russell was sorry he hadn't brought a windbreaker. He took the opportunity to text Felicity with his cold fingers: I miss you, beautiful. I love you. 4 weeks is too long. He added a heart emoji. And then an eggplant. He may have been in his mid-sixties, but he still knew a thing or two.

He watched his phone. Felicity's service in LA was perfectly fine, so he waited to see the dots come up. They didn't.

Ken and Stan drove past them on his right and came to a stop. They all got out, and Russell jabbed his toe in the grass to repair a divot in the turf. It was a relief to be back on dry land. He'd had diarrhea almost every day of the two-week cruise. He was sleep-deprived, dehydrated, and exhausted. Life with a baby was not anything like what Russell had expected.

He wished he could ask Felicity if she felt the same way, but he didn't dare. He was the one who'd insisted on having the baby, promising he would quit his job and take the lead in caring for him. He would have said anything to hang on to this incredible woman who'd swooped into his life and opened up a world of possibilities for joy and youth and sexual adventure. Russell had felt his life was winding down before Felicity came along and revved his whole existence back up again. She energized him. And then came the baby—

"Hey," Glen said, snapping his fingers at Russell. "You're up."

Russell shook off thoughts of Felicity and stood next to his poorly positioned ball, rolling his shoulders back and dropping an ear to his right shoulder and then his left. Golf was all about posture. And stance. And grip. And concentration and stroke and follow-through. It was a mental game. And a physical one. He situated himself and took a few practice swings with a hybrid. He did not want to swing for real. He could already feel the ball slice.

Russell glanced at the flag and then back down at his ball. He swung—wild and out of control. The ball went far but veered sharply left and landed in a bunker.

"For fuck's sake," said Glen. "Is this your first time on the links?"

"Not my day," said Russell. He could take a joke, even if that one stung a little.

"You owe me an apology, asshole," Ken said.

He and Ken were on opposing teams; shouldn't he be thanking him for his horrendous shot? "What for?" said Russell.

"Nancy gave me shit for weeks after you showed up with Felicity at our Memorial Day party," he said. "She started accusing *me* of having an affair."

Russell laughed, which seemed like the right thing to do, given that this was all in jest, yes? "I'm a lucky guy," he said. "No regrets."

Ken cleared his throat.

Glen studied the position of his ball and chose a five iron. Russell wished he would make one damn mistake.

"But a baby?" said Stan, "at *your* age? Honestly, man, I can't even imagine. My kids are twelve and fourteen, and they're killing me. And yours is what, six months old?"

"Three months," said Russell. He would get home that afternoon and take Horatio in his arms. He could feel his weight and warmth already, smell his round little head.

"Christ," Stan said. "I hope you got a good nanny, or you're never gonna take a shit in peace again."

They had, and yet he hadn't.

When Russell got back to New York, the first thing he did was call the nanny agency to ask if Liam could start immediately. The woman on the phone said the contract had been canceled, no refund had been or would be issued.

"But why?" Russell had said in a state of pure panic. Horatio was screaming in his crib, long, sharp wails that made it hard to think clearly. "My wife— I mean, Felicity is going to be furious; she really liked Liam."

"She certainly did," said the woman.

"I don't understand," he said.

"This is her doing."

That made no sense—Felicity had canceled Liam, the perfect, energetic British manny she'd spent months selecting? It was not possible.

"May we please have . . . a new contract?"

But the woman had hung up on him.

He started to call Felicity, to tell her about this catastrophe, but he'd stopped himself. The last thing he wanted was to be accused again of "truncating her dreams." She was trying to focus; she was building on her already successful brand; she was honing her vision for the new, game-changing season of *Felicity at Home*. He couldn't call her right away with a monumental childcare problem. At the same time, he did not dare hire a replacement without her. She was so picky!

No, Felicity would only be gone a month; he would handle the baby on his own—sort of—until she returned. The worry of leaving Horatio with those women loomed large then, and he checked the time on his phone.

"Don't get a *hot* nanny," said Ken. "Our last one was total eye candy from Sweden, but she was a lousy babysitter, and my wife kept accusing me of checking out her ass."

"Dude, we were *all* checking out her ass," said Glen.

"Felicity's letting you play eighteen holes on a *Saturday*?" said Stan. "When the kids were little, my wife never let me out of the house on a weekend. My golf clubs sat in storage so many years I forgot what they were for."

"Felicity's in LA," said Russell. "Something big came up at work." He had been sworn to secrecy and could say no more about it.

"So where are you two living?" said Ken, stepping up to his ball and taking a practice swing.

"We bought a loft on Riverside Drive," said Russell. "Open floor plan, view of the Hudson."

"Nice," said Stan.

"And you're on your own this weekend?" Glen said. "A taste of the bachelor life?"

Russell was quiet until Ken hit the ball. It sailed right down the green and landed with a controlled bounce a putt away from the hole.

Shit, thought Russell.

"Horatio's with me, so not exactly on my own, no," Russell said, trying to sound cheerful. "We had this great nanny who quit on us, so now . . . I'm getting some help from Melinda."

Ken made a sputtering sound, while Stan said, "Whoa, whoa, whoa!"

"Sorry, say what?" said Ken.

"Did you say Melinda?" said Glen. "Like, as in . . . *Melinda*?"

"Doesn't she hate your guts?" Ken said.

"It's not like that," Russell said. How could he make them understand? "We've known each other practically forever." Oddly enough, Melinda did not seem to hate his guts. He'd called her exactly a week ago, saying he was desperate and needed her. He'd explained that the nanny wasn't coming and Horatio barely slept, cried constantly, messed his diaper all day long, and demanded nonstop attention. He could not manage it all by himself. Melinda was quiet at first, and just when Russell thought she'd hung up on him, she cleared her throat and invited him to come over. She'd been a lifesaver, actually.

When he and Horatio arrived at her shockingly small apartment, she'd peppered him with questions: Where was Felicity? How were things going with her, *really*? What made her go to California without him? How long would she be there? Who was this Zach guy? Why was Russell incapable of taking care of the baby?

He explained that everything with Felicity was fine, but Melinda had looked skeptical, almost making him wonder if there was some problem he didn't know about. She offered to help him, so he went back to the uptown loft, packed a suitcase, and came to stay. That part he wouldn't tell the guys, that he was sleeping on her couch.

"Hate to break it to you, pal," said Stan, studying his ball's position on this tricky par 4, "but you can't be friends with an ex you dumped for a younger woman. Life does not work that way."

"Of all the people in the world, why would you ask Melinda?" said Glen. "Why not hire some sitter?"

"We'll get a nanny once Felicity gets back. But Melinda's not bad with the kid. I tried a couple of days on my own, but he's too much work." Russell figured that as dads, they, of all people, would relate.

"Sorry," said Ken, taking off his baseball cap, "I still don't get it."

They were all staring at him. "Look," he said, "it's not a big deal. Melinda was willing to help me out." She'd taken a week off work and even cooked his favorite meals. He felt semi-rested again.

Damn, he really wished he'd asked those two women at her apartment who they were and how they knew her.

"Jesus," said Ken. "Does Felicity know your ex is babysitting so you can play golf all day?"

Russell paused again while Stan swung his club with perfect form, hitting a spectacular shot, his ball bouncing on the green.

They all watched as the ball came to a stop a few inches from the hole.

"And boys," Stan said, a hand on his hip, his stance wide, "that's how it's done."

. . .

Russell had not told Felicity where he was staying. He had not lied, but she never asked him and he simply hadn't gone out of his way to tell her. He wasn't convinced she would mind anyway, so why create a problem if there didn't need to be one?

"Let's not *do* jealousy," she'd said to him the night they set some ground rules, before she agreed to live together. "I hate possessive people; jealousy is so unattractive, don't you think?"

He couldn't imagine Felicity being jealous of anyone. And it wasn't like he'd *planned* to go to Melinda's. He had tried to take care of the baby by himself, but it was impossible. The crying, the endless bottles, and, worst of all, the baby's constant need for his attention wore him out. He did not have that much of himself to give.

At three in the afternoon—after a humiliating loss but a fabulous steak at Glen's country club—Russell pulled Glen aside.

"I was thinking we could grab lunch this week," Russell said, wishing he'd stopped at two glasses of wine. "I've got a proposition for you."

Glen clapped him on the back. "Shit timing, dude," he said. "I'm off to Mexico next week."

"Nice," said Russell. "Family vacation?"

"Hell no. I'm going with the guys to Cancún."

"Cancún," Russell repeated regretfully.

"The annual golf trip. Too bad you can't come along this year."

Russell was not included. It made sense, of course; he wasn't one of them anymore.

"Have I mentioned how much I love my new corner office?" Glen said, backing away from him, winking, and shooting him with a finger gun. "And, hey, enjoy every second with that little one. They sure do grow up fast."

This could not possibly be true. The three months Russell had spent with Horatio had been the longest and slowest of his entire life.

• • •

Russell took an Uber alone back to the city.

On the Pulaski Skyway, he checked his phone, comforted to see a message from Felicity—finally!—and concerned to see seven from Melinda.

Felicity's message said: Babe, ahh, thanks. Hope all ok there. Tell H Mummy says hi.

He sent back heart emojis, about ten in a row.

He scanned quickly through the series of messages from Melinda:

Hey, where'd you hide the kid?

Hello?

I guess baby is with you somewhere?

No baby here AT ALL, just saying. I looked everywhere, even under the bed.

Oh! Got note. Baby's at the bar? How did that happen?

!!!!!! Yikes. Saw the news about your girlfriend & cohost plus royals. Bummer. I won't say "I told you so" but . . . I mean, I did tell you so. On brand for her, no? He's YOUNG. Ouch!

FFS, I guess I have to go to the bar & get the kid.

Russell was confounded. What bar? What bummer?

His stomach dropped; maybe the news of Felicity's show had leaked already. He googled the royal couple and found several pictures taken the night before of the handsome aristocrat and his Hollywood wife heading into some trendy restaurant. Russell zoomed in on one of the pictures. Behind the royal couple, but perfectly in focus, were Felicity and her cohost Zach. In another picture, Zach had his arm on Felicity's back and was whispering in her ear. Zach had a strong jawline and a full head of wavy hair. He had muscles that showed through his shirt. The caption read: *The royal couple was seen dining out at Michelin-starred*

Sushi Bling with celebrity home designer Felicity Wynn and her hot cohost, Zach Murray.

So? What exactly was Melinda implying? Russell didn't love the idea of Zach standing quite so close to his girlfriend, but it was work, and besides, they didn't do jealousy.

He got to Melinda's apartment building and jabbed the elevator button, pulling at the neck of his sweater. The apartment was empty. That was worrisome; where on earth was Horatio, and who *were* those women he'd stupidly left his baby with? He sat down on the couch to call Melinda, when he spotted something. There, on the coffee table, were printouts of pictures that hadn't been there that morning. The first was a slightly fuzzy image of Felicity and Zach embracing next to a car. Over Zach's shoulder, Felicity's face was fully visible, and she was smiling. Russell's hands shook as he flipped to the next picture. In that one her back was turned and below her beautiful blond hair, Zach's hands were grabbing her ass. How could she let him do such a thing? And in public! Russell took an even closer look at the third picture, tapping his pockets and looking around the room for his reading glasses. He couldn't find them, so he leaned in closer to see the image and then held it farther at a distance, willing his eyes to get the image in focus. Even with his lousy, farsighted vision, he could see Zach, shirtless in the shadows, a hand on Felicity's breast.

Russell sank back on the couch, struggling to breathe, his chest tightening, his heart aching from a heaviness, a deep pain in his center. He remembered Felicity talking about Zach while they were still on the yacht. Zach added humor to the show to balance her harsher, more judgmental affect. He was the one who had helped convince the famous couple to let a crew televise Felicity as she revamped their weekend home, an iconic seventies estate they'd bought in the mountains of Palm Springs. He was smart, she said. And a friend.

Was this a publicity stunt to get eyes on the upcoming show? Or was Felicity actually *cheating* on Russell? The thought made him nauseated. He needed to be talked down from an emotional breakdown. Or maybe the physical symptoms he was experiencing (shortness of breath, nausea, a cold sweat) were the early signs of a heart attack? He massaged his shoulder and then touched his cheek. Tears? Russell hadn't cried in years. He'd forgotten what it felt like.

He grabbed his suitcase and began to throw clothes into it. LA would be warm, so he left his navy-blue wool coat on the couch, along with his lug-soled leather shoes and a pile of wool V-neck sweaters. He ordered another Uber, this one to take him to JFK. Where was Melinda? He could use her help packing. Melinda was sensible, practical, excellent at organizing. He felt her absence acutely.

It wasn't until he was sitting in first class, drinking a Scotch and soda after flying west over the very golf course where he'd played so poorly earlier in the day, that he remembered the baby.

• • •

The sky in LA was clear at eleven o'clock that night when Russell's plane landed at LAX. While the pilot taxied, Russell called Felicity's cell phone. It went directly to voice mail, so he left a curt message in his deepest voice: "It's me. Call me back." He hoped she did and soon; he didn't know where she was staying.

Then he called Melinda. She answered the phone in a groggy voice, saying, "Where the hell are you, Russell?"

"I know you're mad," he said, "but I had to go to LA."

There was a pause, which he fully expected because he knew Melinda so well that he was fluent in her conversational patterns. He waited, letting her process.

"Are you fucking kidding me right now?" she finally said, sounding much more awake. "Aren't you forgetting something?"

"I'm sorry I'm calling you in the middle of the night."

"I'm not talking about the *time difference*, Russell," she said. "Jesus Christ."

"No, the baby, I know," he said. He could imagine Horatio sleeping on his back in his travel crib, arms limp at his sides, little lips pouting. "Would you mind watching him for a couple of days?" he said. "I won't be long, but I have to sort things out here."

"How could you just *leave*? Do you know how humiliating it was to have to go pick up Horatio from those women?"

Russell remembered the brusque, buttoned-up older woman and her young friend. "Aren't they friends of yours?"

Melinda coughed loudly. "Forget it," she said. "You better catch the next flight home."

Russell needed more time than that. "My relationship with Felicity is . . . Well, she's cheating on me, isn't she? What am I supposed to do about it? *Forgive* her? No, I can't."

"Well," said Melinda, her voice lighter, "she is a truly terrible person, like I said. But did you really have to fly all the way across the country to tell her that? Couldn't you have just called her?"

"I have to do this in person," he said, feeling very glum. Was he actually going to break it off with this woman he loved madly over . . . an indiscretion? Maybe Felicity was sorry.

"And what are you going to tell her about Horatio? That you left him with *me*?"

Russell had not thought this through. "I'd rather not, no," he said. "I'll . . . I'll tell her he's with that nanny she hired, Liam. It's only for a few days."

The flight attendant came on then, announcing a ground crew shortage that would cause a delay in getting to the gate.

"Shit," Russell mumbled. He was desperate to get off the plane.

"Fine," Melinda said, "I can watch the kid for you, just while you put an end to your relationship with her."

End it? Russell felt downright miserable over the idea. He just needed a chance to talk to her. "You're a saint, Melinda," he said. "I don't know what I would do without you. Is Horatio okay?"

"He's fine," she said. "And don't worry. You know me; I'm reliable, I'm faithful, and I'm not a selfish asshole like some people I could mention."

Russell didn't appreciate the jabs at Felicity. Melinda barely knew her. "It's possible," he said, "that there's been some kind of misunderstanding. Maybe I'll find Felicity, she'll explain herself, and I'll bring her back to New York, where she belongs."

Again there was silence on the line, but this time it surprised Russell. He wasn't sure what Melinda was thinking.

"Either way," he said, "I'll see you soon?" He could hear her breathing. "Melinda?"

"I bet this really hurts," she said, her voice strained, almost as though her teeth were clenched. "I know what you're experiencing right now, the agony of betrayal. The heartache. It must feel like your whole world is falling apart."

It did. And he thanked her for understanding. As they hung up, Russell sat back in his seat, appreciating Melinda for being such a good and decent person. He felt a kind of love for her, even after everything. But he was burning for Felicity, aching to hear her say the whole thing was a huge misunderstanding. He would be willing to believe almost any lie she told.

·   ·   ·

Russell woke up in his golf shirt, boxers, and socks, with absolutely no idea where he was. He blinked in the dark room, looked around, and had a moment of panic, thinking he'd been kidnapped or hospitalized. He stretched then, arching his back and flexing his feet; my God, he'd slept well. And then he remembered everything: Felicity was having an affair with her good-looking cohost. He'd flown to LA and taken a room at the Waldorf Astoria. He sat up and waited for his blood to circulate to his brain, and then he walked across the room and opened the thick drapes, shocked by the sudden bright light and the outrageously unexpected mountain view.

What time was it anyway? He checked the clock on his night table: *Eleven?* So . . . *two in the afternoon in New York?* He'd slept over ten hours? How was that even possible?

He turned on CNN, picked up the phone on the desk, and called room service. He ordered a large pot of coffee, a bowl of steel-cut oatmeal with raisins, and a half grapefruit. An egg white omelet— "No, make that a regular omelet with cheese, ham, and mushrooms. Does that come with potatoes? Good. And a side of bacon, please. Large orange juice. And, let's see, bring a split of champagne, too." Mimosas! This felt like a holiday. No son crying, no wonderful but *intense* woman counting calories and making complicated plans for the day. Just Russell, alone, doing as he pleased.

As he waited for his breakfast, he remembered that this was not, in fact, a vacation. These were grim circumstances; Felicity had betrayed him! He found his cell phone in the pocket of his pants. It was dead, and he'd left his charger plugged in beside Melinda's couch. He called down to the front desk and asked to have one brought to the room, and also, he asked, could someone bring a toothbrush, toothpaste, and swim trunks as well, size medium, or maybe large depending on the cut?

The food came promptly, and he could not remember enjoying a breakfast more. The phone charger, toothbrush, and swimsuit arrived soon after; he plugged in his phone, brushed his teeth, and put on the suit, wrapping himself in a heavy terry-cloth robe. When he stepped out in the sunshine by the rooftop pool, appreciating the perfect temperature of this October day, he thought carefully before choosing a lounge chair. After dozing for a couple of hours, he asked the pool boy for two extra towels, a cheeseburger, a club soda, a beer, a side of fries, and a vanilla milkshake. Russell was having a wonderful day. He dog-paddled. He drank a margarita on the pool steps. He slept under an umbrella with a view of LA. He got a sunburn on his shoulders.

In the late afternoon, he went back to his room and turned on his phone. There were no messages—not a single one. Nothing from Felicity or from Melinda either. It was almost as though no one cared about him. He felt simultaneously hurt and elated and worried.

He texted Felicity: We need to talk. Call me. (Horatio is fine.)

But was Horatio fine? He called Melinda. When she didn't pick up, the reality of what he'd done settled around him: Melinda did not like children. Melinda despised Felicity. What was he thinking to leave his child with her? He tried to calm himself: Melinda was responsible and kind, most of the time. And he would be back soon enough.

Smelling like chlorine, he pulled off the wet trunks and threw them on the bathroom floor. Then he sat naked on the bed and googled Zach Murray. He was thirty-eight years old, staggeringly handsome and stylish, and very masculine. Russell found one shirtless photo that showed deeply defined abs. Feeling a bit bloated from the milkshake, he tried to suck his stomach in, but it was no use. He simply didn't have the kind of testosterone coursing through his body anymore to make muscle like this man had. Russell wasn't in bad shape, but he wasn't young.

As he clicked from one link to the next on his phone, he discovered on TMZ that Felicity and Zach had been together before, on and off during the second and third seasons of *Felicity at Home*. He'd gone to London with her a few times. Felicity had never mentioned Zach as a former lover, not when she discussed the possibility of working with him again, and not when she was on the yacht packing her lingerie to go to LA.

Was it true? Was she sleeping with this man? *But what about me?* Russell punched his fist on the mattress. Maybe Felicity was not who he thought she was.

He took a hot shower, frantically working the shampoo into his scalp. *The baby!* He would sue for full custody. But would he really? He couldn't imagine having or wanting full custody. How would he manage being a single dad at his age?

He dried off with a soft white towel, while his toes made imprints in the plush carpet, and put on clean boxers. Standing on the terrace, he called Melinda to check on Horatio. Again, she didn't pick up.

He gathered his thoughts and sent a text to Felicity:

I am flat out disgusted by you and your slutty behavior. Shame on you, Felicity. I demand that you call me AT ONCE so we can discuss the consequences of your unacceptable behavior. I know what you did and who you did it with. You'd best explain yourself to me TODAY or it's over.

He was sure she would answer that text right away, so he waited, phone in his hand, Wolf Blitzer on the television screen.

He texted again: Call me? I mean it.

When she didn't, he felt a wave of depression and hopelessness wash over him. What would he do if she didn't answer at all? Go back to New York and a life without her? He could not do that. He had to clear this up first, find out if she still loved him.

What a relief when his phone buzzed, and he saw she'd texted back:

Just got your hostile fucked up message—WOW. My 'slutty' behavior? Sod off, Russell. What am I, a child? Your prisoner? You're
'disgusted' by me, making ultimatums? Seriously??? Actually, I'm disgusted by *you* You sound like a complete misogynist prick. Shame on
you. Just take care of Horatio, and NEVER speak to me that way again.
Off to Palm Springs, I'll call you when I get a chance to let you know
where things stand re: us.

This was not the response he'd expected. Where was the apology?
The regret? She didn't seem to feel any urgency to explain herself. Was
she leaving him? Did she not love him anymore?

The first time they'd met, he'd been seated at his broad mahogany
desk in his corner office, a view of Battery Park below and the Statue of
Liberty in the distance. He shook her hand, and she held on to it, longer
than necessary. He agreed to negotiate a dispute over a lease agreement
for her retail space on Madison Avenue, a case he'd taken only because
she was famous, fascinating, and beautiful. They went out for lunch at
Harry's after the successful mediation and drank champagne. She told
him that day—he never forgot the moment because he had a hard time
keeping his eyes from wandering down to the swell of her breasts and
the dip of her cleavage—that she loved how "solid" he was.

"Solid?" he said, frowning at the word and keeping his eyes on her
pouty, perfect lips. "I'm not sure what you mean."

"I meet so many trivial, silly people," she said with a crooked smile
in her sexy, smooth British accent. "But look at you. You've got your
feet on the ground, you've a great legal mind, you're brilliant at what
you do—"

He tried to interject, feeling it was unseemly to accept the praise
too readily.

"Can't you take a compliment?" she'd said, putting her hand gently
on the sleeve of his blazer. "All I'm saying is I'm finding your whole"—
and she motioned up to down with her other hand to indicate his mind,
his face, his Zegna tie?—"brand . . . very attractive. You're a man of
substance."

He'd sat up straighter at that comment, wanting to be exactly the
man she thought he was. She'd taken him home to her apartment in the

West Village that afternoon, and his whole life had changed between the soft, silk sheets of her luxurious bed.

What had gone wrong? Had he stopped being a man in her eyes when he stopped working? Maybe she didn't see him the same way now that he was spending his days changing diapers and pacing the floor with a crying baby rather than putting on a starched shirt and tie and being the "great legal mind" she'd been attracted to in the first place.

He needed to become the man she fell in love with.

Chapter 20

Evelyn Shaw may have been opinionated *as fuck*, as William's children would say, but it was only because she knew a lot about the world, having spent seven decades as one of its residents. And one thing she'd figured out was that people were who they were. A leopard cannot change its spots. Lauren was the same agreeable if slightly eccentric person she'd been as a child, and William was just as tightly wound and persnickety as he'd been since the day he was born. Her suspicion that she was not, in fact, an excellent judge of character was not something she was willing to accept.

Ever since her arrival in Greenwich Village, personalities had become slippery. Phillip was far more complex and vulnerable than she and her late husband had credited him to be. Leo was as odd a duck as ever, but he was emotionally connected in ways she hadn't recognized before. Frances, during her almost daily calls, was beginning to come

across as pushy and inflexible, whereas she'd always seemed caring before, and Harrell, sweet boy, wasn't nearly as simple-minded as she'd
feared, having beaten her in five hands of gin rummy the very day she'd
taught him to play.

But above all, Evelyn found herself having an impossible time getting a handle on Melinda. Who was this woman, really? And how could
Evelyn reconcile the bitter, angry demon they'd been battling for weeks
with the one standing on the stoop in front of her now, tears in her eyes
(from the wind or emotion, Evelyn could not tell), holding a crying
baby in her arms. She could not begin to imagine what would bring
Melinda to show up uninvited at the brownstone on a Wednesday evening, a place where she knew she was not welcome.

As Evelyn stood with the front door open, gobsmacked to see Melinda standing there, Olivia, who was about to leave when the bell rang,
and Lauren came to the entry as well. Evelyn wanted to blurt out, *What
in tarnation are you doing here?* But before she could open her mouth,
Lauren invited the Trojan horse inside and brought her to the living
room, where Melinda took a seat on the couch, trying to get the baby
to quiet down. Bumper came over, sniffed the child, and licked his head
before Lauren got him to lie down next to her.

Melinda sat stiffly with her tote bag still over her shoulder and
apologized for the third time for intruding.

"It's okay," Lauren said, keeping her distance by sitting in the far-
thest chair from Melinda in the room. How could they know if Melinda was there in search of a new, ingenious way to wreak havoc? This
was surely not a social call.

"You're still taking care of Russell's baby?" Olivia said. "That can't
be easy."

Olivia had her fanny resting against the radiator in the other corner
of the room, the three of them forming an isosceles triangle with Evelyn on her feet, floating among them, turning on lights to get a better
look at their enemy's expression.

"Sorry for being such a bitch when I picked up the baby the other
day," Melinda said, staring at her shoes. "I didn't understand how you
ended up with him, and I was pissed off."

"What's going on, Melinda?" Evelyn said, speaking less kindly and certainly more directly than Olivia. "Is Russell off playing golf again? In the dark?"

Startled, Melinda turned to face her. "It's much worse than golf actually," she said.

Evelyn couldn't help but notice that Melinda's hair was unwashed and her shirt had an old, crusty spit-up stain on the shoulder.

"I know you all think I'm crazy," Melinda said, her eyes darting from Olivia to Lauren and back to Evelyn. "And I don't blame you after what happened in the store and with the stripper and everything. I want you to know that I agree with you. I mean, I know I was awful, and I'm sorry. I also know I have absolutely no business taking care of this kid."

"I don't understand this," said Evelyn, trying to decipher the expression on Melinda's face. "Are you taking Russell back? Because once a cheater, always a cheater, that's what they say."

"I've actually been kind of worried about you," Olivia said with a helpless shrug.

Melinda shot her a skeptical look.

"It's true," Olivia said. "You've missed, what? Almost two weeks of work now."

"I've been told I'm getting fired if I'm not at my desk tomorrow," Melinda said. She had dark rings under her eyes. "But what can I do? I don't have anyone to help with the baby."

Evelyn was instantly put off. Was Melinda asking for their help with Hank, after all she'd put them through? Because that would be patently absurd.

"Excuse me," Evelyn said, "but what do you mean you don't have help? Where is that baby's father?"

"I don't know," Melinda said, looking utterly miserable then, her shoulders dropping. Evelyn wished she'd kept her mouth shut.

Melinda stroked the baby's head. "Russell found out that Felicity's cheating on him, apparently—"

"Ha!" Evelyn blurted out. "Serves the louse right."

"So he flew to LA to confront her," Melinda said, "and left the baby with me."

"He did not," said Lauren, slapping a hand on her own knee, appalled.

"He did," Melinda said. "He didn't even tell me he was leaving. He just took off."

"Who's Felicity having an affair with?" Olivia asked, opening her phone.

Melinda kept her eyes on Hank's face and said, "Her cohost?"

Olivia tapped away on her phone. "Unbelievable," she said. "Zach's married. I'm starting to wonder if the pedestal I've put Felicity on is a little too high."

"I thought Russell was going to California to dump her," Melinda said, her eyes filling with tears, "but I guess he's trying to fix things with her."

Evelyn drew in her breath sharply. For the first time ever, her heart went fully out to Melinda. That cad had left town, expecting his ex-wife to care for his love child while he went off to woo his cheating girlfriend. How dare he? Evelyn wanted to give that man a piece of her mind.

She brought a box of tissues from the windowsill and set them on the coffee table. "I'm very sorry to hear that," she said, putting a hand on Melinda's shoulder. "You do not deserve to be treated so badly."

"How awful," Lauren said, her eyes squinting. "But what does this mean exactly?"

"It means," said Evelyn, standing up as straight as her back would allow, "it's time for Melinda to rid herself of Russell once and for all and move on with her life."

"But how can I?" she said, waving her free hand at the baby.

Lauren leaned forward in her chair. She, too, looked exhausted and was worrying her red, dry hands together. "Do you have any idea if Felicity's show is still happening?"

Evelyn didn't say so, but she thought asking Melinda a question about Felicity and her show was not the best move in the moment.

"They're doing publicity already, so I assume so," Olivia said, still scrolling on her phone. "An affair might actually be good for their ratings." She looked up at Melinda. "I can't find anything about Felicity and Zach. Did she admit to an affair?"

Evelyn thought they were both missing the point. "That baby needs his parents, and Melinda shouldn't be stuck with him. Did he say when he'd be back?"

"That's the problem," Melinda said. "He said he'd be there a couple of days, but he's disappeared. His phone is ringing with this weird tone, like he's out of the country. I've left countless messages. I can't decide if I should be worried about him or just plain furious."

"It's time to put your foot down," said Evelyn, pounding her right fist into the palm of her left. "Hank is not your responsibility."

"Who's Hank?" said Melinda.

"Horatio," Evelyn said. "*Horatio* is not your responsibility."

"We gave him a nickname," said Olivia, with a flip of her hair, "because the name his parents gave him totally *sucks*."

Melinda put a hand to her mouth and tried not to smile, but Evelyn could see the corners of her lips fighting to turn up. She imagined Melinda might be quite beautiful if she weren't so miserable.

"I was thinking," Melinda said, as she shifted the baby's weight in her arms, "and this is awkward for me to ask, but could one of you call Felicity?"

"Excellent idea," said Evelyn. "Lauren, call her and tell her she has to come straight home."

Lauren raised her shoulders and winced, looking the way she did at fifteen when Evelyn asked her to wear a dress with ruffles. "But what about the series?" Lauren said meekly. "If she comes home, she can't finish filming."

"Lauren Shaw," Evelyn said, "what is more important here? This child's well-being or some television program?"

"It's not just *some* television program," Lauren said, looking like she, too, was about to cry. "It's my *career*."

"You should call her anyway," said Evelyn gently. "She has a right to know Hank's father is AWOL."

"Maybe something bad actually happened to Russell," said Melinda. "I can't understand why he hasn't called."

"It doesn't make sense," said Lauren. "He must miss his kid."

Evelyn had seen Russell only the one time as he was rushing off to play golf, his hair damp and his fly down. "Is this in character for him?" she asked. "I mean, other than what he did to you, of course, is he the type of man to renege on his responsibilities?"

"I don't really feel like I know him anymore," Melinda said, "but no, it isn't like him at all. He was a good husband, until he wasn't." Melinda adjusted her position again, shifting Hank's weight on her lap. She looked so worn down that no one said anything.

Lauren moved her chair a little closer. "Melinda, I know I've said this before, but I'm sorry for what I said to Felicity. I should have kept my mouth shut. I hate that I played *any* role in your divorce—"

"No," Melinda said, putting a hand up. "Russell made up his own mind to leave me. None of this was your fault."

Lauren was crying. Melinda was crying. Evelyn looked to her left and saw that Olivia was crying too. Well, something needed to be done, a concrete deed to help this situation.

"Is there a bassinet around," Evelyn asked Lauren, "or something that we could put Hank in to give Melinda's poor arms a rest?"

"There's a portable playpen upstairs somewhere," Lauren said, taking a tissue and wiping her eyes. "I'll ask Leo in a bit."

Evelyn stood up. "I'll ask him now," she said. "I'll be back." But a little voice was telling her that these three young women should not be left alone for too long.

As she climbed the crooked stairs, she wondered where Phillip was. He went off like this sometimes, and though it was illogical, it hurt her feelings that he had activities without her, a social life that didn't include her, while she had no life outside this house. He was a mystery. Why was he even home? The situation with his job in Berlin made no sense to her, but she never asked about it. She did not like to think about what she would do after he left.

She found Leo in the boys' bedroom, with all three children crowded around him. They were sitting on the floor making some kind of diagram that involved pumpkins and what appeared to be an explosive device. "I'm sorry to interrupt," she said, "but I need something."

Leo didn't seem to hear her.

"Daddy," said Waverly. "Daddy, Grammy's talking to you."

Leo glanced up from the project, an orange marker in his hand. "Oh, Evelyn! Hello," he said, sounding as though he thought she'd just arrived from Boston and not as though she'd been living in the house now for weeks.

"Do you happen to know where the playpen is stored?" she said.

"My playpen?" said Waverly.

"It was mine, too," said Harrell. He was drawing something on his arm rather than on paper.

Charles, too, was focusing on the project, drawing pumpkin vines down the side of the poster board, an artist like his mother. He was a delightful mix of his parents, the best of both, in fact. But she hoped he would quickly grow out of his need to act superior, especially over his siblings. She wasn't sure who he got that from, but it was not his most attractive characteristic.

"Playpen," said Leo, looking up at the ceiling. "Yes, I think I do."

"Could you get it, please?"

Leo did not ask who needed it or what they needed it for. He simply got up off the floor, went into a closet off the hallway, and after pushing a few boxes to the side, a big one labeled *Slides 1968* and a small one simply marked *Charley*, Leo dragged the playpen out. A broom fell out of the closet along with it and clattered on the floor. Evelyn stared into the closet, horrified to think it was likely Charley herself, or her remains anyway, in the small box with her name on it. She slammed the closet door shut.

"And could you set the playpen up in the living room?" Evelyn said, picking up the broom and leaning it against the wall.

"Why?" said Waverly who had followed them into the hallway. "Is there a baby here?" She squeezed her hands together. "Is it Hank again?"

"Yes," Evelyn said, placing a hand on the top of her head. "You can come with me to say hello, but be very quiet because he's sleeping."

Waverly took her grandmother's hand, and they followed Leo down the stairs, leaving the boys to work on whatever science project Leo had them cooking up.

Leo wrestled with the playpen, and once it was set up, Melinda, with a grateful nod, lowered Hank into it. She shook her arms out and rolled her head to stretch her neck. In her absence, Lauren had turned on music, Bach playing quietly from a speaker Evelyn couldn't see.

Waverly tugged on Evelyn's hand, and Evelyn leaned down as she whispered, "Why is the school desk lady here?"

"She came for a visit," said Evelyn.

"Is Hank her grandbaby?"

"No," said Evelyn, putting a finger to her lips. "He just stays with her sometimes."

"Where's Hank's mommy?" she asked.

That was a fair question. "At work," Evelyn finally said.

Leo gently jiggled the sides of the playpen, as if to double-check that they were locked in place, and then took a step back. "Anything else I can get you folks?" he said, his hands on his hips. "Something to drink?"

"Is it too early for a glass of wine?" Melinda asked, looking at the naked-man portrait above the fireplace.

"Not at all," Lauren said eagerly.

It was, in Evelyn's opinion. But as Waverly sat on the floor, watching the baby sleep through the mesh sides of the playpen, Evelyn went with Leo into the kitchen and got four stemmed glasses and a bottle of red wine. When they returned to the living room, the three women were sitting very close together, deep in conversation. Evelyn had the strong feeling she had missed out on something. Leo put a tea cloth over his forearm and pretended to be a waiter in an elegant restaurant, speaking with a French accent and calling them mademoiselle as he poured them each a glass.

Hank became fussy then, and Melinda slumped back on the couch, looking utterly defeated.

"Can I hold him?" Waverly asked, jumping to her feet and putting her arms out.

Lauren looked at Melinda, but Melinda shrugged and looked at Evelyn.

"Yes," said Evelyn. "And you may need to feed him too."

"Feed him what?" said Waverly.

Melinda reached in her tote bag, saying, "I have formula and a bottle."

"Oh, Leo," called Lauren, catching his attention as he headed toward the stairs, "would you mind making a bottle for Hank?"

"Who?" Leo said.

Good grief, thought Evelyn. Leo always missed the forest for the trees.

"The baby," said Lauren patiently, handing him the empty bottle and the can of formula. "Russell's baby."

"It's been a while," he said, "*mais, oui, bien sûr,*" and he went to the kitchen.

Meanwhile, Waverly arranged herself in a chair, and Lauren brought the baby to her and set him in her lap. Waverly leaned over him and rubbed her nose on his.

"As much as I appreciate the offer," Melinda said, looking rosier than she had earlier, "I can't have you two doing this."

"Doing what?" Evelyn said.

"Nothing much," said Lauren, sitting back down next to Melinda. "Olivia and I just thought we could help out with the baby a bit. We'll make a schedule. If Olivia can take days, I'll take nights. We still have a crib that we can set up in our bedroom."

Evelyn was horrified. "Lauren," she said. "You can't possibly manage another child in this house."

"I agree," said Melinda.

"It's only until Russell shows up," Lauren said.

"You need another baby to take care of like you need a hole in your head," Evelyn said. "You've already taken on a dog that tinkles in the house and a gerbil that bites—"

"The gerbil was my fault," Melinda said. "Sorry about that."

"It's fine. And Pixel doesn't bite," Lauren said. "You just have to hold him the right way."

"You're missing my point entirely," Evelyn said.

Lauren held up her hands, their skin dry and red. "I can't have done all this work for nothing," she said. "I want Felicity to stay right where she is, so I get the publicity she promised me. As long as we're taking good care of Hank, I don't see why we have to tell Felicity anything."

"I'm not following," Evelyn said. "What exactly are we *not* telling her?"

"That she has a childcare problem," said Lauren. "The show must go on."

"I'm in," Olivia said. "I'll babysit Hank during the day so Melinda can go back to work."

"Sorry," said Evelyn, trying to catch up. Olivia hated Melinda after all. "But why would you do that?"

"When Felicity finds out I helped with Hank," Olivia said, "she'll feel like she owes me."

Evelyn hadn't thought of Olivia's own connection to the baby. "You would work for that home-wrecker?"

"For her brand?" said Olivia with a little shrug. "Absolutely."

"Okay, then," said Lauren. "It's settled."

"We get to keep him?" said Waverly, looking up with an expectant smile as she hugged the baby.

"No, sweetie," said Lauren. "This is temporary."

"But this is too much," Melinda said.

"I agree," said Evelyn. The very idea was preposterous.

"Too much by myself, yes," Lauren said. "But it's only until Russell gets back, and Leo can help me. And maybe," she said turning to Evelyn, "sometimes you and Phillip could take a turn or two . . . unless you have to go back to Boston."

Evelyn detected something saucy in her tone. "I was planning to, yes," she said. But Evelyn did not want to go home. Her house was large and empty, and she could not imagine returning to such loneliness after her stay in New York. She also didn't want to drive anymore, which was a problem where she lived. She had not told Frances or William—who would take her keys away in a hot minute if they knew—nor had she told Lauren, but she'd had a few incidents of late with her Volvo. She'd managed to run over her own mailbox at the end of the summer, a mailbox that had sat in the very same spot for forty years, but she hadn't seen it there. It was as if it sprang up in front of her car out of nowhere and scared her half to death. For a split second she'd thought it was a toddler. Then there was the matter of a small fender bender she'd been in the last time she'd tried to parallel park in front of Wellesley Books on Central Street, denting the bumper of an English professor's Honda Accord. They'd exchanged insurance information as well as pleasantries, and next thing she knew, her premiums had shot up. The idea of driving on the Mass Pike, veering down Storrow Drive along the Charles, and getting honked at by reckless and rude Boston drivers was becoming unthinkable. How could she stay in her house if she couldn't drive? In New York, she could walk or take an Uber anywhere she wanted, and it was all perfectly normal and manageable.

She could move to a walkable area of Boston, but she needed *some* distance from her son's family, or Frances would flat-out suffocate her.

Before she could respond, Leo came in shaking the bottle and testing it on the inside of his wrist. "A fine vintage, if I may say so myself," he said, handing the bottle to Waverly and helping her maneuver the nipple in Hank's mouth.

"Back to work for me," he said. "The boys and I are trying to figure out how much interior pressure a pumpkin can withstand before . . . *pow.*"

"Pow?" said Evelyn, hating the sound of that. She looked to Lauren, hoping she might ask a few questions before Leo blew up the house.

"Have fun," Lauren called after him, apparently unconcerned about fires or babies or even Melinda, whom Evelyn still did not altogether trust. Evelyn would have to keep an eye on them all.

"I suppose," she said, "I could stay to help a bit with this lunacy. If it's so important to Lauren that the television show goes forward, then I could lend a hand with the baby. But for the record, I think someone needs to track Russell down."

"Felicity must be trying to reach him," Lauren said, "to find out how Hank's doing."

"I'm pretty sure she thinks Horatio is with a British male nanny she hired," Melinda said.

"What happened to him?" Lauren asked.

"Long story," said Melinda sheepishly. "But Russell hasn't told her that the guy never showed up."

The three began planning ways to send Felicity a signal, through a fake Instagram account or a text from the "manny," so that she would know the baby was fine and keep filming her show. It was all too much subterfuge for Evelyn.

Bumper got up and ran to the door as Phillip—ahhh!—came into the brownstone. Evelyn felt instantly lighter and relieved somehow. She went to greet him at the door.

"Am I interrupting something?" he said, peering into the living room as he took off his wool coat. "I feel like I'm walking in on one of Charley's feminist groups. Is that Melinda?"

"You wouldn't believe it," Evelyn said, taking his coat and hanging it on a hook by the door, "but they've called a truce."

"I had tea with an old friend this afternoon," he said, and Evelyn instantly felt a pang of jealousy.

"What's that sulky face you're making?" he said. "Don't judge my friend before you've even heard who it is."

"I'm not," she said. But she hoped it wasn't a woman, for no reason that made any sense. Besides, she would have liked to have been invited for tea.

"I can't wait to tell you about him," Phillip said, putting his hands on her shoulders. "He's a sculptor, and Evie, I think he's the man for you."

Evelyn sighed in frustration. "I've told you, I don't want a man."

"You may want this one. Let's go out for an early dinner, and I'll tell you about him."

She felt a little sparkle of interest as Phillip reached for the coat he'd just taken off, and then got hers from the hook beside it.

"A baby is moving into your house," she said, turning her back as he helped her into her coat. "I thought you should know."

"What's another person," he said. "I wouldn't even have noticed. Now, where should we go?"

An image of parasitic tapeworms flashed in her mind, but she ignored it, pushed it and her husband's dire warnings away. "Sushi," she said, "but you'll have to help me order."

Speaking of leopards and their spots, Evelyn's were changing.

PEOPLE MAGAZINE
Felicity at Home begins publicity tour for season 7

On this Sunday's episode of *WWHL*, Andy will be in the Bravo Clubhouse with celebrity designer Felicity Wynn and her hot sidekick Zach Murray as they dish about filming a top secret seventh season of *Felicity at Home*. In a major twist from the show's regular format, season 7 has Felicity renovating the second home of major West Coast celebrity clients, but viewers will have to wait to find out whose home will be getting the special Felicity treatment. They're keeping the identity of the homeowners under wraps until the show launches. Stay tuned!

Felicity made waves last week when she was asked in an interview how she was managing to juggle motherhood and her career. "I must say, that question is, at its core, hideously sexist. Would you ever ask a man that question? No, you would not. It's quite insulting actually. I'm a mother, I'm a working woman. I'm doing it all just fine." She and her partner, Russell Dunlop, a retired real estate lawyer in New York City, have a three-month-old named Horatio, frequently featured on her Instagram @FelicityatHome.

Chapter 21

"I'm hoping you all know a thing or two about intraspecific nest parasitism," Leo said to the audience of four children, a dog, and a gerbil who were gathered at the kitchen table, "and, gosh, it's an interesting evolutionary tactic."

"Inter-what . . . ?" said Harrell, his legs swinging under his chair right next to Bumper, who was waiting attentively for any Cheerios to fall on the floor. Pixel, the class gerbil who was still staying with them for some reason, was being passed around the table.

"*Intraspecific*," said Leo, enunciating carefully, "meaning 'occurring within a species'—nest parasitism." He adjusted first his broken glasses, taped at the temple, and then the cushion he'd put under his rear end to make sure that the act of feeding Hank his bottle was not putting undue pressure on his fragile lumbar vertebrae. He should have been working on his code and the very interesting finding he had accidentally discovered, but he couldn't, not with Hank around. The next best use of his time was talking to his kids about biology.

"What's that?" said Charles. He had the gerbil on the table, his arms forming a big circle to make a playpen.

"So, just as an interesting example," Leo said, "brood parasites, like certain birds, intentionally lay their eggs in the nests of other birds."

"Why?" said Harrell.

"So that the bird can be relieved from the difficult, time-consuming work of building a nest and rearing offspring," said Leo, looking at Hank in his lap.

"Why?" said Waverly. She moved Charles's hand so the gerbil could escape Charles and come to her.

"Because then she's freed up to spend her time foraging for food and reproducing again and again. So, the female, well, let's say she's a . . . purple indigo bird, will sneak her eggs into the nest of a Jameson's fire finch, thereby saving herself the time and energy of raising offspring on her own. Isn't that a brilliant act of self-preservation?"

"Can't the mommy fire finch tell that it's not her egg?" said Waverly.

"Excellent question," said Leo, feeling the thrill he always got when sharing surprising scientific phenomenon, "and that's the really astounding part from an evolutionary perspective. It's called egg mimicry. In some cases, the parasitic eggs have evolved to look like the eggs of the host bird. Now, some birds, like pied wagtails and red-faced cisticolas, have also evolved so that they've learned to spot the difference, so— ha!—good luck fooling them. But others, like say a Brazilian baywing, can't detect the impostor, and she'll end up raising a screaming cowbird as her own." He laughed then because it really was a mind-blowing evolutionary adaptation. He'd been gesturing enthusiastically with his hands, which meant he'd accidentally removed the bottle's nipple from Hank's mouth. Leo gave it back to him, and Hank accepted.

"In some cases," Leo went on, "when the mother sneaks in and lays her eggs, she'll break the shells of the eggs that are already in there, just to make sure *her* egg will get enough resources. Clever, right?"

Both Waverly and the gerbil in her hands were staring at him with big, round eyes, another clever evolutionary adaptation: he could not help but find their faces cute and appealing, thus increasing his compulsory, biological need to care for them. Nature was truly amazing.

"And you know what's super rad?" he said. Charles called everything "rad" these days, so Leo was pretty sure he knew what that word meant, and he liked to work it into conversations whenever possible. "Sometimes, when the parasitic baby bird hatches, the first thing *it* does is immediately murder any siblings who actually belong in the nest."

"Murder them how?" said Charles, his spoon stopped halfway to his mouth, his eyes unblinking.

"In various ways," said Leo. "Sometimes they use their bodies to shove the unhatched eggs out of the nest so they smash on the ground. Other times," he said, and he held his own spoon to demonstrate, "they stab the other hatchlings to death with their beaks."

"Rad," said Charles, and he put the spoonful of cereal in his mouth.

"Gruesome," said Harrell.

"That's *mean*," said Waverly, clutching Pixel to her chest. She pulled her legs underneath her. "If I saw some bird, even if he was a baby, and I saw him, going around stabbing other baby birds, I would tell him he's a bad bird."

"Is he though?" Leo asked, forgetting all about Hank. "What an interesting thing to say, Waverly. Based on what metric would you conclude that he's 'bad'? Because you could make the argument that he is actually good."

"How?" said Waverly, squinting, as if daring him to convince her.

"Can we call him 'mean' when he's acting purely on his instincts? Aren't we anthropomorphizing this poor baby bird when we use our human moral code to evaluate his behavior? Or his mother's, for that matter. I would argue that we can no more judge that bird for killing his quasi siblings than we can judge a lion for eating a baby gazelle, or a shark for not knowing how to . . . run."

"I don't get it," said Harrell.

"He's saying since he's a bird," said Waverly, looking at Leo as though *he* were the one doing the murdering, "he can't help it 'cause he's just a bird being a bird."

"Exactly!" said Leo, proud that Waverly was doing some pretty high-level thinking for her age. He turned to Harrell. "When we're out in nature observing the behavior of obligate brood parasites—and I've only given one example, while, of course, there are fish who do this as well, and insects, like parasitoid wasps, which, if they're ectoparasitic, lay eggs or larvae on the host, paralyzing and eventually, of course, killing it . . ." He stopped and took a breath. "As observers of nature, we shouldn't react to these behaviors with *moral* outrage. We should record what we observe, accurately and free from personal judgment, thereby maintaining scientific objectivity. If we remain detached"—and he paused to make sure they were all following—"we can witness and analyze the processes by which the fittest survive, and we can learn more about evolution and the natural world."

"Well," said Waverly, "I still think it's mean." She leveled her gaze at him. "Did you and Mommy put me in the wrong nest?"

"Obviously not, dummy," said Harrell, "or you wouldn't be here."

"Don't call your sister a dummy," said Leo.

Hank had finished the bottle. Leo sat him up and turned him to face the kids. "And that is actually an outstanding question that brings us back to Hank here. Fortunately for us, Hank has neither the musculature nor the urge to throw the three of you out of the nest to ensure his own best chances for survival. He lacks the instincts—or maybe we could say the neural wiring—to say to himself, 'If I get rid of these three kiddos, there will be more Cheerios for me!' He's just a human baby, and we know that the only tool they have to work with is to look cute. Look cute and cry loudly. That's it."

"If he's so cute," said Charles, "why does he have ugly blue veins on his head and everywhere."

Leo looked. "He's well-vascularized," he said. "And due to his lack of pigmentation, his veins are highly visible. Phlebotomists will love him."

"You said bottom," said Harrell, laughing.

"*Phle-bot-o-mist*," said Leo carefully. "A person who draws blood."

"Like a vampire?" said Charles.

"What about Hank's mommy?" said Harrell. "Is she a obvious boob Paris-sight?"

"An obligate brood parasite. No, she's more like . . ."

"She's a Mayzie, the lazy bird," said Waverly. "That's what Grammy said. She's off at the beach while Horton the Elephant has to sit on her egg."

"Grammy is correct," said Leo, remembering the long-suffering elephant up in the tree, "one hundred percent."

"Is Mommy the elephant?" said Harrell.

Leo had to think. Lauren *was* the elephant in this scenario—as were they all—but he did not want his children telling his wife that he'd called her an elephant. "Yes, your mother is the elephant, but only in this very narrow literary sense," he said. "And so are we, right? We're taking care of the egg, AKA Hank. But the point is, as a literal human *and* as a metaphorical elephant, I can't help feel it might be nice if Hank's parents would stop being parasites and return to their own nest, taking their offspring with them."

"Daddy," said Waverly, looking aghast, "you don't like Hank?"

"I do like Hank," said Leo. "What's not to like? But I think he's been here long enough." He patted the baby on the back and bounced him gently. Hank burped, which was quite satisfying, until approximately fifty milliliters of baby formula were ejected from Hal's digestive tract, directly onto Leo. The children yelled, "Ewwww," as he grabbed the first piece of cloth he could find, which turned out to be Lauren's sweatshirt. He was out of practice with infant care; he scolded himself for not anticipating the high probability of regurgitated milk.

"Just a little spit-up," said Leo. "Nothing to worry about."

Leo preferred his own children, who had reached an age where they did not need burping or constant tending like Hank did. Leo's children fed themselves the cereal they'd poured themselves into bowls they got themselves. They entertained one another with science projects and puzzles and movies. They were fun to talk to. They were growing up nicely.

But not altogether nicely: Harrell reached toward Waverly to take possession of Pixel, knocking his cereal bowl off the table, much to Bumper's delight. Without thinking, Leo dropped Lauren's sweatshirt onto the floor to sop up the milk.

"Oops," he said. It wasn't even nine in the morning, and Leo was feeling very tired.

How exactly had he ended up caring for a baby who wasn't even a member of the family? Why was he spending a Sunday morning with curdled milk on his clothes when he had much more important work to be doing? He had tried to follow the story about Felicity and Russell when Lauren relayed it, but his mind had wandered off, as it often did, and then drifted back again, just after some critical piece of information had been shared. Now it was too late. He couldn't say, "Wait, sorry—why are *we* taking care of this baby?" At this point the baby was simply there, and he just had to play along, at least until he could figure out how to push the baby out of his nest. Gently, of course, and into the arms of his mother or father, Leo really didn't care which. He just wanted his life back to the way it was before.

Where were the baby's mother and father? Why was it that no one seemed able to reach Felicity, to convince her to return to New York to collect her child? Hank was easy enough, like when Leo had taken all four children to the other side of Washington Square Park to do a special project at the Center for Architecture. But Leo had wanted to build a marble maze too, which was impossible, since the staff made him leave the stroller in the lobby of the building. He'd had to carry Hank the whole time, standing off to the side with him, while the kids got to plan their maze and then measure and cut up pieces of cardboard. Leo tried to participate by calling out some cool ideas, but they were too absorbed in assembling their maze, and occasionally hitting one another with wrapping paper tubes, to take any of his suggestions. Hank, meanwhile, had been so fascinated by Leo's face, he kept reaching for his glasses and finally succeeded in grabbing hold of them and flinging them onto the floor, where they lay broken. The children kindly abandoned their project long enough to fix the glasses, using first glue and then tape for additional reinforcement. They didn't look very good anymore, but they did have structural integrity again.

Leo picked Lauren's sweatshirt up off the floor as the children cleared their cereal bowls and went off in search of a board game that

Leo would have liked to play with them. Instead, he started a load of laundry, while Hank looked up at him and reached for his glasses.

"Oh, no you don't," Leo told him, holding his grabby little hands. "It's true you have a very attractive, symmetrical face, and I can't help but like you. But if your mom doesn't show up pretty soon . . . What do you say we sleuth around a bit and find her?"

If he succeeded, Lauren would be so pleased.

Chapter 22

Waverly leaned into the playpen in the living room and patted the baby on his tummy.

"Hello, Hankie," she said.

He smiled at her, and she loved him so much she wanted to get into the playpen with him.

But before she could pull up a chair to climb in, Daddy walked in and said, "Let's take Hank for walk," and Waverly thought that was a very good idea.

"What about Charles and Harrell?" she said.

"They're going to stay here," he said.

"Just us?" she said. This was even better. Alone with Hank and Daddy meant more for her of both of them. This was a best day already because it was Halloween and it was also a Saturday, so no school, and

Waverly spun herself in a circle with her arms over her head, careful not to bump into the coffee table.

It was almost warm outside, which was weird for Halloween, and Daddy said she could leave her coat at home. "Climate change," he said, sounding mad. Daddy said climate change was the worst thing there was, worse than monsters even, because the oceans were getting fuller and higher and whole places would be underwater sooner than people thought.

"We should eat more plants," Waverly said, knowing that hamburgers and meatballs made hurricanes worse.

"That's exactly right," Daddy said, and he lifted the stroller with Hank in it and carried it down the stairs and then rolled Hank down the street.

Waverly ran around to the front of the stroller to check on the little baby so he would know she was nearby, causing Daddy to run over her feet. It didn't hurt, but she put her hand on the stroller instead and walked beside it, proud for people to see what a cute baby they had. They walked through the park, from one side to the other, past the big fountain where Harrell went swimming, and past the big dog park and the little dog park. Waverly smiled at a man who said "Wow" at her costume. Hers was the best costume ever, and Hank was looking perfect too in Waverly's old centipede suit. Daddy was wearing his yellow Starship Enterprise shirt with a pair of black sweatpants and Spock ears, and he looked good but not as good as last year, when he sewed an extra pant leg on his pants and stuffed it with newspaper so he could be a three-legged person. Mommy said the leg did not look like what he thought it looked like, but Waverly told him it was a perfect costume because it was.

Hank made a burbly noise then and kicked his legs.

"I think Hank's hungry," said Waverly, reaching into the stroller to hold his hand.

"He's not telling us he's hungry," said Leo.

"Daddy, Hank can't talk yet."

"No, but he has other ways of communicating. He could cry, for example."

"Did I cry when I was hungry?"

"All the time," he said.

A fire truck was approaching, and Daddy stopped, squatted down, and covered Hal's ears. Waverly covered her own.

"Why isn't Hank evolved enough to cover his own ears?" she yelled as the truck went by them. "Or why aren't ears evolved enough to cover their own selves?"

"Some are," said Leo. "Elephant ears come with covers. Cicada ears are on their abdomens, which is very handy because they can lie down on them." They continued their walk and turned when they got to the bigger sidewalk on Mercer Street where Mommy used to buy groceries until the store closed.

"I lie down on my ears," said Waverly.

"Yes, but only one at a time," said Leo, adjusting the pointy ears attached to his own.

"Where are we going?" she said, because this was not the walk they usually took.

"I was thinking we could go visit Mommy's ceramics at the store."

"Oh," said Waverly. "Why?"

"For fun," Daddy said. "And then we'll buy candy for the trick-or-treaters."

This really was a best day ever, and Waverly thought it was sad her brothers were missing out on a good outing.

"And we'll also go to Inkwell," he said, "because we're out of glue."

Waverly stopped in her tracks. "Like *out* out?"

"Completely out," Daddy said.

"Are you sure?" They always had things like glue and duct tape in the house. They sometimes ran out of milk and bread, but never important things that made a thing stick to another thing.

"Yes. And it never hurts to buy more," he said.

• • •

The store with Mommy's plates had a blue door, and Waverly held it open so Daddy could push the stroller inside.

"Hello, welcome to Felicity," a lady said. She was pretty with long hair. "Oh my," she said, kind of breathy and scared when she saw the bloody wounds on Waverly's face. The second lady, who looked pretty like the first, gasped. Waverly knew then that hers was a really very good costume. She had one hand hidden under her brother's ripped flannel shirt, and in the other, she was carrying a pretend one that was covered in fake blood.

Leo gave the ladies the Vulcan salutation and then said quietly to Waverly, "This is one of those *Look, but don't touch* stores."

"Like a museum," said Waverly.

"Exactly," said Leo.

She clasped her hands, the real one and the fake one, together behind her back.

"Daddy," Waverly whispered looking up on a high shelf, "look at that bunny. Can we buy him, not for me, but for Hank?"

The little rabbit was so cute in his green pants. Waverly wanted to have him.

"That is a good-looking rabbit," said Daddy, "but we're not shopping."

"We're just looking," Waverly said.

"Exactly."

Leo pushed the stroller toward the saleswomen. "Hi," he said, "where are the ceramics by Lauren Shaw?"

"All gone," said one of the ladies.

"Gone, like sold out?" he asked.

"I can see if any of our other stores have any. We just shipped everything we had to a customer on the West Coast."

"Wow," said Leo, "sold out." He turned and high-fived Waverly's fake bloody hand.

"Do you want me to call our uptown store to check on stock there?" the other lady asked.

"That's okay," he said. "We've got plenty. No, but do you happen to know where the store owner is?"

"Felicity's not here," said the woman, not in a nice voice.

"Oh, I know that," said Leo. "I mean, I know she's out of town. I don't suppose you could tell me how I can reach her. It's kind of important."

"We took her baby," said Waverly.

"Well, we didn't *take* him exactly," Leo said. "We just happen to have him. This is Hank."

Waverly reached in the stroller and patted Hank on the tummy, where a dozen little legs were sewn in two rows. "Mommy and 'livia took him from the school desk lady," said Waverly. "Daddy says he's like a screaming cowbird, except he doesn't almost ever scream, so that means he's either happy or he didn't evolve very good."

"Very *well*," said Leo, "and I think it's the former."

"That's Felicity's baby?" the first lady asked, with a look that told Waverly she did not believe her daddy. Then she leaned over to look in the stroller. "Oh my," she said. "Is he a . . . worm?"

Wow, thought Waverly, and she slapped her fake hand to her forehead. A worm? This lady had never learned about arthropods in her whole entire life.

"As Spock would say," Daddy said, "'Insufficient facts always invite danger.'"

"Excuse me?" said the lady. She looked a little bit mad and a whole lot of confused.

Waverly had to explain. "Hank's a centipede," she said, "and generally venomous. You can tell because of the lots of pairs of legs and the forticules."

"Exactly," said Leo. "Or almost." He pointed in the stroller at the brown stuffed fabric tubes attached to Hal's head. "Centipedes have these pincerlike appendages known as *forcipules*. They can inflict a pretty painful bite."

"Forcipules," repeated Waverly, hoping she would not make that baby mistake again.

Hank made a loud gurgling sound, and the women took a step back.

"I don't understand," said the second lady. "Felicity named her baby Horatio."

"*Horatio?*" said Daddy.

That was a bad name for a baby.

"As in," and Daddy switched to a voice like Dumbledore, "'There are more things in heaven and earth, Horatio, than are dreamt of in your philosophy'?" He went back to his regular voice and said, "No, this baby is called Hank, like . . . Hank Pym."

"Who?"

"Hank Pym?"

When the lady shook her head, Daddy made a face like he'd eaten a whole handful of Sour Patch Kids. "From Marvel Comics? Full name Henry Jonathan Pym? He's a scientist."

They shook their heads in unison.

"Ant-Man?" said Waverly, trying to help these ladies who must have never gone to a library like *ever*. "Yellowjacket? Wasp? He's a human mutate who—"

"But Courtney said Felicity named her baby after a street in the West Village," the first lady said, interrupting, which was a very rude thing to do.

"No, *I* was named after a street in the West Village," said Waverly. These ladies were mixed up about pretty much everything.

"How do you know Felicity?" the second woman asked them.

"We glued her shoe back together at our house," Waverly said. "Mommy says we don't get to keep Hank. And we have to share him with people like the school desk lady. Sometimes we leave him in the Sweet Spot under our house."

Daddy nodded his head up and down. "He does seem to like it down there," he said.

"But we get to keep the gerbil," Waverly said.

"We do?" Leo said. Daddy sometimes missed important announcements like keeping gerbils or other things Mommy told him, like fold the laundry or pick up Harrell from tae kwon do.

The two ladies were looking at them like they were being bad and touching and breaking things in the store. "How did you say you ended up with him?"

"I'm not sure," Daddy said, "but I think we're taking care of him while Russell and Felicity are in California—"

"No, Daddy," Waverly said. "Felicity has a whole 'nother boyfriend now."

"She does?" her daddy said.

"Felicity's kissing around with a handsomer man named Zach."

"Huh," said Leo. "When did she stop . . . kissing around with Russell?"

Waverly always tried to pay attention when the grown-ups were talking, but she did not know the answer to that question.

Daddy turned back to the ladies and their mad faces. "Why don't I leave you my cell number," he said, "and you can pass it on to Felicity, and then we can discuss what to do about her baby. The sooner, the better."

"Daddy," said Waverly, feeling her voice go high, her breath go bumpy, and her eyes go wet. She did not want to cry in front of these ladies, but it was too late for that. The picture in her head of Hank being gone from them was ruining what was a very best day. She leaned in the stroller and hugged Hank, who started crying then, too, and Daddy told them both that everything was okay and took them out of the store and down the street to the CVS, where they bought a lot of candy for the trick-or-treaters, and then she felt better because she got three Tootsie Rolls all for herself.

They got to keep Pixel. Maybe they would get to keep Hank forever too.

COMMUNITY MESSAGE BOARD
ALERT: October 31, 3:47 p.m.

Notice from local police of a possible child abduction in the 10012 neighborhood: three-month-old baby, reportedly wearing a brown bug costume with multiple legs. Suspect: medium height, medium build, male (forties), dark hair, last seen dressed as Spock and walking north on Mercer. Victim was also in the company of a young female (minor) dressed as a zombie. Proceed with caution and call 911.

**** *If you see something, say something* ****

Chapter 23

Phillip was dozing on the couch, a biography of Le Corbusier open on his chest, when he heard the hullabaloo and got up to find out what the fuss was all about. Evelyn, poor dear, was stricken with terror as the old range spewed flames out into the kitchen. She was ordering the boys to stay back as she got her phone to call 911. The boys were stunned, backs against the wall, as Phillip, with shaky hands, turned off the oven, grabbed the fire extinguisher from its spot on the wall, pulled the pin, and sprayed foam into the oven until the canister was empty and the fire was out.

Evelyn put down her phone and turned to the boys. "Explain yourselves," she said.

What had caused the accident? It was something, they said, to do with baking soda, vinegar, a ziplock plastic sandwich baggie, and a pumpkin.

Phillip was very glad the house hadn't burned down. But the crisis was behind them, and he was having a hard time keeping a straight face for Evelyn, who was taking this short-lived fiasco a little too seriously.

As they began to clean up, Phillip saw Evelyn looking at him with her ever-suspicious eyes, as though he were the one who started the fire.

"Why didn't the alarm go off?" she said. "We all could have perished in the flames."

"Don't be dramatic, Evelyn," said Phillip. "The alarms have worked perfectly well since the seventies; there just wasn't much smoke. And the boys were clever enough to open all the windows."

Charles and Harrell were wearing N95 masks and using sponges to wipe pumpkin pulp off the wallpaper that he and Charley had picked out together in . . . 1972? Charles was wearing a lab coat and goggles, his mad-scientist Halloween costume, and Harrell, who was Phillip's favorite—not that he would ever tell anyone that—was wearing a detective outfit: trench coat, dark glasses, and Charley's old plaid hat.

"What if something had happened to my grandsons?" Evelyn said, one hand flat on the table. "I can't stand even to think of it."

"Like what?" said Phillip. He wasn't really asking. Sometimes it was entertaining to get a rise out of Evelyn.

Evelyn stared at him. "They could have gotten injured on *our* watch," she said, her voice getting louder. "Do I really have to spell this out for you?"

Phillip was sorry he'd been napping when it all happened. But he'd been sleeping so poorly at night, with unpleasant thoughts cycling through his mind, that he welcomed rest anytime he could get it.

Leo came home then, dressed in his *Star Wars* or *Star Trek* (Phillip did not know which was what) costume. As he walked into the kitchen then with Waverly, the boys jumped up and down like little monkeys, telling him how badly they wished he'd been there to witness the pumpkin when it exploded into pieces and burst into flames.

"You shoulda seen it," said Harrell. "The whole thing went ka-powie."

"You did it without me?" Leo said, looking genuinely hurt.

"Sorry, Dad," said Charles. "We can do it again now, only better."

"Absolutely not," said Evelyn, slapping her hand on the table.

Phillip agreed with Evelyn on that one. One explosion a day was quite enough. He didn't have a spare extinguisher in the house.

Waverly was wrinkling her nose at the smell of burnt squash.

Evelyn, a dishcloth pressed over her mouth and nose, was aggressively fanning the room with an old *New Yorker* magazine. "I thought the boys were too quiet in here," she said. "I should have checked on them sooner."

"So," said Leo, putting his shopping bags down on the kitchen table, "what have you two learned from this?"

Charles lifted his safety goggles onto his forehead. His lab coat was covered in soot and fibrous orange strands. "Since we controlled for temperature," said Charles, "we think it was the 350-degree heat that increased the power of the explosion, so it did way more than split the pumpkin's ribs."

"I think we should do it again but set the oven higher, like to 450," said Harrell, taking his magnifying glass out of his pocket and looking at the white fire-retardant foam up close.

"Interesting," said Leo. "Don't forget to write up your process and findings in our Google Doc."

"I give up," said Evelyn, dropping the magazine on the counter. "Where's the baby?" said Evelyn, like she was half expecting Leo to say he'd lost Hank on their walk.

"In the living room," Leo said. "He fell asleep in the stroller."

"It would be better if he napped less, wouldn't it?" said Phillip. "The rascal cried quite a bit last night."

"He certainly did," said Evelyn.

"We're Ferberizing him," said Leo. "We're letting him cry it out and learn how to self-soothe. It worked with our kids."

"It's not working with Hank," said Charles. "Can't we try something else?"

Phillip agreed. He hated the sound of the baby crying and the idea of no one coming to his aid. Phillip had half a mind to pick the baby up himself and rock him to sleep.

"It smells like pumpkin pie and bonfires," Waverly said. That was accurate enough.

The noise from the Sweet Spot was drifting in through the open windows; Halloween was one of their busiest nights, and Phillip knew the rowdiness was going to fray Evelyn's last nerve.

She was looking through the paper shopping bags Leo had brought home. "Candy and glue," she said wryly. "How nutritious."

He hoped she would like Ed, because if she didn't, he would never hear the end of it. "Come on, Evelyn," said Phillip, "let's select a flattering outfit for you, something classic. Tonight's the big night."

"I should stay home," said Evelyn, busying herself by folding the bags.

"And do what?" Phillip said. "I don't think you want to greet trick-or-treaters."

"I can stay in my room and chat with my daughter-in-law. I owe her a call."

"You don't owe her anything," said Phillip, putting his hands on her bony shoulders. "I have a good feeling about you and Ed."

"Phillip is a very good matchmaker," Leo said. "He's the reason I met Lauren."

"Phillip knew Mommy?" Waverly asked.

"No," said Phillip. "Your father went on a trip with me to Santa Fe, and I took him to a bug museum."

"Harrell House," said Harrell, "named after me."

"It's the other way around, genius," said Charles.

"Don't call your brother a genius," said Leo. "I mean, unless you're being sincere. Anyway. Phillip knew I was interested in the intersection of entomology and cognitive science, so off we went to this exhibit, and there was Mommy, sketching dung beetles."

"How romantic," said Evelyn.

"It was sweet actually," Phillip said. Phillip spent the next three days of their trip listening to Leo go gaga for a woman he just met.

"If it hadn't been for Phillip," Leo said, "I might never have met Mommy."

"And then what would my name be?" Harrell asked.

Charles sighed and shook his head. "You wouldn't be here, dummy," he said.

"Why not?" said Harrell.

"Don't call your brother a dummy," said Leo.

"What if I'm being sincere?" Charles said.

Charles was a lot like Charley actually. Harrell looked more like her, especially in her hat, but Charles had Charley's blunt and slightly unforgiving nature.

Leo was studying the baby bottle in his hand as if he had no idea what he was supposed to do with it.

Evelyn was looking nervously out the window.

"You're going to like Ed," Phillip said, worrying Evelyn might actually cancel her date. He wanted her to meet this man; Ed was smart and sensitive. He would appreciate her practical nature, and she, if she gave him a chance, would like his romantic one. Maybe Ed would be a reason to move to New York.

"I doubt it," Evelyn said, crossing her arms tightly across her chest, her hands making little fists. "And anyway, what would I have to say to a sculptor?"

"One date," said Phillip. "Have dinner with him, and you'll never have to see him again if you don't want to."

"Wait, can I even use the stove?" Leo asked, holding a kettle near the burned-up range.

"The cooktop is undamaged," said Phillip, "or I hope so." He loved that old stove. He'd lit hundreds of cigarettes back in the day when he smoked, leaning his head down over the flame, and he'd boiled a thousand pots of water for tea.

Leo leaned back and tried a burner. It lit. "Success!" He clapped his hands together. "Waverly and I went on a mission to track down Hank's mother, and we made some progress," he said. "Isn't that right, Waverly?"

"Huh?" said Waverly. She was sitting at the table, reapplying fake blood to her dismembered hand.

Evelyn spun around. "What mission?"

"Do you want to tell them about our exciting trip to the shop today?" he asked Waverly.

"We bought three different kinds of glue," said Waverly.

"No, the other shop," said Leo.

"Candy," said Waverly.

"No, the *other* one."

"Oh, that," said Waverly, looking up. "Daddy talked to two pretty ladies in a look-don't-touch store and gave them his phone number."

"What ladies?" Phillip said.

"Excuse me?" Evelyn said.

Hank began to cry in the other room. "Waverly can fill you in." Leo started to leave the room just as the doorbell rang.

"I'll get the door," Phillip said, putting a hand on Leo's back and following him out of the kitchen. "You feed the baby."

Bumper ran to the door as well, barking his usual combination of dire warning and ecstatic anticipation. Phillip liked the dog just fine, but he'd ruined at least three antique rugs, one of which Phillip had brought to Charley after a buying trip in Turkey. Phillip reached down and held Bumper by the collar. The kids came running to the door too then, ripping open bags of candy for the trick-or-treaters they assumed were on the doorstep.

And they were right! *Gosh*, Phillip thought, looking at the men on his stoop, these costumes were very good indeed. "Hello, Officers," said Phillip, playing along. Charles offered mini Milky Ways, Harrell offered Twix bars, and Waverly, Twizzlers. He would have to talk to the kids about rationing the candy or they wouldn't make it to seven o'clock. This house got hundreds of hits.

Phillip saw then that there were two police cruisers in the street. The hats and badges of these men were authentic, and the guns in their hip holsters were certainly the real thing. "If this is about the fire, we put it out," said Phillip, stepping in front of the children. "It was just a minor mishap in the kitchen."

One of the policemen said, "We're not here about a house fire."

Evelyn came up behind him. "Can we help you?" she said.

"Is there a Leo Aston here?" asked one of the men.

"Yes," said Phillip, a needling of worry in his gut. "Leo?" he called.

Leo came to the door, still cradling Hank as he fed him his bottle. "Live long and prosper," said Leo. Bumper had become alarmed, and Leo tried to quiet him while adjusting Hank in the crook of his arm.

"What can we do for you, Officers?" said Phillip, and then he remembered what day it was. "We know all about Halloween night at the bar, and we don't mind the noise one bit. We're used to it."

"No, sir, we're here to get some information on a possible child abduction," said one.

"Is that your baby?" said the other, pointing to Hank.

"Child abduction?" said Leo, sounding understandably shocked. "In this neighborhood? How terrible."

"Is that your baby?" the officer said again.

Bumper started to growl, low and vicious. Phillip had never heard the dog make that sound before.

"Only for now," Leo said. "We don't get to keep him."

Waverly was cowering behind Phillip, one hand holding on to the leg of his trousers.

"We're going to have to ask you to come down to the station to answer a few questions," the second officer said. "We got a call, saying a man dressed like Spock had taken a baby."

"Oh," said Leo, laughing, which struck Phillip as precisely the wrong thing to do. These men had deadly serious expressions. "No, no, no—"

"You've got it all wrong," said Evelyn archly, stepping in front to stand beside Leo. Phillip thought that was quite brave. "The baby's father abandoned him."

"That's not what we heard," said the first policeman.

"How about you hand me that baby," said the second, putting his arms out to Hank, "while we get to the bottom of this."

Waverly screamed, a high-pitched sound that went right down Phillip's spine, and Hank started to cry.

Bumper barked and lunged at the man, and Phillip grabbed his collar in the nick of time. The dog strained against him, growling, and Phillip leaned over, trying to calm and shush him.

"It's okay, everyone," Leo said, handing Evelyn the bottle so he had a free hand to put on Waverly's shoulder. "I really don't know how to explain—"

"Should I call my lawyer?" said Phillip. He had a good one, but Bill certainly wasn't a criminal attorney. Maybe he could give them a referral?

The second officer had a hand resting on his Taser, and Phillip felt a stab of genuine terror at the idea of any escalation, of Leo getting knocked to the ground and put in handcuffs. He kept a firm grip on the dog's collar as he gathered his grandchildren and pulled them all behind him.

"I think I may have . . . I mean, there's been a misunderstanding," Leo stammered.

Phillip was about to tell Leo to go ahead and hand the baby over when Lauren arrived, taking the stairs up toward the drama that was unfolding on the stoop.

"What's going on?" she said.

"Hey, honey," Leo said. "These police officers are wondering how exactly we ended up with Hank."

"Who's Hank?" said the cop. "We're looking for a . . . Well, I think the woman said her baby's name is . . ." He checked a little pad in his pocket before saying, "Horatio?"

Lauren said nothing. She had frozen, one step below them, her mouth half open.

"Lauren?" said Leo.

"It's okay, I can explain," Lauren said. But then she didn't. Phillip waited, holding his breath, watching her make a face he recognized because it reflected the way he'd been feeling all the time since a recent infamous night in Berlin: caught, doomed, embarrassed. "This *is* Horatio," she said.

"So tell us how you got him," the cop said, keeping his eyes trained on Leo.

Lauren said in a timid voice, "I know Horatio's mother, Felicity Wynn. We were only trying to help, you see, but if . . . well . . ."

Lauren wasn't communicating nearly as well as she usually did.

"Ms. Wynn was extremely upset when she called the station," the cop said. "She said the baby is supposed to be with his father and a nanny named . . ." And again, he checked his pad. "Liam? Does the baby's father know he's here?"

"Not exx-actly," said Lauren. "But, just so you know, for the record or whatever—*is* this for the record?—we've been taking excellent care of him."

"Who's 'we'?" the second policeman asked, his hand still on his Taser, much to Phillip's horror.

"One of her former employees," Lauren said, "and the ex-wife of the baby's father, and me. And all of us," she said, pointing to her family all crammed together on the stoop: Spock, a zombie, a mad scientist, Sherlock Holmes, Phillip, Evelyn, and Bumper.

· · ·

The police officers came inside and told them all to take a seat. Phillip, who needed to use the restroom but didn't dare say so, had Harrell on his lap, pressing uncomfortably on his bladder. Lauren held the baby, Waverly was in Leo's lap, and Charles and Evelyn shared the reading chair. Bumper was banned to the back porch. The cops called Felicity, and when she answered the phone, her voice high-pitched and angry, the police allowed Lauren to explain why Horatio was living at her house. Felicity was utterly confused but eventually calmed down and then started crying. She sniffled into the phone and—to Phillip's and presumably the cops' surprise—asked if Lauren could keep Horatio just a little bit longer.

"And I swear to God I'm going to murder Russell when I get my hands on him," she said, which Phillip felt was a mistake on a recorded police line.

Phillip paid close attention from his seat, and as soon as he was convinced that no one was going to jail, he caught Evelyn's eye and tapped his watch.

"Excuse me," he said to the policeman who was making notes for his report, "could the elderly grandparents be excused?"

They were granted permission, and the two of them went upstairs to the third floor. Phillip's knees clicking and aching all the way up.

"Never a dull moment," Phillip said when they reached the landing.

"My word," said Evelyn. She held out her hand to show him it was trembling.

"Are you shaking because of the police or Ed?"

"Both," she said.

He was surprised that she wasn't using the chaotic events of the past hour as an excuse to cancel. He himself was exhausted. Phillip used the bathroom and then sat in Evelyn's room with his back turned to give her privacy.

"I'm glad you're going," he said. "Ed's a good person. I wouldn't introduce you to anyone who isn't worth your time."

Phillip wiped a bit of black soot off the cuff of his shirt. He was impressed with how well Evelyn could handle a crisis, the oven exploding, police knocking on the door, children wailing. She had more resilience than he did.

"How do I look?" she said, and she stepped in front of him, wearing a drab calf-length skirt and a turtleneck sweater.

"Oh, come on," Phillip said. "You can do better than that."

She stomped her foot at him and went back to the closet. "I don't even know why I'm doing this," she said. "I'm too old."

"You're not," said Phillip gently. They were old, but Phillip hadn't given up on love, not even after his recent heartbreak. "But I don't see why you have to dress like you're the principal of a Catholic elementary school."

"I'm a grandmother who plays bridge. I'm not interesting like you."

"Not everyone finds me so interesting," Phillip said, feeling sorry for himself.

"Oh, please," said Evelyn. "You have an interesting career, you're well-read, you travel, you have all kinds of unusual friends, sculptors and nudists. You make me feel . . . Well, I'm envious."

Evelyn came around to his side of the chair again, wearing the same skirt but with a gray silk blouse.

"Better," he said. "But don't you have a cocktail dress? Or a skirt that actually fits you?"

"What's the use?" she said, and she sat on the bed.

"You've only got fifteen minutes," Phillip reminded her.

"I haven't been out with a man who wasn't my husband since college."

Phillip was, in fact, facing a similar collapse in confidence. "Do you want to know why I'm not in Berlin already?"

He heard an odd creaking sound in the hallway and turned around.

"Mice," Evelyn said. "I saw one out there the other day." Evelyn was looking at him with her penetrating gaze. "And yes, I do want to know why you aren't in Berlin."

"I'm not sure I can bring myself to tell you," he said glumly, running a hand over his head. "And I'm not sure I can ever show my face at the Kunsthaus Schultz again."

"Is that the auction house? But they're expecting you."

"They were expecting me in September."

"I knew it," said Evelyn. "I thought there was something fishy about your sudden return to New York."

He would tell her part of the story, but not all. "There's a man in Berlin named Martin, an absolutely beautiful German, blond and built like a god. He knocked me off my feet when I met him about three years ago, and we've seen each other a few times since. We texted and emailed all the time and seemed to be forming a connection."

"Is he young?" Evelyn said.

"Why is that your first question? Yes," said Phillip, wiping his palms on his slacks.

"How young?"

"Forty-eight maybe? I don't know."

"That's too young for you," she said, her lips pursed in that superior way of hers. "Honestly, Phillip."

"Go put on a dress," he said, when what he wanted was to tell her to go jump in a lake.

"In a minute," Evelyn said. "Go on."

"I had no intention of ever leaving New York, but I was finding it hard here. This house is a lot for me to manage on my own, and it never used to feel so quiet. And then Martin called one day and made a serious pitch, asking me to come and work for him. He mentioned our chemistry over and over, how much he wanted me there. He was relentless. Who goes out of their way to hire a man my age? I took it to mean he wanted something more, and my crush turned into full-blown puppy love and next thing I knew, I'd accepted the job, handed the house over to Leo, and packed my bags. I felt like I was thirty again. I kept imagining the two of us together, working side by side, traveling through Europe. He insisted on picking me up at the airport! We dropped off my bags at the apartment I'd impulsively rented, sight unseen. I was jet-lagged, but it didn't matter. I'd waited months for this moment. He suggested we go to dinner, and we had a marvelous time that night."

"Sounds very romantic," said Evelyn in a singsong voice he didn't appreciate.

"We were walking out of the restaurant when he started chatting about his nearby flat and his art collection and his fetishes and asked if I was interested. I thought he was inviting me to his place for . . ."

"Sex," Evelyn said, like she was proud of herself for saying the word aloud.

"Yes. So we were walking to his apartment, and I suggested we stop at a drugstore to buy condoms."

"Oh my," said Evelyn, with an expression much like the one she'd had when she tried tuna sashimi, a mix of aversion and bravery. Her hands fluttered up to her head and she retwisted her hair in a knot.

"He asked *why*," Phillip said, "and I thought he was being coy, so I said 'so I can finally get you naked and have my way with you,' and I leaned in to kiss him."

"And?"

"He did not want to have sex with me."

"How do you know?" said Evelyn, dropping her hair, which fell loose to her shoulders. "Maybe he's shy. Maybe he wanted to wait until he knew you better."

Phillip felt a sharp pain in his stomach as he recalled the acute humiliation of misread signals, the look of horror on Martin's face, as they stood on Kurfürstendamm near the bombed Kaiser Wilhelm church. "Martin was . . ." It hurt to describe it. "He was appalled, possibly even disgusted, and he told me I was presumptuous and unprofessional, and that he'd never even for a single moment seen me as anything other than a colleague."

"But he tricked you," Evelyn said, blinking her eyes. "Why did he bring up fetishes?"

"He collects Zuni fetishes, these little animals." He showed their size with his fingers. "Martin appreciates Pueblo culture."

"Ohhh," said Evelyn, and Phillip put his head in his hands. "Well, maybe he's not gay," she added naively, trying to soothe his wounded heart and ego.

"He is. He just isn't attracted to me." He checked his watch again. "Ed will be here any minute."

Evelyn hesitated, but then she got up and went back to change.

"So, go on," she said, from the open closet.

"What?"

"What happened next?"

Phillip wished he'd never started this story. It would forever alter the way she saw him. He was a jackass. "When I showed up at the auction house the next day, he suggested we take some time before deciding if we can work together."

"I am so sorry," said Evelyn, from behind him. "This all sounds terrible."

The worst part was that Phillip liked him so much, maybe even loved him. This was a man he'd uprooted his whole life for. "I don't think I can bring myself to go back there, to stand in front of him and apologize. I'll always be the old fool who made a pass at him."

Martin had looked at him that night with an expression he would never forget.

"Can't you get your job back here?" she said brightly. "What if we got an apartment together, like geriatric stars in a sitcom?"

Phillip laughed. At the moment that sounded preferable to confronting the mess he'd made in Berlin.

"Maybe I'll retire." If he stayed in New York, he would want to live and die in this very house, but Leo and Lauren wouldn't want him there permanently, and he certainly wasn't going to let them leave now, after just moving in. He really had no idea where he was going to go, what he was going to do.

Evelyn came out of the closet again and stood in front of him. She was wearing a simple black dress and low heels.

"That's the one," he said. "Where were you hiding it?"

"It's Charley's," she said. "Do you think she'll mind if I borrow it?"

"Not at all," he said, smiling at her. "I didn't know she owned any-thing that classic."

"That reminds me," said Evelyn, "Charley's been dead over ten years. Don't you think it's high time to take her out of the second-floor hall closet and do something respectful with her remains?"

"You're right," he said. "Charley never told me her wishes. I'll talk to Leo about it. I always wanted to sprinkle her ashes in Washington Square Park."

The doorbell rang.

"He's prompt," Evelyn said in a chipper voice. "Unless that's a trick-or-treater or the police or firemen, or who knows who at the door. Are you coming downstairs?"

"You don't need me. Just go have a good time."

"Are you okay?" she said, frowning in concern.

"Me? I'm fine."

"When the time comes," she said, "I'll go to Berlin with you, and we'll take that silly man out to dinner and make him sorry he ever turned you down."

It would be better than seeing Martin alone, but it wouldn't fix his heartache. "Thank you, Evelyn," he said, standing up and hugging her. "I may take you up on that." He had to go back at some point. He'd left four suitcases in the apartment he'd rented.

"I'll be back in two hours," she said, "maybe less. Stay awake, please? Whatever happens tonight, I'm going to need to talk it through."

"I'll be here."

After she left, he found he couldn't contain himself any longer and he cried. He heard voices and music from downstairs and found the sounds comforting. He thought of Charley's atelier by the kitchen, the room he'd never cleaned out because it was too painful and he felt Leo should be the one to choose what to keep and what to discard. The room was a mess, but it had a lovely view out back and was just big enough for a man who had realized only of late that he desperately wanted family around him, needed people coming and going as they had back in the day when he and Charley were young and unstoppable. What would Lauren and Leo think if he asked them to share the house? What would Evelyn think?

His thoughts were interrupted by the sound of those blasted mice again. There was a crash, and he went out to the landing to find little Harrell on the floor in his detective costume, having fallen out of the armoire.

Assignment: Write a one-page descriptive essay on how you spent Halloween weekend. Remember to include as many details as you can to make your essay come alive. Organize your ideas in paragraphs.

<u>What I did for Halloween</u>
By Harrell Aston

1. Dressed up like a detecktive
2. blew up pumkins in the oven
3. the police came and asked questions about the baby we abduckted
4. Hid inside the armwar to SPY. Phillip is sad that the man he liked did not like him back and that made me sad too. Phillip is my grandfather. He fell in love. By acksident he said "lets by kondumbs and be naked" and now he doesn't want to see the man because it will be embarising. I hope Phillip meets a nice man who likes him.
5. SPY some more. my grandma Charley is in the closet but if daddy says ok, we'll put her body in the park.
7. Mommy said curse words three times. She said "fucking bookends" and "dumb ass deckorative tiles" and "I am so sick of making this shit."
7. We went trick or treating and I ate candy til I almost puked. Hank can't have candy because he's only a baby.
8. Daddy is working on computer code so robots can be as smart as people.
9. Wrote Phillip a letter saying sorry for spying

Chapter 24

Ask anyone. Dan was a laid-back. decent. extremely chill guy.

But today he was . . . pissed. It was not true that the baby, or that any baby for that matter, was "no trouble at all," as Olivia had insisted. If the baby was "no trouble at all," then why was Dan stuck spending a whole day babysitting? More annoying was that when Olivia had asked him to step in for her, she'd promised that Horatio—Dan refused to call him Hank out of principle—was a happy, easy little infant. So why, when Lauren opened the door, was he greeted with a red-faced, screaming tyrant in her arms?

"He's not usually so cranky," Lauren said apologetically over the sobs. "He's almost never fussy, especially this early in the day. Come in, come in," she said, stepping back to make room for Dan to enter. Her dog pushed his way in front of her, blocking the entry and sticking his head in Dan's crotch.

"Bumper! Rude!" Lauren said.

The baby hiccupped and then wailed again.

"Is he sick or . . ." Dan let his voice trail off as he took in the sight of the living room. He hadn't been inside the brownstone in a couple of years, and the merging of Leo and Lauren's household into one that was already bursting at the seams was *a lot*. The combination of memorabilia and seventies decor—making Dan half expect Charley herself to swoop in from the kitchen, a cigarette between her thin fingers—with the trappings of a young family (some kind of volcano-related science project on the coffee table, kid art taped on the walls, and small mismatched sneakers strewn around the living room) overwhelmed him. Lauren, dressed in stained overalls and a long-sleeve striped T-shirt, her hair down in tangled waves, looked overwhelmed too.

Dan liked order. If he had permission, half an hour, and a garbage bag, he would walk through the living room and toss out the chipped hotel ashtrays sitting in the windowsills and the postcards tacked on the walls from Scotland, Greece, and Thailand. He would box up the stack of old Playbills and recycle the tattered *New Yorker*s. There was a fishbowl full of restaurant matches, a wicker basket full of corks, and a long row of empty Almaden Chablis bottles, no fewer than fifteen of them, lining the top of the bookcase, some with half-melted candles sticking out of them, wax dripping down the sides.

But on top of all that, there was also a playpen smack in the middle of the living room and a stroller parked in the corner.

"He's just a little colicky," Lauren said, patting the baby on the back and bobbing up and down. "He does well in a front carrier. I can't thank you enough for helping out today."

"Sure," he said. "I guess his real parents feel no responsibility to him whatsoever?" He was aware of the uncharacteristically nasty edge to his own voice. "Sorry, I'm just annoyed by Russell." Dan had no time or patience for the guy who had dumped Melinda and then returned to her when he needed something.

"Do you want to stay here?" Lauren asked, handing him the crying baby. "Leo set up the old crib upstairs, so it might be easier."

"I think we'll take a walk first," said Dan, putting Horatio over his shoulder. "Can I borrow that baby carrier you mentioned?"

Lauren handed it to him off the seat of a worn-leather chair. He took it, feeling a swell of nostalgia. "You know, I used to carry Olivia around in a carrier just like this one."

Lauren looked at the threadbare BabyBjörn. "I think that actually *is* your carrier," she said. "Olivia said she found it in a box at your apartment."

Dan was taken aback. Was nothing sacred?

"You've got our spare key, right?" Lauren was saying, grabbing her bag off the dining room table where a gerbil was running on his wheel. "Come back whenever you want. Olivia and the kids will show up a little after three, and my mom and Phillip will be in and out all day." She pulled her hair up in a ponytail, saying, "I don't know what I'd do without Olivia. We're shipping a whole set of my pieces to California today."

"I didn't know she was helping you, other than with the kids," Dan said.

"She's been almost like . . . my coach," Lauren said. "I'll be crushed when she goes back to work."

Dan would feel better when she went back to work, better when she settled down. He wondered if she needed money.

He laid Horatio down in the playpen while he slipped the carrier on, clipping it and adjusting the straps. Horatio was fussing, but he got calmer as soon as Dan picked him up again. He was a heavy little kid, sturdier than Olivia had ever been. His daughter had been frail and bony, like a little bird. He would never stop worrying about her, no matter how grown-up she got.

• • •

It was chilly outside, leaves skittering down the sidewalk. Dan pulled his coat around Horatio, who was still fussing. He and Lauren parted ways at the bottom of the brownstone steps, Lauren walking east toward the subway to Brooklyn and Dan walking west toward . . . well, he didn't know where he was going.

He felt a familiar weight of responsibility; taking care of a baby was serious business. Exhausting, even when it was joyful. Relentless, even though it could be fun. Russell was way too old for this shit. Dan himself felt too old. Sure, he had put on the BabyBjörn easily, as if he'd used it just yesterday, slipped it over his shoulders and clipped the buckles, slid the chubby baby in. But for some reason, he didn't trust it anymore. He felt a need to keep one arm under the baby's rear end and the other across his back. Dan watched his step as he walked, checking for cars when he crossed the street, even on a green light, and then checking again, on the lookout for rogue couriers on bicycles.

"Dan!"

Dan stopped walking and turned toward the voice, recognizing a woman who'd worked for him about five years before. Or eight maybe. He could not remember her name. "Hey," he said. "How's it going?"

"Wow, you have a baby!"

"No," Dan said, swaying back and forth to keep Horatio calm. "God, no, no, certainly not. I'm just . . . My daughter needed to work today, and—"

"Oh! You're a *grandfather*," she said, clapping her hands together under her chin, delighted. "How wonderful—"

"No," Dan said, "no, he's not Olivia's either. He's the child of . . ." *How to explain?* "He's the son of, or not really the son—the ex-son?—of an acquaintance of my daughter. An enemy of hers actually. And he's not her son either. He's her ex-husband's son. With some other woman I don't know."

She was staring at him now with her head tilted, trying to follow a thread that was not followable.

"It is what it is," he said, although he hated that expression.

"What's going on with you these days?" the woman was saying, flashing a smile. "You look great."

"Thanks," he said. He remembered now that she had hit on him one night after work, back at his place. She'd been confused by Meg's dominant presence, just as Melinda had more recently, and she'd whispered something in his ear about it: *Is your ex going to come after me if I kiss you?* He'd assured her that he was divorced, that Meg did not care what he did or who he did it with. But he also told this waitress that he wasn't interested in her anyway; she was too young, and he was her boss. He had rules about these things.

"How are you?" he said. "You were breaking into acting last I saw you."

"Still am," she said. "I got a bit part in a film, but they cut me out in editing. It was a bummer."

As she rambled on about her dreams of Broadway or at least off-Broadway, it occurred to him that he could hand the baby to this woman (whose name he still couldn't recall) and walk away and that would not be any worse than what Russell had done when he'd hopped on a plane and left his own son behind. Dan would never—under threat of torture—have done such a thing. He might not have a boatload of money like Russell or the love of a woman, but he certainly had a conscience. A big heart, or at least that's what people always told him.

Russell. What a dick. Entitled guys like him always came out on top, the system was rigged that way. Of course Russell was wealthy, of course he took vacations, and of course he had a beautiful, smart wife but traded her in for a younger one anyway.

Russell was off relaxing somewhere while Dan, rushing out for his babysitting shift, hadn't even had time to shave that morning.

• • •

Dan had the spare key to the brownstone in his hand, but after his walk, he rang the bell, in case Phillip or Evelyn was there. The dog barked and scratched at the door. To his surprise, it was Leo who opened it.

"Dan," Leo said, holding on to the dog's collar and looking almost disappointed to see him and Horatio standing there. There were dark rings under his eyes. "Come on in."

"I didn't expect you to be here," Dan said, hoping he could pass the baton and be done with his shift early. "How's it going?"

"I've got some pretty interesting things brewing with my data," Leo said, rubbing his hands together, whether in excitement or because he was chilled, Dan couldn't tell. "I needed somewhere to work where there would be fewer distractions. I actually canceled office hours for the first time. And I kind of forgot about the baby. Don't tell Lauren."

Didn't sound like any batons would be passed quite yet. "It's my shift," said Dan. "No worries."

"Phew," said Leo, mock-wiping his brow.

Dan had always felt connected to Leo. He'd watched him transform from an awkward youth into a happy, well-adjusted, if still slightly awkward adult. Leo was smart as hell and genuinely kind. Dan could not imagine it had been easy to grow up in a household with a mother who took in stray artists the way some people took in stray cats. (She took in stray cats too, of course.) Back in the day, Leo would come down to the bar after school, saying he needed a quiet place to read; imagine a bar being a better place to do homework than a kitchen table, but it was true. Leo had once said to him, "Our kitchen is too noisy, and the third floor is too quiet. This place," he said, indicating the bar, "is just right." And Dan had decided then to change the name of his establishment from the Underground to the Sweet Spot. The name was somehow sexy and cozy at the same time. Dan had a new sign made.

"How are those crickets of yours?" Dan asked, taking off his coat and angling the sleeping baby out of the carrier.

"Amazing," said Leo. "Doing their thing, making sounds that contribute to our understanding of auditory processes in the human brain."

This made zero sense to Dan; what in the world did crickets have to do with brains? Leo was impressive to be sure, but Dan rarely knew what he was talking about.

"But between you and me," Leo said, his sleepy-looking eyes opening wide, "there's a new development that could be quite exciting."

Dan doubted that. "And how is it living back at home?" he said.

Leo glanced around the cluttered room with a look of satisfaction. "The whole family loves it here."

"Are you planning on making any changes?" Dan said. "Some of this wallpaper is looking pretty . . . dated."

Leo seemed a bit surprised by that comment. "Lauren said the same thing," he said. "That if it were up to her, she'd make some changes around here."

What kind of changes? Dan did not dare ask. Was it possible they were thinking of kicking him out? They could raise the rent on him, double or triple it even. They could terminate the arrangement altogether and turn the basement into an art studio for Lauren or an apartment for Phillip or Evelyn.

All Dan wanted was for everything to stay the same. That bar was his livelihood, his greatest love, his home.

•   •   •

Horatio had just woken up from his nap, when Olivia and the kids ran into the house, dropping coats and backpacks on the floor. How could she possibly manage all four of them? He felt a fresh wave of anger at Russell.

"How's Hank?" she said, coming into the living room and taking the baby from him. Waverly was right at her heels.

"*Horatio*," said Dan. "You can't just rename someone else's baby. And didn't you have a hamster named Hank?"

"Named after my second-grade teacher," she said, batting her eyes. "I think I was in love with him."

"With the hamster or the teacher?" said Dan.

"Yes," she said. "And thanks for babysitting today."

He wanted to tell her Horatio had been cranky and difficult, but he hadn't been, not after the first fifteen minutes. So instead he said, "Just don't get too attached. I don't see how this is going to end well for anyone."

"Can I hold Hankie?" said Waverly, tugging on Olivia's sweater.

"Sure," said Olivia. "Go sit on the couch, and I'll hand him to you."

Waverly sat, and Olivia placed the baby in her lap just as Charles came in, his face pinched and furious. "What's the matter?" she said, putting her hands on his shoulders, which were only a few inches lower than her own.

"I'm mad. Can I go in time-out?" he said. "It's too crazy around here."

Dan 100 percent understood. He was ready for a time-out himself.

"Absolutely," Olivia said. "Go upstairs and take a breather."

"When Olivia was very little," Dan said, "she once got so angry, she ran away from home."

"I did?" said Olivia.

"Really?" said Charles, looking intrigued as he tried to imagine his grown-up babysitter as a child.

"She was maybe six years old," Dan said, recalling the days right after he and Meg told her they were separating. "She packed a pillow, a stuffed dog, and a toothbrush."

"Where did she go?" Charles said, his eyes wide.

"Into the pantry," Dan said, "where she sat on the floor and ate cookies. She closed the door and wouldn't open it, even to talk to me."

Charles laughed and shook his head. "That doesn't count," he said. "She was still home."

"It counted to her," Dan said. "For a whole afternoon we slid notes to each other back and forth under the door."

"I guess we can't all run away to places unknown," said Olivia.

Charles pulled on her hand. "Can you help me with math?" he said, heading to the stairs.

"As soon as Melinda arrives," Olivia said.

Dan was angry with Russell and Felicity, sure, but he was pretty ticked off at Melinda too. "That's my cue to leave," he said.

"You should stick around until she gets here," Olivia said. "Maybe ask her out to dinner. She could use a friend."

Dan scowled at that. "I tried that," he said. "She's not interested in me. It sounds like she's hoping for a reconciliation."

"With her ex?" said Olivia. "She despises him."

Dan disagreed. The amount of hate Melinda had for Russell revealed a whole lot of passion.

· · ·

Dan had an hour before he had to be back at the bar, and he found himself wandering toward Melinda's apartment, wondering what he might say to her if he had the chance. Then, when he remembered that she was still at work, he took a left and went to the school instead.

Perkins was housed in an ornate, prewar building smack in the middle of a residential block. Olivia had not attended schools like this one. Dan paused in front of the glass doors where he could see Melinda. She was listening to a young student, her elbows on her desk and her chin resting on her knuckles, concentrating as though this boy were delivering critically important news. The boy gestured as he spoke, and when he came to a stop, he took a bow. Melinda stood up, towering over him, and clapped proudly. Her hair was pulled up, showing off her high cheekbones and her beautiful mouth.

The boy ran off.

Dan pulled the door open and walked up to the desk. "Drama kid?" he said.

She turned at the sound of his voice, clearly surprised by his presence. He had surprised himself. What was he thinking showing up at her work?

"I feel a joke coming on," she said, flashing him her edgy smile. "A bartender walks into a school . . ."

Dan was still looking at the door where the enthusiastic boy had run off.

"That was Connor," Melinda said. "He's doing one of Puck's monologues from *A Midsummer Night's Dream* for the after-school drama club." She sat back down at her desk. "He suffers from terrible stage fright."

"He looked pretty confident to me."

"Well, *now* he does," said Melinda, "after a week of my coaching." She frowned then and said, "I'm sorry I didn't thank you for the flowers you sent. Everything in my life got a little weird. . . . I guess you know about it."

"It's fine," Dan said, trying to hide his hurt feelings. He straightened up and took his hands from his pockets. "I'm here because I'm . . . in a bad mood."

"Okay," she said warily. "Is this about the baby?" She asked like she was inquiring about an unreliable appliance.

"It has to stop," said Dan.

"What does?" She smiled and looked so beautiful then, his chest hurt. "Carbon emissions? Politically incorrect stand-up comedy? Pumpkin-flavored coffee drinks?"

Dan frowned. He wasn't there about the baby at all. He wanted to ask her out and was going about it in the stupidest possible way. "I didn't particularly want to take care of a kid all day. And Olivia is now responsible for *four* children at the same time. It's too much."

Melinda got up, walked around to his side of the desk, and leaned against it, queen of the lobby. She was standing so close to him that Dan was suddenly aware of his unshaven face and unkempt hair.

"I'm very sorry," she said.

"I just feel—and I mean this," he said, his forehead starting to sweat, "that Horatio needs his parents, even if they are complete assholes."

"You're mad, I get it," she said. "Well, I have good news, and I have bad news."

He waited, trying to relax his shoulders.

"The good news," she said, "is that Russell finally called me today."

She'd gone from referring to him as her "shitty ex-husband" to saying his name with intimate familiarity, and in both cases, what it said to Dan was that she still loved him.

"Okay," he said. "And?"

"And . . . Right, well, the *bad* news is, it seems that maybe he's not coming back anytime soon. He's kind of . . . gone."

"Gone?" Dan said. "Gone how?"

"Like gone . . . off the deep end. He's having some kind of psychological crisis—"

"Don't make excuses for him," Dan said, shaking his head at her and hating that he sounded like such a schoolmarm. "Tell him *I* said to get his ass back to his kid. This is unacceptable—"

"Well, I don't know what you want *me* to do about it. I don't have any idea when Russell's coming back. He called from Cancún."

"He's left the *country*?" Dan said, his voice practically shrieking.

"I think he was drunk," Melinda said. "He was ranting about the guys he used to work with and said something about dancing. Russell does not dance."

"And what did he say about Horatio?" Dan asked.

"He asked if he was okay," said Melinda. "And then he said that if Felicity isn't being a mother, he doesn't see why he should have to be a father."

Dan felt like his head was going to explode. "What a piece of shit."

"No salty language on school premises," she said with a softer tone. "It's in the handbook, page fourteen."

"It's just a fact, the man is a piece of shit." And then he blurted out, "You have to . . . go get him."

Melinda smirked then. "What do I look like—a bounty hunter? I'd probably murder Russell if I had such an easy opportunity. And the extradition laws in Mexico are very lax."

"Every time you talk about him," Dan said, "your cheeks get red." His own felt like they were burning.

She looked at Dan then as though she wished *him* dead. He hadn't meant to ignite her anger, but there it was. He was ashamed to admit he found it incredibly sexy.

"You may have had the world's most perfect, peaceful divorce," she said, "but we're not all as lucky as you and Meg. For some of us, divorce is shitty, horrible trauma."

"I'm sorry. I only—"

"I have zero interest in this new version of Russell," she said, with tears in her eyes.

Dear God, he had made her cry. And at work.

"But I'm still allowed to grieve the death of the old one," she said. "The Russell I knew would never in a million years have had a baby, or a young, hot girlfriend, or a leather fucking bracelet. And he wouldn't dump everything and everyone to go to Mexico."

"I'm sorry," Dan said, handing her a tissue from the box on her desk. He'd really done it now. He wanted to wrap his arms around her. Apologize and take her home. "So—what now?" he said. "We pass the kid around until he's eighteen while Russell lives happily ever after in Mexico?"

"Felicity will come back."

"And if she doesn't?"

"Well," she said, "as much as I'd love a trip to the beach, I couldn't drag Russell back here if I tried."

"I'll go with you," said Dan. Where these words came from was beyond him, but the idea of sitting beside this angry woman on an international flight was very exciting. And Dan despised flying. "We could go get him together. We could talk some sense into him."

"Don't be silly," she said.

"I'm not. I'm being completely serious."

She looked at him with an impenetrable expression. "We bring him the kid?" she said.

"We can't take Hank—*Horatio* to a foreign country," said Dan.

Melinda turned away from him and sat back down at her desk. What was he thinking to propose something so preposterous? She wasn't going anywhere with him.

But then she looked up and met his eye. "What about the bar?" she said, almost like she was daring him.

"I've got people to cover for me," he said, watching her. "What about your job?"

"I can't ask for more time off. And this is crazy anyway," she said. "I'm not even sure where Russell's staying."

"Some resort in Cancún," Dan said, shrugging and stuffing his hands in his pockets. "We could figure it out."

She put her reading glasses on and studied something on her computer.

Dan took the hint and began to back away. "I'll be going," he said. "Sorry to bother—"

"Monday's faculty development day." She took her glasses off and glanced up. "I don't have to be here."

He took his hands out of his pockets. "Are you saying . . . ?"

"It would be short," she said, "but I've got miles from my divorce settlement. I could see if there're tickets available."

"Then I'll find a hotel," he said, imagining palm trees, margaritas, heat. "I have a customer who's an agent at Village Travel. He'll get me a good deal."

"It's still going to be expensive," she said with an inscrutable look on her face. "*Two* rooms, this time of year?"

Dan was breathing so shallowly, he felt himself getting dizzy. Was she implying that they should share a room? He felt a tiny seed of hope plant itself in his gut. "Right," he said. "You could come by the bar tonight, and we could talk about it."

"Are you going to make me pay for drinks?" said Melinda, a little smile at the corner of her mouth.

"Not if you order the bad wine." He put his hand out, the same way he had in front of her apartment that night. He tried not to smile, to keep his expression as neutral as hers, but the adrenaline in his body was making him lose control.

"What?" she said, almost accusingly as she took his hand.

"Nothing," he said. "No big deal."

He walked out of the school with a glorious lightness in his chest, a bright energy coursing through him. This was way better than dinner. *Melinda!* He punched his fist in the air, realizing too late that she could still see him from her post in the lobby.

Dear Mommy and Daddy,

I like Hank a lot, but when he cries at night it wakes me up and I can't go back to sleep. Furberizing is mean and it's not working. Also Harrell is loud and gross and I'm too grown up to share a room with him. I will take Pixel with me to live on the third floor. Don't worry. I won't be lonely since Phillip and Grammy are there. I would rather be with them than with Harrell who smells like farts and drives me crazy. He did a Tae Kwon Do kick today and broke my Star Wars Millennial Falcon lego that took me five days to build. Plus Waverly comes in our room all the time and it's too crowded and I can't even hear myself think.

If you don't say yes, I will run away to places unknown or maybe Mexico. Also I'm starving what's for dinner. Have you seen my retainer?

Charles

Act 3

Chapter 25

To step off the plane into the warm, balmy air of Cancún was like waking up after being stone-dead. When they stepped outside, Melinda pulled her wool sweater over her head, rolled up her shirt-sleeves, and lifted her face to the sun.

"I could get used to this," she said. It was magic really. After everything she'd been through in the past year—the shock of betrayal, the loneliness, the uncontrollable surges of rage—she felt she'd earned this trip, this moment to remember that, in spite of all that pain, she was still alive.

Was it the distance from New York, or was it the sun on her skin, or the company of a man she was hopelessly attracted to—or maybe all of these things combined? Whatever the cause, Melinda could not help but smile.

She and Dan rented a VW Golf, and Melinda held one arm out the open window of the car as they headed to the Haven, where Dan's travel agent pal had made a reservation.

"You look like yourself again," said Melinda, as he followed the signs to the airport exit. "You should have warned me that you're not a fan of flying."

"Was it that obvious?" he said.

Melinda smiled. "You traumatized that poor armrest," she said.

Dan smiled, looking a little embarrassed. "I do better with wheels on the ground."

After only twenty minutes in the car, they pulled up to the valet at their hotel. Dan waved off the bellhop and rolled their suitcases across the floor of the empty lobby to check in.

"Two garden-view rooms with king beds," said the buxom receptionist, a pink poppy tucked behind her left ear. "I've got one room on the second floor and one on the fourth."

Two nights, two rooms. And they weren't even on the same floor. Melinda had hinted—pretty obviously, she'd thought—that she was willing to share. Dan had not taken her up on it, and she was both disappointed and a bit relieved.

He was happily drumming his fingers on the counter while the receptionist activated their key cards. "Can you tell me if there's a Russell Dunlop staying here?" he asked her.

Melinda knew the answer already. Russell stayed in gold-standard, familiar hotels wherever he went, preferably Waldorf Astorias, Four Seasons, or Ritz-Carltons. Finding him would not be the problem.

The woman clicked on her keyboard again, and then—predictably—shook her head. "No Russell Dunlop," she said, and handed him their passports and key cards.

"Well," Dan said with a laugh, "it's not like we thought it was going to be that easy."

They rolled their bags toward the elevator, passing a couple, newlyweds by the look of them, walking with their arms wrapped around each other's waist. Melinda envied them as much as she pitied them. Would the young woman break the guy's heart, or would he break hers? She did not like the feelings of bitterness that coursed through her, but there they were. Russell had destroyed, perhaps permanently, her long-standing belief in true love.

Dan pressed the two buttons for their floors. "What do you say we get a quick bite to eat before we start our wild-goose chase?" he said, as the elevator went up.

"I'm going to change first," Melinda said. "Should we meet downstairs in a few minutes?"

"Sure. I'll take this one," he said when they reached the second floor. He handed Melinda her key. "The view might be better from the fourth. See you in fifteen?" He stepped out and waved while the doors closed again.

Melinda was alone. On her floor she walked down the hall and opened the door to her room. It was perfectly satisfactory, not the kind of place where she and Russell used to stay, but pleasant and clean. She stood at the window for a long time, taking in the view of the palm trees and the pool. It looked so inviting, Melinda was tempted to jump in from her balcony.

Russell wouldn't have liked this room. Russell would have insisted on an ocean view.

She dropped her purse on a rattan chair, wishing already that she and Dan had more time before they would have to return to real life. She opened her suitcase and changed into an outfit more fitting for the tropics.

Before going to meet Dan, she called Russell's cell phone and left a message, letting him know where she was and why. Then she took the stairs down and walked into the lobby in her white linen dress and sandals, looking around for Dan. She did a double take at the sight of a guy wearing a baseball cap, shorts, and flip-flops. She smiled at him. "Look at you," she said, trying not to ogle Dan's flat stomach and muscular calves. He looked so boyish and handsome, she almost had to sit down.

"You're a vision," he said.

"Just don't look at my legs," she said. "They haven't seen the sun in months."

"We can get sandwiches or burgers by the pool," he said, cuffing the sleeves of his button-down shirt, "or were you hoping for something else?"

"Sounds perfect," she said, "but before we do that, I want to stick my feet . . . in there," and she pointed through the lobby and out to the ocean. The water was a color Melinda had forgotten existed.

Was it the salt water that had such a strong effect on them? Or the warm air? She wasn't sure, but they pretty much forgot all about Russell on their first day. Instead, they ate fish tacos and then went back to their respective rooms to change into bathing suits. After taking a swim and fully appreciating the sight of Dan in trunks, Melinda dozed on a lounge chair by the pool. When she woke up, the sun was lower and Dan was sitting next to her with a pile of snorkeling gear on the plastic table between them. "I booked us a boat tour," he said. "You up for it?"

Through the shimmering water, they saw starfish, manta rays, and schools of absurdly bright fish. At one point, Dan took her hand and pointed to the coral reef below where a sea turtle swam by. She squeezed his hand back.

Dan suggested she go to the spa before dinner, so she did. She felt so relaxed, so unguarded, that she burst into tears on the massage table, a kind of deep, cathartic keening that somehow made her feel better rather than worse.

They ordered margaritas with dinner and leaned in to hear each other over the mariachi band. Melinda pulled on the straps of her dress so they wouldn't rub her sunburned shoulders.

"Can I tell you a secret?" Melinda said, the tequila making her loose and light. "When I first met you at the bar, I thought Phillip might be hitting on me, and I'm not going to lie—I found him incredibly charming."

"You're not alone," Dan said. "Phillip breaks hearts everywhere he goes. Can I tell *you* a secret?"

"Sure." She put her elbows on the table, her chin on her fists.

"Meg," he said, "broke my heart in about a million pieces when she divorced me. I hated her for it."

Melinda was stunned. "But you said . . . But you get along so well. You act like best friends."

"We are friends now," he said, "but when she left me, I was wrecked and angry and beside myself."

"How'd you get over it?"

"It took years. I faked a peaceful divorce for Olivia's sake, but in reality, it was hell. I should have told you this sooner. I understand you better than you think."

Melinda was both relieved by his confession and terribly ashamed. "You handled heartbreak with grace and dignity," she said, "while I've been a total nightmare. You don't even know the worst of it."

"Really?" he said, his eyebrows lifting. "So . . . what's the worst of it?"

The waiter brought two more margaritas. Melinda took a sip of hers, thinking it would be best if she kept her bad deeds to herself.

"Go on," Dan said after the waiter left.

"I can't tell you," she said. He would never look at her the same way again. He would know exactly how conniving and bitter she was.

"It's just us here," he said. "What is it?"

Melinda squeezed her eyes shut and took a breath. Then she leaned forward, looking Dan in the eye. "There's this app I got," she said. "I used it to photoshop images of Felicity and Zach to make Russell think they were having an affair." She swallowed, watching him to gauge his reaction. He kept his face completely still. "I left the pictures for him to find because I wanted to ruin their relationship. I thought it would be fair to hurt him as much as he hurt me."

Dan didn't say anything.

"In my defense," Melinda went on, "the pictures were ridiculous, and I was honestly shocked he fell for it. And I never imagined he would respond by hopping on a plane."

Dan was quiet for so long, she assumed he was too appalled to say anything. He had every right to be.

"You're disgusted," she said, folding her napkin and putting it on the table.

"That might not have been your finest moment," he said, with a lift to his broad shoulders, "but I understand."

"I doubt that," she said. "You wouldn't have done something so mean and deceitful."

"I'm on your side here," he said, putting his hand on the table between them. "But it doesn't seem like revenge is making you feel any better."

"Some of it did, temporarily anyway." She had laughed out loud in the copy shop when she'd printed the fuzzy pictures, but Dan was right: she was feeling pretty rotten about it now. "I'll tell him the truth," she said. "I keep saying what a horrible person Felicity is, but I'm such a bitch."

Dan reached over and put his fingers on her bare forearm, sending a tingle down her spine. "You're not a bitch," he said.

Maybe it wasn't the most romantic sentiment he could have expressed, but she would take it. "Thank you, Dan."

"I'm sorry we didn't stick to the plan today."

Melinda wasn't. She'd had a wonderful time.

"Tomorrow," he said, "we'll get up early and we'll find Russell. I guess we better get some sleep tonight."

That was the last thing Melinda wanted him to say.

• • •

She was lying in bed, feeling ridiculous to be wearing the white silky pajamas she'd brought. Her room was so quiet. She had wanted to stay up and keep talking, take a walk on the beach maybe. She wasn't the least bit tired.

She got out of bed and opened the door to the balcony, feeling the warm breeze on her face. The tequila she'd had earlier was making her feel gutsy.

She went back inside and picked up the phone on the desk, dialing Dan's room number. She would ask him to come to her. Fuck it, she would just ask, why not? It rang, four, five, six times. Dan never picked up. Melinda was mortified.

Where was he? Had he gone back down to the bar without her? Was he hitting on women?

She crawled in bed and tried to sleep, the burned skin on her back stinging as it rubbed against the sheets.

• ○ •

The next morning, Melinda woke up early and turned on the BUNN coffee machine in her bathroom. She sat on her balcony and sulked, drinking her coffee as the sun came up over the pool. If they needed to find Russell so badly, then fine, she would find him. She called the three most likely hotels where he would be staying, and sure enough, Russell was currently checked in at the Ritz-Carlton.

Over a late breakfast at the restaurant by the pool, she let Dan make a string of suggestions about how they should go about finding Russell before she looked up from her mimosa, saying, "I already know where he is."

Dan, his mouth full of scrambled eggs, looked up at her and swallowed. "How? Why didn't you say anything?"

"I just found out. It was an educated guess. We've been here before."

"You came to Cancún?" Dan said, looking unreasonably surprised at the idea, "with Russell?"

"Maybe five years ago?" Melinda said. "So I called the hotel where we stayed, and bingo."

"What hotel?"

"The Ritz-Carlton."

Dan put his fork down. "Nice," he said. "Must be pretty elegant."

"No, I mean, sure," said Melinda, "but I like it here, actually. I think this pool might be my favorite place on earth."

"Well," Dan said, wiping his mouth with his napkin, "looks like we're going to the Ritz."

Melinda was loath to leave the peace of this little haven. The idea of finding Russell at the Caribe Bar & Grill by the beach, possibly with Glen and Stan and that asshole Ken, was enough to make her break out in hives. They would be nice to her face and then talk shit about her later, telling one another how smart Russell had been to trade her in for Felicity.

"We don't really have to *go* there, do we?" she said. "I left a message for him at the front desk and on his room phone, and on his cell. I'm sure he'll call."

"I thought we came to Cancún to track him down and tell him in person to go home," Dan said. "Otherwise why did we come all this way?"

Not to have sex apparently. "Fine," said Melinda, sighing as she pushed her own chair back. "Let's go get him."

. . .

They drove about twenty minutes to the Ritz-Carlton, a different kind of hotel—grand and expensive, with fountains, marble floors, and massive urns of fresh flowers—situated on a skinny stretch of beach. She'd gotten in an argument with Russell in this very lobby when they were there together because when they arrived, he'd gotten the luggage from the cab, taking his suitcase out and accidentally leaving Melinda's behind in the trunk. They'd filed a claim with the taxi company, but the bag was gone.

"Wow," said Dan grumpily, gazing at the large, meandering, sculpted pool, "*this* is a heck of a lot nicer than the shitty little swimming hole at our hotel."

"I disagree," said Melinda, thinking of how peaceful she'd felt sitting with Dan on the broad steps of the shallow end. "I prefer ours."

. . .

Searching for Russell at the Ritz—and coming up empty-handed—did not seem to improve Dan's mood. He hadn't said much as they checked the restaurants, walked around the pools, scanned the beach, and left another message at the front desk. He'd said even less on the drive back to their hotel. He'd fallen asleep—or pretended to—on the beach that afternoon while Melinda tried to make small talk, and he'd gone back to his room right after they'd had dinner. Melinda sat on her balcony in her pajamas, wondering what she'd done wrong, if Dan was having his one cigarette of the day on his own balcony two floors below.

She went inside and pulled the sheets back to climb into bed, when she heard a knock on the door. She got up and opened it, hoping she could ask for an extra towel from housekeeping. But Dan was standing there, still wearing his shorts and button-down.

"I'm sorry if I was being kind of a dick today," he said.

She shrugged and touched the buttons of her pajama top. "You were disappointed," she said. "Russell was probably playing golf. If we go earlier tomorrow, we can probably catch him at breakfast."

"That resort was pretty spectacular," he said.

"The Ritz? It's nice," said Melinda. And then she stepped back. "Do you want to come in?"

She opened the door wider, and he walked past her into her room. "It's just like mine," he said. He sat in the chair while Melinda perched across from him on the edge of her bed.

"Are you going to tell me what's bugging you?" she said, squeezing her hands between her knees.

"I'm frustrated," he said.

"About Russell?"

He ran his hand over his head. "No," he said. "Or yes, in a way."

"I wish we didn't have to leave tomorrow. I'd do anything to spend a week here." Melinda looked out the window toward the pool. "You know, I called you last night. I was bored. But you didn't pick up."

"You did?" he said, tilting his head. "I left my room but only for a few minutes."

"Where'd you go?"

"I came here," he said. "I was going to knock, but I thought you might be asleep already."

Melinda felt her cheeks growing warm. "Well, you should have knocked anyway. Tell me honestly, do you regret taking this trip?"

"Not at all," Dan said. "I think what I realized is that I don't actually care if we find Russell. I came here to be with you." He smiled sadly and said, "I mean, you know this already, but I happen to like you. A lot."

He stood up so abruptly that Melinda suddenly felt cold. She watched him lean into the minibar. *Holy shit*, he was attractive. He was built so differently than Russell, who was slightly barrel-chested and knobby-kneed.

"Do you want something?" he said "Water? Ten-dollar chocolate chip cookies?"

"You like me?"

"Melinda," he said, studying a bottle of club soda, "please don't embarrass me."

"What?" she said. "You mean, you *like* me?"

He turned around empty-handed and stood, leaning against the wall. "Isn't it completely and totally obvious?"

"Not at all," she said flatly. She hoped her pajama top was showing a little cleavage. Her heart was pounding. "You've been distant, especially today."

He looked up at the popcorn ceiling. "Maybe I wish I could have gotten us rooms at the Ritz," he said.

"Why?" Melinda said. "I certainly don't want to be anywhere near Russell. I love this hotel."

"I didn't knock because I assumed you aren't ready for anything, like . . . that."

"For you?" Melinda sat up straight and raised her chin. "I'm ready." She tried to steady her breathing. "You have no idea how ready."

"Well," he said, smiling, "I *did* knock tonight." He looked at her, and then he came closer.

"Melinda," he said.

She felt light-headed and licked her lips. "Dan."

He kneeled in front of her, taking her hands. "Why on earth did you think I came on this absurd trip?"

It had been thirtysomething years since she'd wanted a man who wasn't her husband to kiss her. *Ex*-husband, that is. And thank God.

"I'm crazy about you," he said. "I was hoping you would make some kind of move," he said, "or send a signal or something. Anything really."

"A signal?" She leaned toward him, but then she wasn't sure what to do. Should she put an arm around his neck? Put her hand on his face? What did people do? Her nerves were going haywire, giving her skin pins and needles.

"Are you cold?" he said, sliding his hand around her back and leaning in to kiss her.

They both startled at the sound of aggressive knocking on the door. Dan called over his shoulder, "Go away."

"It's pretty late for housekeeping," Melinda said. Dan kissed her then, and Melinda forgot all about the door and put her arms around him, pitching too far forward and almost falling off the bed.

"Melinda?" a voice called out. The visitor knocked again, louder this time. "It's me."

Melinda held her breath. "Russell?" she said.

"Russell," Dan whispered.

"Holy shit," she whispered. They'd hadn't managed to find Russell, but he had found them.

Chapter 26

Russell felt good getting so many things off his chest. He dabbed his eyes and blew his nose into his cocktail napkin. He pushed the little paper umbrella to the side of his glass and finished the last sip of his piña colada, while a warm Caribbean breeze blew past his bare legs. There was a band playing, and Russell found it impossible not to tap his foot to the sound of the guitar and trumpet. The drink was delicious, sweet and tangy. He decided he would have another and raised his finger to get the attention of the waiter.

"Oh, let's not," Melinda said. "I mean, you've had quite a few, along with all the extra shots. Maybe we should get you in a cab."

Melinda looked very pretty; she was glowing with sun and with some kind of youthful energy. He leaned in to get a closer look. "You look happy, Melinda," Russell said. "You're beautiful. Your dress really fits you, like a . . . dress."

"I'll get the check," said the man—who was he?—as he finished his Corona out of the bottle. Russell preferred his creamy drink and its curvy glass. Why was it still empty? That was a problem with a remedy, unlike so many other problems. The man—Don? Doug?—was trying to flag the waiter.

"Another round on me," Russell said. "Where's the fire?" He smiled because of something to do with fires but he couldn't think what exactly. He did not appreciate Melinda's insistence on ending the evening. "I've got nowhere to go and no one to see." From his plastic chair, he tried a dance move, shimmying his shoulders and biting his bottom lip in a way he thought might be attractive, sexy even.

Russell saw Melinda glance over at the man but didn't know what her look was meant to convey, other than maybe it was, in fact, sexy to see him let loose like this?

"Look, Russell," Melinda said, "you know you have to fly back to New York tomorrow. So why don't you get some sleep and meet us back here for coffee in the morning? Doesn't that sound like a good idea?"

It had, when she'd brought it up two piña colada milkshakes ago, but now he didn't like the sound of it. Russell felt the sadness well up again. What was in New York for him? Nothing. No job, no wife, just a helpless baby he wasn't equipped to care for. He cried a little, comforted to feel Melinda's hand thumping his back.

"Just think about how happy you'll be to see little Horatio," Melinda said. "You must miss him. He's a cute kid."

"I wasn't meant to be a father," Russell said, and he felt very sad then because he really loved the little guy.

"Too late for that," the man said.

Russell did not like his tone. He lifted his head and looked at him. "Who are you?" Russell said.

"Dan," the man said.

"Sure, yeah, but *who are you?*"

"I'm Melinda's friend," Dan said, "and I've taken care of your son myself. You're a very lucky guy."

"Lucky?" Russell said. Now that was true. He was lucky.

"But," he said, "I want you to know I *worked* for everything I have," he said, poking his finger hard onto the surface of the table.

He felt a need to impress this man, whoever he was. He had such a nice head of hair. "Why does everyone have such nice heads of hairs?" he asked.

"Your hair is just fine," said Melinda.

"It's thinning," said Russell. "It's *thinning*."

"No," said Dan.

"It is," said Russell. "It's thinning, and I can't stop it. My father was bald, you know. My father died and left me a lot of money but not enough hair."

"Your hair is nice," Dan said.

Russell liked him then and leaned over to slap him on the shoulder. "I like you," he said. "A round of drinks on me." Russell chewed on his pineapple garnish. The juice ran down his chin and onto his crotch.

Melinda sighed in that way she sighed whenever she was annoyed with him, usually about the dishwasher.

"Party pooper," Russell said. "Come on, remember when we were young and we had good times, didn't we? We went on trips to places just like this. Well, not like *this* maybe," he said, looking around him at the dumpy, rectangular pool. "But Cancún! We came here and had fun."

"Yeah, well, you kind of ruined our 'fun' when you started fucking Felicity."

"Now, now," said Dan, "let's not get into all that."

"Why not?" said Melinda.

"Well, no, she's right about that," said Russell, and he tried to sit up straighter to show he was responsible. "I'm sorry, Melinda." Her name was becoming very difficult to pronounce. "Me-lin-da, I'm sorry about what I did that. Or no, wait." Was he sorry? He did not want any more lies between them. "No, I'm not sorry exactly, more like *sorry*, because I should have divorced you sooner than I did because I love you, Melinda, and I didn't mean for this to happen, but I don't *love* you anymore like *that*, not after Felicity came along and, my God, Felicity, I love Felicity, she is so . . ." He could not come up with the word and turned to Dan. "She is so . . . what?"

"I have no idea," said Dan.

"Hot!" said Russell. "She is so hot."

"I wouldn't know," said Dan. "I happen to think Melinda is hot."

"Who are you?" asked Russell again. He looked like a rock star. Or a car mechanic.

"A friend," he said. "But let's get back to the point."

"What's that?" said Russell because he really had no idea.

"Your baby," Dan said.

Again with the baby? "Baby maybe schmaby," said Russell. "Felicity didn't think she could get pregnant, so it was a miracle really. A miracle. Can I tell you something?"

"Sure," said Melinda with a funny little lilt to her voice.

He wondered if she was humoring him, and he squinted his eyes. "Are you just saying that?"

"Not at all," she said. "I really want to know what you have to say."

"I tried to get my job back so Felicity would love me again. I found Glen at the Waldorf, and you know what he said? He said nope, no way, get lost, scram. Shoo fly. He"—Russell started to sob—"he really hurt my feelings."

"Okay," said Melinda, patting him on the back.

"Felicity doesn't want me, and Glen doesn't want me, and no one wants me."

"Horatio wants you," she said. "I think there's a chance you and Felicity will be just fine. But you have to go home."

"No," he said. And he wiped his nose on the tablecloth.

He felt angry. "She's not so perfect. You know why? For one thing, Horatio is a stupid name," he said, and sat back in his chair. "So there."

"I agree," said Dan. "That was a bad choice."

"That's what nicknames are for," said Melinda. "We call him Hank."

"Hank? Hank," said Russell. He thought it sounded nice. "Felicity won't like it."

The waiter came, but as Dan asked for the check, Russell outsmarted him by shouting, "Another round of water for the horses," he said, "but make it piña coladas on the horse. *House.*"

"I'm okay actually," said the man to the waiter.

"Yeah, I'm good," said Melinda.

"You are good," Russell said, because she really was a very good person. "You're the best. Oh, Melinda, I'm so glad we can be friends now. You were so mad at me." He turned to the waiter, handed him his empty glass and nodded for another as he was remembering Melinda's hospitality in her tiny apartment. She made him coffee in the morning. She held the baby so he could spend as much time as he needed in the bathroom. "You hated me so much, but then you took me in when I had no place to go. You gave me shelter. God," he said, suddenly remembering, "where is the baby? I left Horatio with you, but if you're here, then where is he?"

"I told you," said Melinda. She was talking slowly in a tone he did not appreciate. She sounded like a schoolteacher. "He's with Lauren, who's a friend of Felicity. But Horatio needs his parents to come back now and take care of him."

"His parents," repeated Russell. "A baby needs his parents."

"That's right," said Melinda. "And by parents, I mean, *you*."

"You're not teachers," said Russell, narrowing his eyes at them, beginning to grasp something: Dan had his hand on the back of Melinda's chair. Not touching her exactly, but almost touching her. "Wait, wait, wait, hold up a minute. Are you two . . ." He pointed from Dan to Melinda and back to Dan. "Is he . . . What's the deal going on between you two anyway?"

Dan shrugged, but Russell wasn't falling for *that*. And then Melinda shrugged too! It was as though they were choreographing their shoulder movements to be in sync.

"You're together!" Russell said, pleased to have cracked the mystery, and then he started crying again. "I'm happy for you, Melinda," he said, "I really am."

"Okay, then." And again she patted his back. This time it felt condescending rather than supportive, so he did a little shrugging of his own.

"How about we call it a night?" Dan said.

"I'm happy for you," Russell said. "I want you to be happy too, Melinda. Drinks on me." But he had no life. He'd lost Melinda, which made him feel adrift. He'd lost Felicity, which made his heart break.

And he'd lost—as in literally lost—his son, which made him feel like a terrible person.

"Ooops," he said. He was so sleepy that just for a second, he put his head down on the table, halfway into the basket of corn tortilla chips, and closed his eyes.

• • •

He woke up with no idea where he was. When he turned his head to his left and then to his right, he was met on both sides with a set of bare feet, one with pink polish on the nails, one with scraggly hair on the toes. *Dear God, what was this?* Had he had a *threesome?* He sat up, tasting something pineapple and putrid in his mouth, as the previous night began to come back to him: the voice mail he'd finally listened to from Melinda. Frozen cocktails by a pool with her and some man, most with a shot of rum on the side. Melinda telling him to come home.

He was still fully clothed in his Bermuda shorts, golf shirt, and boat shoes. He crab-walked his body, between Melinda and the man, to the foot of the bed and went into the bathroom, where he peed and washed his hands, taking note of the bags under his bloodshot, swollen eyes, his red nose, his thinning hair that was looking slightly greasy. There was—*what was that?*—a corner of a tortilla chip stuck behind his ear. He checked the pockets of his shorts and was relieved to find his wallet, phone, and sunglasses. He could sneak out of here, go back to his hotel, and continue nursing the humiliation of first being betrayed by Felicity and then being blown off by Glen and the guys. Glen had looked at him like he was a stalker.

"Dude," he'd said. "What the fuck?"

Russell slowly opened the door to the bathroom and found Melinda's friend standing directly on the other side.

"Good morning," the guy said quietly, looking younger than Russell had remembered.

"Hello," said Russell. So much for sneaking out. Well, he would make his excuses and leave anyway. He was a grown man, and no one could tell him what to do or guilt him into anything.

"Dan," Dan whispered, a hand on his own chest, "in case you don't remember. How's your arm?"

Russell rolled his left shoulder, noting that it was stiff and sore.

"You rolled off the couch last night," Dan said, "after we got you upstairs. We tried to get you to sleep on the floor, but you got a little belligerent." He smiled and then cocked his head in the direction of the door. "Let's go grab some breakfast and let Melinda sleep a little longer."

"I'm not feeling so great," said Russell.

"I bet."

"I was thinking I'd head back to my hotel, get a little rest."

"I didn't get any sleep either," said Dan with a slightly accusing tone.

Was Russell supposed to apologize for that? Well, he wouldn't. He'd come last night to see Melinda, and it was not his problem this interloper was caught in the cross fire of their conversation. Were he and Melinda dating? Was he worthy of her? He did not look like much in his rumpled clothes and flip-flops.

"I'd really like to talk to you," Dan said.

"Is that right? Sure, fine," said Russell, almost as a challenge, "I could use a coffee."

They headed out together, and Dan closed the door slowly with exaggerated concern over waking Melinda, putting the *Do Not Disturb* sign on the handle.

They did not speak as they took the elevator down to the ground floor and walked through the lobby toward the pool, past terra-cotta pots of pink and purple flowers on the stone-tiled patio. This was no Ritz-Carlton.

"Scene of the crime," Dan said, as they sat at the exact table they'd taken the night before.

Russell remembered being there, he remembered music, but to his dismay, he could not recall much of their conversation. He hoped he hadn't said or done anything undignified.

The place had a very different vibe so early in the morning. There was no band playing now, just some spa music coming from invisible speakers. A lizard sunbathed on the trunk of a potted tree next to him. An exhausted-looking father was sitting on a lounge chair, watching his three children play, argue, and scream in the pool. Russell watched, feeling a mixture of elation and guilt that he himself was not parenting at that moment; how could anyone take care of a baby with a hangover as crushing as this one?

The waiter came over, and Russell ordered a coffee.

"No piña coladas today, amigo?"

Dear God, had this man been here all night? "Not today."

"No dancing either? Too bad, you have moves, man." And he laughed.

Dancing? Well, that was absurd. Russell did not dance. "Just coffee and dry toast, please."

Dan was smiling. He ordered coffee as well, along with a cheese omelet, a side of bacon, and fresh fruit.

After the waiter walked away, Russell said, "I take it you're on a statin? Otherwise a man your age couldn't get away with a breakfast like that."

Dan shook his head. "My LDL is under a hundred, so I'm good."

Russell wished he hadn't brought it up. He felt a competitive urge to dominate this guy, to make it clear that in the hierarchy of men, Melinda's new one was beneath him in every respect. "So what do you do, Dan?"

"I run a bar in Greenwich Village. A place called the Sweet Spot. I've had it since the early eighties. You?"

"Corporate real estate attorney," said Russell, sitting back and crossing his ankle on his opposite knee. "Retired." He scraped at a bit of avocado stuck to his salmon-colored shorts. He hated to think he'd been sloppy the night before. His shoulder ached; had he really fallen off the couch?

"What's it like to be a bar owner?" he asked with a little hint of a smile.

"Well, I don't *own* it exactly," said Dan.

"You said 'have,' didn't you?"

"Yes, but technically it's owned by a friend."

"Technically? You mean . . . factually?"

"Sure, but I've got a pretty favorable arrangement," Dan said. "It works. I've done well."

"I don't see how," said Russell.

"Excuse me?"

"You have no capital investment in the property after all these—what did you say?—thirty-some-odd years?" said Russell. "That's almost tragic."

Dan looked flustered. "Look, buddy, you don't know what you're—"

"All you have to show for your years of work is the income you've earned, rather than a major appreciation of the real estate. You can't retire and cash out."

"It's not like that," Dan said. "My friend never raised my rent, not once, so I have a really great deal—"

"Who pays for repairs? Let's say the floors need replacing."

"It depends, I guess, but in general? I do."

Russell actually felt sorry for him. "Your so-called friend has screwed you out of hundreds of thousands of dollars, maybe more. You should have bought your own place decades ago. Then you'd have a nest egg. What will you live on when you retire? I hope you've invested your profits sensibly."

Dan's neck was turning red, and a little vein in his temple was pulsing. He cleared his throat and shifted in his chair. "I'm not here to talk about me," he said.

That had almost been too easy. But the guy should really listen; Russell's assessment of his situation was sound.

"Oh, really? Well, what's on your mind, Dan?"

"Honestly, I'm disgusted," Dan said with a very matter-of-fact tone.

Russell tilted his head back and smiled; who did this guy think he was?

"You left your baby," Dan went on. "You abandoned him. Felicity is off doing her thing. . . . Well, I'd kind of like to know how either one of you sleeps at night."

"This is a family matter," Russell said, blown away by the nerve of this loser, "and absolutely none of your business."

"Bullshit," said Dan. "My daughter babysits him every day, and Melinda should not have to deal with your shit after what you put her through. Given the amount of rum you chugged last night, you may not remember what Melinda and I had to say to you, but—bottom line? You have to get on a plane *today* and fly to New York to take care of your kid. Let's hope Horatio still remembers you."

Ugh. The mention of rum, planes, and his kid not knowing him made Russell nauseated. He sat back then as the waiter approached with cups and saucers on a tray, pouring the steaming coffee and arranging the creamer and the sugar on the table.

"Leave the pot," said Russell sternly.

The waiter set down the metal thermos and walked away. Russell then aimed his coldest stare at Dan.

"You don't know anything about me," Russell said, "and you don't know anything about the situation I'm in, so why don't you keep your thoughts on my life to yourself?" He put his napkin in his lap, picked up his spoon, and poured cream in his coffee. Feeling bloated from his night of excess and envious, frankly, of this man's thirty-four-inch waist, he opted for artificial sweetener.

Dan was droning on now, drinking his coffee black. "Hank—that's his nickname—likes being carried in my daughter's old front pack. He was cranky when I picked him up the other day, but once we took a walk, I found it was very easy to make him laugh."

Russell knew he was bullshitting because Horatio wasn't even smiling yet.

"And I think he likes it when Olivia brings him down to visit me in the bar: there are interesting people, the smell of hops, dim lighting."

Russell tightened his grip on his spoon. "I'd rather my baby not be brought to some sketchy establishment."

"Oh, I agree," Dan said. "None of this is good for him. So please, with all due respect"—he leaned forward in his chair—"get your fucking ass back to New York and own your responsibilities. Got it?"

Russell heard him but could not respond because he felt like he might throw up. His mouth filled with saliva. He shook his head as the waiter placed the toast in front of him, waving it away. The smell of bacon was both enticing and revolting. He burped into his napkin.

"Mmmm," said Dan, admiring his breakfast. "Perfect, thank you. And may I have an order just like this one to go? With some home fries?" He looked at Russell. "Melinda loves home fries."

"I know," said Russell. "I was married to her for thirty years."

The waiter left, and Dan took a bite of eggs and then salted them. Russell averted his eyes and watched the children splashing one another in the pool.

"I wasn't ready to be a father," said Dan, picking up his bacon with his fingers. "But then my daughter came along," he said with a shrug. "I'd throw myself on train tracks for her. I'm sure you feel the same way about your son."

Russell despised this self-righteous man.

"What if I told you," Dan said, "that Felicity never cheated on you?"

That was the first interesting thing this man had said. "I'd say you don't know what you're talking about. I saw photographic proof." Russell took a small sip of ice water. His stomach was roiling and his palms were sweaty. He needed Pepto Bismol urgently.

"You want to know what else I think?" Dan said.

"No," said Russell, wishing this bartender would shut the fuck up.

"And this actually *is* none of my business, but I think you retired too early."

That comment was the second interesting thing he'd said. It was correct at its core. "As a matter of fact," Russell said, "I was planning to return to my position, but unfortunately, it's been filled."

"That's what you said last night. But if I were you, walking around with all that experience, all that legal knowledge about real estate stuff, I'd take on some pro bono cases, do a little good for mankind and my community. Help people who get unfairly evicted and take on slum lords, stuff like that."

No, Russell would not do that, but he could be a consultant. *Interesting*, he thought. He *was* experienced and knowledgeable. This Dan had made a very good point. He could work freelance and keep flexible hours.

Dan took another bite, wiped his mouth, and sat back in his chair. "I don't know you, Russell, but you're not some deadbeat dad. So why don't you go home and impress the hell out of Felicity, like, really wow her. Be the father and man she expects you to be. What do you think?" Dan asked.

"What I think," said Russell, "is you talk too much, you eat too fast, you're pushy, and you're a lousy businessman. Instead of telling *me* what to do, why don't *you* go back to New York and tell your 'friend' he should sell you the bar at a negotiated rate, somewhere between what it was worth in the eighties and what it's worth today. In case you didn't know, Melinda is accustomed to a certain lifestyle that I doubt you can provide." He looked around at the simple pool and the tacky decor of this three-star hotel. "That's what I think."

Dan blinked at him and tried to smile, but Russell could tell he'd gotten to him.

"Thank you, Russell," Dan said, and swallowed hard. "I will take that under advisement." He sat back from his plate. "I'm surprised you haven't asked to see a picture of your little boy."

Russell wiped his forehead. "I have plenty of my own, of course, but sure."

Dan scrolled through his phone and then handed it to him. There was Horatio—*Was that really him?*—propped up against a large dog who was licking his face. Russell was afraid of dogs, and he felt a little burst of adrenaline then.

Russell zoomed in. *Poor child,* my God, *they had him sitting on what appeared to be the dog's bed.* Horatio had grown; he looked more like a baby than an infant, more like a Hank than a Horatio.

"Is that— Is he laughing?"

"Oh, sure. Kid's got a winning smile."

Russell handed the phone back, his stomach gurgling and his heart doing some kind of irregular rhythm, skipping a beat or two and then making up for it by galloping too hard. Russell needed to go home. "I was planning to leave anyway," he said. "I may as well go ahead and book a flight."

Dan nodded in an understated way, given that he probably felt like he'd won a great victory. "Good," he said. "And if you get in a bind taking care of Horatio on your own, we can help out. I know how hard it is. We, and I mean Melinda and I, could stop by your place—together—if you ever need a hand."

Russell understood Dan's message, and he would not interfere. Let this man have a go at Melinda. It would never happen. Melinda and a bartender? She would crush him. "What time's the flight?" he said.

"You don't have to catch the same one we're on," said Dan.

Russell imagined all the steps he would need to take—and with a hangover: calling the airline, showering, packing, checking out, driving, flying, landing, and finally, holding the little guy in his arms, rocking him to sleep. He imagined Felicity walking into the loft and finding him there, doing his best, doing it well. He loved her so much he didn't know where to put it all.

"Why did you say before that Felicity didn't cheat on me," he said, "when I happen to know she did?"

"Let's get the check," Dan said. "Melinda's got something to tell you."

Russell felt a surge of nausea and put his napkin up to his mouth, unsure he could even make it to the bathroom.

Chapter 27

In Olivia's dream, Melinda pushed her father off the deck of a ship and then jumped in after him. They were deep under the water for a long time while Olivia watched from above, searching for movement, until finally they reappeared, paddling up to the surface.

Olivia emerged from the dream, rolling over and stretching, wishing Todd were there so she could tell him how her dad and Melinda had bobbed in the water, almost like they were dancing.

It would have been nice to see him the moment she opened her eyes. Instead, she saw her mother, sitting in the IKEA chair on the other side of her tiny studio, reading the *New York Times* with a cup of coffee.

"Mom?"

Meg put down her paper and took off her reading glasses. "Good morning."

"Um, okay." Olivia rubbed her eyes. "What are you doing here?"

"I haven't seen you in a while," her mom said. She stood, tucked the front of her black sweater in her jeans, and went to pour a cup of coffee for Olivia.

Olivia sat up, confused; she didn't see her mother regularly. When she was in town, they made time to catch up over a meal, but that might happen four times in one month and zero times the next; it depended on her mom's complicated schedule and the fragile state of the world.

"What time is it?" Olivia asked, stunned her mother would barge in like this. "And whatever happened to boundaries?"

"Seven. And I want to talk to you about this baby."

"I didn't even know you were in town," Olivia said. She watched her mom take the milk from the mini-fridge and add a splash to the cup.

"I flew in from Haiti last night. I've been concerned about you."

"Okay," Olivia said, pushing back the covers. "Well, make yourself at home."

"Seriously, Liv, you've spent the last month taking care of some orphan and those Aston kids. I just don't understand it. Where's my career girl? Why aren't you getting back on the horse?"

"He's not an orphan." Olivia got out of bed, relieved now that Todd hadn't come over.

Her mother took the few steps over to Olivia's little table in her one-room apartment and set down the coffee.

"It's a detour," Olivia said. "I won't be babysitting forever."

"I should hope not. You've got real skills, and I wouldn't go so far as to say you found a *passion*, not the way I'd like to see, but you seemed to get some satisfaction from your work."

"Mom," Olivia said, running her fingers through her tangled hair, "can this wait until I'm actually awake?"

"I'm only trying to help," she said, sitting back down and crossing her legs. "You've suffered a setback, and I'd like to see you deal with the problem and get back on course."

This was, of course, her mother's area of expertise. Her book, *Aftermath*, was an accounting of major disasters she'd studied over the years and an analysis of how the affected communities handled them, before, during, and mostly after.

"You don't have to worry about me," Olivia said. "I got this."

She went into the bathroom and closed the door. The whole time she was peeing, her mother kept talking.

"The mistake people make when life hits them with some unexpected, and often unprepared-for, catastrophe is they think they can just return to the way life was before. They try to rebuild exactly what they lost, but history proves how misguided that is. Disasters change everything, and we have to learn and grow from them, avoid the same kind of complacency that left us open to a blow to begin with."

Olivia flushed the toilet and washed her hands, blinking in the mirror while her mother kept talking. "Hurricane Melinda swept into your sphere and trashed your life, yes. You need to get up and dig out from the rubble. But the solution is not to go back to the same exact job in the same place. Goodness, Olivia, don't you want to come out of this stronger? And I hate to bring this up, but that video on TikTok was fairly damning, and I don't know what makes you think Felicity will hire you back after—"

"Mom," Olivia said, opening the door, drying her hands on a washcloth, "can we please, please, please not talk about the video? Is this why you always insist on having a key to my place? So that one day you can catch me off guard at the crack of dawn?"

"No," she said, pulling her hair back and lifting it off her neck. "I keep a key in case there's ever a full-blown decimation of the North American power grid; I need to know I can get to you."

Olivia had grown up with these kinds of dire warnings, always followed by a comment about the need to live life productively and optimistically in spite of the high probability for apocalyptic doom.

Her mother was fanning herself now with both hands. "Perimenopause," she said. "It's all part of a process, but I can't say I'm enjoying it. So what do you think of this Melinda anyway? I can't help but feel that where she goes, trouble follows."

That struck Olivia as fairly ironic coming from her mom, given the trouble she herself had caused. No one had hurt her dad as much as her mom had. He was good at maintaining a cheerful facade, but Olivia, even at seven years old, wasn't stupid. She saw the change in him after Meg moved out. And although he never spoke badly of her mom, Olivia had been able to see for herself how her mother had failed him. Had failed them both.

"I hated Melinda at first, obviously," Olivia said, getting a flash of the shame she'd felt when Courtney had thrust that cardboard box in her arms. "But I understand her now. I may even like her."

"Do you?" said her mom, her voice full of surprise. "That's good, I guess. Do you think Dan likes her? I mean for him to get on a plane, given how terrified he's always been of flying, which isn't a rational fear, as you know, and to go to Mexico during hurricane season, and to abandon his bar, it all seems so out of character for him."

Olivia sat down and blew on her coffee. "He's got a crush. It's fine."

"I'm just wondering if you think she's good for him. I thought she was very nice when we met at his apartment, but I'd hate to see him get hurt. How serious are they?"

"Mom."

"What?"

"Can we talk about something else? Like literally anything else in the world?"

"Fine," her mother said, and she gave Olivia a respite that lasted all of five seconds. "Let's talk about your student loans."

"Oh my God," Olivia said, putting her head down on the table. "That's the *one* other topic—"

"I wish you'd listened to me when I warned you about—"

"I'm going to need something stronger than coffee if you keep this up."

"I just don't see how you can manage that kind of debt, not to mention rent and other expenses, if you're working as a babysitter." Her mom's brow was furrowed in worry.

"Honestly," Olivia said, lifting her head off the table, "I'd rather talk about dad's sex life."

Her mother put down her cup. "You think they're having *sex*?"

"Wow," said Olivia, "definitely none of our business."

Whether it was on purpose or subconscious, her mom had always sabotaged her dad's chances at romance, including by saddling him with a baby in his prime. Olivia always wondered why he never seemed bitter about that.

Her mom did not want her dad, but she never really wanted anyone else to have him either.

"Let him be happy," Olivia said.

"Of course I want him to be happy. But we're his family; why wouldn't it be our business?"

"How's Jens?" Her mother's boyfriend was a Norwegian climate scientist who lived in a yurt. Olivia had met him one time when he was visiting. He offered her maté served in a gourd with a bombilla. It tasted like she was drinking dirt.

"Jens wanted more from me than I could offer. I won't give up my independence," she said. "No, I'm seeing a new man. I met him when I was protesting at Davos."

"An activist?"

"Actually no," she said. "He's the CEO of a pharmaceutical company."

Olivia could not believe her ears. "Doesn't that make him one of the bad guys?"

"Yes and no," her mother said. "His carbon footprint is absolutely shameful—the man owns a private jet, for God's sake. But his company is doing groundbreaking work dealing with vector-borne diseases like malaria and dengue, all on the rise because of climate change. Liv, you can't imagine the arguments we have. I tell him he's evil; he tells me he's a saint. He's definitely part of the solution, but he's also a big part of the problem, and for some reason I'm pathologically attracted to him. How's Todd?"

Olivia was finally coming to understand one indisputable truth: relationships were hideously, absurdly, almost comedically complicated. Maybe the trick was to stop taking it all so seriously. "Our issues are less categorical than good and evil." She could have mentioned that their sex life had never been better, but that was not an update she would share with her mother. "I really don't want to talk about it."

Her mother threw her hands up. "Well, you don't want to talk about your dad or your debt. I can't bring up TikTok or Todd. So, what *can* we talk about?"

"The Kardashians?" said Olivia.

"Who?"

"Since I'm such a mess," Olivia said, climbing back into bed, "why don't you tell me how to fix my life—but do it quickly, since we're all about to die anyway."

"Don't make fun of me," Meg said, frowning at her.

Olivia had only been joking around, but her mother looked hurt.

"I want a job," Olivia said, "I really do, but honestly, I don't have any options. Felicity might be my only chance because at the very least I can explain myself to her. Who out there is going to hire the girl who went viral for being an asshole?" But then she remembered that there were options, there were people who had said they would give her a chance, all she had to do was ask. She leaned off the bed, picking Melinda's binder up off the floor.

"Here," she said.

"What is this?"

"Something Hurricane Melinda left in her wake. It's a bunch of jobs I'm probably not qualified for."

Her mother started leafing through the binder. "Olivia," she said, "have you called some of these places?"

"No," said Olivia, "not yet. I didn't want Melinda's help before, but you're right, I need to get back on the horse. I'll make some calls today."

"You should," Meg said, her voice missing its usual conviction. "You certainly need a job. . . ."

"There's an environmental nonprofit in there that looks interesting," Olivia said. "That would be more meaningful than what I was doing before." Nothing, Olivia figured, would make her mom happier than if she joined her fight against climate change.

"Melinda went to a lot of trouble," Meg said. But then she closed the binder. "Forget about all this. What do you really want to do with your life? You don't have to find the answer in here."

"Maybe not," said Olivia, trying to be somewhat delicate, "or maybe you don't want Melinda to be the one to save the day any more than I did."

Her mother laughed. "Goodness, Liv, what do you take me for? Each and every one of us will land in a crisis at some point, and that's when we need to accept all the help we can get. Lauren needed help with her kids, and there you were; Melinda certainly needs help surviving her divorce; and you need help getting back on your feet. There's nothing wrong with that. Why do you think your father and I have stayed so close over the years? We know we'll be there for each other, just like we're here for you."

Olivia took the binder from her and opened it, this time without any resentment or bitterness. Melinda had caused this mess. Who was to say she wasn't the very person to help fix it?

Chapter 28

God, but that Russell was a colossal cockblocker. Even now as they were flying at their cruising altitude of thirty-five thousand feet—Dan squeezing his own knees in fear—Russell was snoring loudly in the seat directly between him and Melinda, just as he'd snored between them the night before. Dan had spent that unending night lying on his side, stealing glances at Melinda, trying not to fall off his side of the bed, just when he'd thought they could meet somewhere in the middle of the mattress. As impossible as it should have been to feel turned on at that particular moment, with her ex-husband's feet so close to his face, Dan kept imagining reaching over and taking hold of Melinda's body, kissing her . . .

Now they were finally on the plane, and Dan still couldn't squeeze her hand or loop his arm through hers or kiss her cheek because her ex-husband was literally *in the way*. Russell had been furious—of course he had—that first class was full. As the three of them made their way down the aisle into coach, Dan had stepped back to let Melinda take the window seat, but before he could step in to take the middle seat beside her, Russell, in some kind of competitive, chest-thumping power move, swooped in first, denying Dan the privilege of sitting next to her.

Having long believed that airplanes could not possibly defy gravity, Dan wanted nothing more than to be distracted from his fear of dying by Melinda and her lovely mouth. Instead, he gripped his knees, sipped his ginger ale, and tried not to think of going down in a fiery plane crash and of Olivia inheriting nothing from him because he didn't own his own bar, not technically or factually or in any way at all. Russell had really gotten under his skin with all that talk about real estate and nest eggs.

Just when he decided to swap the soda for a vodka tonic to take the edge off, the pilot came on the intercom, announcing strong winds, turbulence, and a very bumpy landing. Dan tightened his seat belt and tried to remember Meg's statistics about the safety of modern aviation.

· · ·

Queasy and exhausted, Dan walked out of the airport terminal with Russell and Melinda into a stormy night. When he and Melinda left three days ago, it had still felt like fall, but in their absence, winter had arrived in New York City in the shape of a nor'easter. Melinda pulled on a baseball hat, and Dan resisted the urge to stand close enough to shield her from the rain that was coming at them sideways.

As soon as Russell proposed sharing a cab, Dan realized he was planning to stay at Melinda's. He felt his blood pressure rising as they waited in line, the wind was blowing from all directions at once.

Traffic was predictably terrible, and as the three sat shoulder to shoulder, listening to the right-wing talk show the cabdriver had on and watching the wipers whip back and forth, no one had anything to say for the entire bumpy, hour-long ride to Manhattan. Dan's leg pressed against Melinda's, and he felt a fiery physical charge between them. He tried to make eye contact, but she stared straight ahead at the long line of red brake lights in front of them. He would have loved to know what she was thinking.

Finally, the cab stopped in front of Melinda's apartment building, halfway down Cornelia Street. Dan got out quickly and let Russell pay for the cab. *Fuck him.* He raised the handle on his carry-on and turned to leave, cold, wet, and dejected.

"Hey," Melinda called out after him, her hair blowing beneath her cap.

"Yeah?"

"Thanks for all that," she said, stepping out of the way to make room for a couple passing them on the sidewalk. "It was really fun."

"Melinda," Russell said, standing beside her door, shivering in his cotton sweater and boat shoes, "come on."

"Wait," she said. "Aren't you picking up Hank now?"

"It's too late," said Russell, pouting, "and I'm not feeling well. Tell . . . whoever's involved that I'll pick him up first thing in the morning."

Dan stopped himself from pointing out that Russell's lingering hangover wasn't Hank's problem or the Astons' either.

"I have to go to work tomorrow," Melinda said, "so I can't help you with him."

"I don't need your help," Russell said, narrowing his eyes at her. "What I need is Felicity back, and your little stunt with those pictures has made a real mess of things."

"I know, and I'm sorry," she said.

Dan felt she'd apologized quite enough already, but Russell was not mollified. "You've ruined my life," he said.

Oh, the irony. Dan had developed a tiny bit of respect for Russell; his confidence was impressive and he was a successful guy, sure. But what a selfish prick he could be. "Look," said Dan, "I think there's enough blame to go around here."

"I just want to get the rest of my things," said Russell, "and go home."

Well, that was a relief.

Russell reached into his pocket and held up a key. "I'll leave your spare upstairs when I go." He turned and opened the door, rolling his suitcase in behind him.

"Jeesh, finally," Melinda said, turning with a timid shrug. "I thought we'd never get rid of that guy." She was shaking from the cold, watching him.

"What now?" said Dan. The rain was soaking through his sneakers.

"I was hoping you'd invite me to your place."

"You're invited," he said, almost urgently. "You mean it?" He stepped toward her, finally, and put his arms around her, slowly kissing her, wishing his lips weren't so damn cold. The rain was picking up again, and he could hardly wait to get her inside.

"Do we need to stop at Lauren's first?" he asked as they set out toward his apartment.

"No, I'll just text so they know Russell's back."

She reached for his hand, and he stopped, unable to wait for the warmth of his apartment to hold her again. Had he washed his sheets recently? Was the bathroom clean? The wind blew hard down Sixth Avenue, and while they kissed, their suitcases rolled off down the sidewalk without them.

When they finally got to his building he picked up their bags and they took the stairs, stopping on each landing. Dan felt like a college kid he was so eager to get this woman out of her clothes and into his bed. At his door, his shaky hands fumbled with the keys until he managed to turn the lock and push the door open. Melinda pulled him inside, as he kicked the door closed behind them.

• • •

That night, the strong winds and high tide teamed up to cause a storm surge that flooded the New York City subway system. The next day, all five boroughs were at a standstill, and the mayor made the unpopular call to close public schools. At five in the morning, Melinda woke to news that Perkins would follow suit. Dan lowered the blinds in his bedroom, and he and Melinda went back to sleep.

Hours later, after coffee and a shower, they walked to Waverly Place, down wet sidewalks that were covered with broken branches, leaves, and trash, his arm across her shoulder. They stopped at the bar first—where the power was on and the floors were dry—before going upstairs to the brownstone, too late, by now, to witness the handoff of Hank to his father.

"The conquering heroes," Evelyn said, ushering them in. "You dragged home the ne'er-do-well—bravo!" She took their coats and then paused, looking them both up and down. "My goodness, the trip did you both good; you're glowing!"

In spite of the glow, Melinda looked tense as she saw that Hank was, in fact, still there, kicking his legs and waving his little arms from inside his playpen. Not too late for the handoff after all.

"Russell didn't show?" Melinda said.

"Not yet," said Evelyn, "but we're hoping he's on his way."

Dan didn't much like the idea of seeing Russell again.

"Forgive the chaos," Evelyn said then. "We've had some excitement today."

The house smelled like popcorn and mothballs. Dan noticed a change in the living room. What was it exactly? The red velvet curtains were gone, for one thing, making the room feel lighter and less like a brothel. The old rug had been pulled up, and the towering piles of magazines were gone. And yet there was mayhem: the boys, delighted to have a day off school, were running up and down the stairs. Waverly chose that moment to climb into the playpen with Hank, almost toppling it. Lauren yelped and jumped up from the couch to help her get in safely. For some reason, there was a steamer trunk in the dining room with its lid open. And there, next to the trunk, were Meg and Olivia.

"Oh," said Meg, lighting up when she saw them, "you're here."

"*You're* here," said Dan. Having to face both their exes on the same day seemed like some kind of hoax.

"Not for long," Meg said. She was wearing a turtleneck sweater and her black jeans were tucked into tall Hunter boots. "I'm headed to a meeting with the New York City Transit office. They should have known the subway system was going to take a big hit, but they were completely unprepared."

Leo and Phillip came in then carrying boxes, and they all but dropped them on the ground next to the trunk.

"I'm worried about your back, Leo," Lauren called from the couch. "I told you not to lift anything heavy."

"What about *my* back?" said Phillip.

"Do you need a hand?" Dan asked.

"We emptied a closet," said Leo. "These boxes are the last of it."

"You remember Melinda," Dan said, placing a hand on Melinda's back.

"I have to thank you, Melinda," Meg said, twisting her hair into a clip. "Olivia told me about all the jobs you found for her. She was feeling pretty hopeless about her prospects, and you've given her her oomph back."

"It was nothing," Melinda said, waving off the praise.

"I made a few calls," Olivia said, "but I was hoping we could talk before I interview."

Dan was overwhelmed by a sense of relief. They got along now. His girlfriend—*girlfriend!*—and his daughter had come to an understanding, maybe even a friendship.

"I have to run," said Meg, pulling on her raincoat. "It's so rare I happen to already *be* where disaster strikes. How the MTA was caught off guard is beyond me." She picked up her backpack and slung it over her shoulder.

"Climate change," said Leo sadly, ripping the tape off one of the boxes. "As a family we really need to do more to stop it."

"Restoring the oyster reefs in New York Harbor is the key," said Meg. "Those little creatures are a natural storm barrier."

"Oysters," said Leo, sounding delighted. "I've heard about this."

"Read up on the Billion Oyster Project," said Meg. "And if you and Lauren want to volunteer with me, we could go together."

"I'd love that," said Leo. "Thanks, Meg."

Meg went to say her goodbyes to the rest of the family as Phillip and Leo went to sit in the living room.

"How was the trip?" Olivia said.

"Brief," said Melinda, smiling a little awkwardly.

"Yes, brief," said Dan. "Good weather though. Nice pool."

Just then, Waverly began sobbing in the living room. "Oh, not again," said Olivia.

Dan turned to see the adults comforting Waverly, who had climbed out of the playpen and was now lying facedown on the floor.

"What's wrong with her?" Melinda said.

"She's upset that Hank is leaving," Olivia said.

"But just think," Evelyn was saying, rubbing Waverly's back, "Hank will be so happy to see his daddy."

"Hank *wants* to go home," Lauren added, "just like you would want to go home."

Waverly continued to cry. "But I don't want him to leave," she wailed. "I don't like his daddy."

You and me both, thought Dan.

Hank started crying then as well. Dan wanted to grab Melinda's hand and leave, to retreat to the peace of his apartment, to be alone with her.

"Waverly," said Leo, "we told you from the start that Hank would have to go home as soon as his mommy or daddy came back."

"Can't we get the inevitable over with?" Evelyn said, wringing her hands. "The anticipation is too painful."

"Has anyone heard from Russell?" Lauren said.

They all turned to Melinda.

"I'll see what's keeping him," she said. Melinda took her phone and went to the kitchen. The beads that used to separate the two rooms were conspicuously gone.

Olivia began sifting through the clothes in the steamer trunk.

"What's all this?" Dan asked.

Olivia held up a royal-blue velour blazer in one hand, silver stilettos in the other.

"Is this not the coolest outfit ever?" Olivia said.

"Very . . . *Saturday Night Fever*," said Dan.

Olivia leaned into the open trunk and pulled out a brown faux-leather trench coat. "They're doing a purge, and they offered me Charley's clothes," Olivia said. "I'll have to hem all the pants," she said, "but there's some amazing stuff."

Dan pulled out a dining room chair, watching the family pandemonium from a distance while Olivia tried on the coat.

"Oh Lord," said Evelyn, looking at her phone, "another text."

Phillip rolled his eyes. "We all know Ed is crazy about you," he said. "No need to show off."

"Phillip," she said, slapping his arm playfully. "No, it's my daughter-in-law," she said.

"Frances, Frances, Frances," Lauren mumbled.

Dan had never met Lauren's elusive brother or his wife, but he'd gathered bits and pieces over the years and had the sense that they were pretty stiff and extremely wealthy.

"Don't be unkind," said Evelyn. "She's motherless and *very* needy. A bit of a pest actually. She's upset that I've been so out of touch."

"Don't let her guilt-trip you," Lauren said.

"She misses me," Evelyn said with a shrug.

Phillip clapped his hands together. "I'd like to get back to the elephant in the room," he said, turning to Leo. "Are you saying the offer is so astonishing, you're actually considering it? You would give up a tenured faculty position at a renowned university in exchange for less stability and a ton of money? Where are your priorities? I don't understand."

"It would be crazy not to think about this job," Lauren said, pulling Waverly onto her lap. "You don't just turn down an opportunity like this without talking it through."

Dan leaned in toward Olivia, who was trying on a fedora. "What job?" he asked.

"Leo wrote some groundbreaking code relevant to artificial intelligence and got a huge job offer in Silicon Valley."

Why did it feel like everyone else was getting ahead? Lauren's work was taking off. Phillip had gotten a great job in Berlin. Meanwhile, Dan's livelihood was linked to the whims and wishes of Phillip and the Astons. If they all moved away, what would happen to the bar? His fate was not in his own hands.

"But are you actually thinking of taking it?" Phillip asked. "Or are you trying to get a retention offer?"

"You can't leave," said Evelyn, picking up a blanket from the floor and folding it. "You just got settled, the kids are happy in school. You can't uproot them again. Honestly, I'm on Phillip's side."

"Two nays," said Phillip. "I'm not saying I don't understand the allure of a new opportunity. Consider my own opportunity in Berlin—"

"What did happen to your opportunity in Berlin?" Leo said.

"I was wondering that too," Lauren said.

They were both watching him. Phillip looked up, apparently surprised to see all eyes on him. "I thought I explained that already, no?"

"No," said Lauren and Leo at the same time.

"He meant to," said Evelyn, coming behind Phillip's chair and putting her hands on his shoulders. "Phillip's job was delayed because of a visa issue. Some backlog of paperwork at the embassy, which has given him time to think. And . . ."

"That's right," said Phillip, patting Evelyn's hand. "They shifted my start date until the New Year. But to be honest, I'm not entirely sure I want the job anymore. I hope it's all right if I stay on a little longer while I sort myself out."

"It's your house, Phillip," said Leo. "You can stay as long as you like."

"The question is," Lauren said gingerly, "if you stay, I mean, if we *all* stay—are *we* imposing on you?"

Phillip sat forward, holding his slightly shaky, liver-spotted hands together. "If you take the job in California, I'll likely leave as well," he said. "As much as I love this old house, it's too much for me, and I don't want to live here alone anymore. I was thinking—with your help, Leo—I could clean out Charley's atelier in the meantime and move in there. Frankly, my knees can't manage those stairs anymore. I know this isn't what you signed up for, and I would hate to be in the way."

There was a pause following this poignant confession, and Dan sat motionless, concerned for Phillip. He didn't know the Astons well enough to predict what they would say.

"Phillip," Lauren said, "we love having you here."

"'In the way'?" said Leo. "How could you be in the way?"

Harrell came over and hugged him.

"There, you see," said Evelyn, giving his shoulders a squeeze. "I told you. And I'll be the first one in line to help clear out that catastrophe of a room. I already measured, and there's plenty of room for a full-size bed if we get rid of that revolting old sofa."

That was all well and good, thought Dan, but were the Astons staying or going?

Waverly started to cry again. "I don't want anyone moving anywhere," she said, sniffling.

"Moving would be discombobulating," said Leo, "but there are big implications to not taking the job."

"So have you decided?" Dan said. They all turned toward the dining room. He wondered if his face revealed the panic he felt. They likely thought this discussion was none of his business, but their plans could completely upend his life.

"Oh, Olivia," said Lauren, catching sight of her in the brown coat and fedora. "You look just like a police detective from a seventies TV show."

"Are you sure *you* don't want it?" Olivia said.

"Oh, I'm sure," said Lauren. "Take it, please."

Like Waverly, this talk of purging and moving was making Dan feel all the more unsettled. He would need to talk to Phillip about their gentleman's agreement. Why should he invest in a bathroom renovation if he might get evicted at any time? He wished he had a fraction of Russell's knowledge about such matters. How horrified would Melinda be to discover he owned neither his apartment nor his business?

She came back from the kitchen then, her mouth twisted in worry.

"Everything okay?" Dan asked.

"Slight change of plans," Melinda said. "Russell's building lost power last night. He's got no running water, no heat, no elevator, and his phone is about to die. But," she added with an optimistic lift to her voice, "he's on his way here to pick up Hank anyway, and he'll take him to my apartment, where he'll stay until there's power uptown."

Waverly threw herself back on the floor and started to cry again.

Dan was unhappy too. Jesus, Russell was a pain in his ass.

But then Melinda leaned in and whispered in his ear: "Are you willing to take in a roommate again tonight?"

Dan's shoulders relaxed, and he wrapped his arms around her. He didn't care who saw them.

• • •

Russell was over two hours late. It was Waverly who spotted him through the living room window when he finally arrived.

They all crowded on the stoop, ready for the big reunion. Dan wondered how Hank would respond. Would he cry? Or would he smile at his father, whom he hadn't seen in a month?

Russell looked up at them from the sidewalk; his face had a sheen, and he was winded. He put a hand on the stone rail and his foot on the first step. "There were no cabs," he said between breaths. "No Ubers . . . the city cleared all the streets for the utility trucks," he said, all but panting, "so I had to walk."

"Walk from where?" Dan said to Melinda.

"Riverside Drive," Melinda said. "That's—what—five miles?"

Dan was impressed. It seemed Russell was at least trying to do the right thing.

"I had to get here," Russell said. He looked even worse than he had during their hangover breakfast. "I wanted to . . . I need to . . ." Russell began the trek up the stairs, but halfway there, he tripped on a broken step, his knees buckling under him.

"Russell!" Melinda said.

But Russell didn't answer. Instead, he gave into gravity, rolling down the stairs and hitting the back of his head so hard that it made a horrific thud.

Chapter 29

Lauren woke up before anyone else in the house with a mad desire to cook something from scratch. She'd finished—finally!—the entire order for Felicity, every last pencil cup, tissue box holder, and trivet, and shipped the whole lot out to California. She was glad to see it all go.

Would she, Leo, and the kids be shipping themselves out to California in the spring? Lauren stared up at the ornate Victorian medallion on the ceiling above the bed. Now that they'd begun to clear out some of Charley's belongings, the house was feeling more like home. She'd been imagining using some of the money she'd earned from Felicity to make a few changes, strip some wallpaper maybe, or replace the kitchen appliances. But then Leo had gotten his mind-blowing offer to work in Silicon, a leap from academia to the business world that surely would not suit him. Lauren understood his excitement over the collaborative nature of the job, and who didn't want that kind of financial security? But Leo *not* teaching? It was unthinkable.

And how could they leave her mother and Phillip on one coast and take off for the other?

She slipped out of bed, put on sweatpants, and left Leo, Hank, and Bumper asleep in the bedroom. She walked to Morton Williams and returned with two shopping bags, stepping over a bit of dried blood on the broken step leading up to the front door. Russell was recovering, but only a few days earlier, Lauren had actually been afraid he would die right there on her doorstep.

Phillip, worried that Russell would sue, immediately went inside to call his lawyer, while the rest of them got Russell in an ambulance.

"This house is too much responsibility," Phillip said as they awaited news about Russell's condition. "I knew that step needed fixing, but my handyman retired in the nineties, and it's become more than I can manage."

"You should talk to Peter, my estate planner," said Evelyn. "It might reduce your worry to have the house in a trust. When was the last time you updated your will?"

"How morbid," said Phillip. "Never."

"I'll invite Peter to have lunch with us. I'm a believer in making plans, especially when the future is uncertain."

To their collective relief, Melinda informed them a few hours after Russell's fall that he was fine (other than dehydration, a jagged laceration, and a minor concussion) and only needed rest and a few stitches. No one had asked how much longer Hank would be staying.

• • •

At the store, Lauren had decided to make chicken soup in Charley's old enameled stockpot. It would simmer all day, overruling the powerful smell of mothballs that had been released the moment they popped open Charley's steamer trunks.

Bumper ran over to greet her when she walked in and stuck his head in the shopping bags. Waverly was right behind him.

"Mommy," her daughter whispered, taking Lauren's hand with sticky fingers. "Aunt Frances and Uncle William."

"Aunt Frances—? On the phone?"

"In the kitchen."

Lauren did not love this surprise. "But why?"

"Mommy," said Waverly, scolding, "come on."

Lauren looked in the hallway mirror; she had no makeup on, and her hair had tiny pieces of dried clay caked in it. She took off her coat and looked down at her sweatpants, wishing she could run upstairs and hide.

Instead, she followed Waverly through the house to the kitchen. There were Frances and William, standing stiffly, their coats on and their arms crossed, eyeing the Formica as though it were contaminated.

"Hiiii," Lauren said in an octave above her normal voice. Lauren smiled as best she could and set down her grocery bags. She hugged her sister-in-law, who smelled like mint and something vaguely citrus, and her brother, whose face was clean-shaven and whose shoes were cleaner and shinier than anything in the house. Bumper liked the high pitch of her voice and wagged his tail. "Welcome, wow, you're really here."

"We didn't *want* to show up uninvited," Frances said, her lips tightly pursed, "but you don't answer your phone anymore."

Lauren had, in fact, missed several calls at inconvenient moments when she was up to her elbows in clay or dirty diapers. "We've been so busy lately. Leo and I have been working, and Mom . . ."

Evelyn was busy and happy and was apparently avoiding her regular catch-up calls with Frances. Lauren wasn't sure why.

"Mom what?" William said with some degree of hostility.

"She's happy," she said, taking a bag of coffee from the old fridge and filling the coffee maker with water. "How are the kids? It's good to see you." It wasn't really, not unannounced like this, but Lauren tried to rise to the occasion. Would she have to offer breakfast? A tour? She began putting away the groceries.

"We haven't been able to reach Mom for days," William said, tapping his shoe impatiently. "We started to get worried."

"Worried about what?"

"Well, she's practically moved here," Frances said. "It's a little . . . strange."

"She's not young," William said, "and we think, maybe, you've been asking too much of her."

"I have?"

"I'm giving you my opinion, Lauren," he said. "We don't understand why you won't let her go home."

"*Let* her—?" What was he implying? That Lauren was holding their mother captive? "Waverly, sweetie," she said, "go upstairs and see if Grammy's up yet."

Waverly put the Popsicle she was eating—a Popsicle? First thing in the morning?—in a chipped coffee mug and stood up, wiping her hands on her Batman pajama top, a hand-me-down from Charles. She ran off to the stairs.

"Mom is welcome to go home whenever she wants," Lauren said. "I happen to think her time here has been really good for her."

"It's not like her to stay away so long or to be completely out of touch," William said. "What is she still doing here?"

"She told me," Frances said, tucking her hair behind her ear, and touching her pearl earring, "that she had to help you mend fences with some woman who hates you."

"Oh, *that*," Lauren said. "She doesn't hate me anymore."

"You're not in middle school," William said. "You shouldn't need Mom to sort out your girl drama."

"That's rude," said Lauren. On the counter behind her, the coffee maker was making strange, burbly sounds. "Look, things got a little complicated around here, but we sorted it all out, mostly. Kind of."

Frances was standing stiffly in her long wool coat, her black Chanel handbag still over her shoulder.

"May I take your coats?" Lauren said with mock formality. "You two look great, by the way. Must be nice having older kids. You probably sleep at night."

Frances, Lauren realized too late, was crying.

"What the— Are you okay?"

"Mom has really hurt Frances's feelings," William said, rubbing his wife's back.

"It's not nice," said Frances. "I thought Evelyn needed me, but now I never even hear from her."

"I'm sure she didn't mean to ignore you," Lauren said. "She just got caught up in things here."

Waverly came back to the kitchen and stood close, so Lauren leaned over and kissed her on the top of her head. "Is Grammy coming down?" she asked.

Waverly shook her head.

"No?" said Lauren. "Is she sleeping?" Strange, given that the clock on the oven said it was after nine.

"Did you tell her we're here?" Frances asked, looking even more wounded.

Waverly shook her head again and exhaled loudly. "She's not here." She sat down, picked up her Popsicle, and put it in her mouth.

"No sweets for breakfast, Waverly. And what do you mean she's not here?"

William looked up at Lauren. "Well, where is she?"

Lauren had no idea. "Did you see her earlier," she asked Waverly, "while I was shopping?"

"Nope," Waverly said, dropping what was left of the Popsicle in the mug and picking up a crayon.

"I knew it," Frances said, turning to William, "I told you. I told you I had a bad feeling."

"Yes, you did," William said wearily.

"I just had a sense that something was wrong, and I couldn't shake it."

"Okay, Frances," said William, "I heard you the first time."

Lauren didn't blame him for being testy. Frances was being a pill.

Leo came into the kitchen then, looking just as disheveled as Lauren. "Frances! William!" he said happily. "What a fun surprise!" He clearly meant it, as Leo was incapable of feigning anything. "Or did I know you were coming and forgot?"

"No, it's a surprise," said Lauren. She got mugs out of the cabinet and poured coffee for the three of them.

"Hello, Leo," said Frances. "You look . . . well."

"I do?" he said. "How are you guys?"

"We'd like to know where my mother is," William said sternly.

"I have no idea," Leo said, rubbing his eyes. He went to the dish rack and took a clean baby bottle, filled it with water, and got the can of formula off the island. "Sorry if I'm a little out of it. But you know how it goes with those late-night feedings."

Frances and William looked utterly bewildered. "What feedings?" Frances said.

This, Lauren thought, was going to be hard to explain.

"The baby's having a growth spurt," Leo said, "so he's hungry *all the time*. I fed him at what . . ." He checked his watch. "About four a.m.? And he's already—"

"What *baby*?" said William. He looked at Lauren and then back at Leo. "What *baby*?"

"It's just a baby we're taking care of," said Lauren with a little shrug. "A friend's, sort of, but not really. Anyway, it's temporary."

"Although Hank's kind of part of the family at this point," said Leo.

"We don't get to keep him," said Waverly, working on a drawing—possibly of Hank—at the table. "His daddy is an-air-dual, but that doesn't make us the right nest. He hit his head on our stairs."

"A ne'er-do-well," Leo corrected. "And Russell's getting back on his feet."

"Who?" said William. "Why is someone else's baby here?"

"Good question," said Leo, scratching his head. "Why can't Russell pick him up now?"

"He's embarrassed about his bald spot," said Lauren. "They had to shave a big patch on the back of his head for the stitches. Melinda says he doesn't like to leave the house."

"He could wear a hat," said Leo, scooping formula into the bottle.

"What are you even talking about?" William said.

"Good morning, revelers," Phillip said, coming into the room in his navy pajamas.

Lauren could not help but notice that Phillip looked a bit hung-over. And then Peter trailed in directly after him, in borrowed pajama pants and her mother's bathrobe.

"We've met before, of course," said Phillip, "at Leo and Lauren's wedding. And this is Peter, my . . . estate planner."

"Good morning," Peter said.

Lauren could not imagine what Frances and William thought of this scene. She got more coffee mugs and began filling them.

"We've met before too," said William, shaking Peter's hand. "I came to your office to sign papers when my mother made me executor of her will."

This was news to Lauren. "How come you're the executor?"

"Oh, yes, I remember," said Peter, and he turned to Lauren and said quietly, "Evelyn's will is a very straightforward split, nothing to worry about."

"Did you have a sleepover?" Waverly asked Phillip.

"We did," said Phillip, ruffling Waverly's hair.

"I don't suppose," William said, "that anyone here knows where my mother is?"

Lauren looked at Leo. Phillip looked at Peter. Peter looked in his coffee cup.

"Maybe she's . . . getting breakfast?" Phillip suggested.

"Wasn't she out with you last night?" Leo said to Phillip. "You were going to a concert together or something . . . ? A piano trio?"

"Oh, of course," said Phillip. "Yes, we took Evelyn to a Mendelssohn concert. I'm not sure where she went after that." He turned to Peter, who was focused on the black ants creeping up the side of his cup.

"They're eerily lifelike," Peter said. "I feel as though they might crawl right onto my fingers."

"Thank you," said Lauren, pleased with the compliment.

"Aren't you worried?" Frances said.

"What about?" said Leo.

"I'm a little worried," Lauren admitted.

"I don't see what there is to worry about," said Phillip. "Evie is such fun. We've been having a marvelous time rooming across the hall from each other."

Leo began shaking the bottle for Hank and testing it on his wrist. "Wish I could help solve the mystery, but I'm off to feed the baby," he said. "I'll bring him down to meet you guys."

There was the sound of the front door closing, and Waverly followed Leo to find out who had come in. Lauren hoped it was her mother so William and Frances would be satisfied that she hadn't been kidnapped. But Waverly came back seconds later holding Olivia's hand. Olivia wasn't looking her best either. She pulled off her coat as though it was suffocating her and waved, keeping her sunglasses on. She was dressed for the disco in Charley's blue velour suit. Frances was eyeing her and everyone in the room as though they were criminals.

"Oh, Olivia," said Lauren. "Very cool." Lauren introduced her to Frances and William, adding—in an effort to sound impressive—"Olivia is our nanny."

Frances raised one eyebrow, as if she liked the sound of that but did not believe it for a moment.

"I didn't know you were coming today," Lauren said. Aside from giving Olivia Charley's clothes, Lauren wondered how she could express her gratitude to Olivia for everything she'd done to help get the damn Felicity order finished.

Phillip was admiring Olivia's outfit. "I remember when Charley wore that suit to the opening of her play at the Hammerstein. It's quite a getup for a Saturday morning," he added, winking at her.

"I didn't *exactly* make it home last night," Olivia said. "I went out for way too many cocktails with my former coworkers and ended up going to Todd's apartment, so I didn't exactly get a lot of sleep—"

"Bravo," said Phillip, clapping his hands. "I like Todd."

"A nanny with a hangover," Frances mumbled. "How lovely."

Bumper was galumphing from person to person and knocked Frances off-balance.

Olivia turned to Lauren. "My Felicity friends told me that

Courtney's about to place another huge order. Your desk accessories were apparently a hit."

Lauren tried to smile back at Olivia's expectant face but found it impossible. She was burned out and needed a break. "Yay," she said, her voice belying her unhappiness. "What does she want this time? Toothbrush handles?"

"Lauren," said Phillip, "that's great news."

"It is?" she said. "I mean, it is, of course."

Olivia turned to Phillip. "I need to talk to you and Evelyn," she said. "Todd made this insane proposition last night, and I need advice."

The front door slammed again, and this time it was her mother who walked into the kitchen. She was wearing a cocktail dress and high heels. She set her Chanel handbag on the counter; Lauren noticed it was the exact same one Frances was carrying, only Evelyn's stockings were hanging out of hers.

Waverly hugged her, causing Evelyn to wobble. "Did you have a sleepover too?" Waverly asked.

"My goodness," said Evelyn, putting her hand on Waverly's shoulder to steady herself. "I thought I could make a subtler entrance. Hello, everyone. Peter, fancy seeing you here."

"You look ravishing and ravished," said Phillip.

Evelyn smoothed her hair with her hand. But she gasped when she spotted Frances and William. "Oh my," she said. She went across the kitchen to give them each a hug. "William, dear. Hello, Frances. Well, I don't know what to say, this is so unexpected."

"Did you just take a . . . *walk of shame*?" Frances asked.

"A what?" said Evelyn.

"'Shame'?" said Phillip. "What does shame have to do with anything?"

"Where have you been?" William demanded.

"Excuse me," Evelyn said sharply. "I certainly hope you aren't here to judge me." Her mother gratefully accepted the cup of coffee Lauren offered her, as Leo came back in with the baby.

"Hank heard all the voices and got very excited to see everyone."

Hank was indeed alert, his eyes blinking and his legs kicking.

Waverly went over to him and took hold of his foot. Hank squealed at the sight of her.

"Look, Hank," Leo said, showing Hank around the room, "so many people." He held Hank out to William. "Do you want to hold him?"

"No, thank you," William said, keeping his arms crossed.

Olivia walked across the room, raising her sunglasses briefly to kiss Hank on the forehead.

Evelyn also greeted the baby, saying, "Well, well, well, if it isn't my favorite little rugrat. Good morning, Hank."

"*What* is going on around here?" Frances said, her voice slightly shaky.

"Same old, same old," said Leo.

"Well," said Evelyn, "with the exception of one exciting development." She turned to William and Frances. "Leo is too humble to brag about it, but he got a very impressive job offer—"

William turned on their mom. "Where were you last night?" he said. "And why haven't you been returning our calls?"

Lauren started to interject, but her mom held up a hand to stop her.

"I was out on a date with a sculptor named Ed who's taking me to Dia Beacon this afternoon to see an art installation. And as for your calls: I'm sorry. I've been busy here, but I should have answered. Now, are we finished with the inquisition or is there more, because I have a terrible headache."

"There's more," said William, frowning.

"Is *everyone* here hungover?" Frances asked.

"I'm not," said Waverly, letting go of Hank's foot and sitting back down at the table.

"We have an announcement to make," William said with pretentious formality.

"Would you excuse us, please?" Frances said to Phillip, Peter, and Olivia. "This is a confidential family matter."

Phillip put a hand on Olivia's shoulder. "Come and see what will soon be my new bedroom, once I do a little redecorating," he said, leading her and Peter to the back of the kitchen. "You can fill us in on Todd. A proposition, you say? I'm intrigued." They went through the accordion door, and Lauren could hear their muffled talking from the back of Charley's old office.

"What proposition?" Evelyn called after them.

William cleared his throat. "We wanted to tell you our important news before it's public: I'm finally running for mayor."

Only Leo reacted to this statement the way Frances and William were probably expecting.

"Wow, cool!" he said. "Good for you! You've got my vote," and he clapped William on the back.

"Thank you," said William.

"Although I guess I can't vote for you," Leo said, "since I don't live in Boston, but that's exciting stuff."

"We need you one hundred percent on board," Frances said, directing her comments to Evelyn and Evelyn only, as though Lauren and Leo weren't even in the room. "This is a serious decision."

From the back room came the sound of Phillip's deep laughter, just as Harrell and Charles came running into the kitchen.

"Good for you, William," said Evelyn proudly. "I think you'll be a wonderful mayor."

"You're finally going for it" was as much as Lauren could bring herself to say. "A real campaign."

"What's a campaign?" said Harrell.

"It's . . . a race," said Lauren. "A competition, and if Uncle William comes in first place, he'll be the mayor of Boston."

"Is he going to come in first?" Waverly asked.

"Certainly," said Evelyn.

"I appreciate your confidence," said William, putting his hands in his pockets, "but it won't be that easy."

"Our lives will be under the microscope, as will yours presumably," said Frances, still speaking directly to Evelyn. "So we really can't have random babies around or debauchery of any kind or a grandmother having a love affair with a sculptor. I'm sorry, Evelyn, but we just can't have it."

Evelyn inhaled sharply and then adjusted her wrap dress. "I see," she said, running a finger under her mascara-smudged eye.

"It's going to be a challenging year," said Frances, going over to her and taking her hand, "and I really need you. You're the closest thing I have to a mother."

Lauren watched as her mother opened her arms and hugged Frances. "There, there," she said. "I'm sorry I've been out of touch."

"I've been worried," said Frances over her shoulder. "You've been away so long."

"No need for concern," Evelyn said, picking up her purse and tucking her hose inside. "And I'm well aware of what my responsibilities are and to whom."

"Good," said Frances. "So if you pack up your things now, we can drive you home."

"*What?*" said Lauren. "Now?"

"Why not?" said Frances. "You've had her for over two months."

"Mom," Lauren said, finding it hard to catch her breath. "You don't want to go today, right?"

"Why would you leave?" said Leo.

"You should certainly stay for Thanksgiving," said Lauren.

"She'll be at *our* house for Thanksgiving," William said, pointing a thumb to his chest.

"That goes without saying," Frances said. "We're announcing William's run at a private event that weekend, and you have to be with us for that."

Lauren waited for her mom to refuse, to say she wanted to stay in New York. But Lauren could imagine her being swayed. Frances was a force, William was her favorite, and they could persuade her. How surprising that Lauren felt like bursting into tears herself; it was childish maybe, but she did not want her mom to go anywhere.

"Sorry to break it to you," Evelyn said, "but I can't have Thanksgiving with any of you. I promised Phillip I'd go to Berlin with him to tie up some loose ends there and collect his things. But after that, I'll go to Wellesley."

"You can't fly off to Berlin," William said, his voice whiny. "I'm about to announce my candidacy. And you need to stop acting like a restless teenager and get back to your life."

"But I'm not going back to my life," said Evelyn with perfect calm. "I'm going back to find a Realtor to put my house on the market."

Frances looked as though she'd choked on something, her two hands clutching her pearls.

"You can come visit me anytime," Evelyn said.

"But where?" William asked.

"I won't know until Leo and Lauren sort themselves out, but I imagine it might be somewhere right around here. A nice modern building with good heating, a zippy elevator, and a doorman." She patted him on the cheek and gave Frances a hug. "We'll catch up soon, I promise," she said. "But if you'll excuse me, I really have to go find out what's happened with Olivia and Todd."

To their shock, Evelyn left the kitchen.

Lauren took the baby from Leo, and, feeling a little giddy, she lifted Hank high into the air, razzing his tummy. She would have to tell Leo the truth, that she wanted them to stay right where they were, in this house with its creaky stairs and long memory. No job, no amount of money would be worth what they would give up if they left.

"Now gather 'round, cowboys," Leo said with a Southern drawl. "Who's hankering fer some flapjacks?"

Lauren glanced over at her brother and Frances and caught William rolling his eyes at Leo, unamused and sulking.

"This is actually serious business," William said sharply. "Can you act like an adult for once?"

"Yo," Lauren barked at him, doing her strongest New York accent, "shut up, take ya' freakin' coats off already, and show some *respect*. Leo's makin' a yuge breakfast."

The children were delighted. "Who are you, Mommy?" Harrell asked.

"Robert De Niro," she said, beaming at Leo.

It was Leo who'd had the idea to invite Evelyn in the first place, it was Leo who'd given her mother back to her.

Lauren didn't want to move to California, but maybe it didn't really matter. The place she wanted to be, would ever really want to be, was right where Leo was.

To: Elon Musk
From: Leo Aston
Subject: Your kind offer :-)

Greetings, Elon,

I have to say your job offer came as quite a surprise and turned my household upside down for a few days. I'm so pleased that my software is of interest to you. I had hoped my cricket data was contributing to acoustic research and cognitive science, and I was pumped over its (potential) utility in AI/speech recognition, but for Tesla to have enthusiasm for its application is a big honor. The amount you offer for a salary is simply a big fat *wow* (or more likely a typo?). My university made a retention offer, in hopes I'll stay, but the provost can't come anywhere close to meeting your salary. Academia, am I right? After discussing it at length with my family, I've decided based on myriad reasons—some to do with IP issues, some for ethical considerations (possible use of the code in DoD weaponry development, for example, LOL), and most due to the needs of my family that, alas, I must decline your kind offer.

When I told my family about all this . . . well, I don't really know how to explain their reaction other than to say they stared at me the way Captain Kirk looked throughout much of *Wrath of Khan*: with a mixture of shock and bewilderment and something like outrage. In any case, we had some spirited conversations about what moving from New York to California might mean for me scientifically and for our family emotionally and financially, and it was at last decided that I should keep my job, patent my technology, enjoy our life in New York and at the university, and continue on my mission to increase our basic understanding of the brain and auditory systems more specifically.

Long story, but as we were talking through your mind-blowing offer, my father (also a long story) met with an estate planner and signed the family home over to me and my wife. On hearing that the house is officially ours, a family friend asked us to sell him the bar in the basement—space we don't even need!—for a sizable amount of money. So although I don't make a big salary, I did get a windfall to the tune of almost a hundred thousand dollars . . . for doing absolutely nothing! Land ownership is pretty cool. I'm thinking of throwing some of my good fortune to the Billion Oyster Project to prevent storm surges like the one we just had here in New York. As much as I love crickets, oysters are pretty rad, too.

Thank you for the offer, Elon, and I'm sorry to say no because there are some real perks working for a company such as yours. But boy, would I miss having students. All of my code, FYI, is open-source on GitHub, so feel free to use anything you might need.

Best regards!
Leo

Chapter 30

Thanksgiving break at Perkins was over a week away, but Melinda had already managed to find placements for every gerbil in the building. Even the gecko would be spending the holiday with a family.

As Melinda was sending a thank-you to Sylvestra's mother for agreeing to take the reptile, the principal wandered over to her desk, just minutes before the kids were let out for the day. "You seem different lately," the principal said, "but I haven't been able to put my finger on it. Did you get a face peel or something?"

"No," Melinda said innocently. "But I switched to a new shampoo recently. Maybe that's it."

As the nannies and parents started arriving for pickup, Melinda spotted Olivia in the crowd and waved her over.

"You remember Olivia?" Melinda said to the principal.

"Of course," the principal said. "Don't you think Melinda looks simply wonderful? A parent even mentioned how radiant and friendly she's been lately."

"Is that right?" said Olivia, studying Melinda carefully, apparently enjoying her embarrassment. "You know what I heard? There's a new man in her life."

"Oh, really?" said the principal with a lift to her voice. "Details, details?"

"No, no details," said Melinda, pretending to look for something in her desk drawer, "but I can . . . confirm the rumor."

The principal made a little squealing sound before she noticed a cluster of parents waiting to talk to her and excused herself.

"Thanks a lot," said Melinda wryly.

Olivia looked pleased. "My dad's pretty starry-eyed too. It's kind of disgusting." She came around to the side of Melinda's desk then. "Listen," she said, leaning closer, "Lauren told me what you're planning to do this afternoon, and I know it's none of my business, but are you sure about this? I just want you to promise me you're not going to, like, murder Felicity or anything. I don't want to have to visit you in prison, and my dad would be really bummed."

"I'm going to be fine," Melinda said, willing herself to believe it. "I'm simply going to own my part in her argument with Russell."

"I don't envy you," said Olivia.

Lauren had tried to talk her out of it. Dan had offered to come along. But Melinda felt this was something she had to do on her own.

• • •

An hour later, Melinda left work and walked south to Prince Street, taking a table at the back of a café. She took off her coat and rolled her shoulders, hoping to suppress any urge she might feel to punch her nemesis in the face. When the waitress came, she ordered and then sat back in her chair to wait, letting her hair loose from the clip that had held it in place all day.

The door to the café opened, and Felicity came in, rolling a suitcase and unwinding a scarf from her neck. She was tanned and slender, even prettier than Melinda remembered. Why had this gorgeous, successful woman set her sights on Russell when she could have had any man she wanted? She was such a bright presence, and Melinda couldn't help but understand why everyone on earth seemed mesmerized by her.

Melinda stood up and waved, as a flash of irritation crossed Felicity's face. She looked up at the ceiling and then crossed the room to Melinda's table.

"Is this a coincidence," said Felicity, "or an ambush?"

"An ambush," Melinda said, and invited her to sit.

"Where's Lauren?" Felicity said, sounding annoyed the way one might when one's dry cleaning isn't ready for pickup on the scheduled day. "She was supposed to meet me here."

"How was your flight?" Melinda asked. "I bet you're happy to be back."

"We're doing small talk now?" Felicity said. "Where's Horatio?"

"He's at Lauren's," said Melinda. "I wanted to talk to you first. This won't take long."

She gestured to the chair again, and this time Felicity sat across from her, slipping out of her black wool coat.

"I wanted to apologize for all the hatred I threw your way," Melinda said. "I demonized you and plotted against you, and that was wrong. You're a person, after all."

"Gee, thanks," said Felicity.

This was harder than Melinda had imagined it would be. She'd expected Felicity to meet her halfway and apologize for stealing her husband.

The waitress came to the table, placing a pumpkin cream muffin and a latte in front of Melinda. Felicity looked at the muffin and ordered tea and a scone.

"Sabotaging you and your relationship with Russell was wrong," Melinda went on after the waitress left. "The infidelity and the divorce were hard on me, but I know it wasn't your fault you fell in love with each other, and I'm okay now. I've pulled myself together, and it's in no small part because of Hank."

"Who?"

"Horatio. We call him Hank for short. Anyway, I've given this a lot of thought, and I think your baby deserves to have parents who don't despise each other. I'd like to see you back together actually, for Hank's sake."

"Does Russell know you're here?"

"No," said Melinda.

"Because that would be pathetic if he put you up to this. Let me guess: Is he staying at your flat again?"

"Yes," Melinda said, "but only because he wanted you and the baby to have the loft. He says you made a beautiful nursery there." Melinda wanted him out of her apartment now, this minute, but that wasn't what had motivated her to show up in Lauren's stead at the café. She tried to remember all the points she'd planned to make without checking the notes she had folded up in her pocket.

"I did a lot of things I'm ashamed of, like making Russell think you were cheating on him. I messed everything up with the nanny you hired, and I did all kinds of shenanigans to ruin your business. And I'm very sorry."

Felicity's face softened slightly. "I accept your apology. You failed at *almost* all of it anyway." She looked up, her blue eyes focusing in on Melinda. "Actually, I should probably be thanking you: because of you, Russell showed his true colors. He's nothing but a despicable, old-school misogynist. He basically called me a whore, did he tell you that?" She pulled her phone out of her pocket. "I can show it to you—"

"But that was my fault," Melinda said. "I drove him to it. I'm the one who convinced him—"

"Even if I *did* cheat on him," Felicity said, her faced pinched in fury, "he talked down to me like I'm a child, accused me of being 'slutty.' You don't say that to a woman you respect, you don't say that *ever*. There I was, with the biggest opportunity of my entire career, and he couldn't handle the lack of attention. I don't need some patronizing, judgmental, controlling man in my life. No, thank you. I'll just have to raise Horatio on my own."

"It'll be hard," Melinda said.

The waitress came with Felicity's scone and a cup of tea. Melinda waited for her to leave before asking, "Do you have family around, to help out?"

"Don't worry about me," Felicity said, with a toss of her hair. "I'll be fine."

"Because babies are exhausting, even when they're easy, and we've had a whole cohort taking care of Horatio."

"A cohort?"

"All of us. Lauren, Olivia, and me. Leo and Dan. Phillip and Evelyn. Even Todd took a turn with the kid the other day."

"Well, it's just me," Felicity said. "Russell jumped ship. I mean, what the hell was he doing away from Horatio for so long?"

Melinda could have mentioned her concern about Russell's slow recovery—he was frequently dizzy and exhausted these days, a result of the concussion—but she didn't want to make him appear weak. Or old.

Felicity, meanwhile, was looking a little undone. "Russell made a promise that he would retire and spend his time with the baby so *I* could keep working. That was the deal we made. I mean, it's not like having a baby was *my* idea."

Melinda felt a jolt of the old pain at this last comment, tossed out like it was a minor side issue. She took a deep breath, in through the nose, out through the mouth. "Having a baby was Russell's idea?"

"I wasn't even trying to get pregnant," Felicity said. "It just happened."

Melinda felt her heart pounding and had to sit on her shaky hands. This act of pretending like a baby just appeared out of nowhere made Melinda want to stab Felicity with a fork. Russell had an affair with her, while Melinda was sitting blithely in their Upper East Side apartment, clueless and trusting. She clenched her teeth to keep herself from screaming. She closed her eyes and thought of Dan.

"I was pretty floored when I found out," Felicity was saying, "but Russ said he was desperate to be a father, that he would retire and handle everything. But he failed. Leaving the baby with *you*? I mean, no offense, Melinda, but that was a fucked-up thing to do."

Melinda really couldn't argue with that. "Russell is flawed, sure," she said, "just like the rest of us. He's made mistakes. And yes, he broke promises to you and had some kind of meltdown. But he's back. And he wants to be with you. Do you really want to raise a baby all by yourself? That's not what you signed up for."

Felicity made a face then that conveyed a feeling that was familiar. "I never knew I could be so angry," she said.

"Tell me about it," said Melinda. But her rage was subsiding, and Melinda was able to focus on the reason she'd come. "I honestly believe that Russell wants to keep his promises to you." God, this was hard. Melinda looked down at her hands in her lap, willing herself to go on. When she looked up again, she was encouraged to see Felicity watching her, attentively if not eagerly. "The thing is, Russell loves you." Melinda felt a dull ache somewhere in the middle of her being, but she went on. "I mean it. I know him pretty well after all these years, and the truth is, he would never have left me if he hadn't fallen completely in love with you. And the only reason things got messed up between you two is because I meddled. Why don't you go out to dinner and talk to him and see if you can't make it work?"

There was a flicker of a smile on Felicity's face. "You're fixing me up with your ex-husband?"

Melinda clasped her hands together on the table. "Seeing him miserable isn't nearly as fun as I thought it would be."

"How can I be sure he won't ditch Horatio again?"

"Remember when I ran into you and Russell on the street that day?" Melinda said. "I could tell he wanted to be a good dad. This is all new to him."

"I wonder," Felicity said, playing with the ends of her hair, "if some people simply lack that nurturing gene or whatever it is."

Melinda had a feeling she wasn't talking about Russell and was surprised she would be so vulnerable. She felt her own empathy returning, and in that moment, she remembered her former life when she was known as calm, level-headed, reasonable: "You're going to be a wonderful mother. And maybe you and Russell could talk to a neutral party to work out your differences."

"Couples counseling?" She scoffed. "He's the one who needs therapy, not me." She took a sip of her tea, which was clearly too hot. She set it down again. "I only wish I didn't feel like I need him."

"It's okay if you do," said Melinda.

Felicity looked as though she was possibly going to cry. "I'm going to go use the ladies' room," she said.

"Of course." Melinda watched her walk away, half wondering if there was a back door that Felicity might use to slip out and escape again. She took a bite of her muffin, just as her phone rang. Melinda swallowed as she answered.

"We're trying to reach Russell Dunlop's next of kin," the voice said.

"This is Melinda."

"We're at the CVS on Bleecker Street. We just put your husband in an ambulance. He may have had a heart attack."

Melinda looked up and saw Felicity coming back to the table. "Where are they taking him?" Melinda asked the woman on the phone. She pulled on her coat and grabbed her purse.

Felicity picked up her coat too, as if she somehow knew the call had something to do with her.

"What happened?" she asked when Melinda hung up.

"We have to go," Melinda said. "Russell's gone to the hospital in an ambulance. They think it's his heart."

Melinda dropped cash on the table and rushed to the door, holding it open for Felicity. She turned back to see what was keeping her: Felicity was unfolding a paper napkin, wrapping it around her scone, and putting it in her purse.

Chapter 31

The renovated Brooklyn warehouse was possibly the coolest space Olivia had ever been in, with its vaulted ceilings, green art installations, and in-house vegan lunch stand. After her interview at the environmental nonprofit, she walked out into the late-afternoon sun in a state of total disbelief. The interview with the woman Melinda knew had gone almost too well, in spite of the fact that Olivia was ill-informed on issues of sustainability and lacked most of the skills needed to handle the basic requirements of the job.

"Oh, we'll figure all that out," the woman had told her when Olivia confessed that she wasn't familiar with any of the software platforms she mentioned. "You can learn as you go. Melinda says you're smart and relentlessly conscientious. She helped me out with a pretty sticky work situation back at the old firm, and I trust her completely."

The door to this company was opening so easily. *This*, thought Olivia, *must be what it's like to be rich.*

But as she walked toward the subway, she wasn't as excited as she knew she should be. She would take the job if they offered it to her, of course she would. She needed the salary, the benefits, and their mission was one she certainly believed in. She scolded herself for her lack of enthusiasm. How lucky she would be if they actually made her an offer! How shocked Melinda would be to know Olivia was hoping they wouldn't.

Her phone rang, her dad's name appearing on the screen.

"How did it go?" he said.

"Good," she said. "Amazing actually. Melinda clearly put in a very good word." Olivia could hear the bar patrons in the background and checked the time; her dad rarely called her during happy hour. "Is everything okay?"

"There's been an emergency."

Olivia stopped walking. "What happened?" Her first thought was that Melinda had murdered Felicity after all.

"It's Russell," he said. "He had a heart attack this afternoon."

Olivia was, for a brief moment, relieved. And then she thought of Hank. "My God, is he all right?"

"We don't know," he said. "But it looks like Hank's going to be with us a little longer."

"Yikes," Olivia said, and she considered the logistics of the situation. She couldn't start a new job if Hank had no one to take care of him. "Why can't Felicity come get Hank anyway?"

"She's with Russell at the hospital," he said. "And we don't know what's going to happen."

"I'll go straight to Lauren's," she said.

"They'll catch you up on the details," he said over the bustle in the background. "We've been discussing the matter of the scone."

"Sorry, did you say *scone?*"

"I'll let Melinda explain it."

• • •

By the time Olivia got back to the brownstone, it was already dark. Lauren took her coat, sat her down beside Melinda in the living room, and put Hank in her lap. Phillip added a log to the fire and went upstairs, where the kids and Leo were moving Charles's desk, clothes, and books up to the spare room on the third floor. Melinda, meanwhile, told Olivia the story of her encounter with Felicity. While she was talking, Evelyn and Lauren poured wine and offered cheese and crackers. Olivia was grateful; she'd taken the subway on two round trips from Brooklyn to Greenwich Village. She'd interviewed for a job, and she'd barely eaten all day. No way was she going all the way back to Brooklyn again. She got her phone out and texted Todd to see if she could stay with him, as the topic turned to Sconegate.

Melinda had been merely puzzled by the incident at the time because she didn't think someone like Felicity ate carbs, but later it started to worry her too.

"Look, I'm not defending her," said Lauren, taking Hank from Olivia so she could eat, "but maybe she just couldn't process the information about Russell that fast."

"I did tell her he was in an ambulance," Melinda said.

"No one likes waste," Olivia said. "I wouldn't want to throw out a perfectly good scone."

"I don't know," Melinda said. "I know I'm the first one to think badly of her, but I don't think she was thinking of the nation's hungry when she put that overpriced baked good in her handbag."

"If you ask me," said Evelyn, "it speaks to the fact that she's fundamentally selfish."

"That sounds right," said Olivia, remembering all the times Felicity dumped work on Courtney late on a Friday afternoon. "But maybe it's worse than that. What if Felicity isn't capable of love?"

"Ouch," said Melinda. "Poor Russell."

"*Poor* Russell?" said Evelyn, throwing up her hands. "I can't believe my ears."

"I don't feel sorry for Russell," said Olivia. "But I feel bad for you-know-who." She pointed to the darling boy now in Lauren's lap.

Lauren leaned down and kissed him on his cheek. "I wish I knew how to solve this problem for our little houseguest."

Melinda was pale. "We were so close," she said.

They all looked at Hank, his doll baby eyes and sweet mouth.

Evelyn turned to Melinda and held up her wineglass. "I'm impressed with how you handled yourself today, Melinda, confronting your nemesis and maintaining your composure. Taking Felicity to the hospital. None of that was easy for you."

Lauren, her cheek resting on Hank's head, looked worried. "I wonder if Felicity's going to abandon Russell in his time of need."

"I don't think so," said Melinda. "I don't know if she loves him, but I think she knows she needs him."

"Meanwhile," said Evelyn, "can we all manage Hank a little longer?"

"How much longer?" said Lauren, passing the baby to Melinda and refilling wineglasses. "Courtney already sent me a new order, and it's huge. I'm in way over my head, and I don't think I can manage all of this."

"But that's wonderful news," said Melinda.

"Is it?" Lauren said, looking miserable. "Because I'm actually thinking of turning it down. I don't mean to sound ungrateful, but it seems I've lost control over my whole . . . self."

Olivia understood exactly how she felt. "Not your self," said Olivia, "but maybe you're losing control of your brand."

"I only skimmed the list they sent, but it's long, and they want weird, impractical stuff I don't want to make, like decorative doorstops. And even if I liked the idea of making a doorstop, which I don't, the thought of making fifty identical ones is horrible. My job has turned into the worst combination of tedious and terrifying. And I never meant to spend *this* much time away from my kids."

"Maybe they could outsource some of the work," said Melinda, bouncing Hank on her knee.

Olivia knew that wasn't the answer. Lauren's brand was all about being handmade. What Lauren made was art.

"Sure," said Lauren, "and my designs will get sent to some factory to be machine made, and I'll just be a name stamped on the bottom of a doorstop."

"You're between orders," Olivia said, "so before you agree to anything, you should dictate the terms of your arrangement." She wanted Lauren to take ownership. They were her pieces after all. "It might take some negotiating, but you can set the parameters."

"I don't think I can," Lauren said. "I wish I had a partner," she said. "I suck at navigating the business side of this."

Just then, Olivia felt a nudge in her side. Melinda had elbowed her. When Olivia looked at her, Melinda smiled and raised her shoulders.

"That's your cue," Melinda said quietly.

"My cue?"

"No one knows what Lauren needs better than you."

Olivia smiled, a seedling of an idea taking hold.

Her phone pinged. Todd had answered: Come over! I'll be at the studio until around 2am but Jacob or Tom or one of the guys will let you in. I keep saying—if we lived together, we would always end up in the same bed. Wouldn't that be better?

. . .

Sometime in the middle of the night, Todd opened the door to his room and climbed into bed beside her. Olivia, who had been thinking through her pitch to Lauren, rolled over to face him.

"Sorry," he whispered, "I was trying to be quiet."

"I'm wide awake."

"And you're here," he said. "How was your interview?"

"Fine," she said, moving closer to him. "But Hank's dad had a heart attack today."

"Jesus," he said, sitting up. "Is he okay?"

"We think so," she said. She sat up too. "Can I ask you something?"

"Sure," he said. "Oh shit, let me guess: *Why* I can't work normal hours like everyone else—"

"No, no nothing like that," she said. "In fact, I'm starting to appreciate the whole idea of being your own boss. No, I was wondering, let's say you were sitting in a café one day, eating a scone, and you found out that I got hit by a cab or something. Would you immediately leave, like right away, or would you wrap up the scone to take with you?"

"Is this some kind of trick question?" Todd said. "Because I'm more of a bagel guy."

"It's a hypothetical situation," she said. "But fine, you're sitting at a diner eating a toasted bagel. You get word I'm in the hospital. Do you leave it on the plate or take along?"

"This is an emergency?" he said. "Like you're injured?"

"Yes."

"That's easy," said Todd, lying back down. "Fuck the bagel."

Olivia put her arms around him and sighed. "I hoped you'd say that."

Fuck the scone. Fuck the bagel. Olivia kissed him. "And I think you're right," she said. "We should move in together."

To: Olivia
From: Lauren
Subject: you and me

Olivia! I am so proud of you for starting your own venture. If you need a place to work, you are welcome to have an office on the third floor of our house, overlooking Waverly Place. Since we're going to have some freed-up space, I'm setting up Lauren Shaw "headquarters" there—we can keep Charles company :)

I'm attaching the signed contract. I can't tell you how happy I am to have you representing Lauren Shaw Ceramics. Given the success of the first episode of *Felicity at Home*—jeesh!—I'm really going to need your expertise so that I don't lose my freaking mind. In fact, with your help, I'm hoping I can learn to love my work again.

Here is my wish list as you negotiate with Courtney on my behalf:

1. No more bookends or doorstops or paperweights. Can we please stick to tabletop? Mugs and bowls and platters, things people put their hands on, love, and use. It's what I do. I am open to lamps and vases. But never again with decorative tiles, seriously.

2. Artistic decisions need to be mine, and I hereby declare there will be no scorpions henceforth.

3. As everything is and will remain handmade by me and me alone, I can only do so much. No bulk orders at a scale that is unmanageable.

If all of this means that Felicity doesn't want to work with me anymore, that would be unfortunate, but I can live with it. I'm sure you can find me a new vendor.

And no, I have no website, no social media presence, no "platform" of any kind, so you've got your work cut out for you.

Hank may be leaving soon, but how lucky I am that you and Melinda are part of my life!

xoxo
Lauren

Epilogue

When the Uber pulled up in front of the brownstone on Waverly Place, Felicity noticed her fingers were trembling as she reached for the door handle. She squeezed her hands into fists to make it stop. She stood next to the car as Russell got out and—somewhat gallantly—kissed her hand.

"Take it slow," she said, eyeing the very same flight of stairs where he'd fallen not long ago. "You're not supposed to overexert."

"I hate it when you say things like that," he said sulkily. "I feel decrepit."

Russell *was* decrepit.

"You're fine," she said, wrapping his scarf around his neck. "Just remember that you promised me a full recovery. I don't want to see you blow it by taking the steps two at a time." *As if he could.*

"Stop worrying about me," he said. "It's emasculating."

Felicity was very glad Russell hadn't died. When she'd seen him in the hospital, looking pale and ancient, she'd imagined her future alone with Horatio. Of being solely responsible for the well-being of another human for eighteen years and beyond. Well, it was too much. And she couldn't hire her way out of this mess; she couldn't count on a nanny any more than she could count on a cleaning lady or a personal assistant. No, her instinct from the beginning had been correct: she needed a father for this child. She needed Russell.

When he had regained consciousness, opened his eyes, and seen her by his hospital bed, he'd burst into tears. "I'm so sorry I ever doubted you," he'd told her. "I love you so much."

Felicity was relieved to hear him speaking clearly, but she felt physically—not repulsed exactly—but repelled.

"I should have known you would never cheat on me," he said. "You're a good person."

That comment infuriated her. "Of course I am," she'd said firmly. She had cheated on him, but she did not want to upset Russell in his already fragile state. What he didn't know wouldn't hurt him. And regardless, she was nevertheless a good person.

"Slower," she said as he started up the brownstone stairs. "Horatio doesn't want to see you winded and sweaty."

She rang the bell, and when no one came, she knocked loudly.

"Are you nervous?" he said.

"Not at all," she said. "Let's not make more of this than it is. We're picking up our son, that's all."

"I'm nervous," he said. "Or maybe I'm just excited. I've really missed the little guy."

"Well, don't get overly excited." The last thing she wanted was his blood pressure to spike and have him end up back in the hospital.

Felicity had tried to miss Horatio, AKA Hank. But the whole week she'd stayed by Russell's side at the hospital, she'd been consumed with work. And once she brought him home to recuperate, she'd had countless Zoom meetings about the release of the show, which was already a smashing success, and about her store, which was making record sales. She'd been offered a six-figure book deal. All this to manage while also making sure the nurse was taking good care of Russell. She hadn't found much room in her mind to think about the baby. She called the Astons daily to get updates, but when Lauren droned on about his feeding schedule and sleep cycles, she got antsy.

The door to the brownstone opened, and the same little girl she'd met the previous spring was standing there with her big, slobbery dog.

Waverly frowned and squinted her eyes meanly at them before turning away. "The cowbirds are here," she yelled into the room behind her as she walked away.

"The who?" Felicity said to Russell, but he hadn't even seemed to register the comment. *God*, was he losing his hearing? Russell was backing away, eyes wide, as he looked at the dog in sheer terror.

"Come on, Russell," Felicity said, holding his hand. "He's a perfectly harmless mutt."

They followed Waverly into the house, taking off their coats. No one came to hang them, so they draped them over the stair railing and stood there with the dog, waiting. The place had been decluttered since her last visit, but it was still odd. *Odd* was probably the right word for the entire family. How could Russell have left their child with these almost strangers?

Lauren's husband came to the entry to greet them, a birthday hat perched at an angle on his head. "You're here!" he said. "Good to see you, Felicity." He was as animated and unstylish as he'd been when she'd met him; no makeover had taken place in the intervening months. He shook Russell's hand. "Hey, how're you feeling?"

"Fine, fine," Russell said. "I was lucky. As far as heart attacks go, mine was pretty mild. We can't thank you enough for taking care of Horatio. I'm sorry it turned out to be such an extended—"

"Oh, he's a great kid," Leo said, adjusting the elastic strap under his chin. "We've enjoyed having him."

"Whose birthday?" Felicity asked.

"No one's," said Leo. "Why?"

Felicity pointed to the hat on his head.

"Oh," Leo said, "right, it's for Hank's going-away party. And the grandparents are flying to Berlin tonight. My kids are pretty emotional about all the departures, so we thought we'd make a thing of it. Come on in! Watch your step."

Felicity maneuvered around a stack of suitcases and looked into the living room. They had decorated. There was a banner across the wall that read *Bon Voyage!*

"Come into the kitchen," said Leo. "Hank's in here." He gestured with his arm.

The kitchen, still with its heinous orange countertops, was packed full of people. Felicity had not anticipated this reunion to have so many witnesses, all of whom ceased their chatter the second she and Russell walked in.

Lauren came toward her, carrying a child that could not possibly be hers. He was huge, almost grotesquely so. Lauren smiled widely as she handed him over. *This* was her baby? Felicity had no choice but to put her arms out and hold him, waiting, hoping for her heart to react, for her brain to send some electrical impulse, a feeling. Nothing happened. She held him—goodness, he was heavy—did his head still need supporting?—and cradled him in her arms.

"He's so big" was all she could think to say. He was fat and still completely bald, and he was looking up at her with no recognition whatsoever. She felt exactly the same way. *Who are you?* she wanted to ask him. *And please don't start crying in front of all these people.*

But it was Russell who started to cry. "Oh, my baby boy, he's so grown up. He looks just like his beautiful mommy," he said.

Well, that was a ridiculous thing to say. This child did not resemble her in any way. If anything, he looked like Russell, whose hair on the back of his head had not even begun to grow back.

"Look at you, little guy," Russell said, tears running down his face. "You sure seem to be eating well."

"Oh, he is," said Lauren. Why on earth was she crying, too? "He's got a terrific appetite."

Felicity wondered what they'd been feeding him. Cheeseburgers? She hoped that whatever he'd been consuming was organic.

He was looking up at her, and she was surprised to see the corners of his little mouth pull up in a smile. It was endearing actually and yes, rather cute. He was wearing clothes she'd never seen before, hand-me-downs, by the look of them, and he didn't smell familiar. Felicity would have the nanny bathe and change him into something new the second they got him home.

Waverly was standing uncomfortably close, holding on to Horatio's feet. And Russell was leaning into her personal space, baby talking at him. Felicity felt intensely claustrophobic.

"Why don't you sit," Felicity said to Russell, "and I'll put him in your lap?"

Russell obeyed immediately, and Felicity handed him the baby. He held Horatio close, whispering to him. It was touching and reassuring to see how much Russell loved their child. As long as his health improved, she thought, this could work out quite nicely.

"We're just putting finishing touches on the feast," said an elderly man next to the stove. "We're doing Thanksgiving dinner a day early," he said.

Felicity looked around at the people in the kitchen for the first time since walking in. Surely, they weren't expecting them to stay.

"I'm Evelyn," a woman said, "Lauren's mother. And that's Phillip. And our friend Peter. You know the kids already. Have you met Dan? And this is Todd. And my friend Ed. And that's Meg. You know Olivia, of course. And Melinda."

Felicity was overwhelmed. Of course she knew Melinda and smiled tightly at her, and at the young woman, who looked very familiar though Felicity could not place her. She glanced at Russell and tried to catch his eye, hoping they could make their excuses and go. She had a nanny to train.

But Russell made no move to leave. Did he really think she was willing to spend more time with his ex-wife?

There was a flurry of activity in the absolutely hideous kitchen as the motley group began to collect forks and knives, glasses and napkins. They chatted as they went in and out of the kitchen, the dog galloping back and forth. To her horror, one of the boys was carrying a pet . . . mouse?

"Thank you," Felicity said over the din, as graciously as she could, "for all you've done. Perhaps another time—"

"Let's eat," said Phillip. "Go on to the dining room and sit any-where you like."

Felicity gave up. The people—there were fourteen or so including the noisy children—and the dog crowded into the next room, where there were far too many chairs pulled up to the table. Russell carried Hank, watching his step and then pulling out a chair for Felicity. There was some fanfare as the older man—Leo's father?—entered the room with a turkey platter and took the seat on her right. He, Leo, and Lauren began passing plates and bowls, many of which were Lauren's, the kinds of pieces she made that had so delighted the royal couple.

"Looks delicious," Russell said.

"We made some low-fat, low-sodium options," Melinda said, reaching down on the floor and handing the oldest boy what appeared to be a retainer with her bare hand. "How are you feeling, Russell?"

"Fine," Russell said. "Much better now that Felicity, Horatio, and I will be together again. My heart is full."

Your heart is busted. Felicity was allergic to that kind of overly senti-mental talk. When she'd told Russell the previous spring about Lauren's "follow your heart" advice, she realized later that they interpreted that expression differently. She took it to mean that she should listen to her inner voice, her practical side, her instincts. But Russell took it to mean that what they had was true love. She would let him believe it.

"That's wonderful," said Melinda, passing him a kale salad. "We're so happy to hear it."

"I'll wait to eat," he said, pointing to the baby, as if he were some long-suffering martyr.

"Good to see you up and about again," said the man on his left. "We were all very worried."

"Thank you, Dan," Russell said. "I got your email; congratulations on the bar."

Felicity leaned in to see who it was, just as Dan flashed Russell a winning smile. *Gosh*, his eyes were gorgeous.

"Thanks for your advice," Dan said, "and for not charging me for it."

How did Russell know him? He wasn't . . . Surely this handsome, rugged guy wasn't Melinda's boyfriend.

The middle kid chose that moment to knock a full glass of milk over, and Lauren's mother and Leo got up to clean the mess.

"I'm Olivia," said the young woman at the foot of the table, wearing a vintage, color block dress, holding hands with a cute, young guy in a black T-shirt beside her. "I used to work at Felicity headquarters," she said. "I don't know if you remember me."

Felicity looked at her. *The video!* Here was the very girl who'd been caught lecturing a customer on the brand's mission, causing a PR headache that had disrupted her Caribbean cruise.

Lauren passed the platter of carved turkey. "I told you all about Olivia. She's been helping me out in, well, in every possible way."

"You're the one who's been advising on the commission these past few months?" Felicity said. "Whatever you did, it worked. Her pieces are flying off the shelves." She felt like a gesture was in order given that these people had, in fact, been caring for her child all this time. As long as Courtney kept this young woman far away from customers, she might even be an asset. "You know, given how helpful you've been with Lauren and with Horatio, I'd be happy to have you come back to Felicity."

"Oh," said Olivia, "that's so nice, but—"

"I'll talk to Courtney, and we'll find you a position. You were aiming to be a buyer for the store, is that right?"

"Gosh," said Olivia, tilting her head then, almost apologetically, "thank you, really, but I've recently taken another job."

"She's representing me," said Lauren with a bright smile. "I mean, my brand. Olivia will be the one to talk to from now on about any new orders."

"How wonderful," Felicity said. That was unfortunate; Olivia knew enough about the inside numbers to drive a hard bargain. "Courtney will be in touch," she said with a polite smile.

Felicity watched the three women clustered together at one end of the table. "How did you three become . . . friends?" she asked, because that's clearly what they were.

"Well," said Melinda, smiling at Lauren and Olivia, "I guess it was Hank who brought us together." They were watching Horatio as he sat in Russell's lap, making her feel both incompetent as a mother and very alone.

The competitive part of her kicked in, and she turned to Russell. "My turn," she said, and put her arms out.

Russell moved Horatio onto her lap, and she wondered if he'd been changed recently or if his diaper was going to leak on her Nanushka trousers. She put her arms around him, finding his soft, pink skin so lovely, she put her cheek against his.

"Let's have a toast," Phillip said, and he stood up next to her, raising his glass. "On behalf of Hank's entire fan club, I would like to wish Felicity, Russell, and Hank a very happy return to their life together. We will miss you, dear little boy. Cheers!"

Everyone took a sip of whatever they had in front of them, and in that moment of silence, the girl Waverly burst into tears. And then the middle kid joined in. The oldest boy dropped his head on the table and sobbed. Lauren's mother dabbed a tissue beneath her eyes. Felicity couldn't be sure, but it seemed that pretty much everyone around the table was crying.

"I guess we're more attached than we realized," Phillip said.

"Sorry, we're a little emotional, that's all," said Lauren, reaching for her napkin as tears ran down her face. "Happy for Hank, of course. So happy. Aren't we?"

"We're very glad for Hank to be returned to his rightful nest," Leo said, pulling Waverly into a hug. The girl was distraught.

As Waverly continued to cry, Horatio squirmed and looked up, the corners of his mouth tugging downward. Then he, too, began to sob. Felicity didn't know what to do about that. She tried jiggling him on her knee.

"Waverly, you have to stop," the older brother said. "Hank always cries when you cry."

Waverly tried. She wiped her eyes on her shirt and took a few jerky breaths, but it was hopeless. She wailed, Horatio wailed.

"Now, listen," said Lauren, hugging Harrell. "I'm sure if you ask Felicity and Russell nicely, they'll agree to let Hank come over for a playdate sometime."

"And sleep over?" Waverly asked.

"Well," Leo said, "I don't know about that—"

"No," said Lauren's mother, "but he could come play. Would that make you feel better?" she asked her granddaughter.

"We don't get to keep him," said Waverly, sniffling and wiping her face.

"No, we don't," said Lauren.

"He has his own family."

"Yes," Lauren said, "but we'll see him sometimes."

Horatio was still crying.

Waverly sat for a moment with her head on her arms. Then she looked up. "Can I hold him?" she asked.

Felicity had never heard such welcome words. She needed help. She needed more help than even Russell could possibly provide. If it took this many people, young and old, to take care of Horatio for a few weeks, how on earth were she and Russell supposed to raise him by themselves? Felicity felt a panic rising in her chest. She didn't have friends like this, parents to come and stay, neighbors dropping in to help.

"No, Waverly," said Lauren, "Felicity hasn't had a turn in such a long time—"

"Of course she can," Felicity said. Everyone got up and shifted seats so that Waverly could come over and sit in Phillip's chair. The little girl wiped her nose and then put her arms out. Felicity passed the baby as Phillip was pouring her a glass of wine. Felicity accepted it gratefully.

Russell held out his glass, too, but Felicity placed her hand over it. "No, Russell, none for you. You heard the doctor."

Melinda had also switched chairs and was now leaning against the handsome man next to her, looking very relaxed indeed.

Just as the platters were handed from one person to the next, the baby was passed from lap to lap, each person holding him as though he meant something to them. They cared about him. It was hard for Felicity to even wrap her head around, but these people really loved her child.

He was across from her now, facing her from the lap of the young man next to Olivia. He raised Horatio up with his tattooed arms and razzed his neck, to the baby's glee.

Her son, her boy, looked all around the table, flapping his arms up and down, and finally locked eyes with her. He had a sweet expression, a beautifully angelic face. He smiled at her then and made a burbling sound, the little cherub. And at that moment, Felicity felt something, like a longing, almost like hunger. A flicker of warmth, a sweetness growing in the vicinity of her heart. Her baby needed her. She leaned forward and reached out her arms.

Acknowledgments

I am so grateful to Emily Bestler of Emily Bestler Books and so proud to have four novels with the EBB fox on the spine! Thank you very much, Emily and the whole wonderful team at EBB/Atria/Simon and Schuster, including Lara Jones, Megan Rudloff, Alaina Mauro, Dana Trocker, Suzanne Donahue, Jade Hui, and Sonja Singleton. And special thanks to Ella Laytham for the wonderful cover. Thank you, all!

I am extremely grateful to my agent Linda Chester for believing in me. And to Kathleen Carter at Kathleen Carter Communications for all of her relentless hard work, humor, and patience.

Anika Streitfeld, over the course of two years, helped me turn a vague premise about an angry woman into a novel. Thank you so much, Anika, for your hours of attention, expertise, and friendship, along with your insistence that I get it right, no matter how many rewrites it takes. You are truly the best, and I am forever grateful.

I wish my dad could have read this book because he was always my biggest fan. I'm so lucky to have two wonderful sisters, Laurie Woods and Wendy O'Sullivan, and their families, all of whom are early readers and champions. And thanks to David and our three wonderful sons—Alex, Andrew, and Luke—who cheer me on every step of the way. Thank you, Amy White, for always being there for me. And thanks to my friend Felice Kaufmann for reading chapters and talking my ideas through in their early stages. Candy and Mitchell Moss and Donna James are and have always been so supportive—thank you! Also sending so much gratitude to Andrea Peskind Katz, Pamela Klinger-Horn, Lauren Margolin, Cindy Burnett, Zibby Owens, Robin Kall, Jamie Rosenblitt, Ashley Hasty, Donna Davis, House of Books in Kent, CT, Caroline Leavitt, Julie Clark, Elin Hilderbrand, Jane Green, Lisa Barr, Rochelle Weinstein, and so many others in the book world for their support. And to my Thursday author friends, Fiona Davis, Susie Orman Schnall, Jamie Brenner, Lynda Cohen Loigman, Nicola Harrison, and Suzy Leopold: What would I do without you?? I love you *ladies*!

I'm always in need of experts. Thank you, Megan O'Sullivan, for your insights into upscale retail business. Thanks to Kaira Rouda for explaining the particular pressures of political campaigns. So much gratitude to Stephanie Marcus, Karla Andela, Megan Irving, and Rita Seiko Payne for teaching me all you know about the world of ceramics and the many steps of making beautiful porcelain objects. And thanks to Lynda Cohen Loigman for connecting me to this amazing group of potters!

A note about the epigraph: "The sweet spot is where duty and delight converge." This quotation—which rings perfectly true to me—is widely attributed online to Thomas Mann. However, my attempts to find the exact source came up empty. I contacted the wonderful people at the Thomas Mann Archives in Zürich, and they were unable to find the source. I appreciate their efforts! Since I could not find any other person who is given credit for the quotation, I have credited Thomas Mann and will continue my search for its origin.